ALL THE KING'S MEN

RISE OF THE FALLEN
&
MICAH'S CALLING

DONYA LYNNE

Rise of the Fallen
Micah's Calling

Published by Phoenix Press

Copyright © 2012 Donya Lynne

ISBN: 978-1-938991-22-6

This book is a work of fiction. References to historical events, real people, or real locales are used fictitiously. Other names, characters, places, and incidents are the product of the author's imagination, and any resemblance to actual events, locales, or persons, living or dead, is entirely coincidental.

Cover art by Reese Dante.

Licensed material is being used for illustrative purposes only and any person depicted in the licensed material is a model.

ACKNOWLEDGEMENTS

This book would not have been possible without the contributions of so many. Thank you to Laura for being there from the beginning. And thank you to my wonderful beta readers. Your contributions are invaluable. I can't express that enough. Without you all, Rise of the Fallen wouldn't be the story it turned into.

Thank you to my husband, who has given up a lot of time with me and has cooked a lot of dinners without my assistance as I chased my dream. I love you, honey.

Lastly, to every single one of my fans on Facebook, thank you for helping make my vision of Micah jump to the page. There are too many of you to list, but you all know who you are, and Micah would like me to let you know he bows in gratitude to each and every one of you.

BOOKS BY DONYA LYNNE

All the King's Men Series

Rise of the Fallen
Heart of the Warrior
Micah's Calling
Rebel Obsession
Return of the Assassin
All the King's Men - The Beginning

Strong Karma Trilogy

Good Karma
Coming Back to You
Full Circle

Hope Falls Series

Finding Lacey Moon

Stand-Alone M/M Titles

Winter's Fire

Collections and Anthologies

All the King's Men Vol. 1 (books 1-3)
All the King's Men Vol. 2 (books 4-6)
Strong Karma Trilogy Boxed Set
Whispered Beginnings - A Romance Sampler

ALL THE KING'S MEN

RISE OF THE FALLEN

DONYA LYNNE

DEDICATION

For my mom.
I wish she could have lived long enough
to see my writing career happen.

CHAPTER 1

GLASS SHATTERED AS THE HEAVY VASE FLEW across the room and smashed against the wall.

"You can do better than that. Come on, hit me!" Micah goaded the hefty man, wishing like hell the asshole would do more than love tap him with his itsy-bitsy fists. Well, not so itsy-bitsy, but they sure felt like it for all the good they were doing.

"Motherfucker!" The brute charged him again. "This is my house!"

Yes, it was his house. And that was his mangled wife and kid cowering in the corner, bruised and broken. Their blood splattered the walls.

"Well, by all means, defend it, asshole."

When Micah had heard the man beating his wife — from two blocks away — as she tried to protect her son, he had been out looking for a fight. This jackass had sounded like he would be able to give Micah the pain he needed, but so for all he'd gotten was a lot of lip service and pansy-assed sissy taps against his chest, even though it looked like the wife beater was giving it all he had.

Another useless punch landed against Micah's stomach.

"You hit like a girl." He laughed. Micah actually laughed at the guy. What a disappointment this asswipe had turned out to be.

"Oh, yeah, well how does this feel?" The man grabbed his leather belt from the floor and cracked it like a whip against Micah's arm.

Micah's pulse quickened at the snap of leather, and his eyes twinkled with need. "Now you're talking." He lumbered forward, all menace, provoking the man. "Come on! Hit me!"

The belt swung again, and the woman ducked and covered her son's head. A satisfying crack rang out as the leather connected with Micah's torso.

Aaaaahhhh, sweet sting of pain. That's more like it, but still not quite enough.

"Is that all you've got!" Micah stalked the man as he swung again and again, striking him with the belt until Micah grabbed the guy's arm in midair. "You're useless."

"Oh yeah?" the man said through nicotine-stained teeth. Sweat beaded his oily forehead. *Oh yeah* seemed to be his primary vocabulary.

A knife appeared in the man's other hand, and even though the idea was tempting to let the guy stab him, Micah had had enough. He wasn't getting what he needed here. With an easy swat, he knocked the knife away then snagged the belt from the man's grip. Locking one hand around the asshole's throat, he picked him up and slammed him against the wall hard enough to make a picture fall from its fastening and crash to the floor.

"You're not worth my time." Micah grabbed the man's balls with his free hand and twisted, making him scream like the cupcake he was before casually tossing him aside. The guy landed on the floor and rolled over, clutching his family jewels.

Sirens rang out in the distance and Micah had half a mind to stay. Maybe the cops could give him the beating he needed. It was tempting, but then he glanced at the woman and child huddled in the corner and momentarily remembered not just where he was, but what he was. He needed to clean shit up and get out of there.

The woman and boy cringed as he strode toward them and knelt down.

He gripped the woman's mind into compulsion. "You will pack your bags tonight and take the boy with you and never look back. You are beautiful, strong, and confident and will go to the woman's shelter and never regret your decision to leave this man." Micah pointed to the dick holding his crotch and rolling around on the floor. If only there was more Micah could do for them, but he had his own problems. "When I leave, you won't remember I was here."

Micah stood up and turned for the door.

The little boy hazarded a terrified glance at him. "Who are you?"

Micah turned around and leveled his navy blue eyes on the young human. "Nobody. I'm nobody."

He wiped the boy's memory so he wouldn't remember Micah, then he vapored the man's memories and slipped out the back door and into the shadows as police cars screeched to a halt in front of the house. He was gone before they even stepped out of their cars.

Thirty minutes later, Micah was perched like a gargoyle on the banister of his eighteenth-floor balcony. He was naked and his skin gleamed against the lights of Chicago. The cold January wind blew his shoulder-length, black hair over his narrowed, soulless eyes. The fight had failed to give him what he needed to control the ache in his chest, which now expanded and played peekaboo with the suicidal thoughts plaguing his mind.

This was how it felt to lose a mate. Like falling off a cliff into a bottomless pit. But when was losing a mate ever easy for a male vampire? He felt empty, like a surgeon had cut him open, pulled out a couple of vital organs, then sewn him back up with acid. Something was missing and it left a raw scratch on the inside of his skin.

The fight with the wife beater was supposed to have taken the edge off his suffering, but he felt more in need of a beating now than before. He was getting worse, and at an accelerated rate.

At this point, dying would be a gift. And maybe he would die. All it would take was one slip of his foot, and if that happened, Micah wouldn't even try to save himself by dematerializing back to his balcony. A fall from this high could cause enough damage to kill him, and if it didn't, the broken bones wouldn't heal in time for him to escape the sun when it rose in a couple hours. That would finish him. He wasn't a day walker like Traceon or the new guy at AKM, Severin. The sun would fry his ass into dust.

Hooray for the sun.

What had started this decline into darkness? Sometimes he couldn't remember. Oh, that's right. Jackson. Jack had broken up with him. How long had it been since Jackson left? A month? No, it had only been a week. Shit, it felt like longer. He had fallen far in a short amount of time.

The past week had been a waking nightmare. For the first two days after Jackson left, Micah had lived on the marble floor of his bathroom, curled in a shivering ball when he wasn't hunched over the commode. The vomiting had lasted twenty-four hours then became dry heaves and gagging on the second day. Food? No thanks.

He had finally overcome the last of the sickening ache on the third day, but that had opened the door for a dark, dangerous hunger, which grew deadlier by the hour. A hunger for pain that had deepened in the days since and sent him in search of a beating every night. But tonight was the first time a fight had left him still in need, and not because his opponent had been weak, but because Micah's need had worsened. Probably because Micah had lost a mate before and the pain was compounded from losing another.

During the Middle Ages, he had lost a wife, Katarina. He had barely survived Katarina's death, but doing so had come at a heavy price: He had never fully regained his will to live and had turned into one hell of a nasty SOB who people instinctively knew not to mess with. Losing her had changed him and thrust his mind into a world of isolation and rebellion. And now he had lost Jackson. If he'd thought losing Katarina had been rough, losing his second mate was even worse, because it opened up all the old wounds again so they could seep right alongside the new ones and compound his pain into an agony that would kill most mortals.

Jackson had come along nine months ago, right after Easter. He was a male, but that hadn't mattered to Micah.

For the first time since losing Katarina, his heart had stirred, and within a month, he had mated him. Not a full mating, but a bond to Jackson had formed nonetheless. With Jack, Micah had smiled again. Jack had given him hope and happiness for the first time in centuries, even if something had always felt off with him.

Maybe because Jackson had never mated Micah back, which was odd. When it came to mating, a male normally didn't form a bond with someone who wasn't a true mate. It was almost as if Micah had been meant to mate another, but the link misfired to tie him to Jack. But if he'd been meant for another, who?

He couldn't answer that.

Which brought him back to being perched on the banister, overlooking the city like a sentry.

Closing his eyes, he moaned from the cold wind's bite, a kind of pain in and of itself. He wallowed in the hollow place that had once been his soul, the darkness creeping and spreading like a parasite to eat him from the inside out as the brittle cold clawed his skin.

With his arms stretched vertically between his bent knees, he gripped the corner of the banister and closed his eyes, his toes curled over the railing. His senses engaged and stretched out, and he felt everything dark and nasty that seeped in the streets below. He inhaled, savoring its acrid odor.

When he opened his eyes again, his pupils smoldered with malevolence, and he swept his gaze from side to side as if searching for something. He felt eyes on him but couldn't find the source. Or maybe it was just his imagination. Nothing was making sense. He teetered on the banister as he glanced down the side of the building as if a legion of giant spiders were crawling up the side, coming for him. Nothing. No one. He was alone. So why did he feel another's gaze?

From the shadows below, the guardian kept his pale eyes fixed on the eighteenth-floor balcony, watching the naked vampire sway in the cold wind. Micah had to be freezing up there, or maybe he didn't even notice. It was clear even from here that Micah wasn't fully present in his own body. He hadn't been since Jackson had left a week ago, and it only seemed to be getting worse. This wouldn't do. The guardian refused to lose Micah. He had come too far and searched for him too long.

Fuck! The toothpick in the guardian's mouth snapped as he clenched his jaw and watched Micah lean precariously forward. Fast as a rifle shot, he reached his hand into the air and blasted Micah with a gentle push of energy that mimicked a strong breeze. The guardian's mind eased as Micah seemed to come back into himself long enough to climb off the railing and put his naked feet back on safe ground.

Momentarily relieved, the guardian breathed a deep sigh, deciding to stick around for the rest of the night to make sure Micah didn't pull any more near nosedives or worse. Pulling up his collar and securing his skullcap, he stepped back into the darkened entrance of a nearby business, fully shrouded in shadows, his special powers engaged. With closed eyes, he stretched out his senses to keep tabs on the damaged vampire up on the eighteenth floor. He cringed at the pain he felt coming from Micah, but at least it wasn't death. Not yet, anyway. And hopefully never.

CHAPTER 2

THE NEXT NIGHT, Samantha Garrett shoved her feet in her tennis shoes and whipped the laces into double knots before bounding to the kitchen. That was one good thing about a studio apartment, it didn't take long to get from A to B. Two or three good-size steps and she could be anywhere. So, see, her studio really was an asset. Yeah, and if she kept telling herself that she might stop hating the tightly cramped place.

Her eyes darted to the clock. It was almost eight o'clock. Shit. If only she could get a different job — one where she could actually sleep at night and not grind a pole — but dancing at the Black Garter paid well and she'd been able to negotiate being paid in cash, and that was crucial so she didn't leave a trail Steve, her ex, could follow.

She threw together a midshift snack and tossed it in her bag then grabbed a grapefruit from the bamboo bowl on the counter. The citrusy smell that burst into the air as she cut it in half reminded her of her childhood. Mom had always had grapefruits in the house. She even ordered them from the fruit club so that a large box arrived once a month to fill the kitchen with their tangy aroma for days.

Damn. There went the tears.

It was her mom's birthday today. And she couldn't even call her.

She missed her mom and dad, but didn't visit or even call for fear Steve would find out or track her down. Her ex had enough money and connections that he probably had her parents' phones tapped and their house monitored, even though it had been a year since she had left him. But she knew Steve, and he wouldn't rest until he found her. It had been hard enough just getting away from him. Until she could buy a new identity and some protection, she was stuck here.

Hence, the dancing job that kept her up nights. She had thought her dancing days were behind her. At eighteen and at the tail end of her rebellious years, she had spent eight months dancing at the local titty bar, as her dad had called it with a certain amount of disdain. The money had been good, though, and she'd enjoyed it at first, but the way the men had looked at her began to creep her out.

Then 9/11 happened and she felt compelled to serve her country since she wasn't really cut out for anything else, and the dancing had proved to be less glamorous than she thought. So she quit the titty bar and joined the Army to be a medic. She figured the Army could give her a fresh start, and since her new goal was to be a nurse, becoming an Army medic was a win-win.

Six months later, she met Steve, a handsome surgical resident. With dark hair and a body built by the gods, she thought she had found the pot of gold at the end of the rainbow. Steve immediately asked her to marry him, and what girl wouldn't want to marry a handsome surgeon? So they ran off to Vegas and shocked everyone by getting married before she left for the Middle East.

She laughed, because now she knew what a mistake marrying Steve had been. Turned out her pot of gold was only *fool's* gold, and she was the fool who fell for the lie. Her marriage to Steve ended up being a nightmare.

As soon as her eight-year commitment to Uncle Sam was over and she could make a clean break from Steve, she packed a duffel, grabbed a wad of cash, and ran away after Steve had left for a twenty-four-hour shift at the hospital.

By the time he found out she was gone, she'd a good head start, and he hadn't caught up to her, yet. Mostly because she was careful and didn't leave a trail. Hence, the reason getting paid in cash was so important.

She'd never looked back, even though she was always

looking over her shoulder. Freedom without being free was what she called it. But at least she wasn't being beaten, anymore.

Thank God they'd never had children, or she would have been stuck with Steve for God only knew how long. She rubbed her hand over the place on her abdomen where she still had a reminder of his abuse. Thankfully, it was small and didn't detract from her striptease act. If anything, the tiny blemish gave her body character and made her appear more human and not like some fake Barbie. There were enough of those at the club.

Fake was something she wasn't. This bod was one hundred percent all-natural and homegrown tomboy, with one catch. She could work a stripper pole like few women could. It was one reason why she headlined and had been given her own dressing room at the Black Garter and made more money than the other girls.

She didn't have to love her job, though. She just had to do it well and endure it. For a few more years, anyway.

Once she shoveled in the last of her grapefruit and swiped away her tears, she tipped the bowl to her mouth and guzzled the juice then rinsed the bowl. After shutting off the kitchen light, she quickly checked her reflection in the bathroom mirror and teased her boy-short blond hair with her fingertips. *Piecy.* That's what the girl who cut her hair called it. Piecy. Pieces of hair stuck up and out in soft, fashionable peaks.

Time to go. With a quick check to make sure the Beretta she hauled everywhere for self-defense was in her bag, she grabbed her duffel and ran out the door.

"HEY, PAX?" Adam disconnected the call to Micah Black, one of Tristan's enforcers.

"What's up, Probie?" Paxton, the senior dispatcher on duty, spun around and shoved himself across the width of the narrow room, his chair gliding over and ramming the counter next to Adam.

"Micah Black. He's not answering his phone. Should I contact Tristan?" This was Adam's first sustained nonresponse since he had come on board at AKM two weeks ago. Micah hadn't answered his phone in several days and, according to the schedule, he hadn't checked in, either.

"Nah, ignore it."

"What? Ignore it?" Adam turned back to the call log on his computer screen. "But he hasn't answered in..." He counted the check boxes. "Seven days. And according to the schedule, he's missed every shift for the past week. Shouldn't his commander be notified?"

"The past week?" Pax laughed. "No wonder it's been so quiet around here."

"What do you mean?"

"You haven't met Micah, yet, have you, Probie."

The other two in the room chuckled and Adam frowned. Was he missing the joke? "No. Why?"

Pax wheeled himself over to his side of the room and leaned back in his chair. "Look, Micah does his own thing. You stay out of his way and he'll stay out of yours. *Capiche*?"

"What's that got to do with protocol?" According to his training, a nonresponsive agent was supposed to be reported to the agent's commanding officer, but Adam had to go through his supervisor since he was a new employee. And his supervisor was Paxton, who, along with the other two dispatchers, laughed at his question.

"Protocol? Guys, when does Micah ever follow protocol?" Paxton looked at the other two dispatchers. Adam glanced at them as they both shook their heads and chuckled.

"Here's how it is, Probie," Paxton said, "There is no protocol with Micah. He's what we call the Lone Ranger, because he does what he wants, when he wants. He barely even follows Tristan's orders half the time."

"But according to the log, he never misses a shift but has been MIA for a week. Isn't that odd?"

"Fuck no. It's a blessing. Enjoy it, Probie. When he gets back you'll be wishing he'd stayed away." Paxton turned back to his monitor and dismissed the conversation. "Hey, guys, are the Blackhawks playing tonight?"

One of the others piped up. "I'm not sure. I'll check."

Adam frowned at his call log while the others shot the shit about hockey. He didn't feel right about this, but what could he do? If Paxton refused to report Micah's absence, then there wasn't a lot he could do but keep calling.

He opened up a new line and dialed then adjusted his earpiece as he waited for Micah to pick up. The least he could do was leave another message. He didn't know Micah, but he hoped the guy was okay.

AS MICAH WANDERED AROUND HIS APARTMENT wearing only a pair of black briefs, his thumb worked rhythmically over his sternum, massaging the ache that wouldn't go away, his face contorted in a mix of pain and despair. Only one thing could squelch the nauseating pain. More pain. It was like fighting fire with fire. Sometimes, to stop a bigger fire, several smaller ones had to be set. That's what Micah needed. Fire to end fire. Pain to end pain.

It was another night and he needed to find something to ease his distress. He needed to find a fight. No, wait. He had already tried that last night and it hadn't been enough. Getting his ass kicked wasn't cutting it, anymore. Shit. Now what?

His cell rang and vibrated against the kitchen counter for what had to be the third time in thirty minutes. He glanced at the caller ID as he walked past. AKM Dispatch. AKM. All the King's Men. He chuffed softly. He didn't feel very king-worthy right now.

As with the previous calls, he didn't answer and let it go to voicemail. Let them leave a message. Maybe he would get back to them, maybe he wouldn't.

In numb silence, Micah ambled to his bedroom and pulled on black nylon sweats and a black and grey camo muscle shirt. The shirt used to hug his body like a second skin, but now it hung from his six-and-a-half-foot frame like it was two sizes too large. After a week of not eating or feeding, he'd lost enough weight that his sweats slid down and hung low on his waist. But he still refused to eat. Food wasn't what he needed.

Pain. Suffering. Agony.

Those were the things his body craved now.

Before turning off the light in the closet, he caught his reflection in the mirror. What stared back was a skull with skin. Empty shadows filled his sunken face. He looked like hell, but at least he looked how he felt. If anyone didn't like it, they could go fuck themselves.

As he turned away, his gaze swept the collection of knives on his weapons shelf: Next to his two Sig Sauers and extra clips was a twelve-inch Bowie knife, a nine-and-a-half-inch Ka-Bar Big Brother knife, a black Tanto knife—what could he say, he had a thing for knives—and several more various blades. He was about to shut off the light when his gaze landed on his razor sharp, double-edged boot knife. He froze. Four inches of cold steel stared back at him like a seductive temptress.

"Hello, friend." He picked up the small but lethal knife and a tic twitched the corner of his mouth as if he were an addict waiting for his dealer to hurry-up-and-give-him-the-stuff-already.

He slowly turned the knife in his hands, mesmerized as he shut off the light in the closet and drifted back into his room. He didn't even realize he was standing in front of his dresser until he looked up and caught his reflection in the mirror. The stranger that glared back at him sneered.

You're a loser. A waste. A burden. A burden who caused Jackson to leave. It's all your fault. You're worthless.

Self-destructive thoughts pummeled him like Mike Tyson in his prime. Each thought was a body blow, hurting him more, bruising his heart, knocking the air out of him.

Micah's breathing deepened and turned ragged. His eyes flitted in a panic. He was suddenly claustrophobic, his spacious bedroom becoming a six-by-six box. His hands shook. Crazed panic shuddered his lungs. He needed to get out of the box. He couldn't be locked up like this.

Suddenly, his eyes caught that magical, elegant blade once more, and his body calmed. His mind went silent. His breathing returned to normal and he felt a surge of peace.

Aaahhhh, sweet pain waited for him in his hand. He didn't have to go in search of a fight, did he? The pain he needed was right here. It always had been.

With anticipation, he yanked off his shirt and tossed it to the floor. The knife was like a penlight in the hands of a hypnotist — *You're getting sleepy. Very sleepy. Do as I say.*

Somehow he ended up in the bathroom without a clear memory of how he got there, his arm poised over the raised spun glass bowl of the sink. With the underside staring back at him like a sacrifice, his grin widened. The knife — his arm — the knife. His gaze darted back and forth between the two, and a perverse, lusty thrill came over him. He actually pulled a semi in his sweats, he was so excited.

It was as if he were only an observer, and the tip of the knife was about to pierce someone else's arm, and he couldn't wait to see that asshole bleed. But when the blade cut into flesh, it was his arm that bled.

Sweet pain.

His eyes rolled back as he savored the sting, and a content sigh eased out of his throat. As a retired Dom, he had caused plenty of people pain for pleasure, but never once had he given that pleasure to himself. *Mmm.* So this was what his submissives had felt. He could see the allure.

Pleasantly dazed, he opened his eyes and watched his blood travel down his arm and drip into the clear glass sink then slide down the side to the drain, where it pooled around the seam of the metal ring. Then he licked the wound, sealing it with his venom . . . and promptly cut himself again. And again. And still again. Each time, he felt himself tumble further into the abyss of destruction, watching his blood flow like he was rubbernecking a bad traffic accident he couldn't rip his gaze from.

Finally, he looked up at the mirror over the vanity.

Who was that looking back at him? The person in the

reflection was a stranger. The enemy. The one who had destroyed everything and chased Jackson away.

Frowning, he growled at himself. "You're a fuck-up. A fucking loser."

The knife dug angrily into his flesh again and the face in the mirror winced. Micah smiled in triumph. That asshole looking back at him deserved it. But wait, the fucker was smiling. He was smiling at Micah, mocking him.

"What are you smiling at?"

You, asshole. The stranger laughed at him as if he were in on a joke Micah could only guess at. *You're a loser. A no-good, washed-up loser. Nobody wants you. Katarina died because of you. Jackson left you. You ruined their lives. You were never any good for them. Save everyone the trouble and just die.*

Micah grimaced. Who the hell was this asshole who knew him so well? "I hate you. I fucking hate you! SHUT UP!"

The knife clanked into the sink, and Micah smashed his fist into the mirror. Shards of glass exploded outward and rained down to the tiled floor and into the sink as Micah snarled violently, feeling momentarily victorious for shutting up that asshole.

Then Micah shook his head. What had just happened? He blinked hard, trying to focus. The broken glass, the blood, the knife, the stranger in the mirror.

Stranger? God, what was he doing? What was he thinking? He was losing his mind. Going crazy. Fighting against himself. Enough sanity remained for him to realize he had just tried to kick his own ass.

And what was with his arm? He raised it and backed away from the sink until his back met the wall. He sank to the floor. He had cut himself. Blood coated his forearm and his hand.

Then he noticed that the ache in his chest was gone. He huffed out a manic chuckle as he rubbed his palm over his sternum. The pain was gone. Whatever he had done had worked, but now his mind was scrambled eggs. None of that mattered, though. He had found the cure to his pain, at least for now. So what if the cost was his sanity?

Hell and shadows invaded his mind as he stared at his bleeding arm. This was his life now. He'd better get used to it. And if he couldn't? There was always death.

CHAPTER 3

Adam disconnected the phone and glanced at Paxton. It had been two weeks and Micah was still MIA, and Paxton still wasn't concerned.

Pursing his lips nervously, Adam brought up Tristan's schedule. Micah's commander had taken a medical leave the past two weeks, but it looked like he was finally back.

As far as Adam was concerned, this matter should have been brought to Tristan's attention over a week ago, whether it meant interrupting him on his leave or not, but Paxton had sat on his ass and done nothing. Micah could be lying in a pile of sunbaked dust out there, or he could be dead in his home, and the longer they delayed, the harder it would be to figure out what had happened to him.

Adam looked at Paxton again then made a decision. If this cost him his job, so be it. He printed Micah's schedule and a copy of the report showing all the no-reports and nonresponses then quietly rolled them up in his hand.

"I'm going for coffee," he said.

No one even looked at him as he got up and slipped out.

TRISTAN LEANED BACK IN HIS CHAIR. Shit sure had piled up in the last two weeks while he'd been gone. He needed to get through all this paperwork so he could meet with his team again. They usually met nightly before patrol, but after being gone so long, he was out of touch with what was going down.

"Excuse me, sir?"

Tristan looked up to see Adam from dispatch standing just inside his door.

"Yes, what is it, Adam? By the way, how are you getting on in dispatch?" Tristan liked Adam. He was a smart kid, and from what Tristan could tell, he had the chops to be an enforcer someday. Adam was one to watch. And he was a day walker, too. More than a quarter of all vampires were day walkers nowadays with all the mating that had gone on between humans and vampires through the centuries. Hell, from what he could tell, that percentage might even be higher, closer to half. The growing ranks at AKM reflected the ratio, too, attracting day walkers with their mixed-blood powers in droves.

"Um, I like it. I'm learning a lot." Adam fidgeted and looked over his shoulder.

Tristan sensed the kid was nervous about something, and that made him curious. "Why don't you come in and have a seat?" He gestured to a chair.

Adam offered a tight, respectful smile, his straight blond hair hanging down over his luminous eyes. After closing the door behind him, he took a seat.

"What's on your mind?" Tristan said

"Micah Black."

Tristan's blood went cold. This couldn't be good. "What's he done now?"

"Nothing, sir. That's just it. It's been two weeks since he last checked in."

Two weeks? "What?" He rocked forward, slamming his booted feet on the floor.

Adam held out the report. Tristan flipped through the pages and scanned the call log and schedule sheets, noting all the no-shows and no answers by Micah's name.

"Why wasn't I told earlier?" Tristan raked his fingers through his short, sandy-blond hair, unable to comprehend what he was seeing and hearing.

"My supervisor told me to ignore it, that Micah does

his own thing." Adam fidgeted. "But after two weeks of nonresponse, I had to do something. Paxton wasn't doing anything about it, so here I am. If it gets me fired, it gets me fired, but I thought you needed to know."

Tristan's anger rose. Someone might lose his job, but it wasn't going to be Adam. "Don't you worry about your job, Adam. In fact, you might just get a promotion if I have anything to say about it."

"Sir?"

"Nothing. Good work. You did the right thing by making me aware of the situation."

"Thank you, sir."

"Call me Tristan, Adam. I can't stomach the formality."

"Yes, sir — Tristan, I mean."

"Okay, head on back. I'll take care of it from here."

Adam nodded and smiled grimly then got up and left.

Tristan grabbed his phone and dialed dispatch.

"Yes?" Paxton.

"My office. Now."

Dead air answered and Tristan imagined Paxton's face had just drained of all color.

"U-uh, yes. Yes, sir. I'll be right there."

Tristan slammed down his receiver and sprang from his chair. Fuck! What had happened to Micah?

Twenty minutes later, after chewing Paxton a new asshole and sending him back to dispatch freshly skinned, Tristan sent orders to the members of his team to do some checking then pulled them together for a powwow. They were just as at fault for not keeping him informed about Micah's absence as Paxton and the other dispatch supervisors were. Someone should have made an effort to reach him while he had been taking care of Josie.

Tristan tapped the butt end of his pen against his desk. *Tap-tap-tap-ratta-tat.* It tittered like a tiny machine gun.

His last phone conversation with Micah had been right after Jackson had split and right before he had gone on medical leave to take care of Josie. Micah had at least had the courtesy to call and tell him he was going to take a few days off:

"I need some time off."

"Yeah? What for?"

"Jackson split."

"Shit, man, you okay?"

"Fine."

"I'm sending someone to pick you up. You need to be in observation."

"No."

"Micah—"

"I said no. I'm fine."

"You sure?"

"Fuck off."

Micah had hung up on him and that was the last he'd talked to the guy, and then Josie had gotten morning sickness so bad he'd forgotten all about Micah. Now, no one knew where Micah was. Great! The team's loose cannon was fucking MIA, and if Tristan had thought Micah had been hard to control before, he could only imagine how messed up he was now, or what damage he was doing to the shaky truce between the vampires and *drecks*. Micah was the type who could single-handedly end the truce. His cannon really was that loose.

Looking across his desk, his gaze darted from one pair of eyes to the next as he took in the other members of his team of enforcers.

Malek sat directly across from Tristan, the light reflecting blue off his long, jet-black hair.

"Anything?" Tristan asked him.

Malek shook his head. "Not yet."

Iobates chimed in, "Still won't answer his phone, either. And his dorm hasn't been touched."

"Thanks for checking, Io." Tristan's aggravation grew. So, Micah wasn't home, hadn't used his dorm at the compound, wouldn't answer his phone, and hadn't checked in for two weeks.

"Trace, did it even look like Micah had been at his house?"

Traceon leaned against the far wall. He had come from the training center to attend the meeting, and rivulets of perspiration trailed from the top of his shaved head down his neck, making his mocha-colored skin glisten. He stood with his arms crossed, a matchstick between his lips. With a shake of his head, he plucked the matchstick from his mouth. "The milk in his fridge was halfway to cheese and the mailbox was full. What do you think?"

Trace was almost as indifferent and emotionally detached as Micah, but at least he followed orders and didn't ask for special favors.

Case in point, after bonding to Jackson, Micah had talked Tristan into letting him have a second, private residence. No one at AKM knew where the two of them lived together, but at least Micah had spent half his nights at his known address for the past year. Now it looked like he had abandoned his house altogether and fallen off the face of the planet.

Tristan should have known better than to let Micah have a private residence, but like everyone else, he gave Micah more latitude than the others. It was how shit had to be done with Micah. He did what he wanted, anyway, so why fight it? And sure, Micah was the private recluse of the bunch, but this disappearing act wasn't like him.

Tristan's frown deepened. "So, no one has heard from Micah, and no one has bothered to check on him. Except for you, Severin." Tristan addressed the long-haired new guy. "You haven't been here long enough to be in on this ass-chew, but the rest of you," Tristan's gaze flung back around the room, "should have known better."

Only Malek had enough conscience to look down as if ashamed. The rest just stared back. But then, Micah wasn't the most well-liked SOB He didn't play nice with others and had a reputation for being not only the resident loose cannon and recluse, but also the resident dick. He ruffled more feathers than a wolf in a henhouse, always rubbing people the wrong way. Even Tristan struggled to hold his tongue around Micah. Most likely, just as with the dispatchers, the team had enjoyed the peace and quiet while Micah was gone.

But it pissed Tristan off that no one had bothered looking

the brother up. After this much time, someone should have pulled a Sherlock Holmes to track the fucker down to make sure he was safe.

"Fuck!" He threw the pen across the room, and it ricocheted off the wall. Trace caught it with a snap of his hand, and the two exchanged glances.

"Sorry," Tristan said.

"Don't worry about it." Trace tossed the pen back.

Tristan blamed himself for losing track of Micah. He had been wrapped up in his own concerns about Josie and the baby, and before he'd known what was going on, two weeks had passed and he was behind the eight ball.

"I want everyone pulling doubles until we find him. We're on lockdown and no one goes home until we do." A couple of groans broke through—Io and Arion, of course. Tristan glared at them. "You need to crash, use your dorm. You got a booty call, cancel it. You've all sat back and done nothing while one of ours is suffering and missing. So, playtime is fucking over until he's home, you got me?"

Trace chewed on his matchstick and shifted uneasily. Everyone else nodded, even if Io's and Arion's nods were reluctant.

"We've got all this top-notch surveillance shit." Tristan waved his arm like an angry Vanna White. "We've found harder-to-find shit than one of our own. Surely we can tap into some of this fucking technology and find him!"

The pen went airborne again. *Thwack!* This time Trace let it fall to the floor. Tristan turned and paced.

Tristan didn't need this shit right now. He'd been wound tight since finding out six weeks ago that Josie was pregnant. She was as badass as most of the males in the room, but even she had to bow down to biology, and the morning sickness had been terrifyingly bad for the last week. It worried Tristan, but that's how it was for a male whose mate was pregnant, even if he hadn't actually mated Josie, not in the vampire sense of the word, anyway. His biology hadn't fired up a bond with her, but that didn't mean he didn't love her or worry like hell about her being so sick. And now he had

Micah to worry about on top of everything else.

He spun on his heels to face the others again. "Malek, I want you and Trace to hit the streets. Sniff his ass out. If he's alive, I want him back here yesterday."

"What if he's dead?" Arion said.

Trace stepped forward and slapped Ari across the back of the head.

"Hey!" Arion turned and glared at Trace, grabbing his noggin.

Trace growled back, causing Ari to reconsider and turn back around.

"If he's dead, I still want him back here." Tristan hoped he wasn't. As much as Micah got on everyone's nerves, he and Micah went way back — since before Katarina's death — and Tristan thought of the pain in the ass as a friend, even if Micah didn't necessarily reciprocate.

The mood sobered at the thought that Micah could have bitten it without their knowledge. They were so tightly bound to one another it often felt like they shared the same mind half the time, even if they didn't always get along. And with all the shared blood among them, surely they'd have felt it if Micah had died, right?

"Io, I want you to work the computers, try and dig into the records and find his new place. Shouldn't be too hard for a hacker like you."

Iobates half-grinned and fist-bumped Arion. "Fuckin' A." Tristan rolled his eyes. Io was a cocky cuss, but the best hacker Tristan had ever met.

Tristan looked over at the new guy, Severin. "Sev, I want you to go with Arion to Jackson's place. If Micah is staying where they lived together, then Jackson will know where to find him. That's probably our best shot."

Severin cleared his throat as he glanced at Arion, acknowledging the other male with a single nod.

"I'm handing off the rest of our workload to the other teams until we find him. I got word that the VanGruben clan made it to safety out of Sumatra after the earthquake, so we don't have to send a team there to search, and if anything comes across the scanners, I'm routing it to Stryker's team."

Nobody challenged him, which was good, because he was ready to nail someone to the wall. Literally.

He paced back behind his desk, raking his hands through his blond hair before stopping to press his fists down onto the industrial wood surface. If what Tristan feared was true, Micah was in bad shape. Tristan only hoped the fucker hadn't gone and done something stupid. Given how Micah had reacted when Katarina died, it wasn't a far stretch to imagine he was capable of killing himself now that he had lost a second mate.

Fuck! How had Tristan let this happen? At one time, he and Micah had been friends. They had joined All the King's Men — or just AKM — together, soon after King Bain created the enforcement agency, which had bases of operation in major cities all around the world, particularly where large concentrations of vampires lived. He and Micah had worked side by side on security details, policing the drecks to ensure the precarious truce between their races remained intact, and had performed a hundred other types of tasks and missions together. But they had drifted apart as Micah sank further into his self-imposed isolation, and when Tristan had been promoted, the rift between them made it so they hardly knew each other anymore. Even so, Micah was his responsibility, and Tristan still loved him like a brother.

"Go. Find him. Let me know as soon as you have a six on his place. I want to go there personally."

Trace stood to the side, watching him closely while everyone filtered out of the room. Only after everyone else had left did Trace push away from the wall and walk out the door. Tristan often wondered what went on inside Trace's head.

As long as he went out and found Micah, he really didn't care right now.

CHAPTER 4

THE GUARDIAN GROWLED WITH FRUSTRATION as he gazed up the side of the luxury apartment building to the eighteenth-floor balcony. He could feel Micah's inky black imprint, but that was all. Micah wasn't home.

Fucking meeting. If Tristan hadn't called them together, he could have gotten here earlier and followed Micah. All he could do now was follow the cold trail Micah had left behind and hope it was enough. But first, a quick stop inside Micah's apartment was in order. The guardian was curious to see what had been going on up there, and with Micah gone, this was the perfect opportunity.

The security guard looked up as the guardian entered the lobby.

"Excuse me," the guard said. "You have to sign in. You can't just go up."

"Really?" With a glance and a wave of his hand, the guardian gently compelled the guard to sit back down and forget he had ever been there. "Consider me signed in."

The guardian stepped into the elevator, rode up to the eighteenth floor, then unlocked Micah's door with his mind. Not all vampires could pull that trick off, but he was special. He could do all sorts of nifty shit with barely a thought.

Once inside, he closed the door. Silence. The place felt like a tomb. He opened the fridge. No food. He opened the cupboard and found more of the same. What the fuck was Micah living on? He closed his eyes, reached out his senses, and got the answer. Pain. Micah was living on pain and suffering and not a whole lot else.

Shit, what was he going to do? He needed Micah. Or, rather, he would eventually. Even now, he felt himself losing his grip on his power. Micah could help him keep it under control. At least, he could if he didn't wind up dead first. And the guardian still had to gain Micah's trust. So much was at stake.

A quick peek inside the master bedroom found the massive four-poster in messy shambles. Clothes littered the floor. And what was that smell? Micah's blood? He looked in the bathroom and found the mirror had been shattered. Shards of glass littered the floor and dried blood dotted the sink and marble tiles.

Damn! What kind of mind-fuck was Micah tripping on?

He had to find him.

Spinning on his heels, the guardian rushed out the door, relocked it, took the elevator down, and shot past the guard and back out to the streets of Chicago. Micah's trail was weak. He had left a long time ago. Hopefully it wouldn't go cold before he found him.

THE PITCH BLACK IN THE ALLEY matched Micah's mood. It had been two weeks since Jackson had left him. Two weeks of giving less and less of a shit as each day came and went. Two weeks of pain and misery and slicing his forearms to relieve the ache in his chest.

Red, angry cuts covered his forearms. His latest self-mutilation had failed to give him the relief he needed, and he hadn't even bothered licking over the wounds to heal them. He liked the way they looked scoring his flesh like claw marks.

With an acidic gaze, Micah prowled for the pain he desperately needed — pain that would put an end to his suffering. One way or another, it would all be over soon.

Tonight, if he got his wish.

He exited the alley and looked left then right through a haze of fog that diffused the light from the neons. The creature he sought was near, but moving away, as if it knew it was being hunted and didn't want a confrontation.

Come now, don't be shy. Micah followed the trail, his pace quickening now that what he needed was so close.

Shoulders that had once been wide and thick, but which now only halfway supported clothes that hung off his thinning frame, rolled as he marched alongside the busy thoroughfare. The hour may have been late, but this was South Chicago, the part of the city where deals were made in the shadows until the wee hours of the morning, corner taverns entertained well past the legal hour, and nightlife took on a whole new meaning. More than just humans gravitated toward the South Side at this time of night, which was what Micah had counted on.

The trail led him to a run-down corner bar—a dive, but packed. As if the angel of death himself had entered, the patrons seemed to sense him more than see him as he stepped inside. Heads turned cautiously to give him the once-over around longnecks of Budweiser. A group of roughnecks playing pool unconsciously shrank back from him as he passed to take a vacant table in the corner.

Lately, he seemed to have this effect everywhere he went. Must have been his sparkling good mood.

His thick, black brows furrowed and his dark gaze raked the room, searching for the one he needed.

A waitress approached, fidgeting nervously. It was obvious she would rather be alone in the alley with Jack the Ripper than waiting on him.

"Those are some ugly cuts there." She nodded toward his arms, trying to warm him up, pen poised over a tablet resting on a tray propped against her hip. When he didn't say anything, she smiled tightly and sighed. "What'll you have? Kitchen's about to close if you're hungry, but we've got plenty of booze."

"Fuck. Off." Micah said. He was in no mood for her, food, or a drink.

He didn't have to tell her twice. Scurrying away, her relief that she wouldn't have to go near him again washed over his raw senses like saltwater on an open sore, except that Micah was too numb to give a shit.

As he scanned the room, his gaze dug into the shadows. Where was he? The one who could end it all tonight.

A figure stirred in the shadows, a hood pulled over his head. The movement was subtle, but Micah zeroed in on it like a hawk to a field mouse.

Bursting from his chair, he barreled toward the man whose bulky sweatshirt belied his brawny form and the weapons he no doubt carried. No guns, but surely a knife or two, or maybe even a cop's nightstick. Most drecks — at least the bad ones — carried nightsticks, being they preferred posing as cops. A nightstick would be perfect. Something to be beaten with that would cause him the pain he needed.

"You motherfucker. You've been dodging me all night. You and me, outside. Now!"

"Fuck you." Malevolent hatred shot back at Micah.

Unrest rippled through the bar, silencing most of the patrons as George Thorogood's "Bad to the Bone" rocked out from the jukebox. All eyes were on Micah and the man in the shadows, and everyone was poised to beat feet if guns came out — or draw their own guns, as the case may be, because it was a good bet half the customers in this shithole were carrying, not to mention the bartender.

Micah grabbed the dreck by the collar, the cotton fleece bunching in his fist as he pulled the guy up. "I need you to do me a favor, fucker. Consider this a freebie."

The dreck snarled, but nodded a wary acquiescence. Micah slowly released his sweatshirt and turned for the door, expecting the dreck to follow him.

There was no love lost between the drecks and vampires, who lived a tremulous, mistrusting co-existence with each other. Vampires and drecks were closely related, like second cousins to one another, except the vampires came out higher up in the gene pool, stronger and more powerful. And didn't that just make the drecks resent vampires even more? It was also why vampires got the job of policing them and maintaining the peace.

Drecks looked like humans, just as much as the vampires did, but the vampires knew better. When the façade came off, most drecks made nasty shape-shifters.

Moreover, most drecks — including the group this guy belonged to if the scent was right — loved killing vampires, even if there was some fucked up truce between them that prevented it. Which meant that this lucky fucker was about to get an early gift from Santa Claus.

"You been keeping out of trouble, Apostle?" Micah knew the names of every dreck in the city, and he knew this one was particularly fond of giving pain. "Or should I call you Officer John Apostle?"

"Okay, you know me, so who the fuck are you?" Apostle replied.

"Just think of me as the guy who needs a favor."

"Fuck that. Give me a name or I'll bleed you right here, blood sucker."

Micah scoffed. Apostle had balls. If he didn't need the dreck's services so badly, he would enjoy showing him how wrong he was about that bleeding business. "Call me Micah, asshole."

Apostle eyed him warily. "What do you want, Micah? And this had better be good."

"Got any friends nearby?" Micah growled the question over his shoulder as he led John Apostle away from the bar.

"A couple." The dreck followed cautiously.

"Call them."

"Not until you tell me what you want." Apostle's voice was edged with malice.

Micah spun around and came nose to nose with the shifter. "I'm about to be your fairy godmother, asshole. Now, call your friends."

Dark curiosity passed between them as the dreck considered Micah's words. "What do you mean?" But he took out his phone, so he was obviously interested. His gaze never left Micah's.

"You like to kill vampires, right? Well..." Micah stepped back, arms extended to the sides, presenting himself for the sacrifice. "Merry Christmas, Happy New Year, and happy birthday. Oh, that's right, you fuckers don't do birthdays."

"We don't do holidays, either, but, in this case, I think I might make an exception." John Apostle's tone rose with curiosity as he appraised Micah. "Why? I mean, not that I give a shit, but I thought you guys could just walk into the sun if you wanted to pull a Kevorkian. Why do you need me?"

"You're better than the sun for what I need."

"Is this some kind of trick?" Apostle eyed him suspiciously as he dialed.

Micah issued the shifter a cold, dead stare, but he wasn't so far gone to lack understanding of the dreck's suspicion. Of course this would look like trickery to one who was accustomed to the precarious relationship between their races — a relationship in which the vampire usually sought to do the ass-kicking rather than ask for one.

"My reasons are personal, dreck. But I can assure you this is no trick. I'm done. Checked out." Micah took out a cigarette and lit it. He figured now was as good a time as any to take up a bad habit, seeing as he wasn't going to live past the hour.

Apostle's eyes narrowed. "So, you want us to kill you?"

Micah nodded, squinting as he took a drag off the cig. "See, you're not that stupid, after all." He blew out a stream of smoke, scrutinizing the shifter. He refused to go on like this. The nightmare of his life grew more agonizing by the day. By the hour, actually. Not even the brutal cutting was doing it for him, anymore. He was out of control. He didn't want to live. He just wanted one thing before he died.

"But I need you and your friends to grant me one favor."

Apostle tilted his head with suspicious curiosity. "Killing you isn't enough?" When Micah only stared back at him, he sighed. "Fine. What?"

"I want you to beat the living shit out of me before you kill me. You got me?"

One eyebrow cocked on Apostle's face as his mouth quirked into a satisfied smirk. "No problem."

Samantha shut the door to her dressing room and took off her mask then hung it on the wall. Another shift at the Black Garter was over. Thank God.

She wasn't wearing much, just red lace panties which she quickly peeled off and threw in the laundry, then she got dressed to go home. Tips had been good tonight, and she was that much closer to complete freedom.

She grabbed her bag, opened the door, shut off the light, and waved to Ted and Jose, the bouncers, as she slipped out the back.

Her skin crawled as she left the gentlemen's club and crossed the parking lot. She just wanted to get home and shower, as she did after every shift. She didn't have sex with the men — only danced for them. But some still touched. The only way she could endure the degradation was to remind herself that she only needed to do this a couple more years and she would have more than enough money to buy herself a new identity and start a new life.

Still, it didn't make the aftereffects of every shift any easier.

Her keys jingled in her hands as she approached her car. But a sudden burst of laughter from inside the parking garage across the street brought her feet to an abrupt stop. This wasn't normal laughter. This was the raucous laughter of men doing bad things to someone.

Looking around to see if anyone else was near, she found herself alone. Of course, it was almost four o'clock in the morning. Who would be out at this hour besides an exotic dancer and a group of thugs engaged in what sounded like one hell of a beatdown?

A voice in her head told her just to get in her car and leave — to forget what she heard and go. But the ex-military veteran who had been beaten by her husband for eight years cold-cocked that voice into silence and then gave her a shove as if to ask what in the hell she was waiting for. Before she knew what she was doing, she had grabbed her Beretta out of her bag, along with the extra clip, and rushed across the street.

Flat-backing herself against the wall with her gun held close, she peeked around the wall to see what was going on. Damn! Five men—well, she thought they were men, but they looked a bit...*off*—beating a sixth man. The sixth wasn't resisting, even though something about him made Sam think he could easily take all of them, despite his inferior size. Not that he was small. He just looked...well, he was too thin, like he was sick or hadn't eaten in a while. The five beating him had long, black hair and their skin had an odd bluish color. Something seemed strange about them, but maybe it was just the lighting.

"Hey!" She jumped out into the open and pointed her gun at them. "Get away from him."

Five sets of eyes turned on her as the sixth man fell to his knees under one of the garage's overhead lights.

Not backing down an inch, Sam stepped closer, poised to open her own can of whoop-ass if they didn't walk away.

As one of the men started to approach her with a nightstick gripped in his fist, his eyes flashed red. What the fuck? Fear rattled her spine and she shot off a round.

"NO!" The sixth man held up one hand, trying to stop her as he crumpled in on himself.

Stop her? What the hell was going on here? Was this some kind of gang initiation?

"Like hell I will!" She stepped forward and fired again, hitting the one coming toward her in the shoulder.

He flew backward from the impact and threw his head back as an ear-splitting shriek broke the air. Was that him? Sam clamped her free hand over her ear and winced, shying away briefly before glancing back at the sixth man who now lay motionless on the pavement. She had to help him. Resisting the deafening screech, Sam forced herself to stand her ground, her gun trained on the asshole doing a banshee impersonation.

Suddenly, the devil-man's scream stopped and his mouth snapped shut. He fixed Sam with an icy glare that looked abnormally blue, just like the rest of him, then the five attackers turned as one and fled, disappearing so fast Sam actually entertained the thought she had only imagined them. Until she looked back and found the dark-haired man still lying faceup, deathly still. Shoving the Beretta into the waist of her jeans, she rushed toward him.

Micah lay on the ground, looking up at the light shining down like a mockery of the light he had hoped to see as he entered the afterlife and took his final walk into Heaven, or whatever awaited a vampire when he died.

Noooo…nooooo! He was still alive. Someone had saved him. Why? Why had someone interfered? All he wanted was to die. Just die and be done with his horrible, wretched life.

The scent of lilacs, subtle and feminine, wafted over him like angelic perfume as the woman who had saved him against his will knelt beside him.

"Hey…hey, can you hear me? Can you move? What's your name? Can you tell me your name?"

Her intoxicating voice instantly soothed him, but Micah couldn't see her as he blinked against the bright light.

"Who are you?" He groaned, his entire body protesting his attempt to talk.

"I'm going to save you."

As she bent over him, the overhead light formed a halo around her head as it shone through her spiky blond hair and shadowed her face. The smell of lilacs grew even stronger, pleasing Micah's senses.

Whoever she was, she looked, smelled, and sounded like an angel.

CHAPTER 5

JOHN APOSTLE GLARED DOWN at the blue, seeping hole in his shoulder. His four companions hovered nearby, looking on.

"That bitch fucking shot me," he said, poking a finger through his sweatshirt. The bluish hue of his skin looked pale against the darker blue blood that flowed from the wound.

Exchanging glances, the others remained silent for a moment until one asked, "Do you think the vampire set us up?"

Apostle eye-rolled at the guy, his icy-blues filled with a lot of don't-be-stupid.

"I was just asking." The other dreck backed away.

Apostle tossed his long, blue-black hair over his shoulder so he could probe the bullet hole with his finger. He grimaced then said, "No, Tormin, that fuck-face wanted to die. If it had been a trap, he would have had more than some human bitch with a pansy-assed nine milli waiting for us."

With a pained grunt, he pulled the slug out of his shoulder and threw it aside. When was the last time he had been shot? It had been a while, he knew that. And here he had let some weak, human female shoot him. Damn her. And he had been in such a good mood up until then. That bitch had robbed him of the joy of killing a vampire. She would pay for that little misstep once he got better.

"I need to heal, goddamn it, but I want that bitch. You guys find her, but do not fucking touch her. I want to do her good *personally*. Any of you fuck with me on this, and your ass'll make like a boot cover after I shove my foot up it. Got me? Find her. Tell me. Don't. Fucking. Touch her."

The other four drecks nodded cautiously. No one questioned the boss.

"Okay, everyone change back and get outta here," Apostle said.

The five took deep breaths, closing their eyes as the blue tint faded to Caucasian and their long hair receded to the high-and-tight cuts required in the police force where they all worked. Their faces filled out, too, no longer taut and hollow. When they opened their eyes, the ice-blue irises had changed to the human color of their choice. Apostle, a.k.a. Officer John, had opted for brown eyes in his human visage.

"See you tomorrow," Apostle said, giving each of his men a hard look to ensure they understood his previous order.

As they dispersed, John held his shoulder close to his body, already channeling healing powers to the injury. Blue blood had turned to red, but it was all just an optical illusion.

John Apostle was no more a human than a zebra was a thoroughbred.

SAM HAD STRUGGLED WITH THE MAN who was in and out of consciousness, but had finally gotten him to her car, half-dragging him since he could barely stand or move his feet. She couldn't take him to the hospital. They would want her name. And she couldn't give her name to anyone, least of all someone who would put it into an electronic health record for a John Doe. It would just be a matter of time before Steve saw it in the system and tracked her down.

That had left only one other option: her apartment. Her tiny, closed-in, can't escape, studio apartment. By the time she reached home, Mr. Dark and Mysterious had passed out cold and she had to put on her Army hat to heft him over her shoulder and lug him inside. With a grunt of relief, she unloaded him onto her bed then stood back and caught her breath as she looked at him, all wonked out with his gorgeous head of black hair splayed over her pillow.

Why did I have to get involved?

She grabbed her first aid kit—which was a little more than your basic collection of Band-Aids and alcohol wipes, what with her Army history and all—and took another look at the man who still lay unconscious.

Mental note: change the sheets and bedspread before sleeping in the bed again.

He had been horribly beaten, and his face was a mess of cuts and bruises. Sam frowned. She could have sworn his face had looked worse just half an hour ago. There had been a contusion around his left eye that now looked almost healed. And the laceration to his upper lip looked smaller and more cleanly scabbed.

Shaking off the unusual healing injuries as adrenaline-induced delusions, Sam pulled out a pair of shears and cut away his shirt. God, he looked half-starved despite the air of power that surrounded him. The man's ribs showed plainly through his skin, which was covered with nasty bruises from where those men had kicked and beaten him.

"What the hell were you doing back there?" she said, talking more to herself than to him since he was out cold. "You should be in worse shape than you are, if you ask me."

Gently palpating his chest and abdomen, Sam felt for broken bones or evidence of internal damage, shaking her head.

"And why didn't you want me to help you? What? Was this some kind of gang thing? You look too old to be in a gang." She studied his face. He looked maybe twenty-nine at the oldest. His shoulder-length, black hair appeared silky soft, and he had what looked like a few days of growth along the sharp angle of his jaw and across his chin and upper lip. It was a comely look. Sam had always been a sucker for a man with facial hair, especially when it was as manicured as this guy's.

His face looked angelic now that his eyes were closed. Earlier, in the parking garage, when his eyes had been open, Sam had seen a lifetime of pain in their depths, a suffering that ran deeper than the beating he had just endured. It was a look she had seen in the eyes of some of the older soldiers she had treated, and it made her wonder what this guy had been through to hurt so deeply.

Biting her lip, she resisted the urge to run her fingers through his hair to see if it was as soft as it looked. But she did trace the tips of her fingers over his forehead then turned her hand so the backs of her fingers brushed down his cheek. Something about this mysterious man made her want to comfort him.

Suddenly she yanked her hand away. "Stop it, Sam. This isn't time for Florence Nightingale Syndrome." This guy was dangerous. Hell, why else would those thugs want to beat the crap out of him? He must have done something terrible to make them retaliate like that.

A nasty scrape on the man's shoulder seeped blood and he had numerous, angry lashes on both forearms which looked relatively fresh.

She sucked in her breath and frowned. "What the hell are those from?" There was no way those men in the parking garage had done that to him. His clothes hadn't been ripped, for starters, and they had been beating him, not knifing him. She had seen cuttings in the Army, and that's what this looked like. If she was a betting woman, she would lay down a hundred that this guy was cutting himself, which meant he was even more fucked up than she thought.

Sam looked more closely at Mr. Out-Cold's face and sighed. With a shake of her head, she grabbed an antiseptic wipe from her kit. "What have you been doing to yourself, mister?" She ripped open the wipe's wrapper and the faint smell of alcohol permeated the air. "You're a troubled one, aren't you? Let's get you fixed up so I can be rid of you. You kind of freak me out."

As she touched the antiseptic wipe to the jagged scrape on the man's shoulder, the man's eyes shot open wide, his entire body contracting violently as he growled — growled? Yes, he growled as his head snapped around.

Animalistic, navy blue eyes met hers, full of fear and something else, something dark.

The rest happened so fast, Sam didn't have time to react. His unbelievably strong hands latched onto her arm, pulled her wrist to his mouth, and then fangs — *Fangs?* — pierced her skin as he bit her.

MICAH HAD BEEN IN A SEMI-LUCID STATE, aware of everything going on around him but unable to rouse himself. He had felt the woman cut off his shirt, had felt her sure, confident hands ranging his chest and torso before her gentle fingers caressed his face. She had talked to him, too. Well, not really to him, but sort of. Her voice was smooth and low, sultry. He just wanted her to keep talking. The sound of her voice was a balm, an audible salve to soothe his soul.

But then she had grown quiet and sucked in her breath. Micah touched her mind and realized she had seen his self-mutilation. Shame flooded him as his long-absent conscience reappeared, chastising him for what he had done. For some reason, he didn't want this woman seeing the damage he had done to his own arms.

And then everything shattered into white heat as fire stung his shoulder.

Intense hunger raged like wildfire. Micah couldn't recall ever needing to feed this badly. In an instant, his eyes flashed open and shot to the woman tending him. Terror erupted in her expression, but all he could see, think, feel, smell, and breathe was blood. Glorious, life-giving, hunger-sating, heaven-sent blood. With graceless impropriety, Micah yanked her wrist to his mouth as if it were a sandwich — and he had gone way too long without food — then bit down with unceremonious impatience.

When was the last time he had truly fed?

The woman struggled as he locked his hands around her arm and lurched upright with her wrist clenched in his mouth. Her blood flowed like a river of life into his belly, and he moaned in ecstasy even as he fought to restrain her. He had been too wrapped up in his need to feed to compel her into submission, and she grappled, squirmed, and struggled against him, gasping and protesting.

Blood. All he could think about was drinking her blood. She swung at him with her free arm, kicking and trying to pull away, but he stayed with her, using one hand to deflect her haphazard punches, turning his body to avoid her kicks. All the while, his fangs kept her wrist locked in his mouth, her blood spilling down his throat.

He finally overpowered her and bent her back and down to the floor. Crouched like a man kneeling in prayer, his gaze ranged up her arm, which stretched between them, linking her to him like an umbilical cord as she continued to struggle. His feral gaze locked onto the pools of clover green in her eyes as his chest and abdomen heaved lustfully. Bloodlust. Strong and pure and all consuming, it gnawed at him like a jackal on a bone.

The woman tried to cry out, but he slapped his hand over her mouth, stifling her scream, taking his fill of her blood as her body finally stilled beneath his.

It was only then that Micah realized she was crying. Tears streamed her cheeks as horrific sobs convulsed her chest. As his senses ebbed back into him, he gently lifted his hand from her mouth, keeping it close in case she tried to scream again.

"Please, please stop. Don't kill me."

Her fear smelled like sulfur as the words clubbed him. Kill her? He didn't want to kill her.

Where was he, anyway?

Micah's eyes flitted around the room. It was suddenly clear he wasn't in Kansas, anymore. What was this place? He had never been here before. Nothing was familiar. How had he gotten here? His eyes darted back to hers.

After releasing her wrist with a gasp, Micah fell back like he had just seen Jesus wagging a judgmental finger at him, and he ass-planted on her generic beige carpeting.

"Where am I?" he said, wiping his mouth.

The woman trembled in fear, too afraid to move as she clutched her bleeding wrist to her body. In his confusion, he had forgotten to release the dose of venom that would heal the bite.

"Where am I?" Micah's voice rose urgently as he frowned in dazed confusion.

"M-my a-apartment." The woman was shivering.

"What's your name?"

She paused like she was trying to decide whether or not she should tell him.

"Tell me!" He was freaking out.

The woman jumped. "S-Sam."

"Why am I here, Sam?"

The woman frowned at him like his question confused her.

"Why am I here?" Why did he have to repeat everything to get her to answer?

She flinched. "You were hurt. I helped you. D-don't you remember?"

Everything flooded back into Micah's mind with such force he visibly wobbled as if he were in the ocean and a wave of storm surge had just rolled over him. He even sucked in his breath as if he were sinking underwater.

He remembered. Jackson, his fall into misery, his death wish, the drecks beating the shit out of him in that parking garage. And then the crack of a gunshot and a woman's voice, followed by an image of...

"It was you." Micah's awed words whispered out of him as he sat back. She was the woman who had saved his life, even though he had only wanted death.

"Yeah. It was me, you asshole. I saved your life." Her fear morphed into anger.

Sam was a tough little doll. He approved.

"What the hell are you and what did you do to me?" She held out her bleeding wrist. Her expression was half terror, half outrage, and her mind seemed to be dancing over the question of what in the hell she had sitting on her floor in the middle of her apartment.

Micah had screwed up, but he had been so delirious with agony and hunger he hadn't been thinking clearly. He had failed to compel her, and now he could feel dawn's approach. He was never this careless.

"What time is it?" He looked around for a clock, knowing he needed to get home. Fast.

"What?" Sam shook her head as if she couldn't keep up with him. "Are you on drugs? Are you one of those weirdos with a vampire fantasy who went and got his teeth altered?"

Finding a clock and seeing he only had fifteen minutes before daybreak, Micah had to move fast. Sam's blood was already making him stronger, and he could feel his injuries healing quickly.

"Look at me," he said.

She refused, but when he tenderly lifted her wrist to his mouth and licked her skin to coat the bite mark with his venom, her eyes snapped to his. Just as quickly, she sucked in her breath as the euphoria entered her bloodstream. It wasn't enough venom to harm her, just enough to take away the pain of his bite and heal the punctures. Normally, he would have released the venom during the bite so that when he broke away, the mark would heal instantly. Being that he had been so clumsy, this was the best he could do.

He captured her gaze and she fell limp as he locked her into compulsion. Filtering through her memories, he was about to pull the plug on everything that had to do with him when his heart skipped a beat at the way she had reacted to the touch of his tongue on her wrist. The subtle intake of breath and the surprised look in her eyes, as if she couldn't deny her attraction to him, awakened him.

God, she was beautiful. Full of fire, strong, courageous. Micah's kind of woman.

He caressed her cheek with the backs of his fingers as if she were made of fine porcelain, and her warmth rippled through his hand. Something about her was so familiar. Like he'd seen her somewhere before and simply couldn't place where.

He couldn't do it. He couldn't strip away her memories. At least, not all of them. He wanted her to remember him, so the next time he saw her, she would recognize him. The bite memories would have to go, though, so he quickly dashed anything that had to do with fangs and blood drinking, but left everything else.

The healing bruises of his body protested as he lifted her off the floor and gently laid her on the bed then stood over her for a moment to memorize her. She had short—almost boy-short—blond hair that stood out in stylish, feminine spikes like she'd combed and plucked it with her fingers. And she had a heart-shaped face and a daintily pointed chin, her skin smooth and flawless, her body slender and athletic. She looked like a runner, her stomach flat and her breasts small but perky under a rose-colored, long-sleeved cotton tee.

"That's a good color on you," he said quietly, staring at her a little longer before checking the clock. He had to hurry. "Sleep, Sam," he commanded her. "And remember me."

On his way out, he paused as her duffel bag caught his eye. A gun poked out through the top. He knelt and pulled out a nice looking Beretta. That was some heavy-duty hardware for a pretty thing like her. He glanced back at her prone form on the bed and smiled then put the Beretta back in the bag and pulled out her wallet. Samantha Garrett. That was the name on her driver's license. He looked at her again. "I'll be seeing you, Samantha Garrett." He dropped her wallet back in her bag and hurried out.

After gathering his bearings, he dematerialized to his apartment. He hated dematerializing. It always left him disoriented, so he only used the nifty vampire trick when he had to.

As soon as his feet hit the balcony and he stepped inside, he realized that thoughts of Jackson no longer filled his mind. They'd been replaced by an all-consuming need to find out more about his angel, his savior, Samantha.

Jackson's memory was still there, though, and Micah still ached, but those thoughts no longer chained him to a cannon ball dropping into the depths of hell. Micah actually felt okay. He felt like things were going to be all right. The agony seemed to be lifting. He no longer felt the need to mar his flesh to take away the pain, because, well, the pain was merely an echo compared to what it had been just a few hours ago.

In a stunned daze, Micah wandered into the kitchen as the computerized timers engaged the double set of heavy, opaque drapes to close along the dual tracks over the windows.

Standing with his hands pressed against the counter, head down, Micah thought back over the last couple of weeks and wondered what he was supposed to do now? With an angry rumble, his stomach answered. *Eat.*

Fuck, he was famished.

DOWN BELOW, THE GUARDIAN MATERIALIZED into the shadows and looked up at the eighteenth floor. Back at the human woman's house, he had been ready to bust down her door when Micah walked out and dematerialized back home. The guardian didn't know what had happened between Micah and the woman, but whatever it was had been good, because the guardian could feel Micah finally eating again, which was something he hadn't done in two weeks.

One thing was certain: the human female was a spitfire. The guardian had just come across Micah's trail, which led into a parking garage, when he heard gunshots. Five drecks took off out of the garage then the blonde dragged Micah to her car a couple minutes later. She was strong, both in body and spirit. That much he could tell. Micah had been in and out of consciousness, but that woman had muscled him to her car like a pro.

The guardian could have interfered, but his curiosity had held his hand. He had been intrigued and wanted to know more about this woman, so he had followed her home, where she slung Micah over her shoulder like a soldier and hefted him inside. The guardian had felt her caring hands inspect Micah, and then all hell broke loose as he felt Micah take her blood.

And thank God for that, because Micah hadn't fed in two weeks. To know he was eating *and* feeding eased the guardian's mind, and he grinned for the first time since his watch over Micah had begun. Whatever had gone on in that woman's apartment had changed Micah for the better. The feel-good emotions coming from the eighteenth floor told the guardian that much.

As the first rays of sun kissed the eastern horizon, the guardian bundled his coat collar around his neck and dematerialized to his own home. Micah would be fine. Now maybe the guardian could think about working on phase two of Project Micah.

CHAPTER 6

THE NEXT NIGHT, Arion and Severin went to Jackson's apartment.

"I hope he's home," Arion said, walking side by side with Severin down the hall of the luxury apartment building.

"Or that he hasn't moved." Severin folded a stick of gum into his mouth.

"Got a piece for me?"

"Sure." Severin held the pack of gum out for him so he could swipe a piece.

Arion checked the door number as he bit down on the stick of spearmint gum and stopped in front of apartment 9-D. "Yeah, I hope he hasn't moved, too." After all, the address was a year old.

They had scrounged Jackson's address out of AKM's database the night before but had to delay their visit because the sun had been rising and, unlike Severin, Arion couldn't go out in the sun. And since newbies like Sev weren't allowed to hit the field without a veteran along for the ride, they had postponed visiting Jackson until tonight. Tristan hadn't been pleased about that, but what could they do?

Sev's gaze automatically ranged the hall as if he were looking for traps or hidden dangers. Decades of pulling military duty alongside humans had likely created a few habits that would never be broken. Ari could only imagine the life Severin was rumored to have lived fighting alongside humans in generation after generation of wars.

Giving the heavy door some knuckle action, Arion leaned against the doorframe, sizing Sev up.

"So, you were a SEAL?" Ari said.

"Yep."

"Impressive. And you can really go out in the daylight, huh?"

"Yep."

Ari wondered what a specialist like Sev was doing at AKM if he had spent his life fighting with humans. "Fuckin' A. Must be nice." He remembered what sunlight felt like from his youth, before his transition. He'd soaked up as much sunlight as he could and spent every available daytime minute outside before reaching adulthood, because he'd known once he did, he would only see the sun in pictures, never directly. "Trace says he can, too, but I've never seen him do it, or heard tell of it. He says it's because he just doesn't like to. Hurts his eyes or some shit."

Severin chomped on his gum and flicked his long, wavy hair off his shoulders with a shrug. "I don't mind it. Keeps me nice and tan." He lifted his impressively chiseled arms, showing off the golden glow of his skin.

Rolling his eyes with amusement, Arion knocked on the door again, louder this time. "I hope we didn't waste a trip for nothing."

Severin nodded toward Arion's inked up left arm. "Nice tats."

With a glance at his arm, the corner of Arion's mouth quirked upward. "Yeah, Io and I got 'em done together about five years ago. He did the right arm, though. I went with the left."

Sev's brow lifted. "So, you and Io...?" His voice trailed off curiously, as if he were trying to imagine Arion and Io together.

As in, *together*.

Arion chuckled. "No, man. Io and I are like brothers. Just friends, but no sweat. You're not the first to think he and I have something going under the sheets, but we're just tight. I've known Io a long time. But if you knew Io, you'd know he doesn't swing that way. Not even close." Io was the biggest homophobe on the planet, so getting with a dude was the last thing on Io's to-do list.

Severin looked away. "Hey, it's your biz if you swing like that. Nothing wrong with it."

Arion was about to answer when he heard rustling inside the apartment and glanced at Sev before pushing away from the wall. Clearing his throat, he pulled his formal demeanor back into place.

After a pause in which Jackson had probably checked the peephole, the door swung open.

Jackson adjusted his robe, an erection evident under the fabric. "What's up, Ari?" He was breathless, as if he'd been in the middle of something strenuous, and ran his fingers through his disheveled hair before eyeing Severin.

Severin had joined AKM the week before Jackson and Micah broke up, so Jackson had never met the guy. And Arion wasn't in the mood to make an introduction. Honestly, something in the way Jack looked Sev up and down like he was dessert kind of pissed Ari off, but he couldn't place why. It just felt tacky and wrong on a dozen different levels.

"Can we come in?" Arion asked.

Jackson's attention returned to Arion as he pursed his lips. He glanced nervously over his shoulder. "Um, I've got company and…"

"Forget it," Sev said with a shake of his head, not hiding his disgust or lowering his voice. "It's been what? Two weeks and you're already fucking someone else like Micah never meant anything…while he's in such a fucking mess that no one's heard from him since you split on his ass. Asshole. You didn't give a shit about him, did you? Go back and fuck your little *toyfriend*." Sev nodded severely in the direction Jackson had looked just a moment before.

Arion stared at Sev in awed silence. The guy wasn't much of a talker. The outburst had been the most he had heard Sev say at one time, but it had been a doozy. He looked back at Jackson, whose face and neck blanched crimson. Where had Sev's tirade come from? Sev didn't even know Micah that well, having only seen him a couple of times at the compound. And, knowing Micah, seeing him was probably all Sev had done. Micah wasn't known to be social or talkative. So, what made Sev stick up for the guy like that? Was it that he now considered Micah his brother in arms and would defend him regardless? Or was this something personal?

Either way, there seemed to be more to Severin than he first imagined. He was more than just a pretty face with luxurious tresses and a stacked body. The male had substance. Arion approved, even if he would have approached the sitch differently.

Jackson stepped toward Arion as if he thought that would protect him, his now-wary gaze never leaving Sev. "What does he mean? What's this about Micah?"

Sev inhaled like he was about to go off again, but Arion hushed him with a raise of his hand, giving Sev a you-need-to-chill glance as he answered. "Yeah, um, about Micah. We need to know where you lived with him. He never told us and no one's heard from him in over two weeks. We're getting worried. Apparently, he's taking it pretty hard that you left." Understatement.

"Yeah, sure. I'll do whatever I can to help." Jackson nodded nervously under Severin's intense glare. "Micah got us a place at the Sentinel downtown. I'll write down the address."

Jackson stepped away and returned a few seconds later with a pen and pad of paper, scribbling down the address before ripping out the sheet and handing it to Arion. He glanced at Severin as if seeking the male's approval.

He wasn't going to get it. Arion could feel that vibe without looking.

"Thanks, Jackson." Arion lifted the paper and turned toward Sev, giving him a nudge. "Let's go, Sev."

"I hope he's okay. I never meant to hurt him," Jackson said.

Throwing a final, loathing glance at Jackson, Sev tore his gaze away and let Arion direct him back down the hall to the elevators.

"What was that about back there?" Ari said, hitting the down button. "You practically tore him a new asshole."

Shrugging, Sev looked away nonchalantly. "Nothing."

"You sure?"

Sev's pale blues landed heavily on Ari's eyes. "What are you, my mother?"

Shaking his head and sighing, Ari looked away. "Hey, I'm not saying you were wrong for what you said. In fact, I'm glad you said it, because I was thinking it."

"Can we just drop it?" Sev's jaw renewed its gum-chewing intensity as he stepped into the elevator.

"Sure, whatever man."

Discussion over. For now, anyway. The two rode down the elevator in awkward silence.

They needed to get this information into Tristan's hands pronto. Ari could hit Sev up later about the rest when he cooled off.

CHAPTER 7

MICAH HAD SPENT THE DAY EATING the last of the bread, a box of cereal—dry, since he hadn't bought milk in over two weeks—three cans of green beans, a box of crackers with an old block of cheese he'd had to cut some mold off of, and a pizza. With his belly full, he had slept through the final hours of the afternoon, well past dark, in fact.

Now that he was awake again, his stomach felt like an empty pit of feed-me.

He paced in front of the oven, shoving the last piece of another pizza in his mouth and making a mental grocery list, when the doorbell rang.

He brushed his hands together then went to the door and yanked it open. His boss, Tristan, stepped inside, holding—oh glory to Jesus—a large bag of McDonald's.

"Hey, Tris."

He snatched the bag out of Tristan's hands and returned wordlessly to the kitchen, leaving Tristan at the door like he wasn't even there. He tossed the bag on the kitchen counter and ripped it down the side to get at the large fry and a mouthwatering order of McNuggets.

TRISTAN ARCHED AN EYEBROW. What the hell? Micah was usually aloof, but something was different. It was as if Micah didn't realize anything was wrong. Did he even know how much time had passed since the two had last talked?

"Uh, yeah, help yourself there, buddy."

Tristan shut the door quietly and sat on one of the bar stools, a bit aghast at the way Micah tore into not only the bag, but also the food. He was afraid to reach for the Big Mac he had bought for himself, fearing he would lose his hand. Setting down the tray of large Cokes, Tristan popped a straw in one and took a drink as he continued to scrutinize the situation.

He had to admit, Micah looked better than he thought he would. The guy had lost major weight, though. Had he not been eating? Well, he was eating now, scarfing the McD's down faster than a Dyson sucks up dust.

What was wrong with this picture? Everything.

"You okay, Micah?"

Micah flicked the Big Mac across the counter toward him, choosing the Quarter Pounder instead. "You can have that. I don't need it. I know you bought it for yourself, anyway."

"Micah," Tristan said quietly. "You okay, buddy?"

Grabbing the other Coke, Micah's scowl only met Tristan's for a split-second before his eyes shot back to the array of food on the counter. Washing down a half-chewed chunk of McNugget and fries, Micah nodded. "I'm fine. Just hungry."

Concerned but not willing to push too hard, Tristan unwrapped the Mac and took a bite, watching Micah go at it before asking, "So, what have you been up to? We haven't heard from you at AKM, and you haven't been answering your phone."

Pausing with a handful of fries halfway to his mouth, Micah appeared to be trying to recollect what he had been doing lately. "I don't know." He frowned at Tristan with his trademark piss-off face and shrugged then returned to kill off the last of the McNuggets before drinking a long pull of Coke.

Tristan stood up and walked around the apartment, munching his Big Mac and sucking on his drink, listening to the sounds of Micah stuffing himself as he peeked around.

"So, you've just been taking some time off?" He sounded like a suspicious detective. Felt like one, too.

Micah killed the fries and hit the Quarter Pounder with newly invigorated energy. "What do you mean?" He spoke with his mouth full, cheeks stuffed. He looked like a squirrel with a mouthful of nuts. "And, hey, how did you find my apartment? I never gave you this address."

"You've been MIA for over two weeks, Micah," Tristan said. A bewildered frown coated his puss. "Ever since you and Jackson broke up. He told us about this place so we could check up on you and make sure you were okay."

At the mention of Jackson's name, Micah came to an abrupt stop. No chewing, no swallowing, no nothing. The color drained from his face and it looked like he was rethinking which direction his food was supposed to travel as he backed away from the counter toward the sink.

Tristan immediately thought about all the McD's Micah had just packed in. "Fuck. Micah, you okay?" He never should have mentioned Jackson's name.

MICAH FELT HIS GAG REFLEX TAKE HOLD as thoughts of Jackson flooded him. The past two weeks rushed back as if someone had just hot-wired his mind and made all the necessary connections for shit to start working again: Jackson leaving him, the despair, the cutting, the plot with John Apostle to kill him.

His mind kept doing this to him. One minute he had no recollection of recent events, and in the next, the past two weeks attacked him with a vengeance. It was as if his mind couldn't sort itself out, trying to catalog Jackson into the past but constantly throwing him into the present.

Fuck me. He was going to lose it all—his mind and his cookies.

Until Tristan had said Jackson's name, his brain had been in one of its Jackson blackout modes. Tristan had triggered the violent resurgence of all those painful memories.

Just as he felt the overwhelming urge to evacuate his stomach, the last piece of what had happened last night slammed into him, replacing the nausea with the need to breathe. Hard.

The woman. Samantha Garrett. The one who had saved his life, whose blood was like an offering from the gods, a nectar of honey and jasmine wine. He sucked in his breath then started coughing to keep from choking on his food. He reached for his Coke and took a long, steadying drink.

Sam. Who was she? Where was she right now? Did she remember Micah? He had left her memories of him intact, so surely she remembered him. When could he see her again?

"Who?"

Tristan's voice snapped Micah back. "I didn't say anything."

"Yes, you did. Who's Sam?"

"Nobody," Micah said. He returned to his sandwich and took a bite, eating more slowly than before. "I'm delusional," he said indifferently. No way was Micah going to dish the dirt on the woman he had met the night before. No fucking way. She was his. Nobody needed to know about her. His, damn it! Micah wouldn't let anyone else near her.

Micah swallowed heavily and mentally stumbled. When had he decided Sam Garret was his? The realization smacked him in the proverbial forehead, V8 style. What the fuck? Was he already tethering to a new mate? So soon after losing one? It would explain his misfiring brain cells, but he and Sam hardly knew each other. Then again, mating didn't always occur between two people who already knew one other. In fact, a lot of the time, it didn't.

But did that automatically mean he was forming a third mating bond? To Samantha this time? And what if Sam didn't share his feelings?

Fuck! He was a walking disaster magnet.

"Fine, Micah, play that way. But you and I are going to have a long talk real soon about what's been going on with you for the past two-and-a-half weeks."

It was clear Tristan wasn't buying his act, but Tris was the delusional one if he thought Micah would sit through a one-on-one over the matter.

"Quit bustin' my chops, Tris. I've got shit to do." Yeah, like buy a tractor-trailer of groceries to feed the bottomless pit known as his stomach, while trying to figure out what was going on inside his body over this Samantha chick. *Hmm, I wonder if she'd be home tonight if I swung by for a visit.*

"Well, I expect your ass at the compound tomorrow night, Micah. I'll give you tonight, but tomorrow night, you're checking in."

With a roll of his eyes, Micah feigned a salute as he popped the last bite of Quarter Pounder in his mouth then wadded up all the empty wrappers and tossed everything in the trash with the empty Coke cup.

"Fine, chief. I could use the gym, anyway." It had been weeks since he'd done any lifting and his body was craving the burn.

Thoughts of the short-haired blonde he had met the night before invaded his mind. Her green eyes. Her gentle lips. The way her hands had felt so confident and sure as she had palpated him.

Her familiarity. He knew her. He'd met her before, but where? Why did she feel so damn familiar? And why was that so important to how he felt about her now?

"You could use a haircut, too," Tristan said. He was trying to sound authoritative, which was a joke with Micah, and Tristan knew it. Given their past, Tristan knew he couldn't manage Micah, just make suggestions. Micah did his own thing. "I'll see if Josie feels well enough to give you a trim."

Micah leaned against the counter, his stomach content for the moment, even if his mind was a mess of confusion. "How is she?" Micah knew she had been suffering through a rough first trimester.

"Touch and go. She's been really sick, but the doc says that's normal and should pass soon. She was feeling pretty good when she got up tonight." Tristan fidgeted with his keys, looking down at the floor before glancing back at Micah. "She'd love to see you. She's been worried."

Feeling a twinge of regret, because he liked Josie and hated upsetting her, Micah glanced away. Grabbing a pen off the counter, he thumbed the cap off then popped it back on as he fiddled with it. "Tell her I'm sorry. Things were shitty for a while, but I'm better now." It was the most he would say on the subject.

And I'll be even better once I get another taste of Samantha Garrett.

CHAPTER 8

STEVE GARRETT HUNG UP THE PHONE. The last year had been a colossal waste of time and money.

He paced in front of the large picture window overlooking the wooded, sloping hillside behind his home in one of Denver's more elite and secluded subdivisions. His dark-haired reflection stared back at him in the glass, as did the fire flickering in the fireplace behind him.

After his blood pressure normalized, he flipped open the slip of notepaper he had been clutching in his other hand then dialed the number that had been scrawled on it.

"Hello?"

"Is this David?" Steve said.

"Depends on who wants to know."

"My name is Steve Garrett. I was referred to you by a friend."

"What kind of friend?"

"One who runs on the wrong side of the law."

Silence on the other end, then, "You must be referring to Kaplan."

"Maybe." Steve liked David already.

"What can I do for you, Dr. Garrett?"

"How did you—?" This was his first contact with the private investigator-slash-bounty hunter. How did he already know he was a doctor? Well, a surgeon, but whatever.

"Please, Dr. Garrett. Give me credit for being good at my job."

Steve didn't really care or want to know how David

already he was a doctor. Only one thing mattered, and that was results.

"Fine," Steve said. "I need you to find my wife."

"Your wife, huh?" A pause. "Samantha Marie Garrett, date of birth, July fifteen. Ex-Army. Born in Missouri. That her?"

"You're hired."

"We haven't even discussed my rates, Dr. Garrett."

"You can call me Steve. And I don't need to hear your rates. I'll pay whatever it takes. I just fired the last guy who tried to find her. He was useless, so I've already wasted enough money. I want the best, David. You don't mind if I call you David, do you?"

"Nope. You can call me whatever you want as long as you pay the bill."

"Good. Send me your contract and I'll return it to you immediately." Steve rattled off his e-mail.

"I'll get it to you in ten minutes." David paused. "Oh, and Steve?"

"Yeah?"

"I never fail."

"That's what I've heard." His skin prickled. Sam would be his again. Soon. He could feel it.

He disconnected and returned to his bedroom. The naked woman tied to his bed squirmed and bit down on the gag. Her eyes flared with arousal as he picked up the riding crop from the dresser. Her skin was still reddened in patches on her breasts and thighs from when he had played with her before his phone call.

"Now where were we?" he said. "We've got ten minutes."

SAM AWOKE RUBBING HER HAND OVER HER WRIST. It was hard to tell if it ached or itched as she scratched her blunt nails over two red, swollen bumps. What the hell had bitten her while she slept? Spiders? The marks didn't look or feel like spider bites.

Making a mental note to call the landlord later about

bringing in an exterminator, she rolled her head to the side and checked the clock on the nightstand.

"Oh, hell." She half-groaned as she forced herself to sit up.

How had it gotten so late? She should have been up and showered by now.

As she tried to stand, the room spun and she plopped right back down on the bed, wincing at the sudden pounding in her head. It felt like she had the flu, her body achy and weak.

That's when she noticed she was still dressed in the clothes she had worn home from work last night. Sam had slept all day. Over twelve hours. That wasn't like her.

And what about the man? She hadn't dreamed him because the mess of her first aid kit still littered the floor. That man had actually been here, so where was he now? Had he knocked her out? Stolen her purse?

She whipped her head toward her purse on the kitchen counter and paid the price as a bolt of lightning bounced around inside her skull. She winced through the pain, but at least her purse was still here. Her duffel bag was still on the floor, too, and she could just see the butt of her Beretta sticking out. Moving more slowly, she glanced around the apartment and found everything in place.

The mysterious dark-haired man with the amazing navy blue eyes had left her meager home intact but had somehow been able to get up and walk out without her remembering. How had he even been able to move in his condition? He had been in bad shape. Who got up and walked away from such a horrible beating?

Apparently, that guy did.

Steadying herself, she managed to stand and work her way to the kitchen, where she filled a glass with water and drank like the desert in a rainstorm. She was so thirsty, craving orange juice, for some reason.

She grabbed the Tropicana Pulp-Free from the fridge and drank straight from the bottle in heavy gulps, keeping the bottle with her as she hurried to the bathroom and cranked on the shower. The water and juice made her feel a little better and steadier on her feet as she quickly stripped and stepped into the tub.

The hot shower invigorated her back to half-alive, but she wondered how she would make it through her shift. How could she dance large tips into her G-string when she felt like a half-dead zombie? What the hell had happened last night to make her body feel like it had been run over by a bulldozer?

She replayed the events from the parking garage until the time she got Mr. Mysterious home, and then it felt like something was missing. She remembered him suddenly lurching toward her as she had started to clean the wound on his shoulder. The next thing she recalled was the two of them on the floor, him asking questions that made no sense.

Closing her eyes, she leaned into the spray, rinsing her hair. Unbidden thoughts of the man called to her memory, just snippets that had no beginning or end, almost like extra puzzle pieces that didn't fit into the bigger picture. His mouth on her, his tongue laving her wrist. Why had he done that? Sam couldn't remember, but she could recall how it had made her feel. That simple, warm caress of moisture on her skin had touched her to the core. Even now, the memory of his eyes ranging her seductively as his tongue caressed her made her womb clench. Heat flooded the heart of her.

The man's memory tugged at her as if she were a roped calf, helpless to run away or do anything to free herself.

"Who are you?" she whispered to the lightly mildewed walls. "Where did you come from?"

No man had excited her this way in a long time, and she didn't even know his name. Maybe the anonymity was the allure. Maybe the fact that he was a mysterious, sexy stranger was the fuel for her fantasy. *A tall, dark stranger, his gaze like blue fire. His tongue used on her in a way that makes her pulse race. He eases up behind her in the shower. The smooth glide of his arms around her waist makes her yearn to feel his naked body pressed against her back. He's tall, easily six inches taller than she is, so he looms over her like a protective guard, keeping her safe as his large hands range up her torso to caress her breasts.*

Sam could almost feel him against her as her own hands

followed along with his in her fantasy, feeling her taut nipples against her palms.

She didn't care that she was already late for work. Thoughts of him awoke her body, and she suddenly felt almost normal, as if thinking about him served to heal her of whatever ailment she had suffered to make her feel beaten and battered upon waking.

As her hands dove between her legs, she opened wider and dropped her head back as if on his shoulder, wishing — *yes* — that it was him touching her instead.

CHAPTER 9

MICAH HAULED HIS ASS TO **AKM.** He decided to skip the haircut Tristan had suggested, going straight for the training center after checking the dashboard. Thank fuck the place was empty. Micah wasn't in the mood for a whole lot of hey-buddy-where-have-you-been? Which was exactly what he feared he would get when someone saw him. Trace, Malek, and Io would know not to bug him, but Arion didn't seem to get that Micah didn't like to talk, and Micah hadn't figured out the new guy, Severin, just yet. And Tristan was Tristan. He'd be all up in Micah's ass for weeks.

He had been going at the weights for a good half hour and was in the middle of an eight-rep of bench press when Arion appeared at his head, spotting him through the last four. He banged them out, and Ari helped him rerack the bar as Micah sat up.

"Hey, Micah. Are you sure you should be hitting the weights this hard?"

Micah glanced askance at him, his trademark scowl firmly in place. He noted how Ari eyed the loaded bar with concern then dropped his gaze to the faint, almost-healed scars on his arms. Arms that probably looked much too thin to Ari to be pushing that kind of weight.

"You got something to say to me, Ari?" Micah's gruff voice was full of fuck-off-and-mind-your-own-business. It was clear Arion thought Micah's head was screwed on either too loosely or too tightly, but either way, it meant he thought Micah was in no shape to be here working, let alone pumping out eight reps at three hundred fifteen pounds.

Arion shrugged, wavering briefly. The two had never gotten along, and Micah had a way of intimidating those around him. Maybe it was his brooding silence or the ever-present scowl that never left his face. Hell, it could have been the nonverbal fuck-off his body language threw out like a warning beacon — *Leave this one alone, or he'll fuck your world right to hell and back.*

But Arion always seemed to find the courage — or was that stupidity — to go on chasing the devil. Fucking hell, did Ari think he was a priest and Micah was a soul that needed saving? Sometimes Micah wondered if the fucker had a death wish or if he simply enjoyed stirring Micah's pot. Every time they had one of these discussions, Micah thought Arion was ready to back down — that he had finally realized Micah didn't appreciate his invasive prodding. Then he seemed to gather his courage and plod on, pissing Micah off even more. As if Arion had room to talk for the fucked-up life he lived. One of these days soon Micah had a feeling he and Ari were going to throw down if this shit didn't stop.

He just wanted to be left alone. Let his soul burn in hell. As long as it meant he would have his privacy, Micah didn't care.

"Where have you been, Micah?" Arion said, shaking his head in frustration.

Micah turned away and glowered. The little asshole had done it again, keeping on when he should have just walked away.

"Fuck off."

"You look like shit. How much weight did you lose? Thirty pounds? How much? And what the hell did you do to your arms?"

This was how Arion was, a pain in his ass and a thorn in his side. "Who died and made you my conscience?" Standing, Micah blew him off and started to walk away, but that little cuss just got up and followed.

"Nobody, but —"

Micah spun and grabbed Arion by both shoulders and

shoved him against the wall, growling. "Everyone else gives me my space, why can't you?" Giving him another hard shove, he knocked the back of Ari's head against the wall.

A chuckle brought Micah's head around. The door to the gym was propped open and Trace was standing just outside, a spank-ass grin splattered on his puss as he nodded once at Micah. He chuckled again and walked on.

Micah turned back and released Ari, and then smoothed his sweat-soaked hair off his face.

Ari's eyes flashed wide as he reached around and rubbed the back of his skull.

"What's going on?"

Micah turned again and saw Severin enter the training center, his long, blond hair pulled back in a man bun. The new guy whipped the towel from over his shoulder, his eyes flicking between Micah and Arion before leveling an icy glare on Micah.

"Nothing," Micah said. "Ari and I were just finishing. He was agreeing to leave me alone. Weren't you, Ari?" Micah gave Ari a pointed look to emphasize their discussion was over.

"I can see that." Severin stepped in front of Arion and bristled as if preparing for a fight.

Micah picked up the protective energy rolling off Severin like ripples in water after a rock broke the surface. He frowned curiously through narrowed eyes as he glanced back and forth between them. What the fuck was brewing between these two?

"It's okay, Sev," Arion said, stepping out from behind him.

"No, it's not okay." Sev looked over his shoulder at Ari. "He's being a dick."

Micah scoffed, drawing Severin's attention again. "Cool out, pretty boy. I won't hurt your boyfriend. And you couldn't take me, anyway."

"You think?" Sev tossed his towel to the side, taking a step forward like he was ready to throw down.

"No. I know." Micah knew not many could take him. Even

with his massive weight loss, he was bigger, stronger, and more ruthless than most. Severin was a big-ass boy, though, with shoulders wide as a Mack truck—wider than Micah's, even though Micah had him in the height department. Still, Sev was young. But Micah had superior strength.

With a last, lingering glower in Arion's direction, he turned and walked out, leaving them behind so he could escape to the showers, where he hoped to get some privacy. He stripped down and gave himself a hot, refreshing suds and scrub then stood in the raining water for several blissful, quiet minutes. After drying off, he flipped his long, black hair back and walked unabashedly naked to his locker. He squirted a glop of straightener in his hand, rubbed his palms together, and then combed them briskly through his hair before letting it fall freely over the sides of his face. The damp ends brushed his shoulders.

He took out the black military digs that always seemed to find their way back to his locker clean, thanks to Josie and her helpers, and pulled on the canvas pants and wool sweater that now looked and felt two sizes too big.

Ari was right. He had lost a fuckload of weight over the past couple weeks. But thanks to the heavy-duty eating of the past two nights, along with taking Sam's blood the night she saved him, Micah had already gained back six pounds. Nightly feedings for the next several days would also help.

After yanking on his leather combat boots, he shrugged into his leather bomber jacket.

"Where do you think you're going?" Tristan entered the locker room as Micah was checking the cartridge of his gun.

He holstered the piece under his arm and slid three extra clips in his pocket. "Out."

"Like hell you are."

"Stop me," Micah said with nonchalant carelessness. He slipped a set of brass knuckles in another pocket, then sat down and tucked his boot knife—the same one he had used to mutilate his arms—inside the ankle of his right boot.

"You son of a bitch," Tristan said. "You've been gone over two weeks. You look like the walking dead, and it's obvious you've been suffering some major shit. Yeah, I saw your goddamn arms, you asshole. And now you act like nothing's wrong?"

Micah stood, his hair falling over his eyes. "I'll deal with it."

"Like fuck you will. And I thought I told you to get a haircut."

"That was an order?" Micah walked past him toward the exit. "I thought it was just a suggestion."

"Micah, I don't want you going out." Tristan's voice held a warning that Micah knew he couldn't back up.

"If you can stop me, I won't," Micah said, not slowing down or turning back.

Tristan followed him out, giving in with a frustrated sigh. "I want you checking in every hour, asshole."

With a wave over his shoulder, Micah dismissed the command. "I'll be back before dawn."

TRISTAN SHOOK HIS HEAD as he watched Micah leave the compound. He hated for the members of his team to patrol alone, but Micah rarely allowed Tristan to enforce protocol with him. The insubordination was tolerated with Micah, though, because he was the most lethal of all the members of Tristan's team, probably because he was also the one who showed the least amount of give-a-shit about his own life.

"Trace, get your gear," Tristan said to the darker-skinned enforcer as he came down the hall.

Trace was the other quiet one in the bunch, but unlike Micah, Trace took orders, even if his lack of discussion made you feel like at any moment he was going to blow you off.

"What's up?" Trace said. He had what Tristan called a DJ voice. Deep and resonant. Trace had a way of enunciating that charmed both men and women alike. Tristan imagined that Trace never had trouble finding willing partners to feed from, or for anything else, but he kept his private life just that, private. No one knew what he did off the clock or who he did it with.

"Follow him." Tristan nodded toward the door Micah had just walked through on his way out.

Trace shrugged on his coat, already armed up. "Sure thing. I was just on my way out, anyway. What am I looking for?"

This was what Tris liked about Trace. The guy never talked back. "Just follow him. I want to make sure he doesn't go hara-kiri again."

With a nod, Trace pulled a black skullcap over his shaved head and went after Micah. Tristan trusted Trace to keep his distance and not get caught spying. Micah was good and still might realize he was being followed, but that was a risk Tristan was willing to take to ensure his best enforcer didn't do something stupid, like get himself killed.

WITH LONG STRIDES, Micah ate up the sidewalk, deep in thought. Not only had it been too long since he had seen the woman who consumed his thoughts, but now he also had to worry about John Apostle. Micah had promised the dreck he hadn't been out to trick him and that he wanted him to wipe his ass off the face of the planet, but then Wonder Woman had arrived on the scene and changed his fate.

Apostle would be out for his blood now. Drecks didn't like any kind of reneging and took a broken promise personally, even if it had been out of Micah's control.

Moreover, Apostle could have marked Sam, and that shit didn't fly. Micah would break all kinds of truces and peace treaties to keep Sam Garrett protected. Fuck Apostle and his bunch of rodents. If they made a move on Sam, he'd fuck up their world so righteously the galaxy would shift from the gravitational pull of his wrath.

Even now, Micah's fists clenched at the thought of Apostle or his cronies hurting her. He already thought of Sam as his, and it was well known in their world that if you touched anyone claimed by a vampire, you touched the vampire, too. So, best touch lightly, and even then it was best not to touch at all or risk retribution.

As he turned a corner, the golden arches of McDonald's were a not-so-subtle subliminal message for his stomach, glowing like a gateway to gastronomical bliss while proverbial angels sang. His stomach rumbled its approval: *feed me.* Micah had been on eating autopilot since he had met Sam, his appetite roaring back to life like a pride of lions that hadn't eaten in a month and found themselves in the midst of a herd of zebras. Smorgasbord!

Walking through the parking lot and stepping up to the entrance, he hesitated before opening the door for a young, pregnant woman trying to corral her two pajama-clad children.

The woman's gaze lifted when she realized someone was holding the door for her. With a nervous start, she eyed him fearfully. "Oh, I'm sorry. Let me get out of your way." Her eyes took in his black attire and what must have been a scary-ass mug to make her look at him like he was Dracula.

Frowning, Micah ran his tongue over his teeth, ensuring his fangs weren't bared. He normally had this effect on people, both men and women alike, but it was better to make sure he hadn't vamped out without realizing it. After all, he had been off-kilter the last few days.

Averting his gaze, he stepped back and tried to say in his most congenial voice, "No hurry, ma'am. Take your time. Can I lend a hand?"

"No." The word snapped out. She probably thought he had asked if he could help her so he could get her alone and have his way with her or some shit. Sometimes, being the scary-looking, badass vampire with an attitude problem had major drawbacks. This was one of them. Why it suddenly mattered, though, was a mystery.

"Have a good evening, ma'am," he said. She ushered her kids past him and out the door to the minivan in a nearby space.

She ignored him and he sighed with disappointment as he entered and approached the counter. As the barely twentysomething girl behind the counter shrank back, Micah mentally rolled his eyes. Shit. Couldn't he just enter a McDonald's and order some goddamn food without everyone he came in contact with thinking he was going to rape, beat, or rob them?

"W-welcome to McDonald's. C-can I help you?"

Forcing himself to smile, because he knew that humans responded well to smiles, he stepped up and eyed the menu. "Yes, I'd like a Double Quarter Pounder with cheese meal, supersized, with a Coke, an order of McNuggets..." his eyes continued scanning the board. "How about a grilled chicken sandwich, too? Oh, and two apple pies."

The girl responded well to his smile, smiling back and looking him over with new interest. "This all for you?" she said, flirting.

It never ceased to amaze Micah how quickly a smile could transform someone's fear into attraction.

"Yep." He grinned as he fished out his black leather wallet. He lowered his voice and leaned in like they were best friends. "Do you think it's too much? Think I'll get fat if I keep eating like this?"

She giggled and shook her head. "I don't think you have anything to worry about there." A blush rouged her cheeks. Shyly avoiding eye contact, she gave him his total then turned to gather his food.

When she returned with a loaded tray, he paid and thanked her, then stepped into the empty dining area and found a table by the window where he could watch the goings-on outside. Taking off his bomber jacket, he sat down and dug into his meal, his dark eyes scanning the streets. Tristan had to have sent someone to follow him. He knew his commander too well, but hell if he could get a bead on who it was.

Which meant it had to be Traceon. That bastard was like a stealth bomber, flying undetected in the wide-open spaces, finding ways to blend into the milieu and shadows so that even Micah struggled to find him. It was those damn mutant powers of his. Fucking mixed-breed day walker.

Micah hated being followed.

He grabbed his cell phone and dialed Trace's number as

he shoveled french fries into his mouth.

"Fucker," Trace's voice said after one ring. Then Micah saw him step out of the shadows across the street.

Micah chuckled and swallowed. "I knew it was you, asshole."

"How?" Trace crossed the street and headed toward the entrance.

"I may not talk much, but I know my teammates." Micah took a bite of grilled chicken sandwich, and then washed it down with Coke.

Yes, Micah knew his teammates, because he usually kept his mouth shut and his eyes and ears open. He also had a habit of dipping into the minds of those around him. Not so much a habit, really. He just couldn't stop himself. Micah always just found himself wandering through the thoughts of others. Except for Trace. Trace's mind was guarded better than Guantanamo Bay. No one was getting inside his head.

"Tris wants to make sure you don't get hurt."

"Go back and tell Dad I'm fine, I will continue to be fine, and I don't need a babysitter. You catching my drift?"

"You're not the boss, Micah," Traceon said, disconnecting and sitting down across from him.

Micah didn't even look up, just kept eating like Trace wasn't even there as he hung up his phone and set it on the table. "Just go back and stop following me. You'll just piss me off if you don't."

"What's new?"

Glancing up, Micah arched an eyebrow. "You saying I'm moody?" He knew the stories. After all, he wasn't given a long leash for being the most agreeable member of Tristan's team.

Trace clucked his tongue and looked out the window. Very little fazed the dark-skinned day walker. Not that his skin was that dark. More like coffee with a modest pour of creamer mixed in. Not African American, but not Caucasian, either. A racial enigma.

"I'm not even going to dignify that with an answer," Trace said.

Micah actually liked Traceon, at least as much as he liked

anyone. Trace was a cool cat. He was quiet and kept mostly to himself, which worked out fine with Micah's need for privacy. However, despite never causing waves, Micah sensed that Trace could wreak major havoc and unleash hell on earth if he wanted to. Why he kept his nose so clean and flew so close to the arrow was a mystery.

But those were Trace's secrets to keep, and just as Micah didn't like anyone prying into his business, he wouldn't pry into Trace's.

"Go on," Micah said. "Run along back to Daddy and let me have my privacy. I'm not going to hurt anyone."

Trace's eyes narrowed on him. The guy looked like he knew more than he let on, but, as if he understood Micah the way Micah understood him, he nodded and stood. "Just call me when you're ready to go back. That way I can show up after you do so it'll look like I did my job."

So, Trace would dance with Micah as long as Micah scratched his back in return. Clever fellow. It was the first time Micah had known Traceon to be insubordinate. It made him wonder just how many times Trace had bucked orders that he didn't know about. Or was this the first?

After thinking it over for a second, Micah nodded. "I can do that."

Grabbing a fry, Traceon cleared his throat, keeping his eyes straight ahead. "Don't get yourself killed or it'll be my ass, you got that? I'm trusting you."

"I got it." Micah nodded.

Whatever Trace's reasons for helping him, Micah was grateful he was willing to cooperate and skidaddle. It meant he owed him one, but so what? He didn't mind owing Trace if it meant he could be alone.

"Hey, Trace. Here." Micah turned and tossed him one of the apple pies.

Trace caught it and looked like he might actually smile then didn't. "Thanks." Instead, he simply turned and walked toward the exit.

Micah watched him stroll through the parking lot and slip back into the shadows. Now he was truly alone. Now he could do what he wanted to do. Time to go see Sam.

After killing the rest of his food and downing the Coke, Micah pocketed his phone, tossed out his trash, and gave the young, blushing girl behind the counter a wave as he left.

Thankfully, the night was quiet. No dreck skirmishes kicked up that he had to break apart. Even the human thugs on the South Side were behaving tonight, not causing any drama that would require Micah's special kind of interference. He was free and clear to wander where his mind had been pushing him for two days: back to Sam's apartment.

After arriving at the ramshackle townhome-turned-apartment building she lived in, he walked the perimeter out of habit, wanting to make sure nothing was amiss. He didn't like that Sam lived in this part of town. It was a rough neighborhood with a lot of crime, not to mention the amount of dreck activity that went on around here.

His predatory senses tuned into everyone and everything that had been here in the past twenty-four hours. Sam's lilac smell strengthened around her windows, but four other scents told him that four people lived in the building besides Sam. Then there was a dog, a stray cat, and someone who had the inky, papery smell of a mailman.

He glanced around the entrance to the apartment building then entered the dingy foyer. His dark silhouette filled the small space as he inhaled deeply then jolted as the funk of drecks swept into his nostrils.

Drecks had been here—the same ones from two nights ago. Well, two of them, but at least neither of which was John Apostle.

Fuck! Sam! They had found her.

He had been afraid Apostle had marked her, and he'd been right. Apostle had been pissed not to get the kill Micah had promised him, and now he had Sam in his sights for taking away his fun.

Darting for Sam's door, he found the lock picked and burst inside.

"Sam!"

He flew to the bathroom where her lilac scent was strongest then spun back toward the main room in frustration when he didn't find her. The apartment was only one room, so she had few places to hide. All he found were clothes and a few pairs of shoes when he checked the closet. Next, he dropped to the floor and looked under the bed. Just plastic sweater boxes filled with clothes.

Panicked, Micah jumped back up and inhaled deeply again and again. Sweeping his gaze around the room, he picked up what he could of the odors in her home. Had she even been here when they broke in?

Micah didn't sense the acrid smell of fear and there was no sign of a struggle, which meant there hadn't been any fighting. Relaxing only slightly, Micah sighed with relief. They hadn't taken her, at least not from here. The drecks had come for her, but she obviously hadn't been home when they broke in.

But that didn't mean she was safe. As distant cousins to the vampires, drecks were excellent trackers and their senses were just as keen.

So, Apostle's lackeys had been here, but now were gone, which meant they had gone after Sam and had a head start on him.

He had only just found Sam. She had saved his life in more ways than one, and even though he barely knew her, he knew enough that if he lost her, it would kill him. She was his. And if those drecks touched her—if they took her from him—he would make sure every last one of them suffered through their last breath before he walked into the sun to take his own life.

FROM THE SHADOWS, Trace leaned against a cold, brick wall and plucked the matchstick from between his lips then tossed it to the pockmarked pavement. He hated that he had lied to Micah, but he was as worried about the guy as much as everyone else, and he actually liked the fucker. Plus, he needed him. Micah was his kind of people and he didn't want the asshole to do anything to get himself killed. Trace didn't have many friends, but he thought of Micah as one even though the two had never spent a night drinking and watching their pals troll for sex at Four Alarm, the local hangout where all the others on the team spent their off hours. Hell, the two of them had never even caught a Bears game together on Monday Night Football over pizza and Budweiser. Still, Trace felt a kindred spirit in Micah.

Glancing up as the door to the apartment building opened, Trace frowned as Micah shot out and took off down the sidewalk like a man on a mission, grim panic in his step. The woman must have been gone, but why Micah had come back here was anyone's guess.

With a curious glance back at the building, Trace pushed away from the wall and kept his distance as he followed. He had a feeling things were about to get interesting.

CHAPTER 10

SAM'S TRAIL, AS WELL AS THAT OF THE DRECKS, led Micah uptown to the Black Garter, a gentlemen's club with a high-end reputation. Why the hell would Sam come here? Micah bristled, not wanting to think the obvious, that she was one of the dancers. He didn't like the idea of her dancing for men who lusted after her bare breasts and God only knew what else. Surely, she waitressed or tended bar. No way was she a dancer.

For any other woman, though, it would be a good gig. The dancers at the Black Garter were upper echelon women. Healthy and clean. Management took good care of them, especially Scarlet, the star performer. Her act was amazing. Micah had caught it a couple times. Scarlet kept the big spenders coming back week after week with her mysterious, elaborate, contortionist-like shows. And she was treated like royalty. That had been clear during Micah's previous visits.

He had been a regular patron before meeting Jackson, his eye favoring women until Jack came along. Occasionally, he'd come to the Garter with his old friend, Malek. Malek spent one night off a month here. Twelve nights of lust per year was all that male allowed himself, even now, so long after losing his mate during the war.

Still, Malek's coming here didn't make Micah feel all warm and fuzzy about Sam being inside. If anything, it made him want to punch Malek for even being near her, whether she was a waitress, a dancer, or just a lesbian here to watch the girls. Seven hells, Micah sure as hell hoped Sam had a good reason to be here. A reason that didn't include taking off her clothes while grinding a pole.

Taking the steps to the entrance two at a time, Micah stepped into the dimly lit foyer with its elegant furnishings and travertine floor to be greeted by a pair of breasts in a black push-up bustier. Hard-to-ignore cleavage bobbed toward him.

"Welcome to the Black Garter."

Micah pulled his gaze to the woman's face, trying to inhale beyond her to the bodies in the room on the other end of the long, dark hallway that led to the main floor. "Sam Garrett?" he asked.

"Who, honey?" Her eyes danced down his black attire, narrowing as she saw the leather sheath of his Bowie knife. She was just about to wave for the well-dressed bodyguard behind her when Micah pulled them both into compulsion. He wasn't in the mood to waste time.

"You never saw me, I was never here."

The two nodded with blank expressions, and he hurried down the hall. Dim wall sconces lit the way as he followed the sound of music then turned and exited into the main room, which was even darker. A woman spun around the pole on the main stage. The long fringe of her red velvet bra and panties whipped to and fro as she unwound her legs from the pole and stepped down with clear-soled platform pumps, which looked like they were made of glass.

Small, red lamps were set in the middle of cozy round tables big enough for only one person. The men who came here weren't known for big groups or jeering. This wasn't your standard strip club, and the clientele preferred to remain private.

Touching was also strictly forbidden during stage performances, but the rules of the private performances that took place in back were a bit more lenient. If a customer wanted to tip a specific girl—and many did—they could buy a private dance with her in one of the back rooms where they were allowed to touch all but her breasts and crotch, tuck money into her G-string, hold her hand, et cetera. As long as they didn't get rough or too hands-on, nobody got thrown out. Eight minutes cost fifty dollars, or twenty minutes for one hundred.

Before today, the idea of touching hadn't bothered him, because he would have been all about the touching if he'd have been so lucky as to get Scarlet in one of those back rooms, which had never happened despite more than one attempt. But now? Now was a different story, because if Sam was a dancer, the last thing he wanted to think about was her being pawed by other men. In fact, Micah's trigger finger twitched at the thought of another man putting his mitts on her.

This was going to be a long fucking night. He could tell by the way his skin crawled with possessive heat, as well as the need to find Sam, that his nerves would be frayed until he found her, maybe even after he did. Where the hell was she? He could smell her but couldn't see her anywhere.

But it didn't take him long to find the two drecks sitting at a table near the stage. He recognized them from the other night.

One glanced up and saw him, nudging his companion. The two sneered at him as if they knew why he was there. Micah glared back, daring them to make a move, but both stayed firmly seated like they knew what they were doing. Keeping to the perimeter where he could watch them, he quickly scanned the room. He needed to find Sam and get her out of there. Now. His gaze skirted from waitress to waitress then back to the bartenders. There was still no sign of her.

Which left only one other option.

He glanced toward the stage.

With a sigh, Sam prepared for her turn on stage. The house was packed. She had seen that much during a quick peek at the floor after arriving a half hour ago. A couple of her regulars were in the audience, so tips would be good.

Stretching through yoga poses in her private dressing room, she breathed in then out, feeling her body loosen and her tension fade. She had already meditated, a necessary step to help her disengage enough to dance, otherwise she would never be able to take the stage. Every night was the same thing: meditate, stretch, yoga, dress, perform, finish, and go home to take a long, hot shower to wash away the degradation and invisible paw prints left by her private admirers.

"Namaste." Sam concluded her yoga exercises with the traditional salutation.

Rising from her green mat, she removed her robe and dressed in one of the one hundred or so costumes the club provided for her, making the final transition to becoming Scarlet, star dancer at the Black Garter. A long, black trench made of shiny, heavy-duty plastic covered black, zip-up hot pants and a matching top. Beneath that, she wore a black leather bra and leather and spandex panties. Military-style knee-high boots completed the look.

She was in a solemn mood tonight, her thoughts having been steeped in visions of the dark man from the other night. Who was he? Would she see him again? She wanted to see him again. It wasn't like her to fantasize about a man she didn't know, but that was exactly what she had been doing since she met him.

Tonight she would dance for the mysterious man who dominated her thoughts. He was her muse, and he roused her to dress more quickly than usual. She was almost eager to take the stage now just so she could channel her thoughts of him into her performance. When was the last time she'd been eager to dance? Sam couldn't even remember.

She selected a black and red leather mask from her collection. It had black-out plastic eye covers, as most of her masks did to keep her eyes hidden from the audience. Just that simple costuming trick added more mystery and intrigue to her act. She became almost inhuman to the audience, as if she was a mystical creature or an alien sent to Earth to entertain them. When the men—and women— in the audience couldn't see the windows to her soul, she became so much more enigmatic and erotic, and they were able to dive deeper into their fantasies.

She secured the mask to her face then stood in front of the mirror to make final preparations. She wore wigs most nights, and tonight she adorned one made of black hair pulled into a long ponytail.

Completely detached from reality, she made her way backstage to double-check her music with the technician, and then waited for her cue to go on.

THE LIGHTS DIMMED and drew Micah's attention to the stage as a man's voice whispered seductively into a microphone somewhere out of sight, "Scarlet." He drew her name out sensuously as a low hum of near-sinister music cued up.

Scarlet stepped onto the stage, her masked face down at first, then she looked up as she prowled first to one side, then the other. The energy in the room surged as every man seemed to lean forward in his seat, waiting to see what she had planned for them tonight. Damn, that woman knew how to work a room.

She was dressed to kill, too, at least as far as Micah's tastes were concerned. Lots of black and lots of leather. Too bad he wasn't here to watch—wait a minute. Micah's brow furrowed as he stepped away from the wall, his lips parting in disbelief.

Sam? Sam was Scarlet?

"Fuck me," Micah said, his voice low.

With a long, directed inhale, he confirmed what his other senses already told him.

And the drecks were in on the action, too, perking up as they recognized her scent at the same time he did.

A different kind of tension suddenly filled the room. The humans remained oblivious to the danger about to erupt around them. The drecks kept an eye on him as he tracked the edge of the room, looking for an opening to get to Sam while fending them off. Unfortunately, the drecks seemed just as determined to get to her first, flashing him a warning glance to keep back. Like hell he would. They would not leave here with her tonight.

They were in a standoff on steroids.

Sam moved like a graceful dominatrix, using the pole like an extension of her body as she undulated, spun, and bent, flinging the coat to the side before lowering into a seductive squat and unzipping her top.

Micah could barely take his eyes off her, and possessive need riled his hands into fists. He smelled the spike of heated arousal in the room, and he ground his teeth in territorial menace, his jaw clenched. Malevolent threats shot from his eyes to the unaware men sitting behind their quaint, red lamps. Micah saw more than one adjust his cock under the table. Dirty perverts. She was his. Sam—Scarlet—whatever the fuck! She was his, goddamn it!

How many would tip her for a private dance? How many already had in the time she had worked here? And how many would go home and whack off as they thought about her?

With his blood boiling, Micah's anger almost got the better of him, and he took a step toward the stage, intending to grab her by the wrist and drag her from the room. When the two drecks tensed at his sudden movement, it called Micah back to reality and he stilled, his gaze shooting to them as they flung him a warning to stay where he was.

Fuck that.

Apparently, the drecks received his message loud and clear, because as soon as Micah moved to grab Sam, the drecks flew out of their chairs. One went for Sam while the other attacked Micah. The room burst into chaos as the table Micah was thrown on shattered under him and the first dreck took off down the back hallway with Sam flung over his shoulder.

"No!"

The second dreck landed a solid punch on Micah's puss to buy his pal some time then scuttled back and up to take off after his buddy.

ONE SECOND, Sam had been deep in the fantasy of her mystery man's hands caressing her body, and the next she was being yanked off the stage and forced over some asshole's shoulder.

"Stop! No! I said NO! Put me DOWN! You can't do this, asshole!"

Screaming, Sam thrashed and tried to fight the way the military had taught her, but it was useless. The thick arms that held her weren't easing up.

Chaos erupted in the club as men shouted and waitresses screamed. With the black-out lenses in the mask, it was hard to see much more than shapes and shadows rushing around. One of the club's security guards chased her back stage, only to be knocked out of the way by some dick who seemed to be her kidnapper's buddy.

"Is this about Steve?" Sam said, feeling panic rise. Had Steve found her? Were these his lackeys? "DO YOU WORK FOR STEVE?" Fear gripped her.

"Shut up, bitch." The one carrying her didn't seem interested in talking. And then his buddy caught up to them.

"Hurry up. He's coming," the second guy said, rushing ahead to the back exit and throwing open the door.

Who? Who was coming? Steve? Someone else? Sam felt like she was going to throw up as she bounced like a rag doll against the guy's shoulder blade.

"Hold him off while I get her to Apostle," the guy carrying her said.

Who the fuck was Apostle?

"Are you kidding? Did you see him? I think he's her mate. He'll kill me."

"I don't give a shit." Cold air blasted her as she was rushed outside. "Apostle will kill us both if he takes her."

"If he's her mate, he'll kill us, anyway. I'm not fucking with a mated vampire."

Whoa! Vampire? Mates? What was wrong with these psychos? Were they on drugs? And who was Apostle? And why did they want to take her to him?

"I haven't done anything wrong! Let me go!" She tried

again to beat her way out of her kidnapper's grasp. "You've got the wrong person!"

"I told you to shut up." The guy started running, then came to an abrupt stop and turned around and started running back, shouting for the other one. "Shit! There's two! Go, go, go!"

What the hell was going on? All Sam could do was hang on as she was spun around and flung to the ground as the guy who had been carrying her grunted and fell over. She rolled across the dirty, cold pavement, and banged against the wall of the building behind the club, then gathered her bearings and stripped off her mask.

A man with dark skin leaped inhumanly high into the air, seemed to hang suspended for a split-second, then swooped down in a rush of power over the man who had been carrying her. His fist crashed like a sledgehammer against the man's sternum.

And then *he* was there. The mysterious man from the other night. Rushing out the back of the club, he hesitated for only a moment to look her direction as if checking to make sure she was okay then raced after her other attacker. He tackled the guy, leveling him with a body blow.

Fists flew, and all four men took their shots, but her mystery man and his dark friend seemed to have the upper hand, and eventually the two who had tried to kidnap her broke away and fled.

The dark man approached her and held out his hand. She took it, and he pulled her up. "Are you okay?" he said.

"I . . . I don't know. Who were those guys?"

"I'm not sure. Hey, Micah," He turned to address her mystery man, only to be blindsided with a right hook.

Sam screamed, jumping out of the way as the dark man flew backward. Her mystery man—Micah—had come out of nowhere, as if materializing in thin air right beside her. Micah grabbed her wrist and pulled her back as she tried to go after the dark man and check on him.

"What's wrong with you?" she said, yanking her arm away.

Micah's eyes ranged her body with a mix of lust and

disgust. Something in his forbidding gaze both excited and terrified her.

"Stay back," he said, his deep voice clipped. Then he turned his attention on the dark man. "Keep your hands off her, Trace. You fucking liar."

"Hey, fuck you, Micah."

Micah turned his back on the man, placing himself between her and the one known as Trace. "Are you okay?" He had calmed, and his voice actually sounded tender. This guy could shift gears faster than a race car.

"I . . . I think—I don't know. I think so." Her gaze held his and she felt her pulse skip. He was so tall, and he looked better than he had the other night, as if he had eaten and put on a few pounds. Plus, she didn't see a scratch on him, as if all the damage those Cretans had done in that parking garage had looked worse than it actually was. "How are you?"

As if reading her mind, he smiled and said, "Better, thanks to you."

"Good. You, um...you look better. I was a bit worried."

Trace stepped up behind Micah. "Wait a good goddamn minute."

Micah turned back toward Trace, reaching an arm around her protectively. The tension between the two men was so thick it made Sam shiver. Or maybe that was just the cold. She was out here in nothing but leather underthings.

Two bouncers rushed through the back door and the dark-skinned man named Trace lifted a hand toward them. The two men stopped in midstride.

Her eyes bugged out and she practically choked on her breath. What the fuck? Who were these guys? Criss Angel and David Copperfield in disguise?

"What's up your ass?" Micah said to Trace as he gave the two men a cursory glance before dismissing them as if seeing two men frozen in midair was oh-no-biggie.

"You two know each other?" Trace looked between her and Micah, his eyes narrowed.

"Yeah, so?" Micah's hold on her tightened.

"You mind telling me how she remembers you? Because I know you know it's against regs."

Sam peered over Micah's shoulder, hovering closer to him without realizing it. Trace looked pissed.

"Fuck regulations," Micah said.

Trace shook his head. "You're an asshole."

"Talk about asshole. 'Just call me when you're on your way back.' Does that sound familiar? You're like all the rest of them." Micah waved his free hand through the air as if he were dismissing Trace.

"Just wait a second." Trace jabbed Micah in the shoulder, and Sam got the distinct impression that if it weren't for her, Micah would have gone for the takedown on the other man. Her eyes darted to the back of his head and his long, black hair that fell like silk over his shoulders.

"No, you wait a second." Micah swatted Trace's arm away and pointed a finger at him. "I trusted you tonight, and you fucked me."

"No I didn't. Will you just wait a second?"

Micah took Sam's hand and she clasped onto it without thinking, just knowing it was the right thing to do.

"What?" Micah said, snapping at Trace as he pulled Sam into the warmth of his coat. She instinctively knew to keep quiet while they exchanged verbal jabs. Besides, keeping her mouth closed and her ears open might allow her to learn more about what had just happened and who had tried to kidnap her.

Trace's gaze went from Micah to her and back again then he blew out a heavy sigh. "If Tristan finds out about her, you're going to be in deep shit."

"So? When am I not in deep shit?"

"Look, I wasn't going to tell Tristan about what you did tonight, anyway. I only lied about not following you because I wanted you to trust me."

"That's original. You lie so I will trust you." Micah scoffed. "Screw that! You blew it, Trace. I don't give second chances."

"Cool out. I don't have a beef with you, Micah. But I'm just as worried about you as everyone else. You've been majorly fucked up lately, and unlike the others, I actually like you, shithead."

Sam felt Micah stiffen as if he'd been caught off guard. Why did she get the feeling that Micah didn't have many friends? If any at all? She looked up and found him frowning before he realized she was watching him. Then he cleared his throat and simply scowled back at Trace.

"Yeah, I thought that might surprise you," Trace said.

"So, why did you follow me?" Micah loosened up against her.

"Because," Trace said, shaking his head and pausing, "I didn't want to see the one guy on my team who I actually like get himself killed by doing something stupid."

That seemed to take the steam out of the air, and Sam looked back and forth between them before finally speaking up. "Hey, sorry to get in the middle of your lover's quarrel, but can we get back inside? I'm cold." She started to push out of Micah's hold, but he pulled her back.

"You're not going back in there."

"Oh, really."

He met her gaze and nodded. "Damn straight. You're coming with me."

Trace huffed and Sam turned to see him shake his head again.

"Trace," Micah said, "give me your coat. You owe me for lying to me."

"What are you going to do with her?" Trace said, not even hesitating as he shed his coat and handed it over.

"I'm going to take her to my apartment." Micah pulled Trace's heavy trench around her.

"No," Sam said. "If you're not going to let me go back in I'll go home."

"It's not safe there."

"You mind telling me what's going on, Micah?" Trace said.

Micah looked at her as if contemplating what to do then glanced back at Trace. "Okay, meet me at my apartment in an hour." He rattled off the address. "And don't tell anyone else, got me?"

"Deal."

"I've heard that before."

"Well, this time I mean it. I'll meet you in an hour. Get her out of here before those assholes come back." Trace nodded once then headed off in the opposite direction.

Micah led her to the parking lot.

"Which car is yours?" he said.

"Wait a minute," Sam said, stopping. "I'm not comfortable with this. And what about Ted and José?"

"Who?"

"The bouncers. Are they going to be okay?"

Micah glanced over his shoulder at the two men still in suspended animation. "Trace will release them—"

"Release them? How did he do that to them in the first place?" She was barely holding it together.

Micah turned an impatient eye on her. "I'll tell you later. And, yes, he will release them as soon as he knows we're gone." He lifted his face as if sniffing the air then pulled her toward her car.

"Okay, whatever." She rolled her eyes and bobbed her head in a half-shake. "But I'm still not comfortable with this."

"With what?" Micah opened the passenger door and stood aside for her to get in. "I'm an excellent driver. Don't worry. I won't hurt your car."

"What? No. That's not what I'm talking about."

Micah shrugged and made a face as if he didn't understand.

"I mean," she said, "I'm not comfortable with you going to my home then taking me to your apartment."

"You were comfortable having me in your home the other night."

She frowned and looked around. "Hey, how did you know this was my car?"

"It smells like you."

Now that was a first. Her car smelled like her? She sniffed without thinking about it then shook her head as if she were shaking off cobwebs. "Okay whatever. And the other night was different." She crossed her arms and looked away, feeling as if he could see inside her mind at all the fantasies she had been indulging about him.

"Why? Because I'm not so weak now?" He closed the distance between them, making her aware of just how *not weak* he was, and just how alone they were in the parking lot.

"Apparently not too weak," she said, lifting her gaze to range his very strong, very virile body before meeting his eyes as he stepped in front of her.

"I won't hurt you."

It was the way he said it, almost as if he were a chivalrous knight—her own Sir Lancelot—as if he were speaking to Queen Guinevere herself. Before she could stop herself, she took his outstretched hand and let him help her into the car.

"What am I doing?" she muttered to herself as he walked around the front of the car.

He opened the driver's side door and got behind the wheel.

"Wait," she said. "The keys are inside, with my things."

"Don't worry, I've got this." He winked at her.

She watched him hot-wire her car like a natural-born thief.

"Of course," she said, waving her hand and glancing out the window. "Of course you can hot-wire my car." Just what was she getting herself into with Micah?

CHAPTER 11

"LET ME GET THIS STRAIGHT. You had her but she got away?"
John Apostle stood beside his unmarked Dodge Charger
in an alley behind a row of local businesses, rubbing his
shoulder. Thing still hurt like a motherfucker, but at least
the bullet hole had healed.

Tormin and Janus looked at each other.

"What part of 'do not touch her' did you two idiots not
understand? I specifically remember telling you not to
touch her."

"Micah showed up, so we had to alter our plans."

"Micah? What did he want?"

Janus shifted uneasily as if standing were a chore.
Probably was by the looks of him. Micah hadn't been picky
about where to hit the guy. "I think he wanted the girl, too."

"Oh?"

"Yes, and if I'm not mistaken, she's his mate."

"His mate?" This was interesting. "What makes you
think so?"

"Just the way he reacted like a mated vampire when we
went after her."

Apostle rubbed his chin, thinking. "Intriguing. He
certainly didn't act like a mated vampire when he asked me
to kill him."

The three exchanged glances, then Apostle said, "Give me
her information."

"Apostle," Tormin said, "You can't go after a vampire's
mate. That's war, and you know it."

"He started the war, not me." Apostle didn't like being

teased, and being told he was going to kill a vampire only to have his intentions thwarted was a tease. Micah had wanted to die the other night. So Apostle was going to give him what he wanted, one way or another. If it took killing his mate to kill him, then that was what he would do. He would keep his end of the deal.

"Apostle—" Tormin said.

Apostle backhanded him so hard he stumbled to the side before righting himself, holding his already-bruised face. "I will have her, Tormin. Now, give me that bitch's information."

With a reluctant nod, Tormin pulled a slip of paper from his pocket with two addresses written on it. One for her home and one for work.

"Good, now go home. I'll get someone to cover your shifts for a few days until your faces heal."

Tormin and Janus turned and exited the alley. Apostle reviewed the information on the piece of paper then folded it and tucked it into his uniform pocket before getting back into his car and slipping out of the alley on the other side. Looked like he had a new beat to patrol.

Radioing in a fake call to dispatch about a suspect he was tailing, he put Sam's home address into his GPS. If he was lucky he would catch the bitch at her home if that fuckhead Micah hadn't already rushed her off to safety.

Severin finished his shift and decided to stop by Four Alarm for a beer before going home. With the Micah crisis averted, at least for the moment, everyone could relax. Or maybe not, given how Micah had been behaving since returning to AKM, going off like a loose cannon and shirking his orders. Sev had only been with AKM a month, but it was clear Micah was an asshole who got under everyone's skin. The guy couldn't be controlled.

His thoughts shot to walking in on Micah roughing up Arion earlier. Even now, Sev felt the urge to break the guy's face for touching Ari that way. No one touched Ari like that, not even a fucked-up-just-lost-his-mate Micah.

Cool off, Sev. Ari's not your boyfriend. He doesn't need your protection.

But that wasn't the problem, was it? The problem was that Sev was thinking more about Ari than he should, and in ways he shouldn't.

"Hey, this seat taken?"

Sev looked up, and speak of the devil. Ari stood next to him, motioning to the barstool. Topaz, almond-shaped eyes glanced from the stool to Sev.

"Uh, no. Have a seat." Sev cleared his throat and sat a little higher. "What are you up to?"

Ari sat down and waved at the bartender. "Io and I came in to grab a drink before heading home. We come here a lot."

"Oh?" Sev took a drink of his beer, looking around. "Where is Io, anyway?"

Ari rolled his eyes. "One of his many fans caught him as we came in. He's probably in the bathroom fucking her."

The bartender set a brew in front of Ari without him having to order.

"You do come here often," Sev said, eyeing the beer. "Bartender doesn't even have to ask what you want."

Ari laughed. "Yeah, well, we're regulars." He picked up his beer and gave a mock salute, lifting it as if toasting the air. "Io likes the women here." Something in the way Ari said it made Sev frown curiously. It almost sounded like Ari was frustrated or annoyed by Io's behavior. Or maybe he was just frustrated with himself.

They turned around and faced the dance floor, kicking back against the bar, brews in hand. He glanced at Ari sideways. "What about you? Why aren't you back there with him, Ari? You like the women, too, don't you?"

Ari shot him a glance then quickly looked at the floor before looking at him again with a tight smile on his puss. "Yeah, sure. Why not?"

Sev didn't think he sounded convincing or convinced.

An uncomfortable silence hung between them for a couple of minutes. Then Ari looked at him. "So, what was all that about earlier? At Jackson's apartment, I mean. You tore into him pretty good."

"Was I out of line?"

"No. I'm glad you let him have it. I mean, Micah and I may not be the best of friends, but that doesn't mean I think it's okay for someone to pull shit like Jackson did. Micah had mated him for God's sake."

Sev dove into his beer again, taking a healthy sip. He didn't want to remember his own past or how Jackson's actions had reminded him of it.

"So," Ari said, "what gives, huh? You want to talk about it?"

Sev took another drink. No, he didn't want to talk about it. Well, not to anyone else, anyway. Something about Ari made Sev want to open up. "I lost someone of my own about a year ago."

Ari sucked in his breath and Sev felt his eyes on him. "I'm sorry." Ari's hand settled on his shoulder, and Sev closed his eyes at the seemingly innocent gesture, but it felt good on his body. Warm, soothing, and right in every way.

All too soon, Ari took his hand away, leaving a cold emptiness where it had been.

"Was she your mate?" Ari said.

Sev opened his eyes and turned his head to meet Ari's gaze. "No, he wasn't, but I loved him."

ARI'S BROW FURROWED. Had Sev just told him he was gay? "He?"

Sev nodded. "Yes. His name was Gabriel."

Ari didn't know what to think about this. He hadn't known Sev was gay, so the announcement came as a bit of a shock, but unlike Io, he didn't have anything against homosexuals. In fact, he often felt jealous of gay men. They were free to live the lives they wanted. They didn't have to lie about who they were. Ari felt like every day was a lie for him. A lie he couldn't escape.

"Are you gay?" Ari said, leaning in and keeping his voice low. Why did the idea that Sev was gay excite him so much?

Sev's mouth quirked. "Yes, Ari. I. Am. Gay. That's usually what it means when a male dates other males. Why? Is that a problem for you?"

Ari quickly shook his head. "No, no. I'm sorry. I'm just..." What? What was he? Fascinated? Curious? Interested? "I just think it's great that you can talk so openly about it, that's all. So many people feel like they have to hide, you know?" He looked at his own reflection in the mirror behind the bar. Was that what he was doing? Hiding? Was he actually learning something about himself tonight?

Sev obviously felt Ari's vibe because he said, "What are you hiding from, Ari?" Sev leaned forward, pushing in close enough for Ari to smell the light fragrance of his aftershave.

Ari turned and looked at him. Sev was so close that it would only take Ari leaning forward half a foot and they would be kissing. His eyes dropped to Sev's full lips as if in anticipation then he glanced back up into Sev's piercing blue eyes. What was happening to him? Why did he suddenly feel this way? "Everything," he said. "I'm hiding from everything."

He hadn't even realized he had spoken until Sev said, "Why?"

"I don't know."

Io chose that moment to burst from the crowd. He sprang up between them, still buttoning his shirt. "One down, twenty more to go!"

Ari jerked back, as did Sev, but their eyes met in the mirror. Why did Ari suddenly want to take Sev back to where Io had just come from? And what had just happened here between them? He was heterosexual. Wasn't he? Suddenly, he wasn't so sure.

CHAPTER 12

MICAH WAITED IN SAM'S KITCHEN while she changed in the bathroom. As he leaned his ass against the edge of the counter, he glanced around the room. Sam didn't have much, and that was odd for someone who made the kind of money she did. Why the hell did she live in a dump like this making the kind of money she made? She had to pull in major cash at the Black Garter. He knew what a couple of those girls earned, and Sam was the star, for God's sake. She surely earned more than they did.

Growling at the thought, he sneered at the floor. They would discuss her profession later. Right now, he didn't even want to think about those men watching her while she took off her clothes.

His head snapped up as the bathroom door opened.

"I don't like this," she said for the hundredth time. She looked more like herself with the wig off and her face washed.

"What?"

"Going to your place. I don't like it."

Micah pushed away from the counter and followed her to the bed, where he helped her fold clothes into a small overnight bag.

"Would you rather stay here and die?"

She threw down a pair of folded jeans. "What makes you think they were going to kill me, anyway? You still haven't even told me who those men were. And what was all this talk about mates and vampires and that shit between you and…Trace, is it? That was his name, right?"

Micah nodded.

"Well, what was all that shit? How the hell did he do that to Ted and José, freeze them in midair like that? And how do you know how to hot-wire a car? You some kind of car thief? Who are you?"

It seemed Sam had recovered and found her voice again, her adrenaline-induced aggression finally finding an outlet in Micah.

"Okay, just slow down," he said, reaching for her hands. She pulled away. "No. I want answers, damn it."

Micah wasn't used to being bossed around, but this was Sam. She could do anything she wanted to him. He was hers to command. "I'll give you the answers you want, but let's get out of here first. Once we're at my place and you're safe, we'll talk. How's that? Will that work?"

The two sized each other up. Micah could see Sam's mind working over the logic and reasoning, but he held his ground, letting her know they would do things his way or his way. Yeah, not a lot of choice there.

"Fine, but when we get to your place, you're going to start singing, you got that?" She jabbed a finger at him.

Micah grinned, handing her a folded red sweater. "Yes, ma'am." He liked her feistiness.

Sam swiped the sweater from him and stuffed it in the bag. "Don't patronize me."

"Wouldn't think of it."

She threw him a sideways glance then looked away, but Micah caught the quirk of the corner of her mouth. She liked him despite her misgivings. He could tell.

"Okay, let's go. I've got everything." She zipped the bag and flung it over her shoulder.

Micah shook his head and took the bag from her. "I'll get this for you." No female of his was going to carry her own bags.

He led her to the door and made sure the coast was clear before allowing her outside. Using his body as a shield, he got her to the car and into the passenger seat before tossing her bag in the back and getting behind the wheel.

"Once we get to my place, I'll send Trace back to the club to get your things," he said as he pulled away from the curb.

"That'd be great, because then you can stop hot-wiring my car and freaking me out."

"I freak you out?"

"A little." She hesitated and glanced at him out of the corner of her eye. "Well, okay, not really, as crazy as that sounds, but the fact that you can hot-wire a car does. What, are you some kind of criminal? Is that what those guys were doing to you the other night? Beating you up because you stole their car?"

"No, it was nothing like that." Micah made a left, falling silent.

"Well, what is it that you do? I can see you're dressed like full military badass. Nice steel, by the way."

"Huh?"

"Your knives. I mean, all I can see are the sheaths, but I know my weapons and I can tell that's a hell of a Bowie knife you've got there. And that other one, what's that?"

"Ka-Bar Big Brother."

"Hmm, nice." She nodded appreciatively.

"How'd you know that?" Micah glanced over at her before putting his eyes back on the road, impressed all to hell and back that she even knew what a Bowie knife was.

"I haven't always been a dancer."

"I guess not." Micah had to shift to alleviate the ache in his groin. Hearing her talk about knives had gotten him semi-hard. "So, tell me where you learned about knives."

"Huh-uh. You want answers from me then I expect to get some from you first."

For the first time since he could remember, he was at a loss for words. Usually, he simply ignored people or kept to himself, not wanting to talk. With Sam, he wanted to, but she had shut him down so effectively, he couldn't think of anything to say.

"Well, all right," was all that came out.

Neither of them spoke again until he reached his apartment building and turned into the parking garage.

"The Sentinel? Nice," she said. "Whatever you do, at least you live well."

"I get by." He pulled his pass card out of his wallet, waved it over the scanner, drove down into the garage, and parked in the open lot.

After snagging her bag from the back seat, he ushered her toward a set of elevators that took them up to his apartment.

Trace was leaning against the wall by his door, head down and eyes closed. "Hey," he said, looking up as the two got off the elevator.

Micah still wasn't entirely happy with Trace for breaking his word, but if the guy really was sincere about wanting to make nice and hadn't intended on going back to Tristan to report on his nocturnal prowling and Sam, then the guy deserved a second chance, something Micah didn't dole out easily. For Trace, he would make an exception and give him the opportunity to redeem himself. If he fucked him over this time, though, that was it. Trace would be cut off for good.

After setting the suitcase inside the door, Micah flipped on the lights and stood aside to let his guests come in and look around.

"Nice view." Trace looked out the wall of windows. "How'd you pull this off, anyway? Keeping this place a secret from Tristan?"

Micah shut the door and strolled into the kitchen for a bottle of water. "Tris and I have an understanding." His eyes followed Sam as she surveyed his apartment. "Do you like it?" he asked her. He set the bottle of water down and joined her by the bookshelf.

She straightened as if strengthening her resolve. "Look, you promised me answers—"

"And you'll get them, but I need to talk to Trace first. Trace?" With a nod of his head, Micah beckoned Trace to join him down the hall. "Just give us a minute," he said to her. "Help yourself to whatever you want. There's a bar over there, and the kitchen is stocked. Make yourself at home, and I'll be right back."

Micah and Trace disappeared down the hall, and Sam heard a door close. She was finally alone and let out a heavy sigh. This guy lived large. The furniture was the finest quality, and the liquor in the bar was the good stuff, not cheap shit you'd find at some dive. Speaking of which, a drink sounded good. It might take some of the fray off her edges.

She grabbed a glass that looked like it cost more than her wardrobe—which was ridiculous, right?—and poured a double of Jack Daniels. That would get her good and loose. She hesitated, thinking about the men down the hall. On second thought, maybe she should only have a single. No sense letting her guard down around two virtual strangers. Pouring the extra booze down the sink somehow felt criminal, but pouring it back in the bottle would have been tacky and she would have only made a mess.

Did he have some Coke on hand to give her Jack some volume? She opened the mini-fridge under the bar and what do you know, the guy thought of everything. Snagging a can of Coke, she popped the top and splashed about half the can in her glass before fishing a few ice cubes from the small freezer.

Drink in hand, Sam returned to the bookshelf and ran her gaze down the spines of what had to be over two hundred books that looked like they had been collected over the course of three or four lifetimes. And what was with the Excalibur-worthy medieval sword mounted on the wall? She reached up and touched it with the tip of her finger. It was the real deal, not some fake for show.

And damn! Whoo-eey. Was that a real Monet hanging on the opposite wall? No way. Couldn't be. No one could afford art like that. She glanced over her shoulder down the hall. Well, maybe Micah could.

She returned to looking around and stepped up to his music collection. If she thought his book collection was large, he had a collection of CDs on the opposite shelf that dwarfed it. He probably had every one in digital, too. With a tight smile, she sipped her drink and realized the CDs were alphabetized by artist. Aerosmith, Beatles, Flo Rida, Frampton, Jay-Z, Led Zeppelin, Pink Floyd, Rihanna, and U2, among others. But what didn't make sense was the large volume of classical music he had, and not just Beethoven and Bach, but Liszt, Wagner, Haydn, Chopin, Schubert, and a bunch Sam had never heard of. What a mishmash of eclectic taste.

Micah. What an intriguing fellow. He came off like a hard-as-nails SOB on the outside, but inside his home was quite another story. She had expected beer in the fridge, empty pizza boxes and takeout littering the counter, a La-Z-Boy, and a foosball table, not this immaculate museum of civilized luxury and artistic culture. The fact that he didn't look older than his late twenties only doubled her curiosity.

Just what did this guy do that afforded him this kind of lifestyle?

Maybe he really was a criminal.

"OKAY, SO WHAT'S GOING ON? How is it that human knows and remembers you?" Trace said.

Micah shook his head. "She's not 'that human.' Her name is Sam. Sam Garrett."

"Yeah, yeah, whatever. You know what I mean. You had significant contact with her from what I heard, and her memory is still intact. Just what went down?"

They had a rule at AKM that when a member of the team had what they called *significant human contact*, which included injury, feeding, saving one from a dreck, and the like, it was the team member's duty and requirement to strip those memories from the human's mind. It was the only way they could continue performing the work they did.

"I was hurt. She saved me. I didn't strip her." As in, strip her memories.

Trace's head angled as he scrutinized Micah. "You didn't strip her?"

"No."

The two looked at each other for several seconds and then Trace's eyebrows shot up and he barked out a laugh. "Shit, you like her, don't you? You like her."

"Fuck you." Micah turned away and took off his coat then tossed it on the bed.

"That's why you're doing so much better. Shit, man, we all thought we'd lost you when Jackson left, but now I get it—the miraculous recovery and return to the land of the living. It's her."

"Drop it." Micah removed his knives and started to unfasten his shoulder holster then pointed at Trace. "And don't mention Jackson's name again." He may have moved on with Sam's sudden and preternatural appearance, but that didn't mean he liked being reminded of the pain he had suffered for the two weeks after Jackson had moved out. All he had to do was look in the mirror to be reminded just how far he had fallen. He still had over twenty pounds to gain before he was back to his old size.

Trace's voice quieted. "Yeah, got that, okay. Sorry, brother."

Micah's head snapped around. "You're not my brother. Just because you're here and you think we're some kind of chums doesn't mean you're my brother."

Trace swayed backward as if Micah had shoved him. "Fine, whatever. What do you want me to tell Tristan?"

"What do you want to tell him?"

"Don't play that shit with me, Micah. Just tell me what you want me to say."

The two squared off again and finally Micah said, "Just tell him you followed me, nothing happened, and then I went home. You can even tell him you followed me here. Not like I can keep this place a secret from you fuckers, anymore, anyway."

"I won't tell him about Sam, but you've got to take care of her one way or the other, broth—Micah, because she's not something you can keep secret for long, you know what I mean?"

"Sam's none of your concern."

"You're not thinking about mating with her, are you?"

Micah met Trace's gaze without a flinch, giving nothing away.

"Oh hell, you are." Trace shook his head and actually smiled as he rolled his eyes and looked away. "You're a real piece of work, you know that Micah? At least tell me you don't think she's your next mate."

There was a difference between mating and taking a mate. A big one. To a vampire, in casual conversation, mating simply meant having sex, while taking a mate was like getting married, only deeper. Taking a mate could be described as two souls coming together and claiming each other for eternity. The act was uncontrollable and the connection much deeper than anything the human mind could fathom.

Again, Micah didn't flinch, and he watched Trace's face grow somber, the smile fading, his eyes sharpening.

"You'd better get going, Trace," he said, his voice even.

"Fuck. Me. You do."

Micah could almost hear Trace's thoughts. It had been less than three weeks since he had lost Jackson, and Jack had been his mate. At least on Micah's end. All the physiological changes had taken place to bind Micah to Jackson so that when Jack left, those powerful bindings protested and sent Micah into a tailspin of despair. That's how it was for vampires, and many bound males died from losing a mate. It was a male vampire's greatest fear.

"Micah, she's human."

He nodded at Trace. "Yeah, I got that already."

"She'll die someday."

Micah's hand shot out and fisted around Trace's throat. "Don't ever say that again. You got me? If I'm her mate, I have rights." For one, he could petition the king to allow him to change her. To give her his venom and make her his *davala*.

Trace nodded, frowning, and Micah released him.

"Fine. Whatever." Trace rubbed his neck and walked toward the door. "But I won't tell Tristan or the others.

You've got my word."

"Well, your word is for shit right now, Trace," Micah said, following him, "so you've got some ground to earn back as far as I'm concerned."

"Asshole."

"Fucker."

Trace grinned and led him down the hall. "I'll let you know if something happens. Take care of her." He nodded toward Sam. "Nice meeting you," he said to her.

"Same here. Thanks for earlier, and…well, thanks." Sam's eyes darted between him and Micah.

Micah walked Trace to the door. "Do me a favor and go back to the Black Garter for her things, too, will ya?"

Trace nodded. "Sure."

Micah locked the door after Trace left then turned back toward Sam. He could sense the wear and tear on her emotions. It had been a long night for her, and her confusion tore at him like a beggar seeking alms.

"Answers," he said, doing all he could not to caress her cheek as he stepped in front of her. "I owe you some answers. So, tell me. What do you want to know?"

CHAPTER 13

HE MOVED LIKE A BLACK PANTHER stalking her in the shadows, his eyes never wavering from hers when he approached. Sam took a nervous drink, the ice rattling against her glass.

"Who are you?" she asked. That was the first question.

"Micah."

"I know that much already." She glanced around the room to indicate the amount of money that surrounded them. "What do you do to afford all this stuff?"

His eyebrow quirked as the corner of his mouth turned up. "Isn't it rude to discuss someone's income when you've only just met them?"

His words may have suggested impropriety on her part, but his tone indicated he really didn't mind the question.

"Isn't it rude to take a woman from her home without giving her an explanation?"

"Touché."

"So? What is it you do?" Her thoughts took her down every possible path—drugs, trafficking, terrorism, espionage, high-profile blackmail, computer hacking, every manner of crime.

He diverted toward the bar and poured himself a scotch. "Are you hungry? I can make you something."

"Later. Now spill or I'm out of here."

He capped the bottle, turned, and lifted his drink to his lips, barely sipping as he scrutinized her through narrowed eyes, making her skin sizzle. What was it about Micah that stirred her libido as if it were hot soup and he were the spoon? His intense, dark eyes made her think naughty thoughts, and she wondered how would it feel to kiss those shapely lips.

His eyes smoldered even more acutely, and he smirked as if he could read her mind and liked the ideas floating in her thoughts.

"Well?" she said.

He considered her for a moment. "You weren't far off in the car when you said I looked military. What I do is…" He bobbed his head as if choosing his words. "It's sort of military. Most of it is covert, so I can't discuss it."

"So what, you go around killing people and blowing things up?"

"Not all the time." His mouth curved into a humored grin.

"Oh, so just sometimes?" She fought not to smile back. Something about Micah disarmed her usual standoffishness.

"Yes, sometimes." He stayed by the bar, watching her.

"Okay, so how did that other guy, Trace, do that to Ted and José? How did he make them stop in midair like that?"

Micah cleared his throat. "Traceon has some, um, special powers."

"Duh. Obviously."

"What can I say? The guy is gifted." Micah lifted his glass and sipped, keeping his eyes on hers.

It was obvious he was done with that subject. "Okay, so who were those men and why did they want to kidnap me?"

The smile disappeared from Micah's face and he took a gulp of scotch. "They were two of the men involved in the incident the other night."

"No they weren't. They didn't even look like those guys." The men who had attacked Micah had long, black hair. Those guys tonight had short, cropped haircuts, and their hair had been brown, not black.

"Trust me on this, Sam, just because they didn't look the same doesn't mean it wasn't them."

"Oh, so they just changed their appearance. Just like that?"

He nodded. "Yes."

"And would you mind telling me how they did that?" Surely, he was joking, but he didn't sound like he was. It made the hairs on the back of her neck prickle.

Micah took another drink, eyeing her, looking as if he was in a discussion with himself as his eyes darkened and he blew air between his teeth. Finally, he said, "What I'm about to tell you would piss off my commander so badly I'd likely get desk duty for the rest of my life, you understand? And you probably won't believe me, anyway. You ready for this?"

Sam crossed her arms over her chest as if she were chilled. "Sure." What could Micah possibly have to tell her about those men to put such a grave expression on his face? More than just her neck hair prickled as she waited.

After breathing a heavy sigh, Micah downed the rest of his scotch, poured another, and spoke with his back toward her. "There are creatures living in this city, Sam. They're unsavory, evil, and use humans for personal gain and playthings. They're shifters. We call them drecks, and they thrive on causing pain and killing." He halted abruptly and raised his free hand as he turned back around to face her. "Okay, so not all drecks are bad, but enough are that it's easy to generalize. At any rate, because of the history between our two races, it's our job to police them. We make sure they don't get out of hand."

"Wait, you said they use humans. Are you saying they're not human?" And what was this shit about races? Was he talking about humans and whoever these drecks were? And what in the hell did he mean by calling them shifters? Was that a new gang term or something?

A shiver skimmed down her back. Shit had just turned super weird. As in fucking *Twilight Zone* weird.

"That's right."

Sam took a wary step backward. "And what about you?" Sam remembered what her kidnappers—these drecks, as he called them—had said about a vampire.

"You already know, don't you?" Micah's deep blue eyes held her as he drew his glass to his lips once more, slowly sipping, always watching her.

She peered more closely, trying to get a look at his teeth. Then she blinked and frowned, appalled at herself for buying into his load of horseshit and trying to see if he had fangs. But a little voice in her mind told her it wasn't horseshit. That what he was telling her was, in fact, true. That the world she'd lived in for twenty-seven years wasn't all she'd thought it was.

"Why don't you spell it out for me?" She took another step back then looked at the door, weighing the odds of getting out without him catching her, fear rising in her blood.

"I'm not going to hurt you, Sam. I want to protect you."

"Really?"

Micah took a step toward her just as she turned and bolted for the exit, dropping her glass. Micah's hand slammed against the door the moment she reached it as his other arm locked around her waist.

"Yes, Sam, I'm a vampire," he said. "But that doesn't mean I want to hurt you."

His warm, sultry breath caressed her ear and the side of her neck, making her tremble. But not from fear, which scared her even more.

Her heart raced, her lungs pumping hard for air as her fingers fumbled at the lock. "Let me out! Just let me go. You're crazy."

Even as she said it, she knew it was a lie. He was no more crazy than she was brunette. He spoke the truth and her gut told her so, but that didn't make it easier to accept. Vampires and shifters and whatever else out in the city? What dimension had she just entered? What would he tell her next, that werewolves were real, too?

"Stop it, Sam," he said, pulling her hand away from the lock and securing her arms against her body. "Calm down." He rocked her as if she were a scared child and he wanted to soothe her. "Sssshhh, I won't hurt you. I can't hurt you. It would kill me to hurt you." The last he said as he stopped swaying, his voice dropping to a whisper.

What in the hell had he meant by that?

"Why? Because vampires don't hurt humans?"

"Actually, no, not as a general rule. But it's deeper than that with you...for me...us. We're...You're my...I'm—"

He stumbled over his words, finally hushing abruptly in midthought a second before he turned his face so his nose sank intimately into her hair.

He inhaled longingly, his hold on her morphing into one of tender yearning. The simple gesture stirred warmth to pool in her belly, and a soft gasp escaped her throat.

"You are, too, aren't you? You feel it, too," he said.

He wasn't making any sense, but she nodded anyway, bending her head toward him as his nose drew a circle over her scalp and his breath warmed her skin. Whatever Micah thought she was or what she was feeling, she would be it and feel it.

He slowly released her wrists, and, without thinking, she trailed her fingertips over his forearms. "Is this where you drink my blood?" she asked dreamily, lost under his influence.

"Don't tempt me." He brushed his lips against her neck.

Wait. No, no, no! What was she thinking? She yanked out of his embrace and threw herself against the kitchen counter then turned back toward him. He looked like she had just ripped a vital organ out of him. "I know what you're doing. You're screwing with my mind, aren't you? Trying to seduce me. Trying to lure me into your lair or whatever." She waved her hand at him.

Shaking his head, Micah moved toward her, but Sam stepped away. "Just stay back."

"Sam, I wasn't compelling you. I wasn't screwing with your mind, as you put it. What you felt just now was all you, not me manipulating your mind."

Jutting her chin, Sam thought about that. Her body still sparked where he had touched her, and just thinking about his lips on her neck set butterflies tittering in her belly.

"Maybe you should sit down," he said, walking back toward the living room, leaving her to watch him go.

God, the man—vampire, whatever—was sexy. He walked with a swagger most men would kill for, confident with a hint of vulnerability that drew eyes to him as if he were moving art. He was the type who could put fear into his enemies or make a woman swoon just by crossing the room.

"Thank you," he said.

"I didn't say anything."

He looked over his shoulder as he knelt and picked up her glass, one eyebrow popping as he shrugged one shoulder apologetically.

"Oh," she said, drawing the word out. "You can read minds, is that it?"

"Yeah, sorry. Habit." He took the glass to the kitchen and grabbed a towel and carpet cleaner from under the sink.

"Well, quit the habit around me, okay?"

He knelt once more and sprayed the carpet. "Okay. I'll try."

"No, don't try, just do it."

"Damn, you're bossy."

She chuffed. "Excuse me?"

"That's not a bad thing." He held up one hand as if warding off her pending retaliation. "It's just that I'm not used to it. People don't normally boss me around. I like it coming from you, though."

Huh? That was an interesting tidbit, but she could see what he was saying. Micah struck her more as the type to boss others and do what he wanted, not the other way around. She could imagine most people gave in around him.

"Well, get used to it from me," she said, trying not to sound humored.

"Yes, ma'am."

Now he was just mollifying her, but she kind of liked his smarmy sarcasm. Almost enough to make her smile.

She watched him scrub her spilled Jack and Coke from the carpet.

"I'm sorry about spilling my drink on your carpet." She took tentative steps back into the living room, giving him a wide berth in the process.

"It's no problem. You took the news better than I thought you would, to be honest."

"I'm still not sure I believe it, but right now I suppose anything's possible." It all began to make sense, though. The books, the music, the sword, her kidnappers. She frowned.

That part still didn't make sense.

"Okay, so why did those guys try to kidnap me? That part I don't understand."

Micah returned to the kitchen and tossed the towel in the sink. "You interfered the other night." He threw her a concerned look.

"Interfered?"

"You saved my life. You interfered." He went to the bar and poured her another Jack and Coke.

"So, now those...drecks," the word still wasn't familiar on her tongue, "want to kill me?"

"Let me tell you about drecks," he said, handing her the drink. "They take it personally when someone interferes with a kill or fucks—pardon me, *screws* them over. Drecks enjoy killing vampires more than they do humans. You know, a kind of in your face to mommy and daddy, as it were. They don't like us very much."

"Us meaning you and Trace, right?"

"Well, yes, Trace is a vampire, too. A day walker, unlike me. But there are more than just the two of us."

"Day walker?"

He nodded. "There are two types of vampires. Full-blooded vampires like me, who can't tolerate the sun, and mixed-bloods like Trace, who can."

Hold the freak show just a second.

"By mixed-bloods, you mean vampires who are half human?"

"They could be half human, but they can also be part dreck or part lycan, too." That answered that question. "Or all of the above. A vampire's genetic makeup goes back centuries. Although, I should add that you don't see many mixed-blood vampires who have dreck or lycan blood in them. Given the history between our races, and the intense disdain vampires hold for drecks and lycans, vampires tend to prefer other vampires or humans when it comes to mating. But no matter what other races are part of a mixed-bloods ancestry, vampire genes tend to dominate." He held up his index finger. "Oh, and one more point. Mixed-bloods like Trace inherit special gifts from their combined genes. It has something to do with how the DNA combines when more than one race is involved. Our scientists could explain it better than I can."

Sam was barely keeping up with the deluge of information, but she was hanging on. "Are you saying that's how Trace did what he did to the bouncers at the Black Garter?"

"Yes."

"Okay, so…" She took a second to process. "Why don't drecks like vampires? Is this a racial thing? Like human race relations? One side trying to suppress the other?"

And if so, shame on them. It was bad enough humans pulled that shit.

"No, at least not with drecks. Lycans and their distant cousins, werewolves, on the other hand? I'll admit a little racial slurring goes on there, from both sides. Lycans and werewolves don't come around here, anymore, though, so it's not a problem." He rubbed his fingers over the scruff on his cheeks and chin. "But when it comes to drecks, a long time ago—we're talking millennia—we got along. Drecks and vampires were allies." He shrugged. "I mean, there have always been wars, but most of the time, the fighting was among the different vampire races battling for power. Then, a few thousand years ago, something happened that caused the drecks to turn on us. Alliances shattered. War erupted. But we're the stronger race, so we usually came out on top."

She could imagine how the drecks felt about their inequality. Nothing rankled more than knowing you were inferior and always drawing the short straw from the bunch.

"Which made the drecks hate you even more, didn't it?"

"Yep. Resentment grew, creating a permanent rift between them and us. But our king finally negotiated a truce with their leader. Peace has endured, more or less, for several centuries now, since about the late Middle Ages, but we know it's just a matter of time before another war breaks out. There's too much unrest, and it's getting worse every day." He pushed his hand through his hair and sighed. "I'm part of an organization called All the King's Men, which was created during the tail end of the last war as something similar to King Arthur's Knights of the Round Table. We were the elite warriors of our race. The king's personal guards. But during peace negotiations, our duties changed to those more or less of peacekeepers. We monitor dreck activity now and ensure peace is maintained. Even so, AKM is a cross between a military operation and a police force. We disguise our organization to humans as a detective service, which works well since we perform a lot of surveillance and act as private investigators with muscle most of the time. We even have divisions that work with humans on rescue and discovery missions, undercover ops, security, and the like. It helps us keep up appearances."

Sam rubbed her temple. This was a lot to take in, and part of her entertained the idea that this was all just an illusion or an elaborate practical joke. But, surely, someone would have jumped out from behind the wall by now to tell her to smile for the camera.

"Is this all for real?" she said.

He nodded, his expression somber. "I don't want to lie to you, Sam."

He was as deathly calm as a dark storm cloud on the horizon.

Either he was a great actor or he really was telling the truth.

She huffed and ran her palm over her forehead as she paraphrased the main points. "Okay, so vampires and drecks don't get along. Lots of wars, but there's peace now. Got it. So then, why were those drecks trying to kill you the other night?"

That had to be some kind of violation of the peace treaty.

"Because I told them to."

Sam's breath caught, her glass of Jack and Coke stopping halfway to her mouth as her eyes shot to his.

"You told them to?"

He nodded, and she lowered her glass without drinking. "Why the hell would you do that?"

Micah's gaze flicked toward the ceiling as he drew in a deep breath. Then he glanced uncomfortably toward the wall of windows overlooking the city. He looked like a man who was facing his demons. Pain and shame shadowed his face. It was clear he wasn't proud of what he'd done. Something had happened to hurt this larger-than-life man, and Sam's heart instantly went out to him.

"Micah?" She set her glass on the side table and touched his arm. "You okay?"

His face turned toward hers as if he were surprised to see her there.

"Vampires love very deeply," he said. "We don't just love, we mate. It's hard to explain to a human, but it's powerful when a male vampire mates and those binds lock him to the one his soul has claimed."

Her heart skipped a beat. "You're not talking about... well, sex. I mean, not just sex, but more like...partnering?" Something about the thought of Micah with another woman bothered her.

Micah nodded. "I was mated, and my mate left me a few weeks ago."

"Oh." Her mouth went dry as she glanced away.

"When he left—"

"He?" Sam stiffened, not sure what to think about Micah with another man. Was that normal for a vampire?

"Yes, I'm sorry. I wasn't clear."

"So, you're *not* into women?" She thought about what had happened by the door and grew even more confused. Disappointed even. A part of her had hoped he was attracted to her.

"Yes, I am. I mean...okay, wait." He huffed and paused as if collecting his thoughts. "Until Jackson, I'd never looked at males as potential mates. He was the first, and as luck had it, I became bound to him." His eyebrows furrowed as he gazed at her with fresh wonder, his eyes narrowing as he gave her a swift, almost suspicious once-over, as if he were making an invisible connection in his mind. When he spoke again, the words came out more slowly, almost cautiously. "But he

didn't bind to me, so when he left me a few weeks ago, I..."
He paused, and the wary fog gradually dissipated from his
features. "Let's just say I didn't want to live, anymore. I'd
already lost one mate—a wife centuries ago. That had been
bad enough to survive. This time, I didn't want to live."

Had he really said centuries?

"How old are you, Micah?"

"Old enough." His expression said he didn't want to freak
her out any more than she already was.

Okay, maybe she didn't want to know. Perhaps she should
digest one hard-to-swallow topic before taking on another.

"So, that's why you asked those men—drecks, whatever—
to kill you?"

He nodded. Guilt shrouded his features. "But then you
came along and gave me a reason to live again." It looked
like he wanted to say more, but he didn't. Instead, his gaze
dropped to her hand on his arm and he placed his palm
over it.

Warm and sure. Gracious. That's how his hand felt over
hers.

"Well, thank God for that." Her gaze met his and she
smiled at him.

"You were in the wrong place at the right time."

"Something like that. I mean, hell, it's not every day I get
to save a vampire."

He rolled his eyes at her obvious attempt at humor. "Well,
don't get too carried away with your heroism. You pissed
off those drecks."

"Are you sorry I did?"

He stared at her mouth as if he wanted to kiss her, and she
half-hoped he would. "Hell, no."

Then silence engulfed them. For several seconds, nothing
was said, even though a million silent thoughts passed
between them. She felt like they were refugees, on the run
from danger, and they only had each other to count on for
survival. Whether he really was a vampire or not, something
about Micah steeped her in safety.

"Okay," she said, "you kept up your end of the bargain

and answered my questions. It's my turn. What do you want to know about me?"

"Another time." He glanced toward the windows. "You look tired and we both need to rest."

A whirring sound caught her off guard and she darted her head around to see dual tracks of heavy drapes closing over the glass panes.

"They're automated to close before sunrise," Micah said.

"Oh, that's right. Sunlight. Vampire." She nodded. "Got it."

"You sass me."

"Who, me?"

"Come on, funny lady. Let me get you settled in my room. You'll sleep in my bed. I'll sleep on the couch."

He pulled away from her and walked toward the hall.

"You don't have to do that. The couch is more than adequate for me."

Micah turned around and leveled her with a look that made her feel like a rare, delicate orchid. "No, the couch is not adequate for one such as you, Sam. You deserve a bed fit for a queen. I insist you sleep in mine."

The way he looked at her, waiting for her to follow him to his room, made her heart flutter and her breath catch.

"Well," she said breathlessly, "since you put it that way." She picked up her drink and let him lead her down the hall.

Outside the apartment, Apostle stopped at Micah's door and smiled. Luck had been on his side tonight, after all. He had followed Micah from the woman's South Side hovel to the Sentinel. Then, after finishing his shift, he had come back. It had taken getting off on every floor, but he had finally found Micah's and the woman's scents on the eighteenth, which had led him to the door in front of him. Now he just needed to bide his time.

He returned to the elevator, rode down, left the lobby, got back into his squad car, and started planning.

CHAPTER 14

MICAH COULDN'T SLEEP. He just kept playing over and over in his mind how Sam had felt in his arms and the way her hand had touched him with such care. No one spoke to him with such obstinacy. Yet no one seemed to care as much as she did, either, despite only knowing him for less than a week. Sam had his heart in a twist, a tug-of-war to stay put or go to her.

But there was more to her than that. While he'd been explaining about Jackson earlier, an odd thought had occurred to him. One that resonated with increasing truth the longer he mulled it over.

The first time he'd seen Sam dance as Scarlet had been only hours before he met Jackson. He'd been drawn to her and had even tried to buy a private dance with her, but she'd been booked. What if she hadn't been? What if he'd gotten his private dance? Would his call to mate have fired for her instead of Jackson? And if it had, wouldn't that mean he'd never been meant to mate Jackson, but Sam all along? That would explain why he fell into suffering after Jackson left, because he hadn't been with his true mate, only a surrogate who'd fended off his suffering for a spell.

And really, what were the odds that he would mate them both? What he was feeling for Sam was definitely a mating link sharpening his mind, honing his body like a razor in preparation for his *calling*, the fertile time for a mated male. So, had he really mated Jackson? After all, Jack hadn't mated him back, which had always seemed strange. The one-sided mating had always felt wonky. Misdirected even.

What if he'd been meant to bond with Sam all along? What if the first seeds of the mating bond had been planted when he'd watched her dance? But the moment he left the Garter without getting the necessary up-close-and-personal needed to cement the bond, he ventured off to the nightclub where he'd met Jackson, who eye-fucked him from the dance floor before blowing him in the men's room less than ten minutes later. In the sewage processing plant that had been Micah's brain at the time, it wasn't a leap to think mental synapses could have short-circuited and a few wires crossed to make his body think Jackson was his mate instead of Sam.

Anything was possible.

God, he didn't want to think about Jackson, anymore. He was gone, Sam was here. That was all that mattered. Now he just had to convince her to stay here.

He sighed and rolled his head to stare at the drapes blocking out the daylight. If she decided to run out the door right now, he wouldn't be able to stop her. Apostle and his team of drecks were out there...somewhere. And they would be looking for her. The sunlight didn't affect them.

Just the thought made him feel helpless. Maybe making an alliance with a day walker like Trace had been a good decision, after all. Which reminded him...he picked up his phone from the coffee table then texted Trace, asking him if he'd been able to get Sam's things from the club.

Trace returned his text immediately: *Yes. Will give to you tonight at AKM.*

Micah tossed his phone aside and tried closing his eyes, but it was no use.

He needed to know Sam was okay. Not physically okay, but mentally. He already knew she was still awake. He could feel her mind working and worrying. He swung his legs off the couch, pulled on a pair of sweats, then went to the kitchen and flipped on the light. A pot of tea and a snack would do them both good. He heated water for the tea while he made a pair of roast beef sandwiches. He cut them diagonally, loaded everything on a tray, and carried it to his bedroom. He gently pushed open the door.

"I can't sleep," she said as he entered, sitting up as if she had been expecting him.

"I know. Me neither. Maybe this will help." He carried the tray through the dark room to the bed as she pulled the blankets around her. She was wearing a T-shirt and shorts, but maybe just the simple idea of being in bed around him made her uncomfortable. Or maybe the prim behavior was just habit. "We can eat in the kitchen if that would make you more comfortable."

"No, I'm fine. This is fine."

"I hope you like roast beef." He held out one of the triangles. She smiled as she took it. "Love it."

He poured two cups of tea, and for a few minutes, neither of them spoke as they ate.

"I guess I laid a lot on you tonight." He picked up the second half of his sandwich.

"I'll get over it."

"You shouldn't have to."

She shrugged and sipped her tea. "It's okay, Micah. I'll be fine."

He wanted her to be more than fine. Micah wanted her safe, and he wanted her happy. This affair with the drecks wasn't meant for someone like her, exquisite and perfect in every way.

"So, maybe I should answer your questions now." She popped the last bite of the first half of her sandwich in her mouth and shrugged as she grabbed the other half. "Not like we're getting any sleep, anyway, and it'll give us something to talk about."

"The fear of someone trying to kill you and being in a vampire's home has a way of keeping you awake, does it?"

Sam issued a short laugh that made Micah draw in a breath as if he could catch the sound and hold it forever, tasting it and swirling it around in his mouth.

"That's one way to look at it." She took another bite and watched him in the darkness as she chewed. "So, what do you want to know about me?"

"Why do you work at the Black Garter?" That had been

eating at him for hours.

"Wow. That was fast."

"Sorry, but I don't like it." In fact, he hated it.

"You don't like it?" She arched an eyebrow at him. "Well, too bad."

"It's just that you seem...well, better than that place. You're smart, Sam. And what I don't understand even more is why you live in such a small apartment. You can surely afford better. You're Scarlet, for Chrissakes."

She fidgeted uncomfortably then shrugged. "Well, shit. I guess I owe you answers, right?"

"Yeah, that was the arrangement. I answer your questions, you answer mine."

She finished her sandwich and with unceremonious bluntness said, "I'm married."

Married? Micah nearly choked and started coughing. Despite all his poking around in her head, he hadn't seen that one coming.

She held up her hand. "Hold on, don't get your panties in a wad. I left him."

He gulped down tea and got his coughing under control. "Okay, married and left him. Got it. Go on, because I can tell there's more."

"I married him too young. That was my first mistake." She leaned back against her pillows, relaxing. "Then I was an Army medic for eight years, so I wasn't home a lot. But when I was, it was bad."

It took all of Micah's restraint not to probe into her mind to see the whole story rather than the parts she wanted to share with him. She lifted her shirt slightly and pointed to a scar on the side of her abdomen.

"He gave that to me the last time I was home. He had just found out I had been secretly taking birth control to keep from getting pregnant." She stared at him for a second, silent.

His blood boiled.

"He beat me hard. Actually knocked me down on the glass coffee table. It shattered. I got stabbed. He's a surgeon so he just sewed me up right there in the house. Nice, huh? Kept anyone at the hospital from seeing the shape I was in and figuring out his wicked little secret."

"I want to kill him." Micah's voice sounded almost primal, even to himself.

Sam reached out and touched his arm. "Calm down, tiger." What a turn-on. This woman knew no fear. He had to be one scary-looking SOB right now, but she simply touched his arm and told him to calm down like it was nothing.

"Anyway," she said, casually pulling her hand back, "I ran away and work hard to keep my trail invisible so he can't find me. The Black Garter pays well and they pay in cash, and I live cheap so I can save enough to buy real freedom someday."

"Real freedom?" Micah admired Sam more and more. She was a lot stronger than he had originally credited her for.

"A new identity. A fresh start somewhere he can't get to me."

"Maybe I can help with that."

"We'll see." She simply smiled at him then finished her tea.

He moved the tray to the dresser, sat back down beside her, and propped the pillows on his side of the bed against the headboard so he could lean back in comfort. "Okay," he said. "New topic. How is it you know so much about knives?"

"I became acquainted with knives in the Army. It became kind of a personal interest for me."

Micah reached over, took his Bowie off the nightstand, and handed it to her. "Take a look. Here, let me get my KA-BAR." He hopped up and retrieved it from the shelf in the closet where he had stowed it earlier.

Sam already had the Bowie unsheathed when he returned, its silver blade glinting in the faint light from the hall. What a turn-on seeing her holding his knife. Like she knew how to use it, even if she didn't. She glanced up and he handed over the KA-BAR as he settled next to her again.

"These are serious blades," she said, admiring the long, black knife. "Tell me you're not just a collector."

He shook his head, his cock twitching as he watched her handle his weapons. "No, I'm not just a collector. I know how to use them. In fact, I'm what you might call an expert with a blade. Dangerously lethal."

Sam couldn't explain it, but holding the knives in her hands and catching the tone of his voice as he expressed his expertise with them turned her on.

"Show me," she said, flipping the Bowie in her hand so she could give it to him handle-first. "Teach me something."

Maybe Micah could show her how to disembowel someone. That way, if Steve ever did find her, she could have some fun. The thought immediately filled her with guilt. Could she really do that to someone? Even an abusive ass like Steve? Put a bullet between his eyes, maybe, but cutting him up as if she were Jack the Ripper? Okay, so under the right circumstances, she probably could. Better to be prepared.

Micah's gaze shot to hers and he reached out almost tentatively to take the knife. It was as if he wasn't sure he should.

"Oh, go on," she said. "I won't hurt you."

With a smirk, he took the knife and flipped it around, the blade shimmering as it danced in the light. He tossed and sliced it through the air then grabbed it backhand and lunged for her, pushing the blade toward her throat and stopping a couple of feet away. She didn't flinch, knowing in her heart he would never hurt her. Their eyes met and he seemed almost as breathless as she felt, and not from exertion.

Biting her lip, she clutched the Big Brother with the same grip he was using on the Bowie.

"Like this?" She batted his arm away and surged toward him.

He fell to his back as she cut the knife through the air and stopped within inches of his throat. She loomed over him, feeling her pulse quicken as his eyes smoldered up at her.

"Where were you a few days ago?" he said, his voice deep and seductive.

"Apparently waiting to rescue you." She eased the edge of the blade against his skin, biting her lip, liking the thrill she got from the look in his eye. It was a mix of fear and lust, the way she imagined a cuffed masochist looked as he prepared for his master to flog him.

"Any regrets?" he asked.

She shook her head, heat pooling like warm honey low in her belly and between her legs. "No."

Sam felt him relinquish himself as the Bowie thudded to the floor. His free arm swooped around her and pulled her on top of him. She had to swing her leg from under the covers, but with the knife still held to his throat, she straddled his hips and skimmed her other hand over his smooth, bare chest, as surprised at her reaction to him as he was.

"Tell me you're not using some mind trick on me to make me feel this way," she said.

His hands crept up her bare thighs and inside the legs of her shorts. "I'm not compelling you, if that's what you mean."

Raking her blunt nails across his pec, she smiled as he hissed and pushed his chest toward her hand. He was still thin but a little beefier, as if someone had hooked him up to a hose and blown air into him.

"You look better, by the way. The other night you looked like you needed a couple or a dozen sandwiches."

"Oh?" His hands pushed farther inside her shorts and she shifted her weight so he could explore her more intimately if he wanted to, but he only went so far before pulling his hands out to continue exploring her elsewhere.

Sam hadn't reacted to a man like this in a long time. Actually, she had never reacted to a man like this. Was it just the danger Micah represented, or how safe she felt with him despite all the peripheral shit she still wasn't sure she had wrapped her head around? Or was it the knife at his throat, or just the fact she'd been through a lot in the last twelve hours and simply needed an outlet for all that unspent adrenaline? Maybe it was a combination of everything. Who knew? What she did know was her body craved his in a way that felt almost criminal.

Shifting her hold on the knife, she dragged the tip of the blade lightly over his skin, to the hollow of his throat, down his sternum, and over to one dark, gathered, quarter-sized nipple.

Normally so straightlaced and proper, Sam wanted nothing of either right now. Some would say after so long without, her body now felt the need to make up for lost time, spilling over with arousal. A dark, mysterious man, possibly—probably—a vampire, lay under her, bent to her will as she flicked the tip of the knife across the puckered hardness of his nipple.

"Aren't you scared?" She bent forward so her face was directly over his and her hips rose from him. His hands skated up the sides of her legs and into her shirt to blister her skin with desire.

"I'm scared you'll stop." His hips thrust upward to keep the connection between their lower bodies, and his hardness pressed against her.

"I don't want to stop." She strengthened the contact between her legs by pushing and dragging her pelvis along the length of what lay inside his sweats.

The rumble in his chest sounded like the purr of a jungle cat. The sound mixed with a quickened breath as his palms covered her breasts with a demanding grip.

"Do you want *me* to stop, then?" It was clear he was only teasing.

Rolling her pelvis over him again, she bent down farther, moving the blade back to his throat. "If you stop, this knife will cease being a sex toy and you will have to move very fast to make sure I don't stab you. Do you understand?"

MICAH'S MOUTH DREW UP IN A MISCHIEVOUS GRIN and he purred again—the sound of an aroused male vampire. Sam had him harder than a two-by-four. Who would have known that a knife would be such a turn-on? In his Dom days, Micah had tried a lot of kinky shit, but never had he allowed anyone to put a knife to his throat. Usually, he did that kind of thing to his subs.

"Take off my shirt," she said. She sat back so her full weight pressed against his aching hard-on. "Use this." She lifted the knife from his throat and held it out for him.

He had seen inside her thoughts and knew she had never done anything like this. Where this vixen had come from Micah didn't know, but he liked her. He would have to tell Sam to let her out again sometime soon. Like maybe tomorrow. Or in an hour after they'd finished and taken a brief recess to catch their breath.

He took the knife and licked his lips as he gathered the hem of her T-shirt in his free hand and pulled it away from her body. The force drew her toward him again, although she resisted. Her shirt stretched between them, the fabric straining. Never looking away from her heart-shaped face and her twinkling eyes, he hooked the blade under the hem.

"You sure about this?" he said. He felt her desire, but also her fear, so he wanted to give her one last chance to say no.

"Yes." She licked her lips. "It's not one of my favorite shirts, anyway."

He grinned, and with an easy upward thrust, the blade sliced into jersey knit as if it were nothing more than butter. The satisfying hiss of fabric being cut filled the room as he continued the dissection. Watching the blade slice slowly upward held its own kind of eroticism as it parted the fabric of her shirt like an opening stage curtain. More of her creamy soft skin and smooth stomach revealed itself with each inch of the blade's climb. Getting to all that bare skin on a slow reveal had him holding his breath with anticipation until the last inch severed at her collar and the two halves fell loose.

With a brush of his free hand, he pushed the T-shirt off one rounded shoulder and down her arm to expose her breast. Budded with a nipple so pale he could barely delineate the change of pigment, the supple swell of her flesh was natural and firm. And her stomach was smooth and flat with a single, tantalizing ridge down the middle. He ran the tip of the knife down that ridge, watching her shiver at the metallic caress.

"You're a runner or a swimmer, aren't you?"

"Both. How can you tell?" She shirked the other half of the shirt with a seductive dip of her shoulder so the wasted material fell down her back and over his legs.

"I can just tell." He grinned and set the knife on the mattress then undulated beneath her. He needed to touch her, feel her, experience her femininity. Another purr, deeper than before, trembled the back of his throat as he shoved his hands up her stomach and under her breasts so they rose and pressed together in the middle.

The air between them quickly heated, sizzling, crackling, burning, and he flipped her to her back, rolling with her, pushing his sweats down with one hand as his mouth found hers. He nearly came from just her taste and the mewling noise she made as their lips fused together, twisting and holding, drawing in and urging each other for more.

She shifted beneath him, and he felt her hands pushing down her shorts, their mouths never letting go, grunting in frustration that they couldn't get free of their clothes fast enough, urgent to feel the other, wanting, needing, and demanding.

Finally he kicked his pants off and shoved her legs open with his knees, pushing forward and sinking in deep as she cried into his mouth and locked her arms around his back to hold him hard against her.

Giving himself to her slowly, he rocked into her, his back curving as he took her deep and then slowly pulled out, gliding back into her silky heat once more. Each solid thrust was answered with a feminine whimper, each of which he caught on his tongue until he could no longer hold back and dropped his mouth to her throat as he quickened his tempo. SOMETHING CLICKED when he planted his lips against her throat. Vampires drink blood. They drink from their victims' throats, and his mouth was on her throat. Did he intend to take her blood, just sink his fangs—or whatever he used—

into her flesh and take her? Instead of the thought terrifying her into a cold stop, the added risk sent her to the moon and she pushed him over, keeping the intimate connection between them as she took him from the top.

Harder and faster, she ground herself against him with a need she had never felt, her orgasm hiding just under the surface. But it was there, just waiting, rising and gripping her throat from the inside so that each time she exhaled, she cried out a little louder than before, each breath building a crescendo of sound and sensation.

Micah seized her thighs in his large hands. He was stronger than he looked, pushing and pulling her easily as he bucked up to meet her urging thrusts. The look on his face was so feral, and the grunts he made so carnal, she could almost hear the train of profanities running through his mind. Did he hold himself back for her? She could tell the words hung behind his clenched teeth just waiting for an invitation to spill.

"Tell me to fuck you," she demanded, close to going over. "Tell me!"

With a howl that was half-guttural war cry and half-gracious relief, he switched his grip from her thighs to her hips and pounded hard against her, slamming his length deeply into her.

"That's it, Sam. God, yes, fuck me! Fuck me! FUCK ME!"

When had Sam ever felt so debauched, yet so decadent? She couldn't remember. Micah did things to her no man had ever done, drawing out a woman she'd never felt safe enough to be.

Before she knew what was happening, she was on her back again, Micah's large frame driving into her from above, her legs up and over his shoulders.

"Tell me, Sam," he said, an unbelievable quiet coming over him as he stilled. It felt to Sam like the air around them was only getting hotter, supercharged, pregnant with unspent desire that only needed a spark to ignite.

"What?" Tell you what?" she asked, linking her fingers behind his neck, yearning, squirming for him to continue.

"Tell me to come." His dark eyes glittered as they bore into hers. "Please. Hurry. Tell me."

Panting, pulling, needing him, she nodded. "Come for me, Micah. Come inside me." She realized she didn't want him to pull out. She wanted to feel what he felt like deep at her core.

Growling, he thrust hard and fast, hitting the front of her tight core in just the right spot to stir her own stubborn release from the shackles it had locked itself in.

"Come with me." He grunted. "I can feel how close you are. Come with me."

"Yes." She knew she would. He didn't have to worry. "I'm close, so close, don't stop." As if he would, but she needed him to hear her say it. "Now, now. Micah!" Her nails dug into his back as she gripped him and felt the first wave of release sweep over her.

His body stiffened and shuddered, his hips slamming forward as he cried out and his cock jerked against her G-spot to send her crashing in a wave of pleasure that shot through her body like lightning. Her muscles quivered and pulsed around his steely presence inside her, sucking him as he pulsed and emptied himself against her walls, warming her as if he were pouring hot honey inside her.

AFTER SHE HAD MILKED EVERY DROP from his cock, and after the last of her gentle spasms of release had subsided, Micah pulled out and rolled her to her side and lay down beside her, wrapping his arms around her slim waist as if he would never let her go.

"Did I hurt you?" he said, running his nose over the sweat-dampened skin on the back of her neck. "Mmm, you smell even better when you perspire."

"Do I?" Her body shook softly as she chuckled. "That's a first. And no, you didn't hurt me."

Micah felt her body humming with life. "You've never come that hard, have you?"

"No. How do you know these things?"

"It's my spider sense." He smiled into her soft, short hair.

"Yeah, whatever. You're probably digging inside my head again, aren't you?"

"Maybe just a little."

"Well, stop it."

They were silent for a while then Micah said, "You don't enjoy dancing at the Garter, do you?"

Sam's head bowed slightly, as if she were ashamed. "No. But you know why I do it. I don't have much choice."

"What if I helped you? Found you another job? I can be very persuasive." He ran his hand over the curve of her hip.

"I can see that." He heard the smile in her voice, and then she rolled in his arms to face him. Her smile faded. "I don't want to be a charity case, Micah."

"You're anything but a charity case, Sam." He combed his fingers through her short hair. Making love to her had been wonderful, and it had come out of nowhere. Who would have thought showing her his knives would lead to...well, *that?* He felt so full of life all of a sudden. Not even with Jackson had he felt this alive. "God, I loved making love to you just now." The words swooshed out of him on a heady exhale as if he hadn't intended to speak aloud.

Sam snuggled closer as he tightened his embrace. "I did, too. You do things to me...make me feel things — "

"You've never felt before?"

"I told you to stop that." She playfully bit his shoulder.

"Habit. I can't help myself." His fingers brushed over her back.

"Try."

He chuckled. "Yes, ma'am."

They both drew silent once more, breathing against each other, enjoying the postcoital reverie. But soon enough, Micah's thoughts returned to her career and he pulled away enough so he could look into her eyes.

"Seriously, Sam, I'll do what I can to help you if you want to quit dancing. I don't like you working there, anyway." He didn't want her returning to the Black Garter, especially now that they'd consummated their relationship, which strengthened his bond to her. The thought of all those men lusting after her as they jacked off made him want to hurt someone. He stroked her hair off her forehead and ran his fingertips over the curves of her face.

"Big bad Micah doesn't like anyone looking at his girl, huh?" Her hand skimmed over his chest.

He grinned, making sure to flash a little fang. "Damn straight."

She leaned in and kissed him. "That's sweet, but I told you. I don't want to be a charity case. I'll manage."

Damn stubborn woman. Micah would clean his own savings out and give it all to her if she asked him to. "Well, I won't let anything happen to you."

Her smile widened and she placed her hand in his. "Why do I get the feeling you mean that?"

"Because it's true."

"Are all vampires like you?"

"No."

"Well, are they at least as nice?"

If only the other members on his team could have heard her say that. He chuckled. "Absolutely not."

"What's so funny?"

"I'm known as the blankity-blank-so-and-so SOB on my team."

She nodded. "Oh, well, I guess I can see that, too."

"I bet you can."

The two moved closer together, their naked legs intertwining.

"Should I feel honored to have the famous Scarlet in my bed?"

She rolled her eyes and playfully shoved his chest. "I don't do Scarlet off stage."

"I bet I can talk you into it. I've seen how you can bend." He nuzzled her neck.

"Oh, you have, huh?" Her fingers combed through his hair, and he purred against her skin.

"Yes. Will you give me a private show sometime? I've

always wanted one."

Her head bent back and her breasts pressed against his chest. "It'll cost you."

"How much for a whole night?"

"Hmm, we can work it off in trade. How's that?"

Rolling over on top of her, Micah trailed his tongue down her body as he sank between her legs. "Well, let me get started with my end of the deal then."

The last thing he saw before closing his mouth over her swollen clit was Sam's eyes drifting shut, her head nodding as she pressed into the pillow.

"Yes, please," she said.

CHAPTER 15

IT WAS LATE WHEN SAM WOKE UP with Micah nestled behind her and his hand cupping her between her legs as if he had fallen asleep trying to stimulate her into yet another orgasm. How many times had she come before they had finally fallen into an exhausted, sated sleep sometime around one o'clock? She rubbed her palm over her face, trying to remember. Three? No. Four times.

Her body felt well used, but in a good way, and a pleasant ache throbbed at her center. After their first time, which Sam now blushed over—she'd never been one for rough sex like that, but now she wondered why the hell not—Micah had used his mouth like a cunnilingus master before taking her again on top. The loving had been softer and more savory then, and he'd made love to her with the tenderness of a man more in love than in lust.

After dozing for a few minutes in each other's arms, he had awakened and pulled her on top of him. She had been too tired to do much of the work, but Micah had had more than enough energy left in him for the both of them, securing his arms around her as she had laid against him and he pumped into her from the bottom.

Wow, things had moved fast with Micah. She had only just met him and already felt like she was falling in love. How had that happened when she was normally so cautious and distant?

A soft smile touched her lips as she replayed the morning's memories over and over in her head. His breath warmed the back of her neck as he continued to sleep. His leavings still seeped from her, and she wondered if maybe they should have used protection. Or maybe vampires couldn't impregnate humans. But then that couldn't be true, because if vampires couldn't impregnate humans there wouldn't be all those mixed-blood, day walker thingamapeople like Trace running around.

God, was she really thinking like this? Was Micah really a vampire? And were creatures known as drecks really trying to kill her? Maybe she had merely dreamed all that. She had had something to drink, and she rarely drank, so maybe her mind had played tricks on her.

"No." Micah's gravelly voice broke the silence, startling her.

"What?"

He cleared his throat. "No, your mind's not playing tricks on you." He pulled her closer, sliding his hand farther between her legs, purring when he felt what he had left inside her coat his fingers.

"You're not supposed to be in my mind, remember?"

Soft lips found the place just at the base of her neck, just above the bone at the top of her spine between her shoulders. "I'm sorry. I connected with you before falling asleep so I could make sure nothing happened to you while we slept. It's something mated males do."

Something about that made her heart skip. He protected her even during sleep. How sweet. Talk about your chivalrous behavior.

"Your thoughts about what we did this morning woke me up," he said. "I like that you were thinking about us."

"Me, too." Admitting it out loud made it all the more real. "What time is it?"

She felt him turn his head, then he rolled back and snuggled closer. "Almost seven thirty."

Seven thirty! She needed to get up and get ready for work.

"No," he said, holding her tight.

She reached around and slapped his ass. "Get out of my head. And, yes, I need to work."

"No," he repeated, tightening his hold so she couldn't break free. "You call in sick for a while."

"Micah—"

"I'll cover your lost wages until you can go back. *If* you want to go back. How much do you average a night?"

"*If* I want to go back?"

"Yes. Just think about what we talked about earlier. My offer still stands to help get you out of there. Now, what do you average a night?"

Did he seriously want to know her nightly salary? Surely he didn't plan on replacing what she would lose by calling off.

"Yes, I do. Now, how much do you make?" he said.

"Fine. Maybe I should just think the figure since you won't get out of my mind."

"You could do that." He chuckled and pulled her closer, obviously enjoying playing with her like this.

She had to admit, it was fun if not a tad annoying.

"Okay, I'll just tell you. On weekends I've made as much as a thousand dollars in one night. During the week it's closer to five hundred a night."

"I'll give you a thousand a night until I deal with Apostle and the others. Will that do?" His palm rubbed her up and down and she felt his hardness press against the back of her thighs.

"Micah—"

"Don't argue. Yes or no. And don't say no."

Sam sighed. "You're incorrigible. Fine then. Yes. That will do."

"Good, then it's settled." He lifted her leg, and she felt the head of his cock probe her saturated nether lips, parting them.

"Yes, it's settled."

Then he was sliding home, rocking into her as she reached her hand around and held the back of his head. She could get used to waking up like this.

"So could I," he said.

"We need to do something about your disobedience."

"Mmm, what did you have in mind?"

"I'll think of something. Now, shut up and fuck me."

"Yes, ma'am."

And holy heavens, did he ever.

Sam was the damn finest sexiest woman he had ever met. Waking up to feel his cum spilling over his palm and her body molded into his curves as she replayed their sexual pyrotechnics from this morning made him feel like he was seeing fireworks for the first time. He had always loved fireworks, and not just the flares used by the military from ages ago, but the kind that went off every Fourth of July.

It was the one thing his teammates actually teased him over, how Micah never worked on Independence Day so he could watch the fireworks. It took some planning, too, since the sun didn't set until just before, but it was always worth the effort. He'd even tried to take pictures of them to hold onto the memory all year, but pictures never turned out as good as the real thing.

And that's what Sam was: his own personal firework. She amazed and dazzled him, making him feel alive and whole again.

Pressed behind her, he thrust forward, holding her leg in the air.

She gasped in pleasure and slapped her hand down on the mattress from the force of his body. Her inner channel was slick and swollen after the working over he had given her earlier, but damn she was hot against his cock.

"Your body calls to mine," he said breathlessly as he pounded into her once more.

She only moaned and arched her back so that her head lay against his shoulder and her tight, perfect breasts jutted out alluringly.

"Mmm." He ran one hand up her stomach and his palm layered over the perfect handful of firm flesh, topped by her taut nipple. The hard nub pressed against his palm and he couldn't resist swirling his hand in a circle to feel it tease his skin.

"Micah…" Sam pressed her hips back, her ass forming a

perfect seal against him.

Oh God, she was too much. He couldn't hold himself back. In a swift flourish of movement, he threw his pillow over so it was in line with her hips then rolled her to her stomach on top of it. The pillow angled her hips perfectly so that when he rose up behind her, his hard length drove into her right to the hilt.

"Yes!" She cried out, burying her face into the mattress as her long fingers groped the sheet on either side of her head.

"Yes, what?" His inner Dom worked to the forefront as he sank inside her and lowered himself over her body. With his stomach and chest pressed against her back, he thrust again and whispered harshly. "Yes, what, Sam?"

For a moment, she seemed not to know how to respond.

"Say my name, Sam," he said, cluing her in. "I want to hear you speak my name."

Sam shivered beneath him and whimpered needfully. "Yes, Micah. More, please."

He grinned, eager to give her what she begged him for while his need to control the scene stirred his own desire. Micah hadn't felt the urge to Dom anyone in years. Even when Jack had wanted to experiment with submission, Micah hadn't been very interested. But now, here he was itching to spank Sam and more.

His hand slapped down on her ass as he rose up and rammed his erection into her. Sam trembled and her hands curled into fists as she gritted her teeth through the sting.

"You like when I spank you, don't you?" He swatted her ass again, and then again on the other side. Rosy handprints blossomed on her pristine flesh.

"Yes."

He spanked her harder. "Yes, what?"

"Oh God!" She cried out and arched her back before undulating beneath him. She looked like a slender, elegant reed bending in the breeze. She was so flexible and graceful. "Yes, Micah!"

Her tender, inner walls tightened around him. She was going to come, and he wanted to taste her when she did.

Crashing down over her body, he fucked her hard, opening her legs by pushing the front of his thighs against the back of hers. The new position gave him leverage to hit her deep and rough, and each forceful drive forward provoked a tight, feminine gasp of pleasure to burst from her throat.

"Tell me you're mine," he said, his voice a growl as his mouth pressed against her ear. "Tell me you belong to me."

She quivered and groaned, lost in ecstasy. "I'm yours. I belong to you, Micah."

"Your body is mine." He punctuated the command with a demanding thrust of his hips.

"My body — Oh, God yes — my body is yours. Please..."

"Please what?"

She took a ragged breath and groaned as her body tensed beneath his. "Please, Micah."

"Good girl." He gave her everything he had then, thrusting hard and fast, working her G-spot into a quivering rage of delirium. And just before she tumbled into full-on orgasm, he bit her. He licked her shoulder and sank his fangs in deep.

As the euphoria of his venom took hold, she screamed. Her body spasmed and her muscles blew apart as she erupted in a series of violent tremors.

"Yes, yes, yes, YES, God YES!" She collapsed against the mattress as her body quaked ceaselessly.

Only then did Micah allow himself to release his own pleasure. The taste of her blood, the feel of her body jerking under his, the feel of her feminine canal vibrating and gulping like a throat against his cock, and the knowledge that he alone had given her such tremendous pleasure sent him over.

"UNGH!" Never had such a harsh release claimed him, and his fangs sank even deeper as he slammed his hips against the curves of her ass. And once more he unloaded his offering and filled her, layering his scent over and inside her body as her scent drenched his.

He didn't take much of her blood, and soon released her shoulder before collapsing in a sweaty, well-spent heap over her back. Neither could speak for some time, but he slid his arms up and over hers until their hands met and their fingers wound together in two tightly bundled death grips.

When he could finally speak again, he nuzzled the back of her neck and said softly, "I've never met anyone as amazing as you."

"Mmm, right back at you." She turned her head and looked over her shoulder at him. "Promise me you'll do that again later."

He smiled, all fangs and mischievous lust. "Oh, you can count on it. I promise."

Finally, they crawled out of bed and brushed their teeth together in the bathroom. Then he ushered her into the shower where he made love to her again, her back slapping against the wall, her legs locked around his hips, her fingers clasped around his neck.

Micah couldn't get enough of her and hated having to leave.

"I'll only be gone a few hours," he said, sitting on the edge of the bed, bent over to secure his boot knife into the ankle of his combat boots.

"Can I do anything while you're gone? Laundry? Cook you breakfast before you get back?" Her flirty, playful smile unknotted his heart.

He gave her a heady once-over. She looked good in his robe. "You can think about me."

"Well, that goes without saying." She dipped her head to the side as if to tell him he had stated the obvious.

Micah stood and pulled a black sweater over his head then tugged his hair out from the collar. Maybe he needed a trim after all. "Just relax. Soak in the hot tub on the balcony. Watch TV. Order takeout. Make yourself at home. Just don't go anywhere." He leveled her with a stare that warned her not to test him on that last point.

She crossed her index finger over the center of her chest. "I promise."

"Okay, good."

He had already retrieved his knives from the floor and now secured them to his hips. Taking out his Sig, he checked the cartridge and slapped it back in place.

"A Sig? Really?" she scoffed.

"Yeah, yeah, I saw your Beretta, female. Don't dis my Sig. He's sensitive."

Sam laughed and the sound warmed him all the way to his marrow. He holstered the Sig under his arm then leaned down and caressed her face before handing her a cell phone.

"Here's my extra phone. You can use it until I get yours back from Trace tonight. If anything happens, or if you need me, just dial one and it will ring me."

She nodded as she took the phone and ran her thumb over the number one. Then he kissed her once slowly, gently.

"I'll see you in a little while," he said then kissed her again.

She took his hand and got up with him and followed him to the front door.

"I'll be here," she said.

One last kiss good-bye and he left, looking back at her as the elevator doors opened. "Lock the door."

She nodded then went back inside.

The drive to AKM took less than fifteen minutes. Malek was the first to cross paths with him.

"Hey, Trace is looking for you." Malek frowned, wrinkling his nose suspiciously.

"I know." Micah marched past him, not even slowing down.

He passed others from different teams as they prepped to go out or brought back the first catches of the night then headed past dispatch, the training center and the war room, farther on past the data center where they gathered Intel, all the way to the back hall where he came to the elevator bay and hit the button for the third floor. That was where the dorms were for the members of Tristan's team.

Trace's door opened within a couple seconds of Micah knocking on it, as if the guy had been expecting him.

"Jesus." Trace said. "Her scent is all over you."

"Nice to see you, too." Micah barged past him and into the small room. There was just a bed, a desk, a small table and a few things that personalized the room. Trace obviously liked sports. *Sports Illustrated* back issues littered his desk, and his small flat screen was set to ESPN.

"Where's her bag?"

Trace brushed past him and opened his closet. He grabbed her duffel and held it out to him. "She carries a nice piece."

"Huh?"

"Beretta. Impressive for a dancer."

Micah opened the bag and grinned wistfully as he pulled out the gun and stared at it. He thought about how Sam had shocked the hell out of him with the knife this morning and took what she wanted from his body, despite her confusion over all he had told her.

Most women got excited by him because he was scary and brooding. Even for Jackson, that had been part of the charm and excitement. But Sam had clearly not been afraid of him. She had actually made *him* feel afraid, even if only for an instant.

"She's got courage," Micah said proudly. He dropped the gun back in the bag. "Thanks for going back for this." He lifted the duffel between them.

"So now what?"

"You feel like hunting drecks?"

Trace scratched his chin and met his eyes, one corner of his mouth curling deviously. "Hunt, as in off the record?"

"Way off," Micah said.

"Hot damn! We're going to kill some drecks, aren't we?"

Micah chuckled. He actually chuckled. "When did you become so insubordinate, Trace? You're always kissing Tristan's ass like a pansy and being his errand boy."

"That's what I want you all to think."

"Oh." Micah drew the word out, narrowing his eyes. "So, you're not such a good boy after all, are you? What else are you hiding in there?" He gestured toward Trace's cranium.

Trace shrugged with a flippant bob of his head and grabbed his coat. "You going to stand there and give me the sixth degree, or are we going to go kill something?"

Micah gestured toward the door. "By all means, lead the way."

The two headed into the hall and back down the elevator, then swiped their access cards over the magnetic reader at the back door and slipped away before anyone could stop them.

SAM CHANGED INTO A PAIR OF JEANS and a long-sleeved Henley tee after taking Micah's suggestion and soaking in the hot tub. His was the only balcony on this side of the building, so it afforded her enough privacy to truly relax.

So, this was how the rich lived? They could afford apartments that took up half the floor at the top of a building with a phenomenal view. As far as Sam could tell, Micah only had one neighbor on this floor, and that door was at the opposite end of the hall with the elevator splitting the distance. Would she ever be able to afford a place like this? Doubtful, but she would be able to live comfortably, and that would be enough as long as she was safe from Steve.

After finding something to watch on TV, she checked the fridge and grabbed a bottle of water. She really didn't feel like cooking, and she didn't want to mess up his kitchen. Sure, Micah had told her to make herself at home, but it wasn't her home and she felt awkward just thinking about poking around in his cabinets like she lived there.

She could order a pizza just as easily and save the mess. After using his computer to look up the local pizza delivery place, she snagged the phone from the kitchen counter and ordered two large pizzas—he would need food when he got home, right?—an order of bread sticks, and a chef salad with Italian dressing.

"Anything to drink with that?" the guy on the other end of the line said.

"No, thank you."

"Total is thirty-two oh six. Delivery time is about forty minutes."

"Okay, thanks."

"Oh, and please contact the security desk to let them know to let us up."

Apparently they delivered here a lot. Sam would never

have thought of alerting security.

"Oh, that's right," she said. "Thank you for reminding me. I'm new here and didn't even think of that."

"No problem. We get that all the time."

"I'll bet."

She hung up and looked around for the number to building security but couldn't find it anywhere, not even when she dared to poke around in the kitchen drawers and Micah's desk, feeling like a snoop the entire time. Unable to find the number that way, she tried calling the generic number for the building listed on the Internet, but that just looped her into voicemail hell.

With a sigh, she checked the time after spending twenty minutes searching. Maybe she should just call Micah and ask him, but being unable to find a phone number was a lame excuse and she didn't want him to think she was totally useless. Besides, he was probably out doing some of that top-secret shit—killing drecks and blowing shit up. She grinned to herself with a shake of her head as she thought about how preposterous she would have thought all this was just a couple days ago. Her, with a vampire. A vampire who served up a major dose of kick-ass to evil shifters that prowled the city.

Hoo-rah!

Giving up on finding the phone number, she decided to just go downstairs and tell the security guard personally to let up the delivery driver. She grabbed her wallet just in case her order arrived while she was in the lobby.

Shit, she didn't have a key, which meant she couldn't lock the door. At the last second, she grabbed her phone in case the door automatically locked after she left—she was paranoid about stuff like that. Something like getting locked out would warrant interrupting Micah for sure.

Checking her reflection in the mirrored door of the elevator as it took her down to the lobby, Sam fidgeted restlessly, wondering what Micah was doing. Was he out hunting down the drecks that had attacked her? She was surprised at how quickly she was adjusting to all the information he had dumped on her last night. Had it just been last night? Wow, it seemed like a lot longer than that.

Her hand absently ran over her throat and the two tiny marks where Micah had bitten her. How hot had that been? Even now, just remembering how her body had lit up with what he later explained was venom euphoria, she felt herself go warm and moist between the legs. His biting her hadn't hurt, and she hadn't been frightened at all.

Funny, but that was one thing she couldn't bring herself to be: frightened. Micah had a way about him that calmed her, not scared her. Even at the height of his disclosure, when he had told her he was a vampire and she had tried to flee, as soon as he'd put his arm around her to hold her back, a serene peace had stirred deep inside her. Had that just been some kind of vampire voodoo? He had told her he hadn't subjected her to any mind tricks, though, and she felt certain he'd been telling the truth. Which meant her reaction to him was all her.

And then later, when he had come to her in his bedroom. No man had ever given her such incredible pleasure, and none had ever treated her with such reverence. If this was what it was like to date a vampire, she could get used to it. Maybe she had just never been cut out to date humans. The thought made her laugh, and she was still chuckling to herself as the doors opened and she entered the lobby.

"Excuse me," she said to the guard at the desk. "I'm staying with a friend and just ordered a pizza and they told me I should let you know to let them up."

"Certainly, ma'am. The apartment number?"

She gave him Micah's door number and looked up as a police officer entered the building. His eyes met hers and she quickly looked away, suddenly uncomfortable, but she didn't know why.

"I'll send them up when they arrive, ma'am," the guard told her.

"Thank you." She glanced at the police officer again to find him still looking at her, then turned and went back to the elevator. Why was her heart racing?

Looking back, the officer flashed his badge at the security guard, saying something to him but speaking too quietly for her to hear. With a hard smack, she pressed the elevator button, but it didn't open and she looked up to see the numbers flashing over the door. Sixteen, fifteen, fourteen… Sam turned back to see the officer walking toward her, his gaze fixed on her as she smiled tightly.

"Evening," she said, returning his crisp smile with one of her own.

"Ma'am." He tapped the brim of his hat as he nodded.

Eight, seven, six…

Sam felt for the phone Micah had given her, running her finger over what she hoped was the *one* key. Something just felt off about that officer, and her adrenaline was pumping hard, making her fingers tremble. She could swear she had seen him before, but he hadn't been wearing a uniform. Where? Where? At the Garter? Was he a customer? The way he looked at her made her feel like he knew her, too.

Ding.

The elevator doors slid open and a couple dressed in evening attire stepped out, smiling at her and the officer as they passed.

"After you, ma'am." The officer held his hand over the doors to keep them from closing, gesturing for her to go ahead.

Sam didn't want to get into that elevator with him, and she looked toward the doors of the building in hopes that her pizza would show up and she could make an excuse to stay behind. But damn slow pokes, no delivery boy walked in.

"Thank you," she said to the officer, stepping past him and into the elevator.

He pressed the button for the nineteenth floor and stepped back, hands linked in front of him.

Tension strangled the air in the confined space, and when the elevator opened on the eighteenth floor, she practically shot into the hall, trying to hurry back to the safety of Micah's apartment.

"Ma'am," the officer said.

She stopped and turned around to see the officer step out of the elevator. But he wasn't the officer, anymore. His hair was long and blue-black, his face azure-tinged and gaunt. She recognized him as the man she had shot the other night. Only he wasn't a man, was he? He was one of those things — a shifter. A dreck. One of the drecks who had been beating Micah. How had he found her?

"What the hell…?"

Sam stumbled backward, trying to fish Micah's phone out of her pocket.

"Not so tough without your gun, are you?" The dreck rushed forward and she stumbled again.

She was only a few feet from Micah's door. Her hand closed around the phone and pulled it from her pocket, but she was too late. The dreck grabbed her by the throat and shoved her against the wall with a bone-rattling crash. Sam tried to yell, but nothing came out, not even air. Her thumb worked the buttons on the phone, but she couldn't look down to see if she was hitting the one or not. *Please, hit the one, hit the one!*

The dreck's blue eyes swept down her body then shot to the hand holding the phone.

"Uh-uh-uh," he said, snapping his fist around her wrist like a handcuff, squeezing until she grimaced and dropped the phone.

She was going to die. She already couldn't breathe, so it was just a matter of time. Micah wasn't here to save her, and he would come home to find her corpse crumpled like yesterday's garbage outside his door.

Suddenly, he released her throat and yanked her wrist to his mouth, biting her as she gagged and coughed, the rush of air a painful clawing as she gulped. That's when she felt the burning crawling up her arm from where his teeth held her wrist. It felt like he was injecting acid into her body.

Evil blistered her gaze as his eyes met hers, his blue lips curling into a sneer as if he knew how she felt and got off on it.

The burning sensation increased, and she tried to kick

him and raked her free hand over his face, resulting in a bruising backhand across her cheek. *Pow!* Light exploded in her eye as she was flung to the side.

Finally he released her wrist. "Let's see how Micah likes you now."

Sam was too weak to move, her body feverish, her stomach rolling, her vision doubling and going foggy. What had he done to her?

"This is what happens to those who take what's mine. If you're lucky, you'll die by morning, bitch. If not, be ready for a long, uncomfortable death." He knelt down and whispered. "If I was a betting man, I'd put money on the latter. I didn't give you enough venom to kill you fast. I want you to hurt, bitch."

His sinister laugh retreating toward the stairwell was the last thing she heard before she blacked out.

CHAPTER 16

After canvassing the area near the Black Garter, Micah and Trace were closing in on the two drecks who had attacked Sam at the club last night. Trace had been the one to pick up their scent first.

"I think all four are here," Micah said.

"Four?"

"Apostle had four with him."

Trace stopped. "What are you talking about? Maybe you should start at the beginning, because I'm starting to think you aren't telling me everything."

Micah still hadn't told Trace about how he had asked Apostle to kill him via beat down Rocky Balboa style, which is how the bastards knew about Sam in the first place. He flipped a look at Trace and considered whether or not he should just fess up. It wasn't like Micah to let anyone, except for maybe Sam right now, into his world, but then Trace was helping him. Did he owe Trace an explanation?

"Okay," he said, scowling. He didn't like this, but fuck it. "I asked John Apostle to kill me."

Trace glowered, his face instantly eight shades of pissed off. "You mind telling me why?" His jaw flexed and tightened by his ear as if he were trying not to kill Micah himself.

"Why do you care?" Micah started walking again.

"Indulge me, asshole, before I slam you into that wall and force you."

Glancing askance at the dark vampire, Micah huffed out a short breath that sounded like *yeah, right.* "You can't take me and you know it."

"Want to try me? You've seen what I'm capable of."

Okay, right. Maybe Trace *could* take him. Micah regarded the male who'd fallen back into step beside him, the aggression coming off him like an invisible tsunami. With a growl of contempt, Micah stopped abruptly.

"Fine, bust my chops, you fucker."

"Hey, you're the one who needs my help. Maybe I'll just go back and leave you to deal with this shit on your own." Trace turned and started to walk away.

"I don't *need* your help, but—just wait, goddamn it!"

Trace turned around and gave him a spill-or-I'm-out-of-here look, his face set in furious resolve.

Micah stood akimbo and dropped his head as he shook it in frustration. He hated letting people in. He would rather just keep everyone at arm's length where they couldn't get too close. When you let someone in they had the power to hurt you, and Micah didn't need shit like that interfering with his self-sufficiency.

"After Jackson left..." He kept his head down. Avoiding eye contact was good. "I was fucked up, okay? It got bad. I didn't want to live, anymore, so I found Apostle and asked him and his friends to kill me."

"Why not just sit on your balcony and let the sun do it?" Trace said, keeping his distance. Micah gave him credit for having the sense to grant him his physical space.

Micah cleared his throat and raised his head. He turned to the side so he didn't have to look at Trace. "I needed the pain."

The two stood in silence for a while, Micah feeling Trace's eyes on him.

"Don't you go soft on me, Trace," Micah said. "I don't need your sympathy."

"Don't worry," Trace said. "So, how did Sam get involved?"

Micah shifted his weight uncomfortably at the mention of Sam's name. "She stopped them. She saved me." He finally looked back at Trace, whose eyebrows popped up in surprise.

"How the hell did a human stop five drecks?"

"With her Beretta. She shot Apostle."

Trace barked out a shot of deep laughter. "Fuck me. Really?"

Micah nodded, pride welling up for his woman. "You should have seen her, Trace. She didn't back down an inch. She's tough." A fond smile played over his mouth. "Anyway, she took me back to her place and tried to patch me up." He stopped short of disclosing that he had fed from her, and he certainly didn't want to bring up what they had done today, even though it was already evident to Trace, what with her scent shrouding him like a blanket. Man, he just wanted to get home to her and explore her body some more.

Trace looked at him as if he knew what Micah was thinking, those pale eyes scrutinizing him. What went on inside that head of his, anyway? Sometimes he wished he could find a way around whatever barrier Trace had erected so he could see inside his mind. Something told Micah he would find a shit storm of oh-my-God in there.

"Hey, let's hurry and get this done," he said, taking off down the sidewalk again.

"Yeah, time to fuck up some drecks." Just as Trace fell back in step with him, Micah's cell phone went off. He pulled it out of his pocket and frowned at the number. It was building security at the Sentinel.

"Hello?"

"Mr. Black?"

"Yes? What's wrong?" They wouldn't be calling him unless something was wrong.

"We had a problem on your floor tonight."

Micah's heart lurched, and he stopped. "What kind of problem?"

"A woman was attacked outside your apartment. A delivery boy found her. She was unconscious, but alive. Paramedics just left with her."

Micah looked up at Trace, who stared back at him as if he were watching spiders crawl over Micah's face. Apparently he could hear the other side of the conversation, too. Trace took off in the direction of the SUV they had driven downtown, which kick-started his own fight-or-flight response. Until then, his feet had felt planted in dried cement.

Sam!

"Where did they take her? Which hospital?"

"Saint Augustine's. I'm sorry, I would have called you sooner, but I only realized when they took her that she was staying with you. She'd come down just minutes before to let me know she'd ordered takeout and wanted me to let up the delivery boy. Like I said, he was the one who found her."

"Was anyone else with her?"

"Just a police officer who got in the elevator with her, but that's all I saw."

Apostle! Fuck!

"Thank you."

Micah ended the call just as he reached Trace's SUV, and the other male started the engine. "Saint Augustine's," Micah said, throwing himself into the passenger seat and slamming the door. Trace hit the gas and Micah dialed the phone he'd given Sam. No answer. He tried it again. Still nothing.

"Fuck!"

"How'd they find her?" Trace asked.

"I don't know. Apostle must have followed me from Sam's last night. I knew I shouldn't have let her go back there."

The SUV tore through the quiet, late-night streets, tires squealing as Trace hopped the speed bump just inside the entrance to the hospital.

"Emergency! Emergency!" Micah pointed to the hospital's emergency entrance.

"I know!" Trace swerved down a row of cars and haphazardly jutted into an empty space at an angle and slammed on his brakes, throwing it into park.

Both jumped out and sprinted toward the door. They burst through and nearly ran over a patient in a wheelchair.

"Hey! Slow down!" A nurse yelled at them from behind the check-in desk.

"Sam Garrett," Micah said, crashing into the desk and smacking his hand on the counter.

The nurse ricocheted back in her chair and obviously got the clue that Micah and Trace weren't men to be fucked with, diverting her attention to her computer. Her fingers dashed over the keyboard.

"She's with the doctor now. Room C4."

Micah and Trace took off for the double doors to the back.

"Hey, you can't go back there!"

"Stop me!" Micah pushed through the doors and frantically searched for Room C4. Doctors and nurses frowned and scurried out of his way, protesting, but none tried to stop him.

"Got it!" Trace called from the other end of the hall.

Micah spun and ran to join him, out of breath with panic as he looked up at the door number, confirming it.

Pushing against the handle, he walked in, and the doctor glanced up from the chart he was scanning. A nurse was drawing blood from Sam as she lay semiconscious on the sterile gurney.

"Excuse me," the doctor said. "But who let you in here."

Micah ignored him. He seethed with malice that harm had come to his precious female.

"She's mine," he said.

Taking a new tack, the doctor said, "And you are?"

"Micah." Sam's weak voice reached him. Her semi-lucid eyes were barely open.

The doctor turned at the sound and shook his head. "Well, that's the first thing she's said since she got here, so it looks like you get to stay, Micah. But your friend will have to—"

"He stays," Micah said, his voice unwavering and warning the doctor not to test him on this. "What's wrong with her?"

"We're not sure. The bruising indicates she was choked by someone very strong, but that doesn't account for why her body's systems are shutting down." The look the doctor gave Micah indicated it didn't look good. "We're running blood tests to see if her attacker might have injected her with something, but so far we're drawing a blank."

Micah and Trace exchanged glances. Apostle must have bitten her.

The nurse finished filling the last vial and bandaged Sam's arm, collecting the tray of blood-filled tubes—Sam's blood... her priceless, exquisite, life-giving blood—and left the room as the doctor followed her to the door.

"I'll be back as soon as I know more. Try talking to her. See if she can remember anything."

As soon as the door hissed closed, Micah looked at Trace and tilted his head. Trace jumped in front of the door and blocked it from opening.

"He bit her, didn't he?" Trace said, keeping his voice quiet.

Micah turned her arm over, looking for signs of the bite. A dreck's bite healed quickly. A human wouldn't be able to detect it, but he could.

"Nothing on this arm," he said. He turned his attention to her neck. "Sam, I'm here, okay? I'm going to get you out of here and fix this."

"You're not thinking of—" Trace's voice sounded wary.

"Yes," Micah said, cutting him off.

"Tristan will go apeshit."

"I don't give a fuck about Tristan." Micah's only concern right now was Sam. He refused to lose another mate. "Put it this way, Trace, if she dies, you'll have to kill me before I kill you."

"Gotcha." Trace's voice held a grim note. It was clear he didn't like any of the options.

"He didn't bite her neck, either," Micah said, finishing his inspection and reaching for her other arm. His eyes traveled her skin, scrutinizing, picking through each tiny freckle or discoloration. "Got it," he said. "Here, on her wrist."

"You going to do it here?" Trace said. He shifted uneasily, his voice edgy.

"I have to. I don't know how much time she's got."

Trace blew out a less-than-excited burst of air. It was clear he wasn't comfortable with this, but there was no choice.

"After I'm done, we need to get her out of here. Can you take care of the humans while I carry her?"

Trace fidgeted, not answering.

"Trace?" Micah turned pleading eyes on him. "Please."

"You're fucking with the human world," Trace said, his brow furrowed.

"I know, but I can't lose her. I can't. She's my mate, Trace.

Okay? My mate, for Chrissake."

"Your mate? Already?" It was clear Trace was shocked he had bonded to another so soon after Jackson, even though they had discussed it the night before.

"Yes, Trace. She's my mate. I love her."

The two stared uneasily at each other for a few seconds. Trace finally nodded and looked down. "Okay, do it. I'll run cover so you can get her out."

Trace had extraordinary skills when it came to compelling humans. Micah had never seen anything like it, but then again, he was a day walker, and day walkers always came bundled with special abilities. It was suddenly clear to Micah that he had partnered with Trace for a reason. He needed Trace's special abilities now.

"Thank you."

Trace actually looked surprised to hear the show of gratitude from Micah, but then Micah wasn't known for such sentiments, or much of anything else congenial and well-mannered.

Sam stirred and looked at him through glazed eyes. "I'm sorry," she said, her voice barely a whisper.

"Don't be."

"I'm dying."

"No you're not. I'm going to save you. It's my turn to save *you* now."

She tried to smile, but her lips barely moved.

"Just hold on, okay. This will hurt, but I have to do it."

She closed her eyes again, and Micah pulled her wrist to his mouth, studying the faint bite mark. He had to bite as close to where Apostle's teeth had pierced her skin. Triggering the glands in his mouth to release his venom, he licked the bite mark, numbing it.

"Are you ready?"

She barely nodded her head, too weak even to do that.

Micah licked her wrist again, his venom numbing her nerves even further, and with a silent prayer he opened his mouth and bit down. Sam's body stiffened, then relaxed, and then he let his venom flow. Vampire venom trumped dreck venom, but age mattered. The older the vampire, the stronger the venom. And Micah was very old, which was crucial for what he was trying to do.

First came the euphoria then Sam's body began to shiver then shudder. Her teeth chattered, and painful groans gurgled in her throat.

"Her eyes are open," Trace said.

Micah felt Trace's special powers unfurl, and Sam's body calmed. He could only imagine her pain as his venom spread through her, waging war on Apostle's evil offering, eradicating it. Even with Trace's powers wrapped around Sam like a protective cocoon, she eventually began to tremble again, tensing and straining against the burn until finally she let loose a scream that would have awakened the dead.

Trace jumped to attention and stepped back.

Micah wasn't finished. He needed more time. Just a few more seconds, but Sam's screams were about to bring the full force of the emergency department barreling through the door.

The door swung open a second later, and Trace threw his arm up, his fingers splayed in the open air. The nurse flung back against the wall as if he'd hit her.

"Fuck! I didn't mean to blast her so hard," Trace said. "Are you done, yet?" He helped the unconscious nurse to a chair and flung around as the door flew open again. Invisible energy splintered the air from Trace's outstretched hand once more, stopping the two orderlies that rushed in, freezing them in midglide.

Sam screamed again, and Micah could sense more people coming.

"Hurry, Micah!"

Finally, it was done. He'd given her all he had and released her wrist. The bite mark instantly sealed from his venom's healing properties. He threw the white blanket off her and pulled her into his arms.

"Go!" He shouted to Trace.

Trace charged out of the room, holding up both arms and

stopping everybody in the hall. Not a soul moved, and he turned and looked over his shoulder at Micah. "Come on."

Micah carried Sam out and down the hall, dodging around the frozen doctors and nurses who had been in midstride on their way to Sam's room.

"You wiping them?" Micah asked.

"Already done. They'll never remember she was here. Or us." Trace jogged after him, keeping the humans suspended until they reached the double doors that led back into the waiting area.

"Hey!" the lady behind the desk shouted.

"Trace!" Micah shouted back at him.

The nurse suddenly locked up like someone had put on her brakes then Micah and Trace shot out the doors to the SUV.

WHEN THE NURSE CAME TO, she shook her head and looked around, confused. As she sat back down at her desk, she glanced at her computer and frowned at the record on the screen. Who the hell was Samantha Garrett? They hadn't admitted anyone by that name tonight. Suddenly, a black SUV shot past the entrance toward the exit and she scowled with a huff. That jerk needed to slow down or he was going to kill someone.

CHAPTER 17

THE WOMAN FUCKING STEVE was one of his nurses. Young and fresh, her enhanced tits bounced as she bobbed up and down on his dick, squealing and crying out like those girls in the online porn he watched. Couldn't she just be natural and not put on a show. Fuck, he didn't have cameras in his room, for Pete's sake. Did she think men liked this kind of performance when all they wanted was a hard, raw screw? She definitely wasn't Samantha. Sure, she would get him off and rock his balls, but Steve didn't think he would be inviting Sabrina back to his place again.

It was the same with all the women he brought home. Drinks, dinner, and fucking that left him less than impressed, not to mention unsatisfied. But until he tracked down his wife, these tarts would have to do.

"Uuunhh, yes, oohhh, uh-huh, mmmm."

Steve fought not to roll his eyes. He'd be happier with his hand and internet porn right now. Maybe he should cover her mouth and shut her up.

He was just about to do that when his cell vibrated on the nightstand. Thank God! Saved!

"Don't answer it, baby," Barbie doll said, fucking him in earnest to try to keep his attention. If she only knew she had lost his attention several minutes ago, she wouldn't have tried so hard.

"I have to, now stop." He pushed her off, his dick blessedly free of her squishy cunt. She pouted like a child, flopping to the other side of the bed.

Sitting up, he snatched his phone, ready to send a check

for one thousand dollars to whoever was calling him just to say thanks for putting him out of his misery. When he saw the name on his caller ID he changed his mind. Make that ten thousand dollars.

"Yeah. Tell me you've got good news." David wouldn't be calling him at this hour if he didn't.

"A hit in Chicago. A Samantha Garrett was just admitted into a hospital. Everything matches."

Steve snapped his fingers at the Barbie on his bed then pointed to her clothes, making it clear it was time for her to go. "Which hospital?"

"Saint Augustine."

"Why is she there?" Steve frowned at Sabrina, who had sat up and crossed her arms. He gestured again toward her clothes and mouthed *now*. She was going to irritate him, he could just feel it.

"Mugging or something. God I love electronic health records. Makes my job so much easier."

"Yours maybe, but not mine," Steve said, although at the moment he thanked the administration for mandating their use. "She still there?"

"As far as I can tell."

"Anything else?"

"I've gotten in touch with the local police and just found the dispatch record from where it was called in. I've got an address where she was found. Looks like she was discovered unconscious by a pizza delivery boy. I'll put it together and have it to you within the half hour."

David was proving to be well worth every dime. A year with that other PI hadn't turned up even one nibble, but David had flushed Samantha out in a matter of days. He had to be one of the best investigators and hackers in the country.

"You just made Santa Claus very happy," Steve said.

"Think he'll leave something in my stocking this year, then?"

"Is your stocking big enough to hold that much money?"

David chuckled. "I'll buy a bigger stocking."

Steve was already pulling clothes out of his closet, pleased to see that Sabrina had taken a hint and was putting on her dress. She didn't look happy, but screw her. He had a plane to catch.

"Thanks, David. I'll look for your e-mail."

"No problem."

He disconnected and tossed his phone on the bed before going to the bathroom and turning on the shower to let the water heat up.

"You know the way out," he said to Sabrina as he returned to the room and grabbed a pair of briefs from the drawer.

"Yeah. Call me later?"

"Yeah, sure I will." Yeah, like hell he would.

She walked toward him to give him a kiss good night, but he turned away and went back to the bathroom. "See you, Sabrina."

"Uh, yeah, okay."

When Steve returned to his room after his shower, she was gone. Thank God. Now he could focus on packing his overnight bag without her needy, puppy dog hovering. He checked his e-mail, but nothing from David had arrived, yet, so he hopped over to the travel site and found a nonstop that flew out of Denver at six o'clock. He had a little less than four hours. Plenty of time. He could be in Chicago by midmorning.

It didn't take him long to pack. He just needed an extra change of clothes, his toothbrush, soap, deodorant, socks, and underwear. Oh, and proof that Sam was his wife, of course. He could buy anything else he needed when he got there, but he wasn't planning on staying more than a few hours—just long enough to retrieve his wife from the hospital and get her back to the airport for the late flight home. As he grabbed his leather coat from the back of the easy chair by the window, his e-mail pinged.

He rushed to his desk and printed David's e-mail then forwarded it to his phone before grabbing his keys and his bag. After one final glance around the room, he shut off the lights, locked up, got in his BMW, and drove to the airport. While he was driving, he called the hospital where he worked and told them he had a family emergency and wouldn't be in for a few days. Hell yeah, family emergency. He was going to get his wife back.

CHAPTER 18

TRACEON HAD NEVER SEEN MICAH LIKE THIS. He cradled and rocked Sam with a tenderness so unlike anything he had ever associated with the male that he didn't quite know how to react.

"How is she?" he asked, jerking the steering wheel to the left, careening them down a side street toward the compound.

"I can't tell," Micah said then cleared his throat around emotional gravel.

Trace heard the heartbreak bend Micah's voice, cracking it between his words. He hoped Sam didn't die. This soon after Jackson, Micah wouldn't survive it, and Trace didn't want to lose Micah now that he was making progress with him after years of wondering how to break through that shell of his.

"She'll make it," he said.

The buildings were a blur as he sped down the final stretch of road to AKM. They had medics who could monitor her and see her through the change if she faltered or her body tried to reject Micah's venom.

He shot a quick glance at Micah, but the guy's face was turned away, his cheek pressed against Sam's as he continued rocking her, but the scent of tears told him the male was crying.

AKM appeared just ahead and Trace slowed only enough not to flip the SUV as he turned into the parking lot and raced around to the back. After screeching to a stop in his assigned space, Trace jumped out and rushed around to help Micah, even though he doubted the guy needed it. Still,

Micah wasn't himself right now.

They hurried toward the back entrance, Micah practically running him over.

"Get the door," Micah said as he wiped his face and scowled.

Trace passed his key card over the reader and jerked the door open then dodged aside as Micah rushed past him.

"Move!" Traceon yelled at the gawkers who stood in the way. "Medic! We need a medic!"

Tristan bolted out of his office at the uproar, his eyes opening wide. Appalled disbelief filled his expression when he saw the human—well, not quite human, anymore—in Micah's arms.

"What the fuck is this?"

Micah ignored him, but Trace paused long enough to say, "Not now, Tris. Just alert medical. Human bitten by a dreck. Micah gave her his venom to save her. NOW, Tristan!" He wasn't going to let Micah lose his mate. Not on his watch.

Taking off after Micah again, he ignored the members of their team as they rushed out and watched in horror as Micah kicked the doors to medical open and hurried Sam inside.

Arion grabbed Trace's arm as he turned to follow him in. "What the hell is he doing? Bringing a human in here?"

"Back off, Ari." Trace glanced between him and Severin, who joined them in the hall and pulled up beside Arion like he was Ari's protector.

"He's gone too far this time, Trace. This is inexcusable."

"She's his goddamn mate, Ari! You got that! And she's not human, anymore. Not technically."

Arion swayed, stunned. "Fuck!"

"Yeah, so drop it." Trace started to turn away, but Ari stopped him.

"Are you saying he—"

"Yes, that's what I'm saying."

The color drained from Arion's face and Severin shook his head. "What a meathead."

"She was bitten by a dreck. He had no choice."

"Sure he did," Ari said. "He shouldn't have been fucking

around with her to begin with, and she never would have been in danger. He should know better than to pull shit like this."

Trace felt his blood heat. "Oh, and you would know about mates, right Arion? When were you ever mated, asshole?" Arion had never taken a mate. All the females he'd fucked and not a one had fired his biology to take as a mate. "Until you know what you're talking about, why don't you shut the fuck up."

Severin bristled by Ari's side and looked like he was about to slug Trace.

"You can just check that, hero." Trace warned him with a glance that begged Sev to try. Trace had already been through enough tonight and wasn't in the mood for any more shit.

Tristan and Malek ran around the corner.

"Okay, someone tell me what happened," Tristan said.

Ari scoffed. "Wonder stud vigilante in there," he flung his arm toward medical, "gave his venom to a human."

"WHAT?" Tristan slingshot his gaze toward Trace. "Care to elaborate?"

"As I told Ari, she's his mate. A dreck bit her." He threw Ari a malicious you're-such-a-dick glance as Io showed up to get in on the action. "What would you have done if it had been your mate, Tristan? Would you have let her die?"

Painful memories flashed over Malek's face as he stood to the side. He had never spoken of what had happened to his mate or how she had died, but Trace realized that what was going on here was hitting his comrade too close to home.

Just then Micah came out into the hall, and Trace could sense the dread and sorrow wafting from him like sewage.

"Is she…?" Trace couldn't finish the question, fearing the answer.

"She's alive. For now. They wanted me out so they could tend to her."

Ari shook his head and started in. "You asshole! You think you're above everyone else. That the rules don't apply to you. Well, look what you —"

What happened next happened so fast Trace couldn't

track it. One second Ari was pointing his finger at Micah, and the next Micah's fist was around Ari's throat and he was flat-backed against the wall, a foot off the floor as Micah released a shriek so agonizing and feral it even terrified Trace. Was Micah even in there or had he become something else all of a sudden?

Ari flew through the air and landed on the shiny tile, sliding several feet before Micah jumped on him, cracking his fist against the guy's face as the rest of them surged forward and tried to pull him off. Io and Sev each landed punches to Micah's torso before Trace could get hold of him and pull him back. Io and Severin came at them both, fists cocked.

"Get back!" Trace's voice dropped low and deep, echoing in his throat with deadly malice as he raised his hand, fingers splayed. He was ready to ice his own teammates to protect Micah. "I've got him. He's *my* charge." Warnings flashed from his eyes to the others. "I'm his guardian, now back the fuck off! NOW!"

Tristan and Malek stepped warily in the middle of the fray and pushed Io and Sev back as Trace pulled Micah away from them like a lion with its cub, keeping him safe from danger. Only when he was a safe distance did he wrap his arms around Micah and shroud him in warmth, trying to soothe him through compulsion. It worked only so much, but it was enough to bring Micah back into himself and calm him down.

"I've got you Micah," Trace said. "You're okay, but Sam needs you. Stay strong for Sam, you hear me? Don't you go crazy vampire on me, you got that? I'm the one with mutant potential here, not you. Do you hear me? You got that, Micah?"

Mutant. It's what they called mixed-breeds who went rogue. Rogues were day walkers like Trace who fell prey to their powers. Their powers literally took them over and changed them into something else entirely. The official term was rogue. The unofficial slang was mutant. But no matter what they called them, mutants were the deadliest beings imaginable, even worse than the drecks.

Micah panted, growling with every breath, but he finally nodded. "Yeah, yeah. I've got it. Get the fuck off me."

Trace released him.

Micah pushed his hand through his hair, shoving it off his face as he shot a glaring eyeful of this-isn't-over toward Arion.

Meanwhile, Severin helped Arion up and shielded him against the far wall, throwing one arm across Ari's chest as he glared back at Micah over his shoulder. Io hovered nearby, bristling for more shit to fly, while Malek stood in the middle to serve as a roadblock.

Tristan sighed heavily, his face down. Then he shook his head and shot a glare of his own at Micah. "Take care of your mate, Micah, but after this is over, you and I are going to have a long talk. Do not test me on this, you got me?"

Micah glowered at Tristan. "Whatever."

"Yes or no, Micah. Not whatever. This shit has to stop."

Micah turned away without answering, obstinate to the last.

"*Yes or no?*" Tristan got right in Micah's face, his blue-green eyes flashing.

"Fuck! Yes, asshole!"

Trace stepped in and pulled Micah back. "Calm down, Micah." He turned toward Tristan. "Not now, Tris. Okay? Not now."

Tristan fumed but backed off then turned toward Arion, whose lip was bleeding. He had bruises forming around both eyes. "You okay?"

Vampires were tougher than humans, their bodies able to withstand a lot more punishment. Still, it didn't make the pain any better, or the contusions.

Ari nodded, touching his lip. "Yeah. I'm cool." The unspoken *prick* shot from his eyes in Micah's direction. Micah flipped him off.

"Okay, go home and take care of that," Tristan said, motioning him to head out. "Sev, why don't you go with him? I don't want Ari driving with his eyes swelling up like that."

Severin pulled away and nodded then followed Ari down the hall, their booted feet thunking heavily as they took it slow. Ari's noggin had to be throbbing from Micah's fist action. Io tagged along, giving his best friend a shoulder chuck before turning down a side hall that headed back toward the data center.

Tristan ushered Malek to go with him and they headed back toward Tristan's office.

Which left Micah and Trace alone in the hall.

The doors opened and a medic popped out as if she'd been waiting for the commotion to die down. "She's going to be fine, Micah. She's already adjusting. Thought you'd want to know. Give us a few minutes to move her to a room and we'll take you to her." The medic disappeared and Trace clapped his hand on Micah's shoulder.

"You hear that, brother?" Trace winced, remembering that Micah didn't want him calling him that. "I'm sorry—"

"No, it's okay," Micah said. "I think you've earned your stripes. I think we're brothers after this, don't you? You saved my chops tonight."

Trace wiped the pleased grin from his face as quickly as it appeared. "Sam's a good influence on you," he said.

"You think?" Micah turned and smiled at him. The first genuine smile he had seen from the guy in, well...ever.

"Yeah. I do, brother. I really do."

CHAPTER 19

SEVERIN PULLED INTO ARION'S DRIVEWAY and parked, hitting the brake as gently as possible. Arion had spent the drive with his head resting back against the passenger seat and his eyes closed, obviously feeling like a hammered nail.

"You okay?" Sev asked, keeping his voice quiet.

"Yeah, yeah. I'll be fine." Ari held a towel to his lip, which had finally stopped bleeding about five minutes ago, but the scent of Ari's blood still filled the car. It made Sev's mouth water.

"I'll see you in." Sev got out, went around to the passenger door, and stood back as Ari swung it open and slowly climbed out.

"Damn, Micah's a strong fucker." Ari groaned as he stood up and stretched his shoulder with a grimace.

"What's wrong?" Sev asked.

"He just slammed me damn hard into that wall. My shoulder hurts like hell."

"Come on, I'll get you inside and take a look at it."

He locked up the car out of habit, followed Ari to the door, and waited for him to unlock it as his eyes scanned up and down the residential street as if drecks would jump out and attack them any second. Severin had spent his life fighting. It didn't matter whether the war was human or vampire, Sev had found himself in the thick of it, testing the limits of his mixed-blood powers to keep him alive. He had made a lot of enemies along the way, too, so he never knew when one would leap from the shadows. The possibility kept him on his toes twenty-four-seven.

"You coming?"

Sev turned and saw that Ari was holding the door for him. "Yeah, sure."

Ari closed the door behind him and flipped on a lamp then walked toward the kitchen, shedding his coat along the way. His T-shirt hugged his thick arms and broad back like a second skin. His tattooed arm swung at his side as he trudged to the kitchen.

"You want something to drink?"

Sev brushed his long hair back as he sat down on a barstool. "Water's fine."

Ari grabbed him a bottle from the fridge and set it in front of him as he tossed the bloody towel in the trash.

"How does it look?" Ari said, standing on the other side of the counter and leaning toward him before cracking the lid off his own bottle of water with a wince. Apparently, that shoulder was bothering him pretty badly.

Sev's gaze fell to his lips and the tiny cut he just wanted to lick.

"Like you got beat up." Sev shrugged and tried to act nonchalant. "Actually, you look good for a male whose face just impersonated a punching bag.

"Gee, thanks."

"Oh, come on, you know I'm kidding." Sev caught Ari's eye and they both stopped moving and just looked at each other.

Finally, Ari said, "You think I look good?" His tone was serious.

Sev's mouth went dry and he nodded. "Yeah, actually I do." Ari looked better than good. Sev's thoughts tumbled in about ten different directions, all sordid, all forbidden, all sexual. Ari was just about the finest male Sev had ever laid eyes on and ever since joining AKM, he had wondered what kissing him would feel like. How would his body feel? How would he taste? Damn, but Sev shouldn't be thinking this way about a member of his own team, but he couldn't stop himself.

The two stared at each with a hundred silent questions flowing between them then Ari stood back, cleared his throat, and chugged down half the bottle. "He's an ass."

The abrupt change in direction jolted Sev back into the room and out of his fantasies. He sipped from his own bottle. "Who?"

"Micah." Ari gave him a slightly bewildered look.

Oh, that's right. Micah had just kicked the shit out of Ari. Duh. "Why don't you just leave Micah alone?"

Ari laughed tightly and leaned against the counter. "I guess I just like the punishment."

Sev chuckled. "Hell, Ari, if you like being punished, I can think of better ways to go about it."

"Oh, yeah? Like what?" Was that sexual innuendo in Ari's voice?

Sev grinned but decided to keep his thoughts away from the fantasies plaguing him. "Shit, we could put on a pair of gloves and spar sometime, for starters. I'm hell at the hand to hand."

"Really?" Ari turned and leaned sideways against the counter as he eyed Sev with what felt like more than just casual interest. "I didn't know that."

Sev looked down at the soapstone counter and nodded. "Yep. I've scrapped with the best of them."

"So, what's your story? Where are you from?"

Sev loved the way Ari smiled at him then.

"Not much to say really." He didn't want to risk freaking Ari out about his past.

"Bullshit. Everyone has a story, and the ones who don't want to discuss theirs usually have the best stories to tell, so spill."

It was hard to deny Ari anything, especially when his close-set, topaz eyes drilled him so directly. Sev could just stare at those eyes all day.

After taking another drink, Sev sighed. "My life is boring, Ari. I want to hear about yours."

"Uh-uh-uh." Ari waggled his finger and came around the counter and took the seat next to him. "I've been thinking about what you and I discussed at Four Alarm, about how you lost your boyfriend. I think there's more there. You're more interesting than you think, Sev."

"You think I'm interesting?" Sev had been about to take another drink and had stopped with the bottle halfway to his mouth as his gaze shot to Ari.

The other male averted his gaze for only a second then looked back. "Well, yeah, Sev. I do. Really interesting, actually." His face flushed and he looked down awkwardly before meeting Sev's gaze again.

Neither said a word as Sev slowly lowered his bottle of water back to the counter, his pulse quickening as he stared at Arion. "Well, that's good to know."

Ari nodded, holding his gaze as he took a deep, steadying breath. "Yeah."

"I think you're pretty interesting, too."

As he pursed his lips, Ari's face filled with a sense of wonder as he glanced at his water bottle. The color in his cheeks deepened. "Well, looks like we both think the other's interesting, doesn't it?"

Sev could hardly breathe. "Yep."

Silence engulfed them for several seconds as they both fiddled with their water bottles.

Suddenly, as if a starting gun had shot into the air, the two jumped off their barstools and dove toward each other, meeting in the middle as their mouths fused together. The cut on Ari's mouth had re-opened and the taste of his blood was better than wine.

Wordlessly, Sev's fingers began unbuckling and unfastening Ari's belt at the same time Ari did the same to his. A furious give-and-take of need passed back and forth between them, lifting Sev into heaven. He'd been drawn to Ari right from the start, even before going with him to Jackson's apartment, but until now, he hadn't found a way to get close to him. Maybe he should thank Micah for beating the living daylights out of him since it had afforded him this chance to explore his attraction to the male.

Ari's fists grabbed handfuls of Sev's hair and pulled his head back as the other male nipped roughly at his Adam's apple.

"Fuck, yes," Sev said, barking the curse.

He stripped Ari's shirt over his head then rapidly shed his own before both of them shoved the other's pants down. Twin erections pressed together as denim pooled around their ankles. Gripping each other's ass, their bodies slapped together hard. Sev grunted, claiming Ari's mouth again.

"I've wanted you since I met you," Sev said, his lips still pressed to Ari's.

"I didn't know. I wasn't sure..."

"You and Io are so close. I thought—"

"I told you. We're just friends."

Breathless moans passed between them as their bodies ground against each other, their cocks rubbing together.

"You feel good." Sev pressed against Ari's firm body, clutching his ass and thrusting hard against him.

"So do you." Ari's hand gripped his ass with equal urgency.

"Fuck, Ari. More."

"Don't stop."

His pending orgasm tickled the base of his spine. He couldn't believe how hot he was and how fast his climax was bearing down on him.

Ari groaned. "Oh God, harder. I'm gonna come." He sounded surprised, but relieved, as if he had waited his whole life for this and couldn't believe it was finally happening.

Words ceased, replaced by grunts with every demanding thrust against each other.

Sev needed to pinch himself. Was he really here? Was this really happening? He had wanted Ari from day one. How long had Ari felt this way about him?

Suddenly, Ari's body went rigid, and he moaned long and hard as he thrust his tongue inside Sev's mouth. Moist warmth spilled against Sev's stomach and over his cock as Ari shuddered through his climax. In an instant, Sev thrust Ari back against the counter and came. His cock exploded against Ari's stomach as his body quaked violently, the two of them pressed together like they'd been glued front-to-front as their orgasms spent themselves.

"Unh!" Sev grunted again as another powerful wave

claimed him, and Ari's arms tightened around him.

When it was over, the two stood together, utterly still, their foreheads tipped against each other and their eyes closed, breathing, only breathing. Then Ari slowly pulled away and grabbed a wad of paper towels, handing some to Sev as he began to wipe himself off.

Without a word, the two dressed, avoiding eye contact. Sev wasn't sure how to read Ari's sudden silence. And it seemed Ari wasn't sure what to think, either.

After fastening his belt, Sev downed the rest of his water and grabbed the coat he had draped over a chair at the kitchen table. "So…"

Ari didn't move. "So…" Ari wouldn't even look at him.

"Okay, I'll see you tomorrow then."

Ari nodded. He stood with his palms against the surface of the counter, his body leaning forward and his head angled down thoughtfully. It looked like he had been stunned stupid.

The sudden biological need to go to him struck Sev like a fist, shocking the hell out of him. Oh wow, what had just happened here? Why was his body's biology getting in on the act, striking up a mating bond?

"Yeah, okay then." Sev spun on his heel and hurried out before things got even weirder. He rushed to his car and started the engine, threw it into reverse, backed out, and then gunned it. He could pull over and throw up once he got out of Ari's neighborhood, but not here, not yet.

FROM HIS WINDOW, Arion stared in fascination as Sev's Challenger raced away. He ran his fingertips over his lips. What had just happened between them? Was he gay now? Or had he always been gay and had only pretended to be heterosexual? At any rate, no one could know about what he and Sev had just done. No one. If Io found out, he would never hear the end of it. And if his parents found out, they would kill him. Yes, this was a secret he would take to his grave. What had just happened between him and Sev could never happen again. Never. No matter how much he had liked.it.

Why did he suddenly feel like he was only kidding himself?

CHAPTER 20

"**WHAT IN THE HELL WERE YOU THINKING?**" Tristan slammed the door as Micah followed him into his office.

Micah spun around and yanked the door back open. "You might as well leave it open if you're going to yell at me. Everyone will be able to hear you, anyway. Let's just make it easier for them." He glared at Tristan, meeting him eye-dagger to eye-dagger, challenging him without backing down even a tad. No way was he going to let anyone question his decisions where Sam was concerned.

Finally Tristan took a deep breath and calmly closed the door, but it was obvious it took every bit of his restraint. "You had no right, Micah."

"I had every right. She's my mate. End of discussion."

"No, not end of discussion. We have rules, Micah. We have to live by a code of conduct and ethics about who and what we are. Or did you forget that?"

"I'm not forgetting anything." Micah gave him a challenging look.

"Josie's different."

"Yeah, uh-huh. Right."

"Hey, fuck you, Micah. This isn't about me."

"Isn't it?"

"What the hell is that supposed to mean?"

"Just that if you're going to preach to me about giving a human my venom, you might want to look in the mirror first. At least Sam is my biological mate."

The color drained from Tristan's face, and his eyes went cold as he took a step back. He curled his lips in a contemptuous sneer. "You self-righteous motherfucker. How dare you throw that shit at me."

Micah didn't back down an inch. He wasn't into getting slapped by a hypocrite. "Who's being self-righteous, Tristan? You sit there on your golden-boy throne accusing me of breaking the law, acting like what you did with Josie is okay, when it was just as forbidden as what I did. Even more-so, because she's not even your biological mate, you asshole. Not only did you change her without petitioning King Bain, but you changed her when she wasn't even your mate. At least I've mated Samantha!" He thrust his finger in the direction of the medical ward. "Sam's my mate, and I refused to let her die when I knew I could save her life!"

The blood flooded back into Tristan's face as he jabbed Micah in the chest with his index finger. "You ungrateful prick. This is about your complete and long-standing lack of regard for our ways and our rules. Fine, she's your mate. Fine, you saved her life. Good for you. But that doesn't change the fact that for the last several centuries you've operated on your own agenda without regard for anyone else. It's all been about what *you* want, with no thought whatsoever for the team." He paused, dragging in an aggressive inhale. "I get that you've been through a lot of heavy shit, Micah, but I'm tired of bending the rules for you and looking the other way. You're the best enforcer I've got—maybe the best enforcer in the whole damn agency—but I'm tired of letting you get away with shit no one else can even think about doing without getting reprimanded. From now on, no more special favors. No more solo patrols. No more running off half-cocked. And you *will* follow my orders, or I'll kick your ass off the team. You got that?"

Micah sneered. "Fine, but I patrol with Trace. Only Trace." Traceon had firmly cemented his place within Micah's inner circle of trust tonight. If he had to patrol with anyone, it would be him. They had each other's backs and Micah had come to think of Trace as a friend in the last twenty-four hours.

Tristan looked a bit shocked at his rapid about-face, as if he were surprised Micah had agreed, and so quickly at that.

"What? Did you expect me to refuse, Tristan?" He pulled back, eyeing his boss. "You did, didn't you? You were prepared to kick me off the team, weren't you?"

Tristan smirked and huffed before nodding, some of the wind blowing out of his sails. "Actually, I was."

"Well, sorry to disappoint you." Micah looked down at Tristan's desk and saw the dismissal paperwork. Man, Tristan really had been ready to let him go.

"I'm not disappointed, just surprised. I haven't seen you like this since—"

"Katarina," Micah said. Some of his own animosity dissipated, and he suddenly felt like a chump for throwing Tristan's mating issues in his face, no matter how well-deserved they'd been.

"Yeah, since Katarina." Tristan shook his head and frowned. "You're different all of a sudden. I don't feel like you've got a death wish, anymore."

Micah turned toward the door, gazing in the direction of the medical wing. "It's her. It's Sam, Tristan. She brought me back. I can't explain it."

Tristan sighed, and the remaining aggression blew out of the room. "So she's your mate. Still, you could get into serious trouble for changing her without King Bain's permission." He offered a half-grin. "I should know, because, as you so delicately pointed out, I did the same thing with Josie."

"I don't care. She's my mate and she was dying. I had no choice. There wasn't time to get royal approval. I wasn't going to let her die, and I wouldn't have been able to survive without her." He had been on death's front porch, as it was. And that had just been over a half-bond with Jackson. He was fully mated to Sam, and maybe he had been all along if his previous musings about a misdirected mating was accurate. No way would he have survived her death.

"Okay, here's what we'll do." Tristan settled his ass on the edge of his desk and clapped his palms on his thighs. "Write it up in your report that way—that she was your mate and was bitten and all that shit. I'll do the same and ask the others to provide statements that will reinforce your actions. If anyone questions what you did, even if it's the king, you've got my full support." Tristan held out his hand. "Deal?"

Micah looked at his outstretched hand. He and Tristan had been good friends at one time, but that had been long ago. Slowly, he lifted his hand and grasped Tristan's. "Deal."

They shook on it, but Micah wasn't finished. He owed Tristan an apology.

"Look, I'm sorry for what I said about Josie. I know you and she—"

Tristan raised his hand, stopping Micah. "We were both angry. We both said shit we didn't mean. Don't sweat it."

"But I shouldn't have said what I said."

Tristan pushed off the desk. "Neither should I."

"Want to call it even?"

Tristan nodded congenially. "Yeah. Even." The two looked at each other for a long moment then Tristan bobbed his head toward the door. "Okay, get out of here. Go to your mate, Micah. Go take care of Sam."

Feeling their old friendship rekindle, Micah grinned, gave Tristan a mock salute, then hurried out of the room and down to medical where he pushed open the door to Sam's room and found her sleeping. She looked pale, but beautiful nevertheless. He pulled the room's only chair up to the bed and sat down as he wrapped both his hands around one of hers and watched her sleep. She was alive. No matter what else happened, his Sam was alive, and that meant everything.

"KNOCK-KNOCK."

Micah woke from a light snooze then lifted his head from the bed and smiled at Josie as she rapped her knuckles on the door again.

She feigned shock. "Is that a—yes, I do believe that is what they call a smile."

"Hi, Josie." Micah stretched and sat up. He had dozed off while holding Sam's hand, his head resting on the mattress.

"So, it's true then?" She ran her palm absently over her baby bump as she looked at Sam.

"If you mean that I changed a human, yes, it's true."

"I approve, but then again, I'm a female and believe in true love." Josie's dark brown hair was pulled back, making her large, bright eyes look even more luminescent. "I heard Trace helped?"

"Yes, he did."

Trace had finally left an hour ago, claiming he hadn't slept in over thirty-six hours and needed to rest, but Micah thought he just wanted to leave him alone with Sam. Micah refused to let go of Sam's hand and Josie noticed, her eyes twinkling with delight.

"You love her." It wasn't a question.

"Yes."

Josie sniffled as tears blossomed in her eyes. "I never thought I'd see this," she said.

"What do you mean?"

She came over, sat down on the edge of the mattress, and brushed his black hair away from his eyes. Josie was the only other person besides Sam who wasn't afraid of him. Well, then there was Trace, but that fucker was different. It had taken him a while to work up the courage to approach Micah. These females had more bravery than all the males in the compound combined.

"Micah, you've always been one of my favorites," Josie said, her voice soft. "Probably because you're the most damaged by your past. Well, except maybe for Malek. But he's dealt with it better than you have. Not by much, but still better. Anyway, it warms my heart to see you happy." She paused, smiling at him. "The fallen has risen. Back from the dead to walk among the living once again."

It was true. Micah felt different. Not even while he had been with Jackson had he felt so happy. His gaze fell on Sam's sleeping form and he saw her in a new light. She really had saved him in more ways than one.

"That's right, sweet cheeks," Josie said. "You found your mate."

With a fake scowl, Micah rolled his eyes at her. "Only you can get away with calling me that."

"What? Sweet cheeks?" Sam's weak voice drew both his and Josie's attention. She was grinning, her eyes blinking against the light. "Wow, that's a bright light. And a great nickname."

Josie hopped up and turned the dimmer down. "I'll let you borrow it." She laughed.

Micah shook his head. "Great. Just don't let the guys hear you call me that." He turned toward Sam. "By the way, your sensitivity to light will get better."

"What do you mean?"

Josie started for the door. "I should go and leave you two alone."

Micah got the sense she thought it would be better if she left so he could explain what had happened. "No," he said, stopping her. "Can you stay? I mean, I'd like you to stay."

The look he gave her must have made it clear he thought he would need the support himself, because Josie slowly nodded and made her way back to the bed.

"How are you, Sam? My name is Josie. I'm mated to Micah's boss." She held out her hand.

Sam reached out and clasped it.

"Oh," Josie said, flinching. "Wow, that's some grip you've got there."

Sam glanced between Josie and Micah, confusion crossing her face. "I'm sorry, I didn't realize..."

"No, it's okay," Josie said. "You're just not used to your new body, yet."

"Huh?"

He took Sam's hand and brushed the damp wisps of hair off her forehead. "Do you remember at the hospital, Sam?"

Her brow furrowed as if she were concentrating. Then she nodded. "Yes, I think—didn't you bite me?"

He nodded. "I had to give you my venom. It was the only way to save you."

For several seconds, Micah watched the thought processes play across her face, and then, "What are you saying? Am I a vampire?" She started to jerk her hand away from his and Josie took her other one, trying to calm her.

"No, but you're not human, anymore, either," she said.

Sam looked at Josie like she was a martian, then darted her gaze to Micah. "If I'm not a vampire, and I'm not a human, then what am I?"

"Alive," Micah said. "And that's all that matters." He brought her hand to his mouth and pressed his lips to each knuckle, slowly, one-by-one, conveying all his love in each tender caress.

WHEN SAM HAD AWAKENED TO THE SOUND of a strange woman talking to Micah, she had felt different, but she never would have guessed that the reason was because she was no longer human.

"Micah," she said, struggling to sit up. Her body ached head-to-toe, like she had a bad case of the flu. She even felt feverish.

He lifted his face and moved her hand to his cheek, holding her palm against his skin. The gesture melted something inside her.

"Okay," Josie said, hopping off the bed. "That's my cue. You two need to be alone right now. Micah," she flipped her fingers through his long hair. "We need to talk about this real soon. My scissors miss you."

After she walked out, Sam pushed her fingers through his thick, silky hair, loving how Micah dipped his head into her palm and purred. "I like it long," she said.

"Well then, I won't cut it."

"Josie might get mad." She smiled.

"She'll get over it. Your opinion is all that matters."

"Oh? Why's that?"

He stared at her, holding her gaze like she was a cherished treasure. "Because I love you."

Sam's breath caught at the declaration. "We barely know each other."

"I know enough to know that much," he said, crawling onto the bed beside her. He drew her against his body. "I love you. I can't live without you. I haven't felt this whole in a long time, and it's because of you."

She curled into his embrace, laying her head on his chest. His heart beat evenly, a cadence that seemed to call to her. "Vampires have heartbeats?" she said, realizing that this defied what she knew about them.

He laughed and the low rumble seemed amplified in her ears, and not just because she was lying on his chest. All her senses were more acute than they had been.

"We aren't like what you read about in books or see in movies," he said. "We're warm-blooded, have heartbeats, can see our reflections, can eat garlic, don't blister from Holy Water," he paused then said, "And like I explained before, some of us can even go out in the sun. In fact, day walkers are quite common among vampires nowadays." He said it like at one time that hadn't been the case.

"It's not always been that way?"

"No."

"Why the change?"

"Because of people like you," he said, kissing the top of her head. "And because vampires do mate with humans and produce offspring. Trace's parents, for example. His father was a vampire, his mother was allegedly a witch. At least that's what his file says about him. He tends not to talk about himself too much. But he has some unique powers I've never seen in a vampire, as you've already witnessed, but he's got a good heart, so I'm not worried he'll go rogue on us."

"Rogue?" She was so fascinated. Even after all they had discussed yesterday, it seemed like there was still so much more she needed to learn. But she wanted to learn it. All of it. Because she couldn't see herself leaving. Like Micah, she felt whole for the first time in her life, as if she'd finally found where she belonged.

"We actually call them mutants, but it's all the same. We not only have to watch out for drecks, but also the occasional vampire who succumbs to his powers. That's why it's usually the day walkers who turn. They have unique powers full-bloods don't have. But don't worry, it doesn't happen too often, but when it does, it's bad. Something shifts in their biology. The change is physiological, makes their venom poisonous even to us full-bloods."

"I have a lot to learn about your world, don't I?"

"Only if you plan on staying in it, which I hope you do, or I'll die without you."

"We can't have that, can we?"

He shook his head. "I love you." He said it like she hadn't heard him the first time.

"I know. You told me." She smiled and burrowed closer to him, loving how he felt holding her.

He turned her face toward his and kissed her. "You don't have to tell me you love me now, but promise me you'll tell me someday." His navy eyes glistened with adoration.

"Are you going soft on me?" she said.

"Just promise me, and quit being difficult."

How could she not laugh at that? "You'll just have to wait and see, dear."

"Never a straight answer from you." He flopped his head back against the pillow in fake exasperation.

She fought against the protestations of her muscles and pulled herself up to kiss his neck.

"So impatient." She kissed him again as he blinked his gaze toward hers, brow arched.

"You're trying to sidetrack me," he said.

"Uh-huh." Despite feeling like she'd fallen eight stories off a roller coaster, Sam felt ready to take on the world. What an odd way to describe it. She felt like shit, but felt awesome. "Tell me more about what I am. I'm beginning to think there's more to it than just the simple fact that I'm neither vampire nor human."

"Maybe I should blackmail you. Your promise for my information."

She playfully slapped him and he winced. "Damn, Wonder Woman. Fine, I'll tell you. For starters, you're a lot stronger now."

"Oh." The word dragged through the air as it all clicked into place. Josie flinching as she shook her hand. Now Micah rubbing the place on his arm where she'd slapped him. "Good to know."

"You'll get used to that. But, here's what you'll really have to get used to." Micah's face sobered and he waited until he had her full attention to continue. "You won't age, anymore. You won't die. That's the gift of my venom."

Sam rewound and played his words over, not quite sure she heard him right. "Are you saying I'm immortal?"

He nodded. "Something like that. As long as I live, you live. My life is your life now."

Wow. Immortal. Sam thought about all the possibilities. No fear of dying.

"Oh, you can still die," Micah said.

Sam glared at him. "I thought we had decided that my mind was off limits to you."

He shrugged. "Sorry, habit."

"Like I said before, break it." She would get him to stop poking around in her head if it killed her. Bad comparison since she couldn't die, anymore. Well, according to him she still could. "Since you brought it up, though, tell me just how I can die so I can be sure to avoid said mortal bombardments."

"Drama queen." He ruffled her hair. "Well, the standard decapitation or knife through the heart kind of shit. That would kill you."

"Ah, I'd better sell my guillotine, then, because you know how dangerous that can be around the house."

He chuckled then kissed her. "And, as I said, if I die, that would do it, too. My venom. My life. You're bound to me forever."

"Hmm, so I guess I'd better protect you then, huh?"

"What? With that puny Beretta?"

She smacked him. "Hey, I think that puny Beretta already saved your life once."

Micah laughed at her, rubbing his arm where she had hit him. "Have I mentioned that I love you?"

"Once or twice." She smiled. Oh, she loved him, too. She knew it in her heart. But what fun would it be if she just came out and told him when he was expecting it?

"How about that you're moving in with me. Have I mentioned that, yet?"

Sam should have known that was coming, but it still caught her off guard. "What?"

"Move in with me," he said, his eyes pleading with her, full of longing and love.

Sam thought about her tiny, humble apartment with the paper-thin walls and cramped bathroom. She was comfortable there, wasn't she? Just barely so, though. There wasn't much room to move, no privacy — she *could* hear her neighbor snoring upstairs, after all. But it was home. What exactly was he offering her? A place to live? A domestic partnership where she just lived with him and they had sex? Or, after only a few days, was he ready to make their relationship a more permanent arrangement? Going by the look on his face and the sincerity in his voice, she suspected the latter.

"I know we hardly know each other, Sam," he said, apparently attempting to win her over, "but love works differently with vampires."

"So I'm gathering."

"It's not that I want to spend the rest of my life with you — well, I do, but with vampires it's more a matter of need. I *need* to spend the rest of my life with you. The want is implied." He took her face in his palms and held her with a tenderness she had never known.

No one, not even Steve in the early days of their doomed marriage, had touched her with such deference.

"I need you, Sam. I'll do whatever it takes. You can have your own room if that will make you more comfortable, and besides, now that you're...well, not the same person you were before...I can help you adapt better if we're living together, and — "

"Stop. Just stop, Micah." Sam sighed and shook her head. "You don't have to try so hard to convince me."

He looked at her like he wanted to ask what in the hell she was saying, the unspoken *Is that a yes or no?* shooting from his gaze in a silent question.

"That's a yes, Micah," she said.

"Are you reading my mind?" The grin that spread across his face was a better gift to her than the Mercedes Steve had bought her on her birthday. She had sold that car for cash within a week of leaving his ass and had never looked back.

"If you can do it, so can I." She smirked innocently. "But I have a couple of stipulations if I'm going to move in with you."

"Such as?" He gathered her closer. The aches in her body were slowly dissipating. Moving around was working the pain out of her muscles.

"Such as," she said, "We share a room, for starters. If you give me my own room, the deal's off." She pulled herself over his body, straddling him.

"Done." Micah sank into the pillow, situating himself under her.

"And you have to make love to me anytime I want." She rotated her hips over his. Mmm, he was already hard, and with her new bionic senses, the sensations vibrating through her core felt even more delicious.

"Okay, I can live with that. Anything else?"

She shook her head. "No, but I reserve the right to add to this list whenever I see fit." Her hands eased up his shirt and revealed his ridged stomach as the fabric bunched against her wrists.

"Okay, my turn," he said, tugging her forward. "When?"

"Is tonight too soon?"

"Mmm, I was just thinking that. You sure you're not reading my mind?"

"Positive." She unfastened his belt. "Does that door lock?" She jerked her head toward the door.

"No."

She paused for a minute, then grinned and unzipped his fly. "Fuck it. I want you."

"Now I know you're in my head." He flipped her to her

back and pushed aside the medical gown she was wearing as she shoved down his pants. In one smooth, fluid motion, he surged forward and sank himself inside her, grunting as their bodies connected.

The loving was fast and furious, her body needing his in a way that bordered on desperate. It appeared he needed her just as badly, working furiously, shoving one leg up as he angled his body for deeper penetration, as if he couldn't get close enough to her.

She wasn't sure, but at one point she thought she heard the door open, right at the point where she commanded Micah to fuck her harder. What sounded like the door hissing shut followed, but Sam hadn't cared that they had been seen. If anything, it turned her on even more.

In a matter of only minutes, both announced their simultaneous release with shouts of pleasure, his body stiffening briefly then falling on top of her as his cock spent itself and emptied its contents with a series of luscious contractions that tripled the strength of her own orgasm.

A spent heap of flesh, Sam gasped for air. Her arms locked around Micah's back and her legs trembled through a last wave of release. "I love you."

Micah shuddered against her and buried his arm between her and the hard medical mattress, pulling her against him as he turned his face into her neck. "Thank you," he whispered. "Thank you for loving me."

She wasn't sure, but the single jerk of his shoulders and the burst of breath against her skin felt more like a sob than his body finishing its orgasm. Tightening her hold on him, she smiled. She had found where she belonged. She was Micah's and he was hers.

CHAPTER 21

TRACE LOOKED OUT THE WINDOW of the house situated back from the main road, holding the curtain aside so that sunlight spilled over the four dead bodies scattered around the room. His wraparound sunglasses hid his eyes, the only part of his body that was sensitive to the sun, and he waited.

If the drecks had been telling the truth, Apostle would arrive home any minute. Then he would join the other four corpses in death.

Dropping the curtain over the window, Trace stepped over the bodies and contemplated the events of the past two days. He wasn't quite sure how to feel. He had finally made a friend in Micah, but now the male was mated. Would he have time for Trace? Not that he needed a lot of attention, but the idea of having a friend who understood him, and who Trace felt would get him for who he was, was a nice one. And, well, it went deeper than that. He needed Micah. Maybe not right now, but soon enough he would need what Micah could give him. He could already feel himself needing more than he was getting elsewhere.

He had heard the stories about Micah. The brooding vampire had not only been a notorious loner, but also a hardcore Dom at one time. Years ago, he had learned through a mutual acquaintance what Micah was capable of with a whip and fire, among other accoutrements. That's when Trace had taken to watching him, learning and looking for a way in.

And then Trace had bumped into Jackson at Four Alarm a couple of months ago. The male had been bragging to one of his friends about the equipment Micah had in his home. Some way kinked out shit that would have been right up Trace's alley from the sound of it.

He absently wondered if Sam knew exactly what she was getting into with him.

Damn, he liked Sam. She was perfect for Micah. They complimented each other well. She wasn't a thing like Jackson, either.

At any rate, Trace had known immediately after Micah had half-bonded to Jackson that Jackson would break Micah's heart. And after Jackson's rookie bragging session at Four Alarm, Trace had become even more convinced their relationship was doomed to fail, and he knew when the end came, Micah would need caring for.

So he had taken to following Micah, playing guardian, looking after him. He had known two months ago the location of Micah's secret apartment. Hell, he had been there the night Jackson had walked out. Trace had been watching and waiting for the inevitable, and he had felt Micah's anguish that night as if it were his own.

Trace had even been there the night Micah had nearly nose-dived to the ground. He had used his powers to push him back so he didn't fall off his balcony's banister. But even if Micah had fallen, Trace would never have let him die. Catching him would have been simple enough, but it would have outed him before he was ready.

And then Tristan had called that meeting. Trace had sat in that room over a week ago, biting his tongue when the others were going crazy trying to find Micah. Tristan had even blamed himself. But Trace had kept his mouth shut. It had pissed him off that no one else bothered to notice Micah's absence. So while they all pussy-footed around, he ensured their team's best asset kept topside and breathing. Trace protected those he thought of as friends, and he had considered Micah a friend for a long time. And now Sam was added to that list. Trace would do anything to protect them both.

Which was why these assholes lay dead at his feet. They

had fucked with the wrong guardian angel.

Trace paced back to the window and looked out once more. Micah was through the worst of his troubles, and just like that he was mated again. Lucky him. Why didn't Trace feel all warm and fuzzy about Micah's good fortune? Probably because it threw a glaring spotlight on his own lack of a mate, which was something Trace badly wanted.

Just as he had pointed out to Arion earlier, he had never been mated, either. Unlike Arion, though, that bothered Trace. It wasn't for lack of trying on his part. Trace had had a variety of lovers, some men, some women, but all who satisfied his need for pain, submission, degradation, or all of the above. So far, though, none of his liaisons had spawned a lifemate, and the emptiness left a hole in his heart. Maybe he just wasn't made for a lifemate. Maybe God had other intentions for him.

At any rate, his unusual sexual tastes had little to do with finding a mate. Submitting himself and giving up all control was the only way he could keep himself grounded and his immense powers in check. It wasn't so much that Trace liked being confined, it was that he *needed* to be confined. He needed to be smacked around, punished, gagged, and otherwise abused.

Sure, he got off on being dominated, but the scenes he engaged in kept him in control of a power that would otherwise consume him and tip his internal scale toward going mutant. That was something he couldn't let happen. He would kill himself before changing to darkness. And with Micah's help someday, he hoped to stave off the transformation.

The glare of sunlight off a windshield caught Trace's eyes and he perked up as an unmarked police car slowed and turned onto the winding driveway. He closed the drape, stepped over a dead dreck, sat on the couch, and crossed his legs. He was as calm as sitting water on a windless day. The drecks' pack mentality worked in his favor on days like this, when he could take out a whole trove of them without moving more than twenty feet in any direction.

He loved his job.

Keys jangled at the door, and then John Apostle stepped inside, still in uniform. His gaze swept the room in horror before stopping on Trace. Trace held up his hand, fingers splayed. Apostle halted and froze just as he tried to turn and run.

"Please, do come in," Trace said, slowly moving his fingers, manipulating Apostle as if he were a puppet. "Close the door." The dreck did as he was compelled to do. "Now, come here and get on your knees in front of me."

Apostle walked like a zombie. The only part of him showing any animation were his eyes. The rest of him seemed void of feeling. Stopping in front of Trace, he dropped to his knees with a resounding thud.

"Before you die, I want you to know that Micah saved the woman. She's one of us now." He leaned forward and grinned at Apostle. Trace could feel the dreck's hatred and anger pushing through his fear, but it didn't matter. He was as good as dead already. "Micah and I are her guardian angels, now. And I am his. I won't let anything happen to either one of them, but if anything should, I will single-handedly crush your entire race before I take my own life. Do you understand?" Trace pressed closer, his mouth curling into a malevolent sneer. "You failed, you miserable fuck. What I will do to your race, should I be tested on this matter, won't even compare to what's about to happen to you."

With that, Trace stood and loomed over Apostle then fisted one of his hands. The bones in Apostle's neck began to snap and pop, his spine crushing. Then for good measure, with his other hand Trace squeezed and felt Apostle's evil, blue heart explode inside his chest.

"That's right, fucker," Traceon released Apostle and stepped over him after he fell over dead. "I'm their guardian angel, and you picked the wrong hand of God to fuck with." His anger charged powerfully through his muscles and he stopped, turned, and punched his splayed hands into the air in front of him. A deep, echoing boom sounded and the floor pulsed like it was a trampoline. The crackle of snapping bones filled the air. All five bodies slumped then burst open as the furniture exploded and wind whipped like a cyclone around Trace before slowly calming. Only then did Trace lower his hands.

The beast was coming alive inside him. He needed a fix. Now. He pulled out his phone and sent a nine-one-one text to his provider then took a deep breath. He left the front door open as he walked out into the late morning sunlight and disappeared.

CHAPTER 22

FLIGHT DELAYS CAUSED STEVE'S PLANE TO LAND in Chicago two hours later than expected, and by the time he picked up his rental car and got on the highway, it was nearly noon. His stomach rumbled for want of food, but as a surgeon, he was used to going long periods without a meal. Right now, it was more important to retrieve his wife than fill his belly, so he passed by the fast food chains in favor of following his GPS to the address of the hospital.

David's information had included three addresses. One for the hospital, one labeled home, and one for where she had been found after being attacked.

What the hell had she done to deserve getting mugged? He was sure it was something. Maybe the guy who had attacked her was her pimp and she had been trying to swindle him out of money. At any rate, it was nothing compared to what he would do to her once he got her home. Sam would get a lesson in submission and obedience that would make her think twice before taking off on his ass again. At least he would be able to put that ankle cuff to work now. He laughed. Let her try to leave with that on. She wouldn't make it past the front yard, and he had the only key for the thing.

Yes, Steve had learned from his mistakes, and so would Sam for hers.

Arriving at the hospital, he went to the administration desk.

"I'm looking for a patient," he said.

"Name?"

"Samantha Garrett. She was admitted last night. I was

told it was a mugging."

The elderly, black nurse gave him a look after punching in a query and scanning the screen. "Looks like Ms. Garrett has been discharged."

"What?"

The woman looked perplexed as she frowned at the computer screen as if something didn't make sense.

"What is it?" Steve said. He was already perturbed that he wouldn't be able to one-stop-shop and get her now. Damn it. He had already booked his return flight for this evening. He didn't have time to dick around in Chicago playing hide-and-seek with his bitch of a wife.

"I'm not sure, probably nothing. You should see the doctor who treated her. Dr. Rose. He's in the ER."

"Thank you."

"You need directions?"

"No, I can find it." Steve was already walking away crisply, waving the woman off. He didn't need directions to find his way around a hospital. He worked in hospitals for Chrissake. Directions! Ha!

Fifteen minutes later he realized he probably should have taken the nurse up on her offer. To get to the ER required pulling back out of the parking lot, maneuvering a one-way street, and pulling back in on the other side of the campus. Good thing he wasn't having a heart attack, despite the pulsing vein at his temple and the death grip he had on his steering wheel, or he might have died trying to find the emergency entrance.

He marched into the waiting area and up to the reception desk. "Dr. Rose. Where is he?"

The nurse eyed him impatiently. "And you are?"

"Samantha Garrett's husband."

Her expression morphed into one of concern. "Excuse me a moment." She bustled through the double doors and disappeared.

What the hell was wrong with everyone at this hospital? Were they all retards? Mental incompetents? What kind of people did Chicago have running its medical institutions?

He glanced around the crowded waiting room, receiving a couple of angry glares.

"What are you looking at? You'll get your turn."

"Sir, I'm Dr. Rose."

Steve turned to see a tall man with dark circles under his eyes walking toward him, the nurse in tow. It looked like the good doctor had had a long night and an even longer morning.

"Dr. Garrett," Steve said, taking the other doctor's outstretched hand.

"Oh, you're a doctor. I didn't know."

"Surgeon, actually, but yes. What happened to my wife?"

"Let's talk in my office." Dr. Rose gestured for Steve to follow him into the back. This wasn't good. He could already tell by the tone of Dr. Rose's voice.

Still, he followed him to an office crowded with files, medical reference books, and patient charts. He took a seat as Dr. Rose closed the door then leaned against the edge of his desk.

"Dr. Garrett, I won't waste your time. We have record of your wife being here last night. We have a chart for her, too. I even have blood samples for her." Dr. Rose paused, shaking his head.

"So, what's the problem?" Steve was feeling worse about the situation. There was just something in Dr. Rose's tone that raised his hackles.

"None of us can remember treating her. The nurse who took her blood can't remember drawing it, I can't remember examining her, and the nurse doesn't remember entering her data into the chart. It's like she was never here, but we all know she was."

Steve looked at the doctor like he was yanking his chain. "Did she put you up to this?" He laughed unbelievingly. "Did she tell you that if I showed up to pretend you didn't know her?"

"I'm sorry?"

The smile faded from Steve's face and he stared at Dr. Rose for several seconds, looking for any sign that the guy was kidding. "Oh, come on! You can't be serious. You can't just forget a patient."

"I wish I were kidding, Dr. Garrett. None of us know what to make of it. She was here, but we don't remember her."

Deflating, Steve sank back in his chair. How did someone just disappear from the memories of so many people? He looked around the office as if Sam would suddenly materialize, and then glanced back at the doctor.

"Well, thank you for your time. I'll just…" What? What would he do? Go to the next address on his list, that's what. "Thank you, Dr. Rose. I've taken enough of your time." *More like you've wasted enough of mine.* He stood and shook Dr. Rose's hand and went to the door.

"I'm so sorry about this, Dr. Garrett. We've never had anything like this happen before. I wish I knew how to explain it."

"Don't worry about it. I'm sure it'll come back to you in time." Steve still wasn't sure he believed the doctor's story, but what choice did he have? He was wasting time here and had other places to search for her.

"I hope you find her," Dr. Rose said as they reached the double doors to the waiting room.

"Oh, I think I know where to look," Steve said. Sam would turn up. One way or another, he would get her back.

CHAPTER 23

SAM COLLECTED HER THINGS FROM THE BLACK GARTER and packed the masks and costumes that belonged to her in a box while Micah stood guard at the door. The manager had been beside himself when she gave her notice, begging her not to quit. *The club needs Scarlet,* he had said, grabbing her wrist as he pleaded with her. Micah hadn't liked that and now her manager — ex-manager — nursed a busted lip in his office.

"I like this one," Micah said, picking a club-owned mask off the wall. It was red with slanted eyeholes that made the mask look sinister. Black streaks that looked like claw marks ran up both cheeks and down the forehead.

"That one's not mine," she said. "Sorry."

He sidled up beside her. "I saw you dance once wearing this mask."

Something in the tone of his voice drew her gaze to his and her pulse quickened. "Oh?"

"Mm-hm. I tried to buy a private performance that night, but you were booked up."

"Really? I'm sorry." She turned toward him. "Were you hurt by the rejection?"

He nodded. "Excruciatingly so."

"But you somehow managed to survive."

He growled and inhaled deeply then leaned down and brushed his lips over her ear as he whispered, "Just barely. Do you want to know what I did when I got home that night?"

Sliding her hands up his chest, she closed her eyes and swayed dreamily toward him. "Yes."

"Then take this mask and I'll show you later." He licked the curve of her ear and she felt the leather mask push gently against her hand.

"That's stealing," she said, taking it.

His hand slid around to the small of her back and his lips worked a spell on her skin until she thought she would explode. "Just take it," he said, pulling away. His gaze burned hers as he backed toward the door.

Suddenly breathless, she looked down at the mask, then back up at Micah, who had turned around and stood sentry once more, his gaze sweeping up and down the hall. With a grin, she tossed the mask in the box with hers. The club wouldn't miss this one mask. They had no one to wear it anymore, anyway. As a matter of fact...Sam snagged a couple more of her favorites from those the club owned and threw them into her box, too.

STEVE COULDN'T IGNORE HIS NEED FOR FOOD any longer and ran through a McDonald's drive-thru on his way to the second address on his list. By the time he reached the luxury apartment building with a marble placard that read *The Sentinel*, the sun was setting. So, okay, maybe it wasn't her pimp that had attacked her, but a John she was likely whoring herself to *for* her pimp. She certainly had the look of a high-priced call girl who could get clients who could afford to live in a place like this. And how else would she have been able to live off-the-grid for so long doing legitimate work. It only made sense Sam had taken to selling herself to survive.

Unfortunately, the tight-assed security guard wouldn't let him up the elevator. Fuck! He would have to contact David and have him pull some strings with the local police department. That would take more time, but if that's what it took, then he had no choice. Meanwhile, he could check the address labeled *home*. He probably should have gone there before checking the address for the Sentinel, but he wasn't thinking straight at the time. Lack of food will do that to a person.

Dialing David as he drove to Sam's home address, he waited for the detective to pick up.

"Yeah, you got her, yet?" David said when he answered.

Steve shook his head. "Not yet, but soon."

"She wasn't at the hospital?"

Steve didn't want to get into that debacle. "No."

"Wow, they sure got her out of there fast."

If he only knew. "Yeah, I know. Hey, I need a favor."

"Anything. You're paying the bills."

"I need you to contact the local police and see if you can pull some strings. That address where she was attacked? Well, it's a luxury high-rise and security won't let me up. I'm on my way to her house, but I don't want to wait to see if she's there or not. I don't have a lot of time, and if she's not at her home, whoever lives in that apartment might know where I can find her." He was on the last flight out, only a couple hours from now. The sun had already set and he was running out of time. His patience was wearing thin. If he didn't get Sam in the next thirty minutes, he would have to change his flight and bunk down in Chicago for a night. Fuck, he might as well make plans to fly out tomorrow at this rate.

"Okay, I'll get on it."

He hung up and followed the GPS directions into a part of town that made Steve uncomfortable. Abandoned townhomes and row houses with boarded up windows lined the streets. Groups of hoodlums congregated on stoops and stared at his car like it didn't belong, which, of course, it didn't. Steve was better than these lowlifes.

He drove past a block of run-down businesses. One of the buildings had a bright yellow sign with three X's on it and the words *Naked Girls* blinking in pink neon. Sam lived in this dump of urban shit?

A few more blocks and his GPS indicated that he was there. He shut off the engine and sat back, checking the address on his list. Yep, this was it. God, how low had Sam fallen?

He got out and stepped around a large, pebbled pothole then crossed the street to her building and yanked the weathered, paint-chipped door open and hurried inside. The sooner he got her and left this hellhole, the better. He pounded on her door, double-checking the address again when no one answered. Again, he pounded.

"Hey!" someone shouted from upstairs. "Shut up down there, goddamn it. I'm watching *Dog the Bounty Hunter*."

Of course you are. "Sorry," he forced himself to say. "Maybe you can help me." He looked up the staircase and saw an obese woman wearing a stained sweatshirt that didn't look like it had been washed in over a decade. She had a cigarette hanging from her lips. "Uh, hello, um, does Sam Garrett live here?" He gestured toward her door.

"I think that's her name. Why? You her next customer or her dealer?"

"She does drugs?" That surprised Steve. Sam didn't seem the type.

"Hell if I know, but no one lookin' like you comes 'round places like this unless they pushin', buyin', or lookin' for a ho. I figure she gots to be one of the above."

"No, I'm her husband." Steve tapped his fingers impatiently. "Have you seen her?"

The lady looked like she was excited to have the chance to gossip. She probably lived off Jerry Springer and Maury.

"I ain't seen her today, but she usually sleeps during the day. She works nights." She grinned wryly, and Steve saw she was missing three teeth.

"What do you mean?"

"What you think girls 'round here do when they work nights, mister? Just wait 'round for a half hour or so. You're *wife*" — she chuckled like she didn't believe him for a second that he was actually Sam's husband — "will be up soon. And she don't show up, you can always come up and I'll give you what you want. I'll do you real good. Only cost you twenty bucks." She cackled and blew smoke out her nose then turned around and closed her apartment door.

Nice neighbors.

Sam apparently wasn't home or awake, so all he could do was what the woman had suggested. Wait. But the fat lady's words didn't make him feel any better. If anything, it confirmed his suspicions. He'd have to make Sam get tested before he stuck his dick in her again. He didn't want to get AIDS or any other variety of sexually transmitted disease just from fucking his own wife.

Half-expecting to find his rental car stolen or stripped by thieves, he went back outside and found, to his surprise, his car still intact.

Shit, he needed to piss like an elephant. He hadn't stopped all day and the coffee and large Coke from McDonald's were talking back. Getting behind the wheel of his rental, he rolled down the window and tossed the rest of his Coke out then unzipped his pants and whipped out his dick. He sighed as he pissed in the empty cup then shook out the last drop and opened his door to set the cup on the curb. People in this neighborhood were probably used to finding piss, shit, and vomit littering their sidewalks, anyway. So who cared.

He shut the door and settled into his seat, started the engine, and turned on the heater. It was fucking cold.

A couple of houses had cheap, tacky Christmas lights still in their windows. Didn't they realize Christmas had been three weeks ago? Closer to a month, really. These people were probably the types who were too lazy to take down their Christmas lights, leaving them up all year and only turning them on during the holidays.

His dick still hung from his pants and he closed his eyes, thinking about Sam fucking other men. At first he didn't like it, but then he realized it turned him on. Maybe he could turn her into his own sex slave and command her to fuck his friends while he watched. If she liked sex so much, he could accommodate her and maybe make a little extra cash in the process.

His hand found his hardening cock and stroked it as he imagined Sam bound and gagged, legs splayed wide while his friend from the gym fucked her. Opening his eyes, he looked down at himself, stroking harder. Soon he would have her back, and soon thereafter, he would make her his slave. Soon, yes, oh yes.

His toes curled and he quickly grabbed his McDonald's bag, positioning it just in the nick of time in front of his dick. His cum spewed into it as he shuddered. Steve used the leftover McDonald's napkins to wipe himself off, tossed everything in the bag, including his sandwich wrapper and fry box, then crumpled it up and tossed it out the window to join his piss-filled cup. What was a little semen to these people? He was sure that was something else the residents here were used to finding on their sidewalks or even their front porches.

Headlights turned down the street and Steve hunched down as a black Suburban pulled up in front of Sam's building. He peeked over the dashboard just as Sam hopped out of the passenger side. Ah, the harlot returns.

She'd cut her hair. Otherwise, she looked the same. Tall, lean, small tits.

Steve watched her walk around to the driver's side and frowned as a tall, dark-haired man got out and joined her. They exchanged a quick word, she went inside, and he went to the back of the Suburban and pulled out a stack of broken-down boxes and a roll of bubble wrap before following her.

"I DON'T HAVE MUCH I NEED," Sam told Micah, opening her closet. "My clothes, my books." She grabbed several shirts and pushed them together, then lifted them as one from the bar and set them on the bed.

"How about anything in the kitchen?"

She turned as he started opening up the cabinets. "Maybe that bamboo bowl. And there's a set of China plates my mom gave me on the top shelf in the last cabinet."

Clothes, books, a few dishes, and what else? Well, her computer, of course, and the few CDs she owned. And the stacks of money she had saved under the mattress. Other than that, she didn't need the furniture.

Sam was pulling another bundle of clothes from the closet when someone knocked on her door.

"I bet that's the landlord," she said.

"Probably wants your keys."

"Well, he'll just have to wait until I'm done packing and moved out, won't he?" She smiled innocently at him as she went to the door.

But when she opened it, the person on the other side wasn't her landlord.

"Steve." Her throat constricted around his name, and she was sure her face had turned stark white. How had he found her?

"Hello, Samantha."

Sam's fear jolted Micah as if it were his own, and in an instant he was by her side, pulling her back. "Who the fuck are you?"

"I'm Sam's husband. Who are you?"

Micah looked at Sam, whose fearful gaze turned back to him. "I told you about him. This is Steve."

Ah yes. Steve. The man who enjoyed beating women.

"I know who you are," Micah said. "What do you want?"

"My wife."

"Well, you can't have her." His arm slithered around the front of Sam, easing her behind him.

Steve pulled out his cell. "Well, let's let the authorities settle this then."

He snatched Steve's phone before the other man even knew he had grabbed it, his index finger dialing empty air before he frowned and shot Micah a dirty look. "You asshole."

Steve was beginning to irritate him. And when Micah got irritated, bad shit happened. "Fine, let's ask her. Sam, do you want to go with Steve."

"No," she said without hesitation.

"There you have it." Micah began to close the door, but

Steve's arm shot out, his hand slamming against the door. Micah grinned like the guy had just made his day. If he wanted to, he could snap Steve's arm like it was nothing more than a dry branch, but okay, he'd play.

"You're starting to piss me off, Steve."

Sam stepped around to Micah's side, and he picked up a new feeling from her: aggression. He could feel her anger and the desire to show Steve a thing or two now that she had a new and improved — and much stronger — body.

"No, Micah," Sam said. "It's okay. Steve has a point. I am his wife, after all."

He saw into her mind and liked what she was thinking.

Moving aside, he gave her space. "Okay, but I'm here if you need me, honey." He crossed his arms and grinned as he took a few steps back.

"How are you Steve?" Sam said, her voice pleasant enough.

"Tired, impatient, ready to get out of this hellhole." Steve's gaze shot to Micah. "Not pleased to find you with another man. What? Is he your pimp?"

Sam laughed and looked over her shoulder at him. "Who? Micah? No, he's not my pimp." She winked at him and he tried not to grin, taking a deep breath and clearing his throat.

She turned back to Steve and looked at his hand and sucked her tongue, making an exaggerated, affectionate sound. "Oh, look. You still wear your wedding ring. How sweet. Here, let me take a look at that." She took Steve's hand and wrapped hers around it, then squeezed. Hard.

Steve grimaced, crying out as he fell to his knees in obvious pain. Micah shot to the door, closing it as Sam dragged him in with her new super powers. He knelt down beside Steve and leered. "How do you like your new wife, Stevie? She's gotten a lot stronger, hasn't she?" He was proud of his mate.

Sam squeezed again and he heard a knuckle pop as Steve jerked and whined like a baby.

"I'm not the same woman you used to beat up," Sam said, finally letting go.

Steve clutched his hand to his body, looking from Sam to Micah and back as he sat up and scooted backward on his ass, putting distance between him and the two of them. "What did you do to her?" Steve looked at Micah.

"That doesn't matter." Micah locked his eyes onto Steve's. His fangs extended and he grinned. Micah left him lucid just long enough so he could watch the terror flash in Steve's eyes. Then he locked him into compulsion.

An hour later, Micah packed the last of Sam's things in the SUV and returned to the apartment.

"What should we do with him?" Sam looked at Steve's hypnotized body sitting on the edge of the bed.

Micah had kept Steve compelled while they had finished packing, and now he stepped in front of him. Sam took his hand and he looked down at her.

"I'm going to remove you from his memory," he said.

"You can do that?"

"Of course."

Her eyes brightened as if she had an idea. "What else can you do while you're in there?"

A sardonic quirk turned up the corner of his mouth. "Why? Do you want me to implant a suggestion?"

"Can you?"

"Yes. What did you have in mind?"

"Just one or two things."

Micah turned his attention back to Steve and sneered. "Let's hear them."

The power of suggestion could have a strong influence on a human mind.

THREE DAYS LATER...

Sabrina pushed Steve back on the bed. He didn't really know why he had invited her over. She made such fake sexual noises, but sex was sex, and she had called earlier saying she wanted to finish their date from the other night. He remembered she had been over, and then he had gone to Chicago—he couldn't remember why—but now he was home and Sabrina's nimble fingers worked open the fly of his slacks and pushed them down.

"Oooooooo, uuunnnhhhh, so good," she squealed.

Would she just fuck him already? His dick was as hard as steel and he just wanted to get off. He reminded himself never to invite her over again.

She stood up and stripped out of her dress as he stroked himself and watched. She had nice tits. Fake, but he liked her nipples. They reminded him of someone, pale and small to the point where he couldn't tell where the nipple began and the rest of her tit ended. Who was it she reminded him of? It was just on the tip of his tongue, but he couldn't remember. It wasn't like him to forget stuff like that.

She turned and peeled her thong down, bending over as she took it off, showing him her shaved, glistening slit. Mmm, he wanted that.

"You want my pussy? You like my hot little pussy, don't you?"

Okay, well, maybe if she didn't talk he would enjoy himself more, but what the hell, he would play along just to get it over with.

"Yeah, baby. Give me that hot pussy. That's right, climb up here and put that hot cunt on my dick. That's it, fuck me, baby."

"Oooooooo, yeah, yeah, oooohhhhhh, so good, so—baby, what's wrong? What's wrong?"

Steve stilled abruptly as his dick shriveled and went limp just as she lowered herself on him. "I don't know. This has never happened before."

She hopped off. "That's okay, baby. I can get you hard again." She began to stroke him with her hand, but to no avail. He slapped her hand away and began stroking himself. Ah, yeah, there he was. His dick inflated again, lengthening and standing at attention.

Sabrina hopped back on and her verbal dramatics started again, "Yes, yes, that's right, give me that big cock. Give me that big—baby! What the hell?"

Once more, as soon as she lowered herself on him, he

went limp. "I don't understand."

She jumped up and started dressing as he whacked his peter back into readiness. "Wait, Sabrina. Try it again. Look, I'm ready for you now."

"Screw you. Forget it, Steve. I'm out of here."

"Sabrina!"

She was still pulling on her clothes as she barged out of his bedroom. A few seconds later, the front door slammed shut and he heard her car start, her engine rev, her tires squeal, and then she was gone.

He looked at his dick. "What the hell is the matter with you?"

Six more times with six more women, he tried to have sex, but each time, as soon as he pushed inside her, he wilted like old lettuce. He tried having them give him blow jobs, then hand jobs, but nothing worked. He could get off with his own hand just fine, but nothing a woman did helped him achieve orgasm through any other means. She could get him hard, but as soon as they tried to do the deed the air blew out of his balloon.

And he was in for a surprise the next time he laughed in public. Hopefully his bladder wouldn't be too full when that happened.

CHAPTER 24

IT HAD BEEN A WEEK since Sam had moved into the apartment with Micah. She tucked a stack of underwear into the top drawer of the dresser then glanced up into the mirror. The tiny marks on her neck made her remember the night before when Micah had bitten her again. If sex with Micah was good, sex with Micah while he was feeding was even better. She brushed her fingers over the almost invisible mark, smiling to herself before arranging folded socks next to her underwear.

Micah had not only moved her into his apartment, he had taken her to his house, too, a mansion — well, to Sam it was a mansion after where she had lived for the past year — in a manicured community in the suburbs. And he had shown her the basement in his house, as well as the room that took up half the basement. Where he had a collection of equipment that Sam had only heard some of the harder-core girls at the Black Garter talk about in passing. So, that's what that stuff looked like. Admittedly, she had been turned on a few times by what she had heard, and had often wondered about using whips or ropes or nipple clamps. What did they feel like? Did people really get pleasure from that kind of thing? It surprised her that she wanted to find out.

"Which are you? A top or a bottom?" Micah chuckled and walked into the room with folded laundry.

Sam jumped, startled. "Will you stay out of my head?"

"Sorry, habit."

She laughed. That's what he always said. "You're never going to stop that, are you?"

He shook his head, wrapping his arms around her waist. "No." His grin was unapologetic. "I can't help it. I like the way you think. Especially when you're thinking about my special proclivities."

Sam's eyebrow arched. "Proclivities? My, what a big vocabulary you have."

"I'm just full of surprises." Micah pressed closer. "And I'm very well educated."

Sam's heart raced. "I can see that, and I'm sure you are." She still didn't know how old Micah was, but she could bet he had matriculated more than a few times. His intelligence was a huge turn-on, and over the past week, she had become more and more aware of just how immense his mental faculties were.

"Your intelligence turns me on, too." Micah bent his head and skimmed his lips over the side of her neck.

"Would you stop that?"

"Huh-uh. Nope. Never." He opened his mouth and closed it over her flesh, sucking gently.

Damn him, but he was persuasive.

"Well, can you at least stay out of my memories?" She shivered from the heat he lit inside her.

He released her neck and straightened. "I can do that. Maybe." He grinned and his lips pressed against hers, holding her there for a long moment as if he was stripping off her clothes with his mind. Then he slowly pulled away and growled as he got himself back under control. "I'm going down to the corner store for beer. I'll be back in fifteen. Need anything?"

It was Saturday and the playoffs were on. Trace was coming over to watch the late game. So, yeah, maybe they didn't have enough time to play just now.

"Maybe some pretzels?"

"Will do." He kissed her again then dragged himself away to grab his wallet off the dresser and shrug into his coat.

"Which are you?" she asked as he started to leave the room, referring to his earlier question. He had only shown her the room in his basement. Interestingly enough, they hadn't talked about it. She got the impression he wanted to ease her into the idea slowly.

He stopped and turned his blistering navy eyes back to her. "I'm a Dom, but I also top. With you, I think I might actually bottom, though. But I'll never submit."

"What's the difference between a Dom and a top?" She had so much to learn about the whole BDSM scene, but she wanted to learn. It excited her.

"A Dominant requires submission, a top doesn't. As a top," he slowly stepped toward her as if he were hunting her, "I provide physical stimulation without requiring you to submit." He reached around and slapped her ass. Hard. "See, if you didn't like my slapping you as a top, you can stop me, or basically top me from the bottom. But if I was Dom'ing you, I wouldn't allow you to do that. I would have control and your complete submission. Do you understand?"

Her ass stung in the most erotic way where he had spanked her. "I think so. Topping and bottoming allows for give and take between the two, but between a Dominant and a submissive, one gives and one takes. There is no give-and-take."

He grinned mischievously. "Very good. You've just completed your first lesson."

The air smoldered between them. "I look forward to the next one."

"So do I." He backed away, grazing his fingertips over her cheek. "I'll be back. I love you."

"I love you, too."

She turned back to the dresser and took the clothes he had brought her and tucked them into a drawer then headed to the kitchen to check on the chili. Trace and Micah loved her chili. It took six hours to cook, but it was worth every minute. This was already the second batch she had made since moving in.

She looked toward the windows. It was snowing again. It had snowed earlier and an icy mix was forecast for tonight so Chicago would be a mess. Trace would probably spend the night rather than drive home. She didn't mind. He and

Micah were becoming good friends, and Sam had to admit, she liked Trace. He and Micah were so similar, it was hard to like one and not the other.

She grinned to herself. When Apostle and his crew had turned up dead, Trace had acted like he had known nothing about it, but she could tell Micah knew better. And, so did she. Maybe it was something about the secretive glint in Trace's eyes when she had asked him about it, but she was sure Apostle's death had been Trace's doing. The scene had been pretty gruesome from the sound of it. It made her wonder what kind of power Trace kept hidden under the surface. It also made her thankful he was on her side.

Going back to the bedroom, she hunted through the closet for her old Chicago Bears sweatshirt. She was still getting used to where her things were, and as she shuffled through the hangers in the part of the walk-in closet Micah had cleared for her, something fell from the shelf above and bounced off her shoulder. She jumped back and looked down. The red and black leather mask she had stolen from the club looked up at her, giving her an idea.

MICAH RETURNED TO THE APARTMENT with a bag of pretzels and a six-pack of beer. He didn't drink much, and neither did Trace. Sam might have one bottle.

"Sam?"

The apartment was unusually quiet, the TV droning on with pregame stats. The spicy scent of chili was so strong he had smelled it in the elevator on his way back up.

Sam didn't answer him and he instantly went on alert, setting the beer and pretzels on the kitchen counter before walking cautiously down the hall toward the bedroom.

Opening the door, his mouth twitched and his eyebrow ticked upward.

Sam stood in the middle of the room, wearing a black lace bra and panty, black garter and stockings, and the black, high-heeled ankle boots he had wondered if she would ever put on for him. The black and red leather mask covered her face except for her mouth. Her blood red lips grinned coyly.

"Close the door," she said and smacked the rounded end of a wooden spoon against the palm of her hand with a loud crack.

His cock strained against the seam of his jeans, his chest pumping. Fuck, she was hot.

"I told you to close the door."

"Our lesson gave you ideas, did it?" he said, reaching back and pushing the door. It swung and latched, shutting out the light from the living room, but the lamp behind her by the bed was on, and it threw her into shadowy silhouette.

"Take off your clothes."

Micah could feel her uncertainty. She wasn't used to this kind of play, but the mask gave her courage, allowing her to play a role.

"You're doing wonderfully," he said, trying to reassure her.

He felt her pleasure from his compliment, but she only smacked the spoon against her hand again and stepped to the side. "I told you to take off your clothes."

Micah had only ever bottomed once when Jackson had wanted to experiment with topping him. And even during that entire scene, Jackson hadn't gotten him as hot as Sam had in only a few seconds.

He watched her walk a half-circle around him as he untucked his shirt and calmly pulled it over his head. He was back to his old weight, his body filled out and strong. He couldn't see Sam's eyes behind the mask's lenses, but he could feel her gaze razing him and hear her appraising thoughts. His body turned her on.

"Would you like to assist?" He asked, turning toward her and unbuckling his belt.

She stood in place, watching. "No. And turn away from me while you undress."

He did as he was told, slowly rotating in place to face the bed before the metallic sound of unzipping his jeans broke the silence. As he pushed them down, along with his boxers, he toed off his boots, pushing them aside before stepping out of his jeans. Finally he bent down and pulled off his socks, his hard-on jutting out like a third arm as he stood back up, calm, his back to her.

"You're so fucking sexy like this," he said, testing the boundaries of the scene.

The spoon thwacked against his ass and his body jerked as the pain registered on his face, his eyes blinking from the sting of the strike before he breathed and calmed himself again. So, no speaking unless he was told to speak, he was guessing.

Her nails raked down one side of his back from his shoulder to his ass as her tongue left a heated trail down his spine and she sank to her knees behind him. He stood stoic, still as a statue, his cock weeping as she gripped his hips with both hands and bit the place on his ass that she had struck with the spoon. He fought back a moan, daring to look down and behind him. The spoon sat on the floor beside his left foot and her long fingers dug into his flesh, holding him as she switched from biting to licking. This time he did moan, drawing his head up and letting it fall back. The combination of sharp and soft, pain and pleasure heightened his arousal. So this was what it felt like to be a submissive. Well, maybe not exactly, but she was doing a damn fine job going Domme for her first time.

"Turn around," she said, letting go of him.

With pleasure. Turning around, he looked down at her. She knelt on the floor like a loyal subject worshipping at his feet. He felt the power shift briefly, almost as if she slipped and handed it over to him before taking it back as she sank on her heels and simply looked at him.

He didn't move because she hadn't told him he could. So, they were at a stalemate. He saw inside her thoughts, felt her wanting to lean forward and take him in her mouth like she had last night. And maybe that was the scene. Yes, it was, wasn't it? She knew he would crawl inside her mind and follow her thoughts. She knew it would drive him mad with lust to see what she wanted to do to him while she refrained from doing it. And she was right. Knowing what she wanted to do to him, but not experiencing it in the physical, was torture. Raw, unforgiving torture.

When she picked up the spoon again, he saw the image in her mind right before she flayed the side of his thigh, and again, and then again. The pain didn't stop as she switched hands and abused his other thigh. Through it all he didn't flinch. He took her punishment, gritting his teeth, fighting the sting in his eyes. When her mouth finally wrapped around his hard length, he nearly passed out from the combination of sensations. Grunting as his legs shuddered precariously, she had him within an inch of his sanity, the boundaries of reality blurring into gray as his mind shattered.

There was no stopping the almost immediate, mind-blowing climax that ruptured every nerve ending in his body as he filled her mouth. But somehow he managed to remain standing. Through it all, he kept himself on his feet.

Pulling away, she licked her lips and lay back on the floor, opening her legs wide as she propped herself on one elbow. Her swollen labia protruded around the black lace, which she bunched up and pushed aside, allowing him to see her rosy pink lips as she played her fingers up and down her slit, her honey glistening her skin and coating her fingers.

She didn't speak a word, and she didn't free him to move, only forced him to watch as she dipped her fingers inside then pulled them out to massage her clit in rapid, tiny circles with her slick offering.

Her arousal was as thick as an inferno, overwhelming him with its heady, musky scent, like smoke permeating the air around him. Tiny gasps burst from her throat, and the stiletto heels of her boots pushed into the carpet as her legs tensed and her stomach quivered. But she refused to look away from him, those blacked-out lenses tilted toward his face, her red lips parted so he could see just the edges of her teeth.

Faster her hand moved, her finger pushing back inside her as her palm massaged her clit. Harder she finger fucked herself, her hips gyrating and grinding, her gasps bursting into harsh moans, until, "Ungh!" Her hips shivered abruptly, rising off the floor as she squirted just ever so little against her hand, which pumped several hard times, milking her orgasm.

Fuck. He almost came again. He'd never been with a female who squirted, and even though it hadn't been much, it had been enough to soak her hand and wet a spot on the floor. It took every ounce of obedience not to drop to his knees and fall between her legs to lick her clean.

Collapsing to the floor, she rolled her hand forward and back over her nether lips, smiling, pleased with herself. Then, as if reading his mind, she commanded him, "Come. Taste me."

Micah wasted no time, diving head first between her legs, licking, sucking, drinking down her feminine offering as she rocked against him. He heard her mind give him one final command: *Tonight, while Trace is here, know that I will be wearing no panties under my pants. I will be wet thinking about you. I will be thinking about your cock inside me. And after we've all gone to bed, you will take me out to the couch and fuck me like you've never fucked anyone before, where Trace could come out and see us at any moment.*

He grinned against her nether lips, pulling back only long enough to say, "Yes, ma'am," before continuing to lap away every remnant of her release.

Twenty minutes later, Micah hopped out of the shower and wrapped a towel around his waist. Sam was already dressed in sweats and a Bears sweatshirt and he stopped, his eyes dropping to inspect her for panty lines. There were none. His eyes met hers and a secret grin passed between them as she blushed and darted into the bathroom.

He was reaching for a pair of sweats when the doorbell rang. That must be Trace.

Sweats in hand and the towel still around his waist, Micah flipped his wet hair back and went to the door.

"Hey, Trace, come on in..." His voice trailed off when he looked up and saw who it was. "Jackson."

The male nodded and smiled nervously. "Hey, Micah."

"What are you doing here?"

"I was in the neighborhood."

That was a crock. Jackson had no reason to be around this part of town. His place was miles from here, and so was his job.

The elevator dinged while the two stood and stared at each other. Trace appeared, slowing slightly when he saw Jackson standing there, then he resumed his pace, trying to act cool about the scene, but it was obvious he didn't like the uninvited guest.

"Hey, Mike." Trace's gaze dropped to the towel around his waist as he pushed past Jackson like he wasn't even there. "Nice pants. Where's Sam?"

"She's getting ready," Micah said.

"Mmm, smells good," Trace said before disappearing into the kitchen. "Chili."

Micah turned back toward Jackson. "Really, why are you here, Jack?"

Jackson fidgeted as if it was becoming clear things were different now. "I was hoping...well, I miss you."

"Hi, Trace." Sam's voice reached him from the kitchen then he heard the low murmur of Trace's voice and Sam said, "Who? Jackson?" Then she came around the corner. "Micah, is someone—?"

Micah turned to see her stop. Then she smiled and hurried forward. "Hi, I'm Sam." She held out her hand politely enough, but Micah felt her tweak with possessiveness as her other hand slipped over his back. She wanted Jackson to know Micah was spoken for now. Not that she needed to worry. Micah wondered what he had ever seen in Jackson now that his true mate had been revealed. And it was becoming clearer every day that he'd been meant to mate Sam along. Jackson was never meant to be part of the equation.

"Jackson, meet Sam." He looked at her, love and adoration filling his eyes as he leaned in and nuzzled her. Not a month ago, Micah had been ready to die over the male who now stood at his door. He had been a mere shadow of who he was today. In fact, he had been for centuries. Sam had given him purpose again. She had given him life and love. And with Trace's help, Sam had pulled him back from hell.

The next words he spoke were for Jackson's benefit, but he spoke them to Sam. "Sam is my lifemate. She is my life now, always, and forever. I love you, my precious Sam."

Josie had been right. He had fallen. Long ago, after Katarina's death, he had fallen hard. But with Sam and Trace, but especially Sam, he had come back.

Yes, the fallen had risen to live again.

ALL THE KING'S MEN

MICAH'S CALLING

DONYA LYNNE

ACKNOWLEDGEMENTS

Once again, my first acknowledgement goes to my readers. Thank you for sharing Micah's journey with me. He and I were lost souls together at one time, and it was the readers who helped bring us both back as his story began to unfold on Facebook in the realm of roleplay.

Thanks once again to Laura, my editor, and to Reese, my cover artist. The two of you make my books better than I could make them by myself. Your hard work is much appreciated.

And to everyone else who has helped along the way, there are too many of you to list, but you have my gratitude, as well.

Much love to you all. Enjoy the book.

DEDICATION

To you. You helped me through my own dark
time, and now I will help you through the rest of
yours. You deserve happiness.

PREFACE

Dear Reader,

When I wrote Rise of the Fallen, I knew there was more of Micah's story to tell, but it didn't fit with the story presented in Rise of the Fallen. Rise was about Micah's rise from his own inner hell and his victory over his self-created demons. For me to have ventured into what occurred after Rise's conclusion would have come off as awkward, because what happened next was a completely separate story.

Working the rest of Micah's and Sam's story into subsequent novels in the series wasn't an option, either, because doing so would have lessened the significance of what happened between them while intruding on other characters' stories.

The only solution was to write a novella. This way, the relationship between Micah and Sam is given the importance it deserves, the rest of their story is told, the rest of the series is enhanced, and all the remaining stories can focus on their main characters without Micah intruding more than he already does (because Micah sticks his nose into everything, anyway).

For those who have read Rise of the Fallen (and I hope that's all of you), this novella picks up about a week before the end of that book, and continues past the final scene. You will recognize one of the scenes early on in Micah's Calling, since it appeared in Rise of the Fallen at the end of the book, but I have rewritten it here from opposing points of view.

I hope you enjoy this supplement to the AKM series.

Happy Reading!

Donya Lynne

CHAPTER 1

MICAH BLACK STEPPED OUT OF THE BATHROOM, toweling himself off from his shower, and looked at the lithe female sprawled on his bed. She was beautiful, with pristine, near-alabaster skin so fair she appeared to be made of porcelain. Except for the two red marks on her shoulder where he had bitten her and taken her blood—again—and the scar on her abdomen left over from her life before they'd met, she was the picture of unblemished perfection.

She was his. She belonged to him. Fate had deemed it so, and Micah took the responsibility of having a mate to heart. He would cherish this female, watch over her, tend to her needs, protect her, feed from her, and be utterly helpless to resist her if she needed him. That was the way of a mated male vampire.

Micah sat on the edge of the bed and stared down at Samantha—Sam—then brushed back her short tufts of blond hair. He liked her hair short. It showed off her slender neck and gave him an unobstructed path to her vein when he needed a fix.

Now that she had his blood in her system, she reproduced her own blood much faster than when she had been human, which meant he could drink from her more often. And that was a good thing, because during the past few days, he had regularly exercised that right.

But now, Sam needed rest. Micah had used her body thoroughly during the past several hours. And once she had slept, he would feed her so she kept up her strength. As harsh as the *calling* was on male vampires, it was just as harsh, if not worse, on their mates, who had no choice but to give themselves over to the *calling's* demand. It was Micah's responsibility to take care of Sam during this crucial period.

He slipped on a pair of flannel pants and quietly snicked the door closed behind him as he left the bedroom.

Micah watched TV for a while then went to the kitchen to prepare a light meal for them both. Raw vegetables, cheese, cold cuts, and a jar of green olives. Sam had told him she loved green olives. He piled the veggies on the counter then grabbed a cutting board and a Chef's knife and got to work.

He might have been standing at the kitchen counter in his eighteenth-floor luxury apartment, cutting vegetables and cheese into bite-size pieces, but his thoughts were anything but culinary. He wore a secret smile as his mind traipsed along the memories of what he and Sam had been doing to each other in the four days since he brought her home from the AKM facility where he worked as an enforcer. With his *calling* finally unfurling to full strength, demanding he impart his highly fertile seed into her at regular intervals, he had become quite the expert on her body. And what a body it was, and not just because she was now a stronger, immortal version of what she had been before.

She was smooth and sleek, with supple muscles from long hours of dancing and working a stripper pole. And every time he touched her, she quivered ever-so-slightly, but enough to let him know that he excited her as much as she excited him. Her sultry voice was a song that needed to be made into a soundtrack that played inside his head on repeat so he could associate everything he did with her voice. Her taste and scent should be bottled as perfumed aphrodisiacs custom-made only for him. And the sight of her naked body was far too fetching and exquisite for even the Louvre to display.

But as much as he loved her physical affections, it was her mind that excited him the most. From their first meeting three weeks ago, when he had awakened in her tiny studio apartment after nearly dying at the hands of that dreck, Apostle, Sam hadn't let him intimidate her. She had taken tit-for-tat to the level of art with him, sassing him at every turn, and that was something no one had done to Micah for centuries.

Sam. His spunky, feisty mate. She was a marvel, and even now he didn't feel worthy of her special beauty.

He was about to cut a carrot into spears when his twelve-inch Bowie knife shot around the front of him toward his throat as a warm body pressed against his back. Sam's arm darted around his waist to hold him securely as the blade came to rest just over his Adam's apple.

"What are you thinking about in here all by yourself?" Sam's sexy voice danced provocatively to his ears.

Micah's eyes flicked to the cutting board covered in carrots, sliced cucumber, and celery sticks. A grin curled the corners of his mouth.

"You." A gentle purr pulsed in his chest.

"You're purring, so I guess you're having good thoughts."

Male vampires purred when aroused. And her knife action had definitely aroused him. As if he needed any help in that department right now, with his *calling* driving his body relentlessly into hers.

"Very good thoughts." He grinned as she pressed the knife more firmly against his throat. "You trying to draw blood, love?"

Her lips found his bare back and kissed a trail up his spine. "Mmm, no. Just letting you know who's boss."

Even with her new, immortal body, Micah could easily take her. But when it came to his heart, she *was* the boss. She ruled his heart as well as his soul. As her mate, he would do anything she asked. The biological lock she had on him would never allow him to defy her.

"Feeling cocky, are you?" Micah's body quaked from her lips on his bare skin.

"Absolutely." Her free hand skimmed his torso to the waist of his flannels and dipped down to wrap around his erection. "Seems you are, too."

He groaned and stiffened as she gave him a gentle stroke. "Yes, I'm very cocky."

She kept the Bowie knife at his throat and her tongue heated a slow trail up his spine.

"Push your pants down for me." She sounded like a bossy little vixen, which itched Micah's Dom side. He suddenly wanted to take her to his house in the suburbs, show her his dungeon, and show her exactly how bossy he could be when he wanted to play.

His enjoyment of BDSM had faded years ago, so he had stopped practicing. But now that he'd met her, he could feel himself wanting to don the Dom persona again. How would she look chained to his Titan spanking bench, her ass rosy from his hand or one of his riding crops? Or spread eagle on his wrought iron bed, legs open, wrists cuffed? Jesus! Just the thought made his dick throb.

The blade at his throat pushed in. "Do I have to tell you twice?"

Damn! She was good. He would definitely take her to his house. Tonight. But first, he did as he was told and pushed down his pants, freeing his erection.

Her nipples pressed firmly against his back as she pushed forward and got a good grip on the stiff column between his legs.

"Tell me more about this...*calling* thing." She nibbled the back of his shoulder and smoothed her palm up and down his shaft.

He had mentioned the *calling* to her earlier, but they hadn't talked about it much. Just enough to let her know it was why he was so sexed up right now.

He dropped his head back. The knife lost contact with his throat, but that was okay. The effect was still delicious enough to sizzle his toes.

"The *calling* is what a male vampire goes through when he mates." He closed his eyes and turned his face toward hers as she licked his shoulder.

Stroke-stroke.

"Yes, I know that part." *Kiss-lick.* "How does it work?"

If Micah hadn't been so turned on, he would have laughed. It wasn't like the *calling* was a machine that you could turn on and off. It was a living entity that consumed a male, right down to his balls. *Especially* his balls.

"The purpose of the *calling* is to propagate the species." He reached his hands back and found her bare hips. "When a male's mating instinct fires as mine has with you, the *calling* kicks in and makes him want to have sex." He paused and his voice lowered. "A lot of sex. Almost constantly."

"A lot, hmm?" Sam's voice sounded lustfully drowsy, likely in response to the hormonal heat his body had begun to throw.

"Uh-huh. A lot." He swatted her hand away from his throat and broke free from her grasp long enough to spin around and take her by surprise. In a flash, she was in his arms. He pressed his erection against her lower stomach.

She gasped as he claimed the side of her throat with a nip of his teeth. Then he slid his nose up her jaw and kissed her earlobe, making her shiver. With a dark chuckle that made her shudder again, he continued with his explanation.

"I'm at my most sexually potent — my most fertile — during my *calling*, Mrs. Black."

Sam tsked. "Do you see a ring on my finger, Mr. Black? I don't think so."

He swiped his tongue over the tender spot just below her ear. "It doesn't matter." His voice was a low drawl of sensuality and possessive confidence. "Ring or no ring, you're mine."

"No one owns me." Her fingertips danced down the backs of his arms as she laid her head back. Apparently, she had abandoned the Bowie knife, likely to the kitchen counter behind him, because she wasn't holding it, anymore.

Micah cupped her breast briefly before slipping his palm into the middle of her chest. Gently, he pushed her back and glided his hand up her sternum to her throat as she bent like a sinewy reed, exposing her slim, nubile body to his gaze, which lit like blue fire from his navy irises.

"Mmm, I do believe this body belongs to me," he said appreciatively, drawing his hand back down between her breasts, pressing his palm firmly against her as his fingers curled around her breast.

Sam grinned and pulled herself back up until her mouth hovered only millimeters from his. Her green eyes sparkled with aroused humor as she met his gaze. "Until I have a ring, Mr. Black, you may call me Sam or Miss Garrett. I may no longer be human, but I still want the ring."

Touché.

"I don't like the name Garrett," he said, meeting her stare.

Garrett was the name she had inherited from her ex-husband, Steve, the second asshole Micah had saved Sam from a week ago.

That asshole, Apostle, had been the first.

Sam had been unaware that Micah had asked for the beat down Apostle and his crew gave him the night she found him. She'd walked into that parking garage and saved his life, unknowingly declaring war on Apostle in the process. Micah had known Apostle would come after her, but he had thought he could protect her. How wrong he'd been. That mother fucking dreck had managed to track her down and bite her, nearly killing her with his venom. Micah had been forced to break vampire law and give Sam his own venom and transform her into his immortal *davala* to save her life.

As if her experience with Apostle hadn't been enough, her abusive ex, Steve, had shown up to try and reclaim her. Over Micah's dead body! Steve had picked the wrong guy to fuck with and had gone home empty handed.

Well, not quite empty handed. Micah had made a few mental modifications in Steve's noggin. For example, ol' Steve-aroony could count on his hand being his only action for the next six years, because if a woman tried to do the honors, limp dick would be the best way to describe what happened to his manly parts. And if he laughed in public? Well, let's just say Steve better buy stock in Depends, because he wouldn't be able to laugh in front of others without pissing his pants. But that's the shit you got when you stomped on a mated vampire's territory.

As for Sam, Micah had removed all trace of her from Steve's memories. He would never bother her again.

"If you don't like my last name, you know how to change it." Sam flashed her ring finger and smiled oh-so-innocently.

"You tempt me, female." Micah licked her mouth, grinding his hips against her.

The *calling* was rising within him again, urging him to plant more seeds in an attempt to create a new life inside Sam's womb. A new life he doubted would take root after all she had been through, what with her body being newly immortal after his venom had warred violently with Apostle's to save her, wreaking havoc on her organs. But just because her body was too new with immortality to hold a child didn't make his hunger for her lessen.

Grabbing her under her arms, he lifted her, and she easily swung her legs up and around him without hesitation. She wanted him just as badly.

"We'll continue this conversation later," he said as he turned around, dashed his Bowie knife aside, and set her on the counter. "Lie back."

"So bossy." Her eyes glinted with lust.

"Oh, you have no idea how bossy I can be." But if all went well, she would learn soon enough.

He yanked her toward him as she lay back on the counter, letting his mind briefly wander to his dungeon. Would she let him boss her around down there? He hoped so.

Within seconds, he was inside her, pushing and pulling her on the counter to meet each of his eager thrusts. The *calling* didn't allow for much in the way of long and luxurious fucking. The *calling* pushed a male to quickness, sharpening his sensations to a needlepoint of lusty need that made him come fast and often.

For nearly one week, he and Sam had lived inside each other's bodies like this. The first couple of days home, they had made love almost non-stop. Micah hadn't even bothered to count how many times they had made love, but it had been a lot. Well, fucked is more the word for what they had done. Despite love being at the heart of every urgent coupling, it was hard to refer to rough, physical, body-bruising sex as making love.

With the goal of creating new life, Micah's *calling* had been too powerful to resist. Even when his conscience wanted to let Sam sleep, his body refused to obey, and when the ache to mate became a small war between pain and agony, he had been forced to take her.

Since those first couple days, the sex had tapered. This was the sixth time today they'd made love, and his body was beginning to allow him to luxuriate more. If things went well tonight, they would get in one more healthy dose of one another before nodding off again, and he wanted to savor the hell out of her if his body would just let him.

Her small, pale-tipped breasts bobbed forward and back as he thrust again and again, feeling the quick build of release at the base of his spine. His hands dug into her hips as he increased his tempo, and Sam reached down and latched on to his wrists. Her gaze met his, and she cried out as she came.

God love her, but she was the most responsive female he'd ever met. Sure, her body was reacting to his mating heat, making it easier for her to find her own pleasure each time they joined, but he could tell that even without the hormonal trigger she would still be an orgasmic tidal wave. It would just take her longer to reach her climax without his heat to spur her on.

"Fuck!" Micah slammed into her once more and let loose a torrent of fertility. His entire body warmed, and his nerve endings danced and exalted with yet another successful release of his highly potent offering. The extra special glow and rapturous tingle that cascaded in a chain reaction to every muscle in his body was the *calling's* gift to him for sowing his seeds. The afterglow of orgasm would never feel quite as pleasurable as it did during a *calling*.

"Mmm." Sam released his wrists and sat up. She was all fluid motion and feline finesse as her arms encircled him and her mouth found his chest.

His cock was still pumping inside her, filling her with his potency as her lips and tongue took turns gliding over his skin, flicking one nipple then the other. Needing her closer, he pulled her in, tucking her against his body as the last of his ejaculation ebbed.

Micah didn't want to move. He didn't want to pull out of her. After each session with Sam, it was the same thing. He simply wanted to stay wrapped inside her warm, moist sheath. His cock felt perfect there. At home. Where it belonged. He had never experienced this feeling with his first two mates.

"I love you." He burrowed his nose into her short, silky-soft, blond hair. Mmm, lilacs. She always smelled of lilacs.

"I love you, too."

CHAPTER 2

SAM DIDN'T FULLY UNDERSTAND THIS THING Micah called the *calling*, but she liked it. And she liked her new body, too, because it bounced back and healed itself quickly, readying her for the next time he needed her.

At first, the frequency he required sex had scared her, but then he explained that was normal for a newly mated male. That had been his first attempt at explaining what a *calling* was. Unfortunately, all the chatter about mating and sex had awakened his body, and before he could give her a proper run-down of this mystical, vampire mating behavior, he'd thrown her on the bed and claimed her again.

Miraculously enough, she seemed to peak with arousal every time he did. Was that part of this *calling* thing, too? It seemed too coincidental not to be.

She still had so much to learn about Micah's world. It was hard to believe she had only known him a few weeks.

She kissed a trail up his chest then his neck and over his jaw until he turned his head so his lips met hers. He was still breathless, caught up in whatever aftermath this ethereal force he referred to as the *calling* left him in each time they had sex. She couldn't explain it, but he seemed to be filled with some inner glow that made his chest swell with pride, as if coming inside her made him more of a man—male, whatever. She needed to get used to the idea that Micah was not a man. He was a male. Big difference. A man was human. A male was...well, Micah. Vampire and distinctly *not* human.

She gazed at his beautiful face. His eyes were closed, and

his shapely lips were slightly parted, the corners barely turned up in a reverent smile that softened his features. When his eyes lazily opened, and he found her gazing up at him, his smile widened to show off perfectly straight teeth, as well as the tips of his fangs.

"You look drunk." She couldn't hold back her own awe-struck gaze. May she never get used to how unbelievably gorgeous he was.

"I am drunk." He nuzzled her neck. "Drunk on you."

"I think that's the *calling* talking." She giggled as he nibbled below her ear.

"And the *calling* is only responding to what you've done to me. So see, it's all your fault."

She laughed and gave him a playful shove. "Cuff me, officer. I'm guilty as charged."

Micah purred hard and deep at her words, his whole body tensing sensuously, his arms trembling as they secured her more possessively.

Whoa! She hadn't expected that reaction from him so soon after what they'd just done.

"What the hell was that?" She shot him a wide-eyed look as he pulled back and leveled hooded eyes on her.

"What you said. I liked it."

"Which part?"

He drew in a long breath, practically smoldering. "About cuffing you."

She tilted her head. "Oh really?"

He nodded, purring again. "Oh, yeah." He licked his lips and burned holes through her with his sexy stare.

This was new. When had Micah become so into bondage? Was there something he wasn't telling her? Before she could ask, he was moving inside her again.

Being that he had never withdrawn, it wasn't such a shock, but the fact that he was ready again so soon was. Even with the *calling* thingamajig, Micah had never come at her again before he had even pulled out.

"Really?" She arched an eyebrow at him, feeling her insides warm in response to him.

He growled, hastening. "You have no idea."

His deep, animalistic voice burned and liquefied something in the depths of her belly. Faster than she could say "Tie me up," she was hot all over and ready for another round.

He lifted her from the counter, and she locked her ankles around the backs of his knees as he fucked her hard and fast standing up. Sam had to hang on for dear life, strapping her arms around his shoulders and grabbing hold of his long hair.

He shuddered and stumbled before spinning her around and slamming her back against the pantry door. And he was coming again. Just that fast.

Yeah, she needed to get to the bottom of why the idea of putting her in handcuffs had just prompted the almost immediate eruption of his personal Mount St. Helens. Why putting her into bondage was such a turn-on could prove to be a useful bit of information if she ever needed to bribe him.

The idea alone made her grin.

"Oh, no you don't." Micah spoke against her shoulder, breathing heavily, his voice ragged. "I will not have you using bribery on me, woman."

She smacked him. "Get out of my head."

He huffed and gasped for air as he pulled back. "Damn, you're sexy."

"Don't change the subject."

He grinned his sexy smile at her. "I'm not." He feigned innocence, but Sam knew better.

Still, she was getting to the point where she didn't think he would ever be able to stay out of her mind. Small price to pay to be with the one she loved, but it still caught her off guard.

"Grab me a towel?" He had come twice in one shot, so she knew as soon as he pulled out it would get messy.

He reached and tore off a paper towel and handed it to her before slowly sliding free.

She took the towel and shook her head at him. "You are really beginning to make a mess of me. You know that, don't you?"

With an intimate flourish of his hand across her forehead and through her hair, he swept in and locked lips with her with enough fire to light up Chicago. Then pulled away, leaving her slightly stunned.

"I like you messy." He licked his lips as if pulling her taste from his skin, those soul-shattering navy-blue eyes cutting her to the quick.

"I see."

One side of his mouth curled into a sexy smirk before he glanced at the food-filled counter.

"Come on, let's eat something. You need to keep your strength up." He gestured to the cutting board covered with sliced cheese and veggies.

She tossed the towel in the trash and washed her hands.

His half-hard cock bobbed distractingly in front of him. A week ago, their Adam and Eve attire would have made her seek out a robe or at least an oversized T-shirt to cover herself, but spending four days more-or-less nude had kicked prudish restraint out the window. Cozying up beside him for their quaint counter picnic felt as normal as brushing her hair.

"I have somewhere I want to take you," he said a couple of minutes later, biting a celery stick in half.

"Oh? Where?"

He held out a cube of cheese for her, and she took it between her teeth.

"My home." He tossed the rest of the celery stick in his mouth.

"Yeah, your home." She looked at him and waited for the punch line.

He ate a cherry tomato then held one out for her, frowning at her quizzical glance. "What?"

"I'm waiting."

"For what?"

She gaped at him and laughed. "What about your home?" She looked around his apartment and shrugged.

They were in his home, so what more could there be to show her? She'd pretty much seen the entire apartment by now.

Micah stammered and shook his head. "No. My *home*. This isn't my home." He gestured toward his apartment.

Hold up. So, Micah had more than one residence, and this luxury pad worthy of the almighty Oz wasn't the one he called home?

"This is just where I stay," he said. "My home is in the suburbs. I want to take you there tonight." He crunched into a carrot stick.

Well, well. Micah had a house. How about that?

She settled her hip against the edge of the counter and grabbed another cube of cheese as she glanced into the living room. As nice as this place was, his home had to be even nicer. Or maybe not, which was why he stayed in the apartment. But then, if the apartment was the better of the two, why would he seem so eager to take her to his house?

She nibbled on the cheese, considering the man—male, whatever—stuffing a slice of smoked turkey in his mouth beside her. What kind of house would a vampire live in? It would have to have a basement, for sure. A place to keep his coffin. She fought back a giggle at the thought. Micah wouldn't sleep in a coffin unless it was part of some kinky sex act.

His gaze slid surreptitiously to hers, and she knew he could see what she was thinking.

She merely shrugged one shoulder coquettishly and popped the rest of the cheese in her mouth.

"No coffin?" she asked, sliding past him as she grabbed a handful of carrot and celery sticks.

"I guess you'll just have to wait and see."

She tossed him a flirty over-the-shoulder grin as she lazily strolled into the living room. "Large house or small house?" she said, her tone rhetorical. "I think large."

He turned to face her. "Why do you think that?" He sounded curiously amused.

She shrugged, turned away, and skimmed her free hand along the spines of his books. "I just can't see you living in a small house." She paused, flicked her gaze to his, then added, "Your ego needs a lot of space."

He tossed back his head with a hearty laugh then turned his dazzling gaze back to her as he continued chuckling. "Yes, my ego does require room to breathe."

She lifted one shoulder as she nodded once in affirmation. "I know. So, the question becomes, exactly how large of a home is it? Like, is it mansion-sized or just moderately expansive?" She bit into a carrot stick. "And does it have a pool? A big yard? Lots of shady trees?" She turned and eyed him. "A pretty little flower bed bordering the walkway to the front door?"

As she made her way back to him, she took in the exquisite living room furniture, the antique sword mounted on the wall, the classic novels that looked like originals on his bookcase, his alphabetized CDs. The Monet for God's sake. Did he have more of the same in his home? She got the feeling this sampling in the apartment was but a small collection from a much larger cache of collectibles.

Her gaze flicked curiously toward him as she drew near. What else hadn't he shared with her?

He grinned and slyly averted his gaze from hers as he picked through the cheese on the cutting board. Obviously, he was inside her head again, humored by her rambling thoughts.

She narrowed her eyes at him. *You fuck like a stallion.*

One eyebrow shot up and his grin quirked.

"I thought so," she said, rejoining him and picking up a cherry tomato.

He laughed. Dark, rich, and lovely. She loved his laugh. From what he had told her, he hadn't laughed in a long time. Centuries, really. However, in the short time she had known him, he seemed to be laughing more and more.

They finished the meal he had prepared for them then he swatted her playfully on the ass.

"Come on. Let's get going. I want to hurry and get you back here so I can fuck you again."

"Micah!" She smacked his chest.

"Hey, it's your fault, remember. *All* your fault." His navy-blue eyes glinted with amusement as he goosed her toward the hall.

She jumped and slapped his hand. "Yeah, yeah."

Ten minutes later, she was in the passenger seat of his black Audi A8 as they pulled out of the Sentinel's parking garage. Nice car. She finally knew what he drove. It sure beat her late-80s Toyota Corolla.

"I'm going to buy you a new car," he said.

Sam rolled her eyes at him. He was inside her head again, as always.

"You don't have to do that, Micah."

He took her hand and lifted it to his lips. As he kissed it, his manicured, black facial stubble tickled her skin.

"I want to."

He released her hand and she slipped it into his hair, combing her fingers through all that long, black silk.

They rode in silence for a couple of minutes, and she thought more about what was happening between them, her curiosity returning to this whole mating phenomenon thing.

"Okay, so this…*calling*. It affects you when you take a mate, right?" She really wanted to understand this.

"Yes."

"And, when you're in this *calling* phase, you are at your most fertile. Is that right?"

"Yes."

"So, should I be using protection?" Bad time to think about that, but it really hadn't come up until just now. They'd been too busy getting busy to stop and think about the trivial stuff, such as preventing an unplanned pregnancy. You know, nothing big.

Micah cleared his throat and glanced at her. "I don't think so."

"Why? If you're at your most fertile, and we're having all this unprotected sex, won't I get pregnant?" The idea of having his baby was appealing, but she wasn't sure she was ready for that. Especially since that meant she'd be giving birth to a vampire and didn't yet understand all that went along with that. Would an infant vampire need blood? Would it drink breast milk like a human baby? She had so many questions before she was ready to be a vampire mommy.

Micah shook his head, keeping his eyes on the road. "After what's happened to you, I don't think you can get pregnant. At least, not right now. If anything, you would have been pregnant before Apostle bit you, because I was already entering my *calling* phase with you before then. That first night we were together. I felt it then." He paused. "And if you were pregnant, his venom would have pretty much...." Micah didn't finish the sentence, but Sam didn't need him to for her to understand what he was saying.

She put her hand over her belly introspectively, wondering if she had been pregnant and lost the baby after Apostle's attack. "Oh."

"And then I added my venom into the equation to save you, and now...your body is so new that I don't think it's capable of taking a fertilized egg. *Yet.*" He said that like he had every faith in the world that she would one day be able to have his young. But she didn't miss the disappointment in his tone, either. He obviously wanted a child and was heartbroken that her body wasn't ready to give him one.

Sam's mind jumped back to that night. Had it really been only a week since Apostle had tried to kill her? But Micah had saved her. He had broken all kinds of vampire laws to transform her into an immortal, but at least he had saved her life, binding her to him forever in the process of combining his venom with her blood.

"Do you think I'll ever...?"

Micah took her hand and hushed her, obviously knowing what she was thinking. "It's only temporary, Sam. Once your body adjusts, you'll be able to bear children. I know you will."

The two sat silently for a minute, and Sam wondered what Micah was thinking. He could see inside her thoughts, but she couldn't see inside his.

"Do you want to have children with me?" His voice was soft, almost hopeful.

"Yes," she said without hesitation.

Micah pulled over and put the car in park. He unfastened his seatbelt and in an instant had her in his arms, swooping her up and kissing her hard.

Wow, she needed to remember this. Handcuffs and children. Those were Micah's hot buttons.

He pulled back and chuckled self-consciously. "I'm sorry," he said. "The *calling* makes us males a bit emotional."

"I can see that." Sam palmed his cheek as they stared into each other's eyes. "I like it."

"I'm not so sure I do, but I'll live." He grinned.

"Tell me more about this *calling*." She felt like they had only scratched the surface of all the *calling* entailed.

"Well, for one thing, it makes us *really* want to have children." Micah made a face and nodded before pointing to himself as if he were Exhibit A. "As in, it's all we can think about besides sex, which is why hearing you say you want to bear my children pleases me so much." He caressed her face with the backs of his fingers. "My goal while I'm in my *calling* phase is to get you pregnant. It's why I physically can't *not* have sex with you. And it's why the phase lasts for so long. Because by lasting two weeks or more, the *calling* ensures I hit your ovulation."

"So female vampires? They have monthly periods, too?"

Micah nodded. "More or less."

"And does this mean that when you aren't in a *calling*, you can't get me pregnant?"

"Well, yes and no." He shrugged. "It's a lot harder to get you pregnant when I'm not in my *calling*, but it can happen." He grinned. "Think of it this way: Outside my *calling*, my sperm count is meager, to say the least. In my *calling*, I become Super Sperm Man." He absently made a little squiggly gesture over his chest as if he were drawing a sperm on himself.

Sam laughed at the visual. "Do I need to make you a little red and blue leotard suit, Mr. Super Sperm Man?"

Micah face flushed as he shook his head and glanced away. "That would be a no."

She pressed her finger against the center of his chest and

drew a slow squiggle. "Awe, I think it would look cute."

With a dramatic sigh, he leaned back in his seat and buckled up. "Do. Not. Even. Think about it."

She laughed again. Micah was so adorable when he was miffed.

"Well, if I do think about it, I'm sure you'll be the first to know." She was in the midst of a fit of giggles now, unable to hold back as he scowled playfully at her.

"Funny, Miss Garrett."

She held up her hands, still giggling. "Whoa! Wait a minute. I thought I was Mrs. Black."

"As you so eloquently pointed out, *Miss Garrett*..." He pointed to her left ring finger. "I don't see a ring on that finger."

She stuck her tongue out at him. "Well, you can fix that, you know."

"Maybe." He coyly fixed his gaze on the road.

A moment later, after she had finally gotten her giggling under control again, she asked, "So, how often do you have these *calling* phases? I assume it happens more than once if it's the main form of propagating the vampire race."

"Mated males experience a *calling* once every five to ten years."

"What happens if his mate isn't around to accommodate him?"

He gave her a look as if to suggest she better not be getting any ideas to run off and play hide-and-seek. "It's agony. Pure agony. The only thing more dangerous than a mutant is a mated male in his *calling* without his mate. The mood swings are violent, the agony unbearable. He will do whatever he has to do to get to his mate when he is in the *calling*." He paused. "You would be wise to take my word on this and not test me on the matter."

Duly noted. But what was that other thing he mentioned? Mutants. Hadn't he mentioned them once before?

"Remind me. Mutants are...?"

Micah grinned patiently. "Some vampires are what we called mixed-bloods. They are not full-blooded vampires.

More and more often, vampires are mating with humans, so we get these cross-breeds, like Trace. He's a mixed-blood." Micah kept one hand on the wheel as he briefly gestured with the other, palm up, as if he were holding a hologram of Trace in his palm. "Anyway, when a human and a vampire mate, their children are born with unique powers. It's like a genetic mutation takes place and heightens their abilities in a certain area. Take Trace, for example." Micah quickly glanced at her as he slowed down to take a turn. "Trace has this unbelievable power to mass compel. I've never seen anything like it. He can bring an entire room of people to a standstill and pick through the minds of multiple people at once. I don't even think I know the extent of his power, either, which I think he got from his mother, but I'm not sure."

"Can't you see inside his mind?" Sam frowned curiously.

Micah shook his head. "Not him. For some reason, his mind is locked up tighter than Guantanamo Bay. Either he has consciously locked me and everybody else out, or it's another of his powers and he's simply a closed door. I'm not sure. All I know is that I can walk into the room and see everyone else's thoughts but his."

"Wow." Sam was beginning to realize that Trace was a formidable vampire. "And you think he had something to do with how Apostle and his friends were killed?"

Micah had told her that Apostle and the other drecks who had been after her had been found mutilated inside a house in the suburbs. At least the authorities and enforcers who had gone to the scene thought it was Apostle and his cronies. There wasn't much left of the bodies to identify them. They were more-or-less pools of ruptured organs, decimated bones, and flesh. But if Trace had been responsible for their deaths, he wasn't fessing up.

"It had to be him." Micah appeared awed by the idea. "I can't imagine anyone else having a motive or being capable of that kind of massacre." Micah paused. "That's why I said I don't even know the extent of his power. If it was Trace who did that, he's more powerful than I thought."

Silence stretched for a second. "Okay, so about mutants."

Sam prompted him to continue.

Micah nodded. "Yes. So anyway, occasionally one of the mixed-bloods loses control over his or her power. Their power is caused by a genetic mutation to begin with, amplifying a segment or multiple segments of their brains or nervous system, or what-have-you. Imagine this mutation, or you can just refer to it as power, being more like a parasite. This power feeds off its host. Most of the time, the power lives in harmony with the host, and other times it doesn't. As long as it's living in harmony with its carrier, the power is harmless to him or her. But when the host and the power — or mutation — are constantly at odds, all hell can break loose and the power consumes the host. The mutation takes over, and a physiological transformation occurs. The mixed-blood vampire becomes more or less a monster, or what we call a mutant, even though the official term is rogue. Their strength magnifies, and their venom becomes pure poison. A mutant's bite is more deadly than anything else."

Sam had sat in rapt silence as she listened to Micah explain yet one more aspect about the new life she had entered by becoming his mate. Would she ever get used to this world he lived in? A world she never even knew existed until she stepped into that parking garage to find a handsome, mysterious stranger being beaten to death by a bunch of would-be thugs. Only he hadn't been just a regular stranger and those hadn't been regular thugs. He had been a vampire, and the thugs had been drecks, and when she shot Apostle, she had sealed her own fate.

"Having regrets?" Micah said softly, his profile unreadable.

Obviously he could see what she was thinking. At least there would never be dishonesty between them. "No."

"You sure?"

She reached for his hand and squeezed it. "Yes."

Micah squeezed her hand back. "You're not in Kansas, anymore, Sam. It's a scary world I live in."

"I don't want to be in Kansas. And I don't care how scary it is."

They pulled up to a stop light and he turned toward her,

his eyes searching her face. "Why not?"

Sam smiled wistfully and glanced down at their joined hands. "Because you're here. And I want to be with you."

She glanced back up, and he blinked and smiled at her with a gentle nod.

"And I'm so glad for that," he said.

"Why?"

"Because if you weren't here with me, I wouldn't be here, either."

CHAPTER 3

MICAH GAZED AT SAM, HIS SAVIOR. He had been ready to die before she stepped into his life. After Jackson had left him, Micah had been ready to check out. For good.

But then Sam had shown up, smelling of lilacs and looking like an angel. She had saved his life and given him a reason to live again, and he could feel himself slowly morphing back into the male he had been centuries ago, before his first mate's death. Maybe now he would rise up to become what he had seemed destined to become back then.

If things had happened differently, he would be the team's leader right now, not Tristan. Because that's what he had been before. He had been Tristan's commander. Now it was the other way around. So much was lost after Katarina died. Such was the way of things.

He gazed at Sam, reflecting a moment longer, then caught the glow from the light as it turned green. He returned his gaze to the front and hit the gas.

He still found it hard to believe that he had changed so much in the past few weeks. And he couldn't believe fortune had finally smiled down on him after centuries of misery after losing Katarina in the late Middle Ages. But all that was behind him now, and he could finally see a future of happiness. One where he could actually smile and laugh again.

He'd been laughing a lot with Sam.

But he also couldn't forget how dangerous the world he lived in was. And now Sam was part of that world.

They held hands in silence as he took them out of the city and into the burbs. Her mind was processing everything he had told her, chewing it up, mulling it over, and filing it away.

"Okay," she said out of the blue. "So how many mixed-bloods are there, proportionately speaking?"

Micah shrugged. "I don't know. I know there are more pure bloods than mixed-bloods. Maybe a four to one ratio. Possibly even three to one. Mixed-bloods are becoming a lot more common as time goes on. Why do you ask?"

She sighed as if she were trying to figure something out. "Well, it just seems like since humans outnumber vampires—and I assume they do since you vampires keep yourselves so secret from humans—there would be a lot more mixed-bloods running around."

Micah was impressed. What an astute observation.

"Okay, so what's your question?"

She smiled sweetly. Too sweetly. "Can't you just poke inside my head and see it?"

"Yes, but it's so much nicer to hear your sexy voice." He grinned sweetly back.

Sam laughed and shook her head. "You're incorrigible."

"So they tell me." He turned the Audi toward the north. "Do you want to know why we aren't overrun by mixed-bloods? Is that your question?"

"Yeah, I can't figure that one out. If male vampires are only fertile during their *calling* – "

"Not only," he said, correcting her. "But they are most fertile at that time."

Sam nodded. "Okay, so if that's the case, are male vampires mating humans and *not* having their *calling*? But that doesn't make sense because you're having your *calling* with me, and I'm human."

"Not technically. Not anymore, that is."

"Well, you know what I mean."

"I know. And that's a good question." Micah paused as he pulled into a manicured subdivision with massive houses that sat far back off the road. Each plot was at least two acres or larger. "*Calling* or no *calling,* it's harder for a male vampire to impregnate a human female. And even harder for female vampires to become pregnant by human males.

But there are exceptions, and it happens. And when it does, you have yourself a mixed-blood. I know a couple of mixed-bloods who have two or three siblings to the same mixed set of parents, which is unheard-of. Most mixed couples never have children of their own and have to adopt. But as with human evolution, vampires and their mixed progeny are evolving, too. One day, it could be easier for mixed couples to have young of their own, but right now, as a general rule, it's harder. But a lot of them end up in some kind of enforcement capacity because of their powers. It's why AKM has so many on staff. Their powers come in handy on the job."

Micah slowed and turned into a long, curved driveway that led up to a dark-windowed home surrounded by mature trees still waiting on spring's warmth so they could once again leaf out and shade the magnificent home.

"Does that mean you and I might not have kids?" Sam sounded concerned, and didn't that make Micah love her even more? She wanted his babies, didn't she?

"It's a possibility, but I'll be damned if I'm going to stop trying." He slowed the car as he approached the garage. "We're here."

Sam gasped as if she had only just realized they had arrived at his home.

"This is your home?"

Micah parked the car outside the four-car garage and shut off the engine as he peered out the windshield at the luxurious monolith. "Yup. This is home."

After he and Jackson had gotten together he had spent less time here and more time downtown. But then Jackson had split and Sam saved him, and...well, he wanted to start spending more time here, now. With her.

And not just because of what was in his basement.

He wanted to make a home with Sam, and he didn't think they could do that at the apartment. Sure, the apartment was a great hangout and was closer to AKM, which made it convenient, but this was home.

And he had to be honest with himself. Sam had awakened a part of him he couldn't let out at the apartment. A part of him that some would call depraved. But he valued the trust and honesty required for such depravity. And if Sam was going to be in his life, she needed to know what she had stirred back to life inside him. She needed to see it for herself. Because he wanted to play. With her. Hard. But he wasn't sure if she could take — or even *wanted* to take — as much as he wanted to give. There was only one way to find out.

"Sam..." He took a deep breath. "I want to show you something here, okay?"

Her brow furrowed as if she'd picked up on the concern in his voice. "Okay."

"And I need you to have an open mind about it."

She nodded. "Okay, I will."

With that, he got out of the car and joined her as she stepped out and shut the passenger door. He hoped this went well, but if it didn't and his lifestyle wasn't for her, that was okay, too.

He took her hand and led her to the front door, unlocked it, and stood aside as she entered. Someone came in once a week to clean and make sure everything was taken care of, but they knew not to go into the basement. Only he was allowed down there, and he had the only key, so unless the help picked the lock, they had no idea he had a dungeon.

Sam's gaze swept the open foyer leading into the recessed living room. A pair of glass sliding doors led to a patio and deck that surrounded a custom pool out back, which was closed for the winter.

He followed her as she walked from the living room, her hand running along the back of the plush moleskin couch, and into the ultra-modern kitchen. He had ordered custom cabinetry when he remodeled last year, when he'd been more amenable because of Jackson's presence. Rich and elegant, the cabinets brightened the entire living area with their antique, brushed off-white color and brass hardware.

The kitchen had been a key factor in why he had bought the house in the first place. It was huge, with granite counters and top-of-the-line stainless steel appliances.

"Wow." Sam's gaze danced as if she was struggling to take

it all in. "This is some kitchen."

"I like to cook." He quietly settled the side of his hip against the island in the center of the room, his gaze following her. He remembered what they had done earlier and grinned. "Can you imagine the damage we could do to each other in here?"

Sam's head turned toward him, and her green eyes twinkled, but she didn't reply. She just smiled her secret, sexy smile and continued her tour.

"Come on," he said, pushing away from the counter. "Let me show you the rest of the house." *Yeah, as in, let me show you my dungeon of dastardly deeds.*

Hopefully, she wouldn't run away after paying that part of the house a visit.

She took his hand and followed him as he led her through the rest of the main floor then upstairs. There wasn't much upstairs since he didn't spend a lot of time there, but perhaps she would change that. Unlike him, she could dwell in the daylight. The upstairs floor would make a nice daytime retreat for her. Lots of windows. Lots of light.

But her decorating plans weren't why they were here. It was time to reveal the debauchery that had been such a huge part of his life before he lost the passion for BDSM several years ago. It had simply lost its appeal, getting old and stale—a stagnant fog that had begun to weigh him down every time he donned the Domination persona.

But now he was back, and it was time to show her his even darker side.

Standing in front of the basement door, he took out his keys and turned toward her.

"I won't go down there with you," he said.

"Why not?" She cocked her head to the side.

He inhaled slowly, deeply, drawing in her luscious scent. "Because the *calling* is calling me, and I don't want to get carried away."

"Carried away?" She narrowed her eyes and pursed her lips. "Just what am I going to find down there, Micah?"

He pressed the key into her palm. "You'll see."

MICAH'S EYES DARKENED IN RESPONSE to her question, and it made her heart skip a beat. Whatever was down in the basement was something that stirred his blood…in a good way.

She recalled her handcuff comment and how it had aroused him.

"Micah?" She prompted him again, waiting for an answer.

He took a deep breath, leaned in, and gently kissed her…a soft, lingering connection between their lips. "My trust in you is down there." He dipped his head toward the closed door.

Not exactly the answer she was looking for, but apparently he didn't want to taint her first impression with details.

She unlocked the door then gave him back the keys as he pulled it open.

He flipped on a series of light switches just inside the door, and the stairwell lit up. He looked at her expectantly, and Sam recognized a hint of hope in his gaze.

She took the first step down.

"I'll wait in the kitchen." His gaze flicked down the stairs as he took a deep breath, and then he walked away, leaving her alone with whatever awaited her in the depths of his impressive home.

Micah was behaving so strangely all of a sudden, as if he was both nervous and excited. Clearly, he wanted her to like what she found in the basement, but he was worried she wouldn't.

Curiosity over what could stir such a reaction spurred her down the stairs with barely a backward glance.

The first room she encountered was a bedroom. Micah's from the bacheloresque minimalism and neutral colors. It was huge, though, easily taking up half the square footage of the basement and containing a sitting area facing a massive wall-mounted flat screen that looked more like a small movie theater screen. The bed was enormous, with an ornately carved wooden headboard and footboard. And pillows. Lots of pillows in lots of fabrics and colors. They were everywhere. Micah seemed to be a bit of a pillow freak.

The walls were a rich creamy color. The motif was light, airy, and comfortable. Almost earthy.

Except for a pair of wooden doors on the far wall.

The doors looked like a modern version of something out of medieval times, with black, circular, iron handles set within similar hardware bolted to the wood. The doorway was arched and reminded her of the entrance to a cave, but something told her Fred Flintstone didn't reside on the other side of that imposing entrance.

After making her way across the room, she grabbed one of the heavy round handles. It swiveled into her grasp like a doorknocker. Should she pull or push?

Giving it a yank, nothing happened. Okay, so let's push.

The double doors creaked and whined as if the hinges needed a good oiling. Talk about your scary noises. Maybe he had built a haunted house in his basement. The thought made her grin.

But the moment she got a look at what was inside this new room, her mouth dropped open. This so wasn't a haunted house.

What world had she just entered?

First of all, the room felt like a cross between romantic Tuscany and Medieval Saxony. The walls were painted a deep, yellowish-gold with texturing that reminded her of fresco-style paintings. The floor was matte gray. She scuffed the toe of her shoe across the surface. Non-slip paint.

But it was the ceiling that took her breath away. A fresco of a richly-colored bowl of fruit, large and overflowing, surrounded by nude Renaissance men and women engaged in every manner of debauchery, adorned the ceiling. Except for one area where hooks hung in a grid pattern, and another where a ceiling-mounted mirror reflected a second massive bed, this one made of wrought iron. It would have looked more like a torture device if not for the red satin comforter over the thin mattress.

The bed was only one of a few pieces of furniture in the room that looked normal. Hell, was some of this stuff even furniture? Sam gaped as her gaze swept the giant room that had to be at least twenty-five-hundred square feet, maybe — probably — more.

Where did she start? There was so much to look at. Other than the lavishly dressed bed, there was a leather couch and a pair of wooden, straight-backed chairs, along with a large bureau with shallow drawers that reminded her of something butterfly or stamp collectors stored their prized collectibles in. But that was where her familiarity ended. Every other piece of furniture was foreign to her. Well, she couldn't call it furniture. More like…contraptions.

A built-in beam that looked about twelve feet long ran along the ceiling. Two heavy-duty hooks sat inside a track that spanned the center of the beam, and on the floor beneath was another built-in apparatus with similar hooks. Everything looked to be attached to pulleys and it reminded Sam of a fancy curtain rod. Somehow, though, she didn't think curtains were what got hung from those hooks. Maybe it was the impressive set of floggers hanging nearby on the wall beside one of the many floor-length mirrors hanging throughout the room that gave her that impression, but, yeah, that beam in the ceiling with the hooks and pulleys wasn't for curtains.

And the floggers! There had to be a hundred of them. Cat o' nine tails, riding crops, short ones, long ones, ones that looked like horses' tails, leather, plastic, ping-pong paddles, bamboo rods, canes. Oh my God, there were even a couple of coiled whips displayed.

She walked slowly through the room, afraid to touch anything but fascinated at discovering Micah had a kinky — well, kinki*er* – side. And here she thought that whole knife thing had been sexy.

Lame-o!

This place made the Bowie knife she had used on Micah earlier seem like a foam sword. Weak.

She opened a drawer in another bureau and found an impressive array of vibrators and dildos. Jesus! He had a Hitachi Magic Wand. Um, no. Make that three of them.

One eyebrow shot up mischievously. He could those on her any time he wanted. The thought of Micah inside her with the wand stimulating her clit was a fantasy she wanted to see come to life. Absolutely.

After closing the drawer and inspecting the others to find all manner of toys, silver balls, cock sleeves, stimulators, and an assortment of other playthings, Sam spun and took in the rest of the room. Hell, she had no idea how to use half this stuff. And what was up with the giant glass tank that looked like an empty fish aquarium? And the large dog cage? And were those leashes and collars hanging on hooks beside the cage? What? Did he like treating people like animals?

She stepped over to what appeared to be an odd sitting bench. It looked like a booth in a restaurant, only there was a bench on both sides, it was smaller, covered with black leather, and had heavy-duty hooks bolted to it in several places. She climbed on and inspected it. Hmm. Was this some kind of spanking bench? Sam had heard the girls at the Black Garter, where she used to work as a dancer, talk about stuff like this. A few of her coworkers had been into some serious kink, and she had sometimes enjoyed hearing them talk about the stuff they let men do to them...or that they did to the men, as the case sometimes was.

Was this the kind of thing they had been talking about? She bent over the leather portion of the bench. Uh-huh. Perfect position to be spanked. Oh, and look. Hooks. Right where her hands were. If she were cuffed, she could be attached to the bench and helplessly prostrated.

Why did that suddenly make her get all creamy hot at her core?

After hopping off, she inspected a couple of other benches and a contraption that looked like a mini-guillotine, but not. The hole in the side was much too large for a head, and there was an angled platform. Was she supposed to lie down on that? And somehow...? She frowned and tilted her head left then right, studying the odd apparatus. Micah would have to show her how to use that thing.

She loved the mirrors. Something about watching herself and what was being done to her in this room appealed to her, especially in the mirror above the bed. If he let her watch, that is. She had noticed an assortment of blindfolds in his stash of toys. Along with gags, bindings, ropes, cuffs, chains, and a lot of other stuff.

Shit, Micah was a freak. But he was *her* freak.

She wasn't sure she could handle everything in this room, but enough of it was already turning her on enough that she thought the two of them could rock each other's world pretty well down here.

For the next fifteen minutes, she worked her way through the room, investigating the benches, contraptions, and St. Andrews Cross before ending up on the bed, where she laid back on the semi-firm mattress and gazed up at herself in the mirror.

Damn, but she was turned on. She squirmed and reached over her head to grab the wrought iron headboard. How would it feel to be tied to this bed? How exciting would it be to gaze into that mirror and watch Micah make love to her or go down on her? To look up at the mirror and watch what was happening to her as if she were watching an X-rated movie where she was the star? The thought alone made warmth bloom deep in her belly and spread like slow-moving lava into her core, heating her body.

Micah, Micah, Micah. Look what you do to me.

With Micah, she wanted to explore her sexuality. Never before had she imagined doing the things she suddenly wanted to do with him. Was it the trust she felt with him? Because she trusted him implicitly, despite knowing him less than a month. But she knew he wouldn't hurt her. With Micah, she felt safer than she'd ever felt with anyone, and wasn't that just the biggest fucking turn-on *ever?*

For the first time in her life, she wanted to explore her fantasies. She had never felt comfortable opening up like this with Steve. Her abusive ex had been too much into hurting her for his own pleasure than to give any pleasure to her, so she had withdrawn into herself. Sex in her doomed marriage had become nothing more than a burdensome chore.

Now, all that was behind her. With each passing moment, she felt herself re-opening and rediscovering her sexuality, as well as her sensuality. And it was because of Micah and their incredible connection, based on honesty and openness.

Did Sam want Micah to tie her down and strap her up? Spank her? Flog her? Bend her over that funky bench thing? She glanced at the St. Andrews Cross and bit her lip. God, yes. She did, didn't she? She wanted all that and more. Why? Because she trusted Micah, and she loved him, and the idea of him doing those things to her blew her sex drive into orbit.

What was it he had said to her before she descended the stairs into the basement? *My trust in you is down there.* Yes, that's what he had said. She suddenly knew what he meant, because her trust in him was here, too.

With a contented sigh, she glanced back up at her grinning face in the mirror on the ceiling. *Oh, Micah, the things my mind is imagining.* She didn't know what half the stuff in the room was, but she wanted Micah to teach her. Hell, did she ever want Micah to teach her!

Pushing up off the luxurious bed, she gave one final look around the sin chamber of lust and sensuality, laughing at herself and ducking her head in amusement as the words scrolled through her mind, and walked to the doorway that led back to Micah's bedroom.

As she stepped through and glanced back up, the smile disappeared from her face, instantly replaced with hunger. Micah stood against the far wall by the stairs, his body tense, his eyes hooded and dark.

"You said you were going to wait upstairs." She licked her lips and took a tentative step toward him.

"I heard every..." Micah paused and inhaled deeply, as if he were inhaling her scent. And he probably was, picking up the essence of her arousal. "I heard every thought in your mind."

His shadowed eyes razed her from head to toe, his chest rising and falling lustfully as he pushed away from the wall. Sam got the distinct impression he was exercising extreme restraint.

Maybe she could change that, because the last thing she wanted him to be right now was restrained.

She kept walking toward him. Slowly. Her steps measured

and seductive as she pulled her sweater up and over her head. "And you couldn't stay away?"

Micah's breathing quickened, and each breath brought with it a deep, titillating purr. She loved when he purred. Not only did it tell her he was aroused, but the sound did something carnal to her insides, making her muscles clench with anticipation of what she knew was about to happen.

"No." The single syllable vibrated through his chest, his voice low and primal.

Damn. Handcuffs, children, and thoughts of being worked over in his dungeon of sadomasochism. Her list of things that seemed to get Micah going just got longer and longer.

Sam unsnapped her jeans and slowly peeled them down her legs as she toed off her shoes. All she had on was a white, satin bra and matching panties. Nothing sexy, but then she hadn't expected this or she would have worn something lacier and racier.

"No. You look...." Micah panted, breathing in and out in shallow breaths as his gaze danced up and down her body. "Perfect. Like an angel." He stepped toward her. "An innocent angel."

Who's having very naughty thoughts. Sam couldn't help wondering if that was the allure. Her dressed in pure, virginal white while pondering torrid, lurid fantasies.

"That's part of it, yes," he said, drawing nearer as she crawled over the low footboard, turned around, then sank seductively onto his bed. The normal one. The bed that wasn't designed for bondage. She scooted back, keeping her eyes on him as he prowled to the foot of the bed and turned his body, watching her as she lay back, reached up, and took hold of the ornately carved headboard. Shifting, she sank her head into the pillows and pressed her knees together demurely, feigning fear in her eyes.

He purred again, louder, and pulled off his shirt. His long, black hair flared and settled over his shoulders, and he quickly unfastened his black jeans and undressed, his eyes never leaving hers.

In an instant, he was on her, pushing her legs open, biting

through the front of her bra to release her breasts as he gripped her panties and yanked them off with a satisfying rip. And then he was inside her, claiming her, pulling her hands free of the headboard so he could hold her arms down against the mattress.

He was insatiable, growling, moaning, purring, the pleasure overwhelming.

"Micah!" She cried out as she climaxed.

And before she knew what was happening, she came again, and yet again as Micah sank his fangs into her neck and plunged one final, harsh time inside her and stilled.

His cock pumped hard, and warmth filled her, his fertile seed spilling and falling on what he had already informed her was infertile terrain. Still, she wrapped her arms lovingly around him, the euphoria of his venom loosening her muscles so that she fell into orgasmic spasms one final time beneath him, her body quivering and quaking as he drank her blood.

She might not be able to carry his baby, yet, but one day... yes, one day she would have Micah's child. She didn't know how she knew. She just did.

CHAPTER 4

MICAH DROVE SAM BACK TO HIS APARTMENT in silence, neither of them discussing the room in his basement. He wanted to wait a day or two to go into the details of what he did there and what he hoped to do to her, as well, but tonight, he was too torqued to broach the subject. But that didn't mean Sam's mind was quiet. On the contrary, her mind was a dazzling display of wonder and fantasy over all she had seen and what they'd done to one another after her tour of his dungeon. Even now, Micah could sense her arousal, thick and fragrant to his sensitive nose.

Truthfully, he had been caught off guard and shocked when Sam's thoughts had so openly accepted what she had found in his dungeon. Or the *sin chamber of lust and sensuality*, as she had called it. He liked how that sounded. And he had liked how excited his basement getaway had made her. She was eager for him to show her around the room and how things worked, and he was more than willing to teach her.

After parking his Audi in the garage, he took her hand, and they walked to the elevator bay. The tension between them was like a third person, drawing them closer together, making them walk with a little more urgency, making their breath quicken.

As soon as the elevator doors closed, Sam shoved him against the wall and planted her mouth hard over his. He groaned against her lips, sliding his arm around the small of her back and pulling her against him as if his very existence depended on getting her as close to him as he could.

He knew she'd still been aroused after leaving his house.

And hallelujah and glory to Heaven, he was ready to have her again.

They barely made it out of the elevator and into his apartment before falling into a naked heap on the floor in a twist of arms and legs. He rolled to his back and pulled her on top of him as she sank down on his cock, taking him deep, already thrusting and riding him before he was fully inside her.

She was lost in wanton abandon, her pupils dilated, her nipples taut, her hands pressing against his chest for stability as she fucked him with every fiber of her soul.

Fuck, but he wished her body was capable of taking his seed and making new life. She would make an amazing mother to his young, but he knew it was futile to think such thoughts. At least for now. Maybe at his next *calling* things would be different and he would finally be granted the family he had always wanted.

In unison, they both cried out, coming, their bodies shattering yet again through another powerful climax. Sam collapsed on top of him, spent.

Except for Micah's fingertips lazily trailing up and down her spine, neither moved for several minutes, remaining sprawled on his plush carpet. Finally, he lifted his head and kissed the top of hers.

"Trace is coming over tomorrow night for the game," he said quietly, setting his head back on the floor.

"Mmm?"

"Do you think we'll be able to keep our hands off each other while he's here?"

"Maybe." Her voice was muffled with her cheek pressed against his chest.

She lifted her head and propped her chin on her hand against his sternum. "We can always slip away at halftime for a little pick-me-up if we have to." A crooked grin crossed her lips.

"True." His own mouth lifted at the corners, and a mischievous arch played over his brow.

"As a vampire, Trace should understand this *calling* thing

you're going through, right?"

"Uh-huh. He should. But wouldn't that make us bad hosts?" His grin widened. He liked her suggestion to slip away at halftime.

"Nah, just handicapped."

He laughed. "Handicapped with lust."

She started laughing with him. "Something like that, yes." Sam pulled herself up his body and kissed him, letting her lips linger against his. "Your laugh is so sexy."

"Is it now?"

She bit her lip. "Uh-huh."

"Well, I'm glad I'm laughing again then."

"Me, too."

They lay like that a few seconds longer, then Sam pushed herself up. She stood, helped him to his feet, and then they gathered their clothes. Morning was approaching and the timer on his blinds and drapes engaged to make them close automatically and block out the coming light.

"You know, at my house, we can renovate the upper level and make that your special place," he said, following her to the bedroom.

They tossed their clothes in the hamper and flipped on the light in the bathroom.

"Don't you use the upstairs?" Sam reached in and turned on the water for the shower.

"No. Not really." He grabbed them a couple of towels out of the linen closet. "I figure you can make that your day haven or something. After all, you can still be in the sunlight, and you should have a space all your own."

"Like a man cave?"

"Call it a Sam cave."

She chuckled as she stepped into the shower with him. "A Sam cave. I like that."

He brushed his fingers through her hair as she leaned back into the water. "I want my home to be your home. *Our* home. I want you comfortable there, and I want your personal, decorative touch in every room, but especially upstairs. That's your area." He liked the idea of seeing how she would arrange it. What colors of paint would she use? What kind of furniture? Would she prefer more modern décor or a something cozier? All those small details would tell him so much more about her, and he wanted to know everything there was to know about his Samantha.

Sam contemplated for a moment then smiled. "Are you sure you don't mind?"

"Not at all. I want you to be comfortable, baby." He grabbed her lilac-scented shampoo as she dipped her head again under one of the multiple sprays of water. After squeezing some of the shampoo into his hand, he stepped behind her as she turned, and then he began massaging it into her scalp.

Micah loved tending to her like this. Not that it was unusual during the *calling* for a male to dote on his mate. This was when a male nested, when he began caring for his mate's physical needs in preparation to bear his child. He bathed her, prepared nourishment for her, wrapped her in a blanket if she was cold, tucked her into bed to ensure she rested, brought her tea and water or whatever else she needed.

He grinned as he worked his strong fingers over her scalp, letting the thick suds coat his hands and forearms. He always used too much shampoo to wash her hair, but he liked how the scent lingered on him after the suds coated his arms like this.

As she rinsed her hair, he poured a healthy dollop of lilac body wash onto a loofah, worked the soap into thick, aromatic suds, and gently but meticulously washed every inch of her body, even kneeling to wash her feet as she lifted one then the other, leaning down and placing her hands on his shoulders for support.

Only after she was thoroughly washed did he quickly shampoo his own hair and bathe himself.

Then they stepped from the shower, and he grabbed one of the plush towels and dried her. The first couple of times he'd taken her through this routine, she had resisted, not understanding his need to fawn over her. But now she knew this was all part of the *calling*. He was compelled to worship her and treat her like the precious vessel she was. And one day, when—yes, *when*—she became pregnant, this was the kind of behavior she could expect every day. As her mate, he had no choice but to obey the instinctual signals of his body, and his instincts would demand he take care of her. Besides, she would need his help when she became pregnant, because carrying a vampire's baby was exhausting. Even in the early stages.

As he dried her, he paid extra attention to her slim, flat stomach. God, he wanted to see her belly swell as the weeks passed. He wanted to be able to place his hand against her tummy and feel a tiny life—a life he had helped create—moving inside her. What would that be like? He and Katarina had never had young of their own. She hadn't been able to. Even after several *calling* phases, her body wouldn't accept his offering. A child was the one thing Micah had always wanted and never thought he would have. Now, he had another chance with Sam.

Reverently, he knelt in front of her, wrapped his arms around her waist, leaned forward, and kissed her stomach. And again. Then again. He wanted a baby with Sam. He knew it was just the *calling* speaking through his consciousness, but he couldn't help the desire for a child from springing tears to his eyes.

"Someday," she whispered.

He looked up at her. "Are you reading my mind?" He tried to smile, but he knew he probably looked as pathetic as he felt.

"I don't have to," she said. "You're showing me what you're thinking."

At her words, he nodded and pulled her close, tightening his arms around her before resting his forehead against her stomach as her fingers pushed through his hair to hold him against her.

"Yes, someday," he said, closing his eyes.

THE NEXT DAY WAS SUPER BOWL SUNDAY, and Trace was coming over to watch the game.

Micah and Sam spent the better part of the day tidying up and getting ready for company when they weren't lost in each other's arms, and somehow Sam managed to put together a batch of her famous chili. It was the second batch she'd made since they'd been together, and he and Trace both loved it. The spicy, meaty aroma made his apartment smell like Heaven.

While Sam put away a few things in the bedroom, Micah took out the last load of laundry and started folding it. He needed to make a quick run to the store for beer, and Trace was due in about an hour-and-a-half, so it looked like he wouldn't get any more play time with Sam until after they all went to bed, unless Sam was serious about making their own halftime entertainment.

And to make things even more complicated for his sexual itch, it looked like Trace was spending the night. Snow had started to fall, and an icy mix was forecast for later on. By the time the game ended, at least six inches of the stuff would be coating the roads.

Micah liked Trace. The guy had turned out to be good people and an even stronger ally. Throughout Micah's ordeal with Apostle, Trace had been a stalwart bodyguard.

He still couldn't get over how Trace had defended him at AKM that night he had almost lost Sam. Micah and Arion had been going at each other, and Arion had stuck his nose yet again into Micah's life where it didn't belong, as he always did, and Micah had snapped. His fully-mated side had exploded and unleashed itself on Arion. Fuck, he had pounded the hell out of the guy, but Trace had stepped in to pull Micah away and keep the others from coming after him.

Something told Micah then that Trace's protective nature had more to it than just his desire to keep a friend out of trouble. He felt like he and Trace were tethered together on two different paths that were aligned to collide. But when? And how?

It would help if he could get a look inside that head of

Trace's, but his thoughts were securely locked away. There was no cracking that safe. No matter how easily Micah got into the heads of everyone else, he wasn't getting inside Trace's mind unless Trace wanted him to.

Still, the idea that he and Trace were bound somehow hung over him like a portentous shadow. Trace needed Micah for something. But what?

He supposed he would find out soon enough, but he knew instinctively that whatever Trace needed from him, he would give it. So, it wasn't just Sam he had connected to. He had connected to Trace in a completely different way, as well. Sam was his mate, and Trace was his best friend and then some. Blood brothers was more how it felt. Whatever it was, he would break all kinds of rules and laws to protect them both if it ever came to that.

Micah folded the last of the clothes and carried them to the bedroom.

As he got closer, he tapped into Sam's thoughts. She was thinking about his dungeon again. She had been thinking a lot about his playroom today. Seemed she was excited to get back to it and see what he could do to her.

He would go easy on her at first. He wasn't sure she could handle all that he could give. He hadn't developed a reputation in the local BDSM community as being a Master Dom for nothing. In his day, his reputation had been legendary, and he had garnered quite a following. And not just for the pain he could give, but for his creativity, ardent trust, discretion, respect, and the way he took care of his subs after a scene.

"Which are you? A top or a bottom?" He chuckled as he entered the room and made her jump.

"Will you stay out of my head?" She always said that, but she knew by now he couldn't.

"Sorry, habit." That was his patent answer every time she reprimanded him.

He put the clothes away as she laughed.

"You are never going to stop that, are you?"

With a shake of his head, he wrapped his arms around her

waist. "No. I can't help it. I like the way you think. Especially when you're thinking about my special proclivities." In fact, he was getting aroused at the thought of her thinking about his dungeon and what he could do to her there. Too bad, since they didn't time to play right now.

"Proclivities?" Sam's eyebrow arched at him. "My, what a big vocabulary you have."

He pressed the hand more firmly against the small of her back and eased against her body like a predator. "I'm just full of surprises. And I'm very well educated." Micah had studied in more universities than he could remember. No wonder his vocabulary was so expansive, although he did try not to use such big words on a regular basis. Most people didn't understand them.

"I can see that, and I'm sure you are."

He saw inside her mind and grinned when he saw how much his intelligence turned her on.

"Your intelligence turns me on, too," he said, leaning in and skimming his lips over the side of her neck. Mmm, she tasted good. Smelled good, too.

"Would you stop that?"

He wondered if she was referring to his mental break-ins or his mouth on her skin. A peek inside her thoughts revealed the former, as he suspected, and he smiled to himself.

"Huh-uh. Nope. Never." His lips closed over her neck and he gently suckled her.

She loosened with warmth and arousal ever-so-subtly in his grasp. "Well, can you at least stay out of my memories?"

Micah wasn't one to dig into memories, so he figured he could accommodate her request. He was more into the here-and-now of people's thoughts, not what had happened before.

He released her neck and pulled around until his lips were so close to hers they were almost touching. "I can do that," he said. "Maybe." He grinned and kissed her, holding her there as his gaze smoldered into hers. He really wanted to take her to bed. Now. And stay there. But Trace would be over soon, and they still had a few things to do.

He pulled away. "I'm going down to the corner store for beer. I'll be back in fifteen. Need anything?"

She looked like she wanted the same thing he wanted, and it wasn't something he could buy at the store. Damn. "Maybe some pretzels?" she said, sounding just a bit dejected.

"Will do." After kissing her again, he reluctantly left her side and grabbed his wallet off the dresser then put on his coat and headed for the bedroom door.

"Which are you?" she suddenly asked.

Her question made him stop. She was referring to the question he had asked her when he had walked in. About whether she was a top or a bottom. Was she ready for his answer? He knew she had fantasized about what he could do to her, but fantasizing about it and hearing him say the words were two different things.

When he turned, her innocent green eyes didn't look so innocent anymore.

"I'm a Dom, but I also top. With you, I think I might actually bottom, though. But I'll never submit." He saw her next question before she asked it, and the corner of his mouth turned up wryly.

"What's the difference between a Dom and a top?"

He could sense her excitement, and he sauntered toward her, almost stalking her.

"A Dominant requires submission, a top doesn't. As a top, I provide physical stimulation without requiring you to submit." Stopping in front of her, Micah reached around and spanked her, harder than he'd intended, but she had him so worked up he couldn't help himself.

Her eyes flared at the physical contact.

"See," he said, "if you don't like my slapping you as a top, you can stop me, or basically top me from the bottom. But if I was Dom'ing you, I wouldn't allow you to do that. I would have control and your complete submission. Do you understand?"

She nibbled her bottom lip and stared up at him, totally enthralled. "I think so. Topping and bottoming allow for give and take between the two, but between a Dominant and a submissive, one gives and one takes. There is no give and take."

Yes, now she was getting it. "Very good. You've just completed your first lesson."

Electricity sparked the air between them, and Micah was sooo tempted to forget the beer and pretzels, but he knew he should get going. All this foreplay would make for a much more satisfying postgame show in the privacy of their room later. If his *calling* could last that long, which he was seriously beginning to doubt it would. Halftime was sounding more and more enticing every second.

"I look forward to the next one," she said, her voice sultry.

"So do I." He forced himself to pull away from her, touching her face. "I'll be back. I love you."

"I love you, too."

Micah headed out and down the elevator to the store on the corner, where he picked up a bag of pretzels and a six-pack of beer. He and Sam weren't big drinkers, and neither was Trace, so a six-pack was plenty.

After paying, he made his way back out into the snow. It was just flurries so far — the heavy stuff would hit in about an hour — so before he could get powdered in white, he was back at the Sentinel and riding the elevator to the eighteenth floor.

He could smell Sam's chili before he even stepped out into the hall. Damn, she sure could cook.

Shifting the beer and pretzels to one hand, he pulled out his keys and unlocked the door. The apartment was unusually quiet. Sam wasn't in the living room or the kitchen, pandering around to prepare for Trace's arrival.

"Sam?"

His body filled with tension. The last time he had left her alone in his apartment, Apostle had found her and bitten her, almost killing her. The memory was enough to make him bristle, and he quickly shut the door then set the beer and pretzels on the counter before heading cautiously down the hall to the bedroom.

SAM STOOD WAITING IN THE ROOM for Micah, slightly nervous. She had never done anything like this. After he left, she had changed into a matching black lace bra and panty, black garter, stockings, and high-heeled ankle boots she thought she'd never have the opportunity to wear. They'd been a splurge on a careless shopping trip several months ago. She had almost returned them, but now she was glad she hadn't.

But it wasn't her clothing she hoped would spark Micah's blood to the boiling point. After he left, she had been in the closet looking for her favorite sweatshirt when one of the masks she had taken from the Black Garter had fallen from the upper shelf. It was the black and red one Micah had said he liked so much and had pushed into her hands on the day she quit. Micah had told her he'd seen her perform once when she'd been wearing that mask. So, of course, it was his favorite.

When the mask fell on her, her mind had run off on a tangent, urging her toward an idea that explored this new world Micah had exposed her to with his dungeon of debasement.

So now she stood in the middle of their bedroom, clothed in scanty black lingerie, sexy high heels, and a black and red leather mask with black-out lenses. She was holding a wooden spoon she had swiped from the kitchen. It was the closest thing to a flogger she could find in the apartment.

Micah opened the bedroom door, and her heart clenched. Could she really go down this road? When Micah's gaze landed on her in the dimly lit room, his eyebrows perked up and the barest of smiles flirted with his mouth. Instead of feeling self-conscious, his reaction and the growing bulge in his jeans made her stand a little taller, emboldening her and fortifying her resolve.

"Close the door," she said, smacking the wooden spoon into the palm of her hand.

When he only stood there, gaping and awe-struck, she arched an eyebrow which he couldn't see, being that it was hidden behind the mask. But she was sure he could feel her mock irritation.

"I told you to close the door."

Finally, he reached back and gently pushed it shut. "Our lesson gave you ideas, did it?"

As the door latched, the room was robbed of the light being cast in from the living room. Fortunately, she'd turned on the lamp on the nightstand.

He was right, though. Their lesson had given her ideas. A lot of ideas.

"Take off your clothes," she said.

Would a professional like Micah sense her nervousness? Hell, he was probably in her head right now. If he was, he didn't let on. So maybe he was making a point to stay out of her mind for once.

"You're doing wonderfully," he said.

Mmm, maybe he was in her head. If he was, she didn't care. His compliment boosted her confidence. It told her she was doing something right. Well, that erection obscured by his jeans told her that much, didn't it?

Still, if she was going to do this, she needed to sink into the part. And he needed to obey her. As she stepped to the side, she smacked the spoon harshly against her palm, showing her irritation that he still wasn't undressing.

"I told you to take off your clothes."

He calmly began untucking his shirt, watching her as she slowly walked around him in a semi-circle, inspecting him.

As he revealed more of his body, it became harder to stay in character. When she first met him, he had looked nearly starved. She had since learned that he hadn't been eating or feeding back then, which was why he had looked so gaunt. But now...? Mmm-mm-mmm. Micah was twice the man — male, whatever — he had been when they'd met, in that he had put on at least twenty-five pounds, maybe more, of pure muscle.

But then, he'd been feeding from her nearly every day. At first she had been concerned he would drain her, but then he'd explained that her new body could regenerate blood almost as quickly as he took it. And didn't that just work out beautifully?

Micah wasn't body builder big. Sev and Tristan were wider in the shoulders than Micah, but Micah was taller, leaner, and stronger. Hell, his physical form was the sexiest thing she'd ever seen.

"Would you like to assist?" he said, his tone and his gaze giving away that he was inside her head, enjoying her appraisal of his body.

Sam stopped and cocked her head to the side. "No. And turn away from me while you undress."

Two could play at this game. He might be inside her head, but she could take away the thrill he got from watching her.

Unbelievably, he did as she commanded, turning away, unfastening his belt and unzipping his jeans. Then he pushed them down his long legs and kicked off his shoes before peeling his jeans all the way off, taking his socks with them.

Which left him gloriously naked.

"You're so sexy like this," he said.

Oh, now…she hadn't given him permission to speak. She needed to punish him for his transgression. Inwardly, she cringed. She had never struck anyone, not even playfully. But that's what the game required.

Thwack!

The spoon connected with his ass, and he flinched. She bit her lip and hesitated to see if he would turn and stop her, but he remained in place, stoic and unmoving, so she stepped forward and, unable to keep from touching him any longer, raked her nails down the left side of his back to his ass, following with her tongue down his spine as she knelt behind him.

Micah's skin was smooth and supple, and he tasted slightly of salt, as if he had been sweating just a little bit.

She eyed the spoon-shaped red mark on the right cheek of his ass. He'd probably left plenty of such marks on those who'd been lucky enough to enter his dungeon over the years. Well, no more. The only person who would be getting marked at his hand from now on was her.

After setting down the spoon, she dug her fingers into his hips and held him in place as she bent forward and bit the spoon print. Hard. Micah tensed provocatively, and a moan caught in his throat as if he'd purposely bitten it back.

Mmm, Micah. Sexy, hot Micah. She licked where she had just bitten, then bit him again. Back and forth she licked then bit, licked and nibbled...until she decided it was time to lick and nibble something else.

"Turn around," she said.

As he turned, it wasn't his magnificent hard-on she saw first. It was his dark gaze. He was looking down at her, appearing as if a god, and for just a moment she felt like she was worshipping at his feet, kneeling before him. But then she caught herself. She was in control here, right? At least, that was the role she was playing.

And she would let Micah know it, too.

Sinking back on her heels, she gazed at his hard-on, her eyes obscured by the dark lenses of the mask, and thought about taking him in her mouth. She knew he would be inside her mind, reading her thoughts, and she wanted him to see all the things she wanted to do to him. She wanted him crazy with lust, seeing all her torrid imaginings, yet not experiencing them as she simply sat back and looked at him.

His breathing increased. His body tensed even more. Yes, he was listening to her mind. She knew he couldn't resist. And now her thoughts were driving him mad.

At least she'd found a way to use his tendency to read her thoughts to her advantage. Maybe his mind-reading habit could turn out to be an asset.

After a couple of minutes had passed, she picked up the wooden spoon again and immediately smacked the side of this thigh. Again and again, and still again. Then she switched to the other side and continued flaying him. But Micah didn't so much as flinch. He took the stinging strikes in stride, not moving, not making a sound. If not for the way his body tightened with each strike, she never would have known she was causing pain.

As she smacked his thigh one final time, she pushed forward and took his cock in her mouth, sucking him in hard, licking and swallowing him down her throat.

Micah's legs practically gave out as he grunted, coming almost immediately. His entire body quaked, and his knees wobbled precariously, but somehow he remained standing as he unloaded everything he had against her tongue.

Fuck, but she was turned on. She was on the verge of coming herself, and as soon as his orgasm reached its end, she lay back on the floor in front of him, opening her legs and propping herself on one elbow as she shoved her black panties to the side and touched herself. She was wet and ready for him. So slick and swollen.

He'd told her that he'd tried more than once to buy a private performance with her at the Black Garter, but she'd always been booked. Now, every performance belonged to him, starting with this one. And this was a very special private performance, because she'd never done anything like this for her clients at the Garter. She'd never done anything like this period. Only he was worthy enough to see her splayed, aroused, and masturbating, because he was the only one who'd ever made her feel decadent and daring enough to completely lose her inhibitions. The fact he had earned her trust simply sealed the deal.

Faster her fingers worked, circling her clit, dipping in and out of her slick opening, returning to her clit again.

His gaze nearly devoured her as he watched, clearly wishing to be between her legs, doing the honors with his tongue. Oh God! The thought made her moan. Each breath expelled on a gasp as her stomach clenched, announcing the first wave of her release.

Unbidden, her hips thrust into her hand, gyrating and grinding circles against the rhythm of her fingers until...

With an abrupt shiver, her hips rose violently off the floor and she felt moisture squirt against her hand.

What the hell?

She had heard of women who could ejaculate, but this was a first. She had never ejaculated her orgasm before. Micah's eyes nearly popped out of their sockets as his mouth gaped. He seemed as surprised as she was.

Collapsing to the floor, she massaged herself with

gentle forward and back motions, pulling her orgasm out, prolonging it, smiling contentedly as she stared up at him. Her Micah. He was awakening her inner sex goddess. This was a side of herself she had never experienced, even though she'd always known it was there.

"Come. Taste me." She beckoned him with her glistening hand and lay back as he practically plunged between her legs and lapped away her feminine orgasm.

Tonight, while Trace is here, know that I will be wearing no panties under my pants. I will be wet thinking about you. I will be thinking about your cock inside me. And after we've all gone to bed, you will take me out to the couch and fuck me like you've never fucked anyone before, where Trace could come out and see us at any moment.

Sam felt him grin against her nether lips before he lifted his head and said, "Yes, ma'am."

She rolled her head and grinned as she arched her back off the floor and languished under his oral caresses, stretching her arms over her head. Why did the idea of being caught having sex with Micah excite her so much? And why was it even more exciting thinking Trace would be the one to catch them?

Twenty minutes later, she hurried and got dressed after the two of them grabbed a hasty shower. He still had a towel wrapped around his waist and was reaching for a pair of sweats as the doorbell rang.

With his sweats in his hand, he tossed back his hair and looked at her with a shrug.

Trace was here. Playtime was officially over. But at least they'd shared a last-minute fix. The promise of more to come later hung over them like an erotic shroud.

Micah disappeared down the hall, and Sam quickly skimmed her fingers through her still-damp, boy-short hair. After brushing on some lip gloss, she shut off the light and headed to the kitchen to check the chili.

She heard voices at the door, and a moment later, Trace walked into the kitchen.

"Hi, Trace."

"Hey, little lady." Trace leaned down and kissed her cheek.

He was such a sweetheart, but she could tell he was dangerous. Still, she felt safer when he was around.

"You might want to check the front door," he said quietly, leaning over the pot of chili and taking a deep whiff. "Mmm."

"Why? What's at the front door?"

"Jackson's here."

"Who? Jackson?"

Trace arched an eyebrow and dipped his head in the direction of the foyer.

Sam frowned and hurried out of the kitchen.

"Micah, is someone—?" She hesitated when she saw Micah talking to a man she had never met. Well, male in this case, since Jackson was a vampire. She knew that much.

Jackson had been the reason why Micah had wanted to kill himself a month ago. Micah had partially mated Jackson, but Jackson had left him. And from the way it sounded, mated vampires—even partially mated ones—didn't take well to their mates breaking up with them.

Case in point: the beautiful, sexy male standing in front of her, with the navy-blue eyes and black hair that cascaded in wet tendrils over his shoulder.

Micah had nearly died from the pain Jackson's leaving him caused.

Thank God she had come along to save him.

Micah turned and those gorgeous eyes of his smiled at her as his face lit up. Yes, she was Micah's mate now. So, why the hell was Jackson here?

She hurried forward and wrapped one arm around Micah and pressed her palm against his back as she extended her other hand to Jackson.

"Hi, I'm Sam."

"Jackson, meet Sam," Micah said, looking at her with what she could only describe as complete adoration.

His loving gaze made her whole body tingle.

Suddenly, it felt like Jackson wasn't even there, even though Micah's next words seemed more for him than for her.

"Sam is my lifemate. She is my life now, always, and

forever. I love you, my precious Sam."

Sam felt her face heat. She was sure she was blushing.

Micah turned back to Jackson, who looked positively forsaken. Clearly, Jackson had hoped for a different outcome to his surprise visit.

Your loss, my gain.

She didn't dislike Jackson, even though what he'd done had practically killed the male she'd come to love in such a short amount of time. Part of her felt sorry for him. Jackson had realized what he'd lost too late. If not for Sam, Micah wouldn't even be alive right now, and then where would Jackson be? Staring at a headstone in a cemetery, most likely.

Sam imagined this was the lesser of two evils.

"So, as you can see, Jack, I'm spoken for now." Micah didn't sound as compassionate as Sam felt.

Jackson nodded and glanced between them. "I'm happy for you." He brushed back his wavy, black hair and glanced toward the elevator before looking back at them. "Congratulations. Um…" he gestured toward the empty hall. "I guess, um…I guess I'll head on out. I just wanted to say hi."

"Okay. See you Jack," Micah said, tightening his grip around Sam's waist.

"It was nice to meet you." Sam smiled at him.

Everyone made mistakes, and she couldn't fault Jackson for his.

"Nice meeting you, too." He smiled wanly at her and lifted his hand in a weak wave as he turned and made his way down the hall toward the elevator.

Micah shut the door and turned toward her. "Now that I have you, I don't know what I ever saw in him."

"He meant something to you once."

He nodded. "Yes, he did. But all that's past now."

She gazed up into his eyes for a heartbeat. "Come on, lover. You need to get dressed before the game starts." She took his hand and began to walk away with him in tow.

"Lover?" He stalled and pulled her back, a big grin on his face.

"Mm-hm. You got a problem with that?"

He shook his head and kissed her. "Nope. Not at all, Mrs. Black."

Sam groaned playfully and lifted her left hand. "No. Ring. See?"

Micah chuckled and kissed her ring finger. "You're. Still. Mine."

Oh yes. She was.

CHAPTER 5

MICAH QUICKLY CLASPED HANDS WITH TRACE as he passed the kitchen on his way to the bedroom.

"Hey, brother," Trace said. "You gonna dance around in that towel all night? Coz if you are, I'm overdressed."

Micah flipped him off. "You only wish, fucker." He nodded down the hall toward the bedroom. "I'll be back in a sec."

Trace gave him a nonchalant once-over with his pale green eyes and chuckled. "Thank God. Coz I wasn't sittin' next you if you weren't gonna put some clothes on."

Micah smirked and flipped him off again then departed for the bedroom to change.

Jackson showing up had been unexpected. For almost a year, he and Jackson had been a thing. An item. A couple. Micah had sexed up with males during his darker days, specifically the years after Katarina died when his blood felt like raw sewage churning in his veins, but Jackson had been the first male Micah was attracted to. Then he'd felt the pull to mate him. What a surprise.

But now he suspected Jackson had never been the target of his body's biology. The more he thought about how the first time he'd seen Sam dance as Scarlet was the same night he met Jackson, the more convinced he became he'd been meant to mate Sam all along. Jackson was just in the wrong place at the right time, and the mating link misfired, binding him to Jackson instead of Sam.

But now everything was as it should be. Jackson was out of his life, and Sam was in it. Problem solved. She was his lifemate, and for the first time in several centuries, his thirst for living, rather than the need to keep moving, was what drove him to get out of bed every night. Food was no longer tasteless. The world no longer seemed coated with a grey film. Flavors burst on his tongue now, and vibrant colors met his gaze everywhere he looked.

And it was all because of Sam.

He would die instantly if he ever lost Sam. His heart would simply cease to beat. And not just because she was his third mate — well, his second-and-a-half — and it was a miracle he had survived the loss of his first two. No, he would die for the simple reason that one couldn't live without their most vital organ, and for Micah, Sam was just that. She was more important to his survival than his heart or his soul. She *was* his heart. She *was* his soul. Nothing was more important to him in this entire world than her.

After pulling on a pair of boxer briefs and the pair of nylon sweats he'd been holding, he snagged a black Under Armor shirt from the closet and pulled it over his head before heading back out to the kitchen.

Sam was spooning chili into bowls, and he walked up behind her and wrapped his arms around her waist, hugging her tightly as he dipped his nose into her fragrant hair.

"I love you," he whispered.

She giggled and pressed into him, placing her delicate hand over his arm. "What's gotten into you?"

"I just wanted to tell you that." He grinned into her hair and inhaled before leaning his head to the side to capture her mouth in a tender caress.

Trace cleared his throat and Micah turned and gave him a smirk. "What? Do you want a kiss, too?"

With a harrumph and a frown, Trace shook his head. "Fuck no, shithead."

He and Sam laughed at him. "Awe, what's the problem, Trace?" Sam reached out and pushed him playfully on the arm. "Is Micah too much man for you?"

Trace ran his large hand over his shaved head as he turned and reached for some crackers. "Hell, no." Then he grinned out of the corner of his mouth and glanced at them sideways. "He's not *enough* of one to get with this." Trace waved his hand down his body then turned and shook his ass side-to-side twice before leaving them in his wake to take up residence on the couch.

Micah and Sam laughed as he went.

"Trace, my man, you have no idea how much of a man I can be!" Micah called after him then kissed Sam on the cheek and grabbed one of the other bowls of chili.

"Yeah, yeah." Trace waved his spoon over his head without turning around, and then propped his feet up on the ottoman. "Shut up, you braggart, the game's about to start."

Micah caught Sam's eye then trailed his gaze down to her ass as he ran his hand over her behind. "No panty lines." He kept his voice quiet and popped his eyebrows at her.

"I told you I wasn't going to wear any," she whispered.

"Mmm, I like it." He leaned in and nibbled her earlobe.

"Stop." She giggled and tried to pull away, but he clutched her and pulled her close. "Micah!"

He pressed his lips to her ear. "You were serious then? You want me to fuck you out here later?"

She looked up at him through her lashes and bit her bottom lip, obviously aroused and a little surprised at his use of the f-word. Not that she should be surprised. He said fuck all the time. But when it came to what they did together, they usually referred to it as making love. Somehow, though, making love didn't sound right for what she apparently wanted him to do to her, because hadn't she herself referred to it as fucking instead of making love earlier when they were playing.

After a moment's hesitation, she grinned and nodded. "Yes."

"Why, Miss Garrett, I do like how you think."

"Why, thank you, Mr. Black."

He gave her ass a gentle squeeze then grabbed two beers and led her to the living room.

"Here you go." He held the beers out to Trace for him to take one.

"Awe, you do care." Trace grabbed one and set it on a coaster.

"Only a little, but don't tell anyone." Micah sat down on the sectional and dug into his chili as Sam settled in next to him, tucking her feet under her.

Trace glanced over at her. "This is fucking awesome, Sam." He pointed his spoon at his bowl, which was half empty already. "I want the recipe."

"You cook?" Sam took a drink of her beer then set it down next to Micah's.

"Sometimes. Surprised?"

"Surprised you're talking when you were the one who told me to shut up," Micah said, throwing him an amused glance.

"Eat me." Trace shoved a spoonful of chili in his mouth.

"I don't do dark meat, bro."

"Micah!" Sam smacked his arm.

He flinched and laughed.

Trace chuckled and grabbed his crotch. "I've got your dark meat right here, brother."

Micah grinned and shook his head. "Hey now, don't be fondling yourself like that in front of my girl. You'll give her ideas." He winked at Sam as she turned and gasped at him.

"I reckon it's too late for that already, isn't it?" Trace countered. "After all, she's been hanging with you for the past week."

"Yeah, but I don't like competition."

Trace chuckled. "You worried she might like my dark meat better than your pasty white ass?"

"I'm not pasty white."

"Denial much?"

"Fuck no. And maybe you need to look in the mirror, Trace." Micah waved his spoon up and down, aiming it at Trace. "You're not as dark as all that."

Fact was he wasn't sure what Trace's lineage was. He didn't look African American, and he didn't look Caucasian. His skin was darker, but his pale-green eyes, thin lips, and narrow nose left him racially ambiguous. Was he Cuban?

He'd heard that Trace's mom had been a Jamaican witch, but that didn't sound right. His look was more Cuban than Jamaican. Then again, maybe his father had been Caucasian, which would make sense since his father had given him his vampire blood and Trace's human side had come from his mom.

Any way Micah sliced it, Trace was an enigma. A melting pot of physical traits from multiple cultures. At least, that's how he appeared.

Sam shook her head and stirred her chili. "I swear you two are like adolescents."

Micah leaned over and kissed her cheek. "We're as horny as adolescents, too. You'd better watch out."

Trace chuffed. "As if you'd even let me get close to her, Micah." He took a bite and chased it with a swig of beer. "I'd probably lose an arm or my head if you even caught me looking at Sam like that. Not that I would, but I'm just sayin'."

A visual of Trace and Sam together popped unbidden into Micah's mind. Dark against pale. His friend and his mate.

And fucking sexy as hell.

Whoa.

That wasn't the reaction a mated male was supposed to have to the thought of another male touching his mate.

Perplexed, he glanced at Trace then Sam before dashing his gaze into his bowl of chili. Why did the idea of Trace and Sam together turn him on instead of piss him off?

He looked back up and caught Trace's eye for just a second before glancing toward the flat screen. But his mind couldn't register what was going on in the game. It was too busy freaking out.

If anyone other than Trace had made such a comment about looking at Sam lustfully, Micah already would have been up and off the love seat, beating the holy living shit out of him. Everyone knew you didn't even joke about such a thing. Male vampires didn't take to their mates being looked at, touched, or coveted by other males. Yet Micah was not only cool as a cucumber about the whole situation, he was hot in the crotch at the thought of Trace and Sam together.

This was a first.

Trace frowned curiously at him. "What? No snappy comeback there, stallion?"

Micah looked at Sam, who grinned as she ate another bite of chili. Then he turned back toward Trace. "Not this time, bro."

Trace's frown deepened, and Micah buried his gaze in his bowl of chili as if he'd find some answers in there. All he found was culinary bliss.

What had just happened here? Was this part of what he felt between him and Trace? Was this part of the inevitable collision course they were on with one another, showing itself in his willingness to accept Trace in every aspect of his life, even where Sam was concerned? If so, what did it mean?

Micah turned his attention back to the game and ate. He had a feeling that all would reveal itself soon enough. And when it did, their lives would change forever. He only hoped it was for the better. Micah couldn't take another dose of bad news after what he had just been through. Sam and Trace were the two people he cared about most in the world, and he refused to lose either of them.

CHAPTER 6

AT HALFTIME, Sam excused herself to clean up the kitchen and put away the leftovers. She knew Trace would want to take some home with him, so she pulled two bowls of Tupperware from the cabinet. One for him, and one for her and Micah.

Speak of the devil, Micah entered the kitchen. His hooded gaze told her all she needed to know about what he was thinking.

"Hey you," she said as he stepped up behind her and corralled her within his arms, pressing his hands against the counter on either side of her.

"Hi." He nudged against her backside, his semi-erection caressing her ass.

Sam leaned back against him. "Is your *calling* calling?"

He nodded and kissed her neck. "It definitely has my number."

"It won't let you hang up, is that it?" She ran her hands down his arms.

"Nope. Damn fucker just keeps calling me back."

She sucked her tongue to make a mock sympathetic noise. "That's too bad. We have a whole second half to watch."

He pushed his groin against her ass and groaned quietly. "No halftime entertainment then?"

From what he had told her, she knew if he didn't succumb to his *calling* within a certain amount of time, he would have to endure increasing discomfort until he did. "Only if you can't wait."

He nuzzled her neck and nibbled. "I can wait. It will make

it that much better when I get to have you again."

"Do I stand a chance?" She turned and met his gaze, grinning.

He shook his head. "None."

In other words, as soon as he was able, he was going to be on her and in her in every way imaginable.

His lips meshed with hers, and he ground his erection against her one last time before pulling back and grabbing two more beers. With a quick adjustment between his legs, he flashed his sexy smile and left the kitchen.

"About time, asshole," Trace said.

Sam peeked through the entrance to the kitchen to see Trace reaching for a beer.

"Sorry," Micah said. "I got sidetracked."

"Uh-huh. I know what's got you sidetracked."

Sam smiled to herself as she listened to them trade jabs while dividing the chili between the two Tupperware containers.

"You take a mate, and then let's see how much smack you talk." Micah sat down as Sam shut off the light in the kitchen and re-joined them on the sectional.

"You know, I don't have to be here," Trace said gently, his tone humble and compassionate.

"Hey, Trace, I'm just kidding around. I didn't mean anything by it." Micah leaned forward and playfully punched Trace's arm.

"Yeah, Trace," Sam said. "It's okay. We want you here."

Something in the way Trace's gaze danced down modestly then shone with affection when he glanced back up made him look sad. Or maybe gracious was a better word. He just seemed moved by her words. As if he wasn't used to people wanting him around.

"That's not exactly what I meant." Trace ran his fingers around the label of his bottle of beer. His face appeared flushed. "I just meant that I know what's going on. I know you're in your *calling*, Micah." He paused. "I was actually surprised you still wanted me to come over tonight. I figured you two wanted to be alone."

Micah leaned back and put his arm around Sam, kicking his feet up on the ottoman. "It's not so bad now, Trace. Just be thankful we didn't have you over the first couple days. You might have gotten caught in the crossfire."

Sam was surprised at how normal it felt to be talking about such a personal subject with Trace. Maybe it was because he was a vampire, too, and to them, talking about what happened during a *calling* phase wasn't such a big deal.

"You know," Trace said, looking up at them. "I envy you two."

She leaned in toward Micah, feeling shy all of a sudden.

"Why?" Micah gave her his beer after taking a sip.

Trace shrugged. "Because you have each other." He looked down at his beer. "I've always wanted a mate. I'm not sure it's ever going to happen for me, though." He paused then lifted his head. "What's it like being mated?"

Sam glanced up at Micah as he turned toward her, his eyes reverent and full of adoration.

"It's the best feeling in the world, Trace." He took a deep breath as if he were breathing in her very soul as he held her gaze. "She's more important than anything else. She's my breath, my heart, my soul, my better half. I couldn't live without her."

"Jesus," Trace said with a soft chuckle as he shifted on the couch. "I can't believe you're the same person I knew only a few weeks ago. Holy fuck. You've gone from being a hard-ass son-of-a-bitch to Chaucer."

Sam pressed her hand against Micah's chest and felt his heart beating as he inhaled long and deep again. "Trace, someday you'll know what I mean. Someday, you'll take a mate and then you'll be fucking Chaucer. You'll see." He lowered his voice and smiled at her. "You smell like lilacs."

"You do," Trace said, confirming Micah's statement as he lifted his beer for a swig.

Sam glanced over and laughed as Trace shot her a sideways glance.

"Seriously, you do." Trace lowered the bottle. "It's nice."

Micah purred quietly, sounding perfectly content. "Are

you sniffing my girl, Trace?"

Trace shook his head dramatically and grinned. "Wouldn't think of it."

"Uh-huh." Micah threw a pretzel at him and chuckled before sinking back on the couch and pulling her down with him. "But he's right," he said to her. "It *is* nice."

"Must be my shower soap." She laid her head on his shoulder.

Micah kissed her hair. "Or maybe it's just you."

Trace picked up the pretzel and ate it.

CHAPTER 7

THE GAME ENDED and they watched the post-game, then the news, then a movie, and before long it was almost four o'clock in the morning.

"Well, I should be getting home." Trace slapped his hands on his thighs and stretched as he stood.

Sam was still lying on Micah, listening to his heart beating hard and fast in his chest. The *calling* was pushing him to the brink, and she could feel it. Heat practically poured out of his body, both physical heat and hormonal heat, and she was nearly delirious with arousal, especially with his hard-on pressing against her thigh.

Micah rolled his head to toward Trace as he pointed to the window. An ice and snow mix was coming down hard and fast and had been for several hours, the ice crystals blowing against the windows on violent gusts. "Um, no dude. Look outside. We already agreed, you're staying here."

"I'm a big boy." Trace looked down at him. "I'll be fine. Besides, you two need to be alone."

Clearly, Trace could sense Micah's state as well as she could.

"Like hell." Micah's voice broke as he spoke. "We'll be fine. You can take the spare room."

Trace was about to object, but Micah cut him off. "Don't push me, Trace. I'm not letting you leave. And that's final. Spare room." He pointed. "Take it. We already put fresh sheets on the bed for you."

Sam forced herself to sit up, and she grabbed the remote and turned off the TV before getting off the couch and stretching out the kinks from lying on Micah for so long.

Then she walked over and gave Trace a loose hug and kissed his cheek.

"Good night, Trace."

Decision. Final. Trace was spending the day here.

"Come on, Micah. Time for bed." She held her hand out to him.

He sat up, his erection evident in his sweats. No use trying to hide it, right? Not like Trace didn't already know what was going down, anyway.

"Okay. Fine." Trace sighed. "I'll stay."

Micah took Sam's hand, and Trace gave them a simple wave before yawning and turning to follow them down the hall.

"Good night, you two. Don't do anything I wouldn't do." Trace opened the door to the spare room.

"Oh, we won't," Micah said.

"Yeah, that's what I'm afraid of." Trace closed the door, leaving Sam alone with Micah.

She grinned at him and quickly ducked into the bedroom as he followed and shut the door. He was on her in a heartbeat, his hands shoving her sweatshirt up and off as she gave in to him.

He pushed her sweats down, revealing her nudity. "Do you still want—?"

"Yes." She grabbed two handfuls of his hair and blistered his mouth with hers.

"Fuck!" He pushed her backward, re-engaging the lip lock, backing her into the wall.

Her body was a sunrise of desire, a glow breaking through her as the sun breaks the horizon each day, casting light and warmth over the earth. Every cell in her body called for him, and she knew it was because every cell in his was calling to her. She was beginning to understand the essence of the *calling*. This was it. His body called, and hers answered. What a magical, wondrous feeling this was.

Together, they worked him out of his clothes and he lifted her up so she could wrap her legs around him.

"Sssshhh." She smiled at what they were about to do as he

carried her to the bedroom door.

Quiet as a mouse, he opened the door and carried her past Trace's room and back into the living room as she rode herself up and down the hard column of flesh pressed against his stomach.

"Female, you're going to be my undoing," he said quietly as he sat down on the couch and situated himself beneath her.

"Mmm, well, I'll be sure to put you back together again when I'm through." She lifted herself up, eager to feel him inside her again to quench this fire of hormonal heat baking her core like a kiln.

Impaling herself on him, they both expelled their breath on quiet moans. Yes, this was what they had both needed for the past six hours. Now he was where he belonged. Inside her, locking into the place reserved only for him now. Micah was her mate as much as she was his. She felt the way her body responded to his. If she were a vampire, she was sure she would have formed the same biological link to him that other female vampires formed to their men—males, whatever. Gah! She needed to remember, Micah was not a man. He was pure male. One hundred percent animalistic male vampire.

"Yes I am, and I claim you, Samantha."

She bit her lip, locking her fingers behind his neck as she rode him, rocking against him, up and down, forward and back, needing to feel his release as much as her own.

"Not if I claim you first," she said, keeping her voice quiet.

"Oh, baby, you have no idea how I want that."

"Ssshhh." She grinned and glanced toward the hall.

Trace was only just a short distance away. At any moment, he could come out for a glass of water or a snack and catch them in the act.

"It excites you." Micah bucked up against her, gripping her hips and pulling her down hard as he rose to meet her body with his.

She saw stars and gasped. "What does?"

"The thought of being caught." He did it again, slamming into her, making her fight to keep from crying out.

"Yes," she whispered breathlessly. "It does."

"Mmm." With renewed energy, he fucked her hard, making her bounce with every rapid thrust of his hips. "It does me, too."

TRACE COULDN'T BELIEVE WHAT HE WAS HEARING. Lying in bed, wearing only his boxers, he wasn't imagining the obvious sounds of sex coming from the living room.

He closed his eyes and rolled his head back, trying to ignore them, but he couldn't.

Micah had what he so desperately wanted. A mate. And Sam was perfect, so perfect for him.

Trace wanted a mate like Sam. A female who would know how to turn him on and turn him off as needed. Someone who could control his intense power when it grew out of control and threatened to consume him. A mate who was made expressly for him.

He feared he would never find such a female. As the enigma and freak of nature he was, Trace didn't think God could create one being who could fit everything he needed, if God was indeed in charge of such things. Which he wasn't entirely sure He was. What God would allow someone like Trace to be created in the first place?

One with a sense of humor, that's for sure.

Trace had been with both males and females in the past, depending on the Dom who could arouse his interest enough in that way, but none of them had provided everything he needed. They gave him the pain, but not the understanding, and certainly not the love.

Was it possible that Fate intended a male for him? Trace didn't think so. For some reason, he knew that if he ever took a mate, it would be a female. He was too drawn to the feminine to mate a male.

Which made it even more unlikely that he would find a mate, because what female could dish out the pain and degradation he needed to keep his power at bay while supplying the purely feminine energy he craved? What he needed physically and psychologically wasn't something most females could provide.

When he had discovered Micah years ago and learned of his reputation in the BDSM community, he hadn't been interested in sex with the guy. He had wanted what Micah could give him in the scene. Trace saw in Micah someone who could control the beast that loomed inside him and threatened to consume him every day.

Ever since losing his brother, who had been his sense of balance, Trace had been off-kilter. He no longer had a countermeasure to even him out. That had been what his brother had provided, and he had lost that long ago. And now Trace's power grew stronger and darker and harder to control every day. The only thing that collared it was submission. When Trace submitted to pain and humiliation, his power diminished to the point he could actually feel free for a while. But then his power would slowly creep back in after the scene was over, which meant he had to be vigilant against it twenty-four-seven. Consequently, the only time he could harden sexually was during a scene.

Well, wait a minute.

Trace looked down to find a semi-tent in his boxers.

What the hell?

He couldn't remember the last time he had gotten hard outside his Dom's dungeon. And yet, he was suddenly aroused.

His sorrow over not having a mate had been enough to push back his power, and being subjected to Micah and Sam taking pleasure in each other had added to the mental beating. Their love and closeness made him ache for companionship he didn't think he would ever have, and that, combined with his sorrow, had shoved his power into the shadows so his body could awaken.

If just hearing them was enough to send his power into time-out, what would watching them do? Could it give him just enough of a fix to sustain him a little longer before he required another visit to his Dom? If so, he needed to use it, because his power was growing harder to control. Anything that helped him maintain control was fair game in his arsenal.

Trace sat up and looked at the door then swung his legs over the side of the bed. Was he really considering playing Peeping Tom on Micah and Sam? He rubbed his palm over his shaved scalp and took a deep breath.

He had to know. He needed to know if watching them have sex could give him a reprieve from his cursed power. But he couldn't let Micah catch him. To look upon Sam like that could mean his death. The two of them had joked earlier, but when it came right down to it, Micah surely wouldn't tolerate Trace staring at her naked, with a giant hard-on to boot.

Fuck. Damned if I do, damned if I don't.

Trace took a deep breath and blew it out as he stood, and then he made the short walk to the door and carefully opened it. He couldn't even breathe, he was so nervous. And yet, something drove him onward. Hope that he'd found another weapon against his beast.

After entering the hall, Trace quietly followed the sounds of their muffled grunts and gentle, rhythmic gasps. A soft cadence of slapping flesh beckoned him forward, and his cock kicked to full mast as he thought about the two people dearest to him making love in the way of true mates.

He kept to the shadows, using his power to partially cloak himself, which wasn't hard to do in the dark hour before dawn. The blinds and drapes hadn't even closed over the windows, yet, and no lights were on in the apartment. Only the lights from the city, brightened by the snow, illuminated the room.

And then he saw them.

On the couch.

Their coupled forms faced each other, and their bodies moved in perfect synchronization. Sam was on top, her hands pressed against the back of the couch on either side of Micah's head. Her body churned and bounced aggressively as Micah took her hard from the bottom. She faced Trace, but her eyes were closed. Her face was the picture of bliss with her bottom lip dropped open as she breathed heavily. Her breasts were small but buoyant, and they jiggled with the urgency of Micah's thrusts.

Trace pressed his back against the wall and gaped at them, his cock straining.

The two of them together were beautiful. So in love. What did it feel like to love someone like that? And to be loved the same way in return? To want someone so badly you didn't care about anything else?

Micah suddenly changed tempo, slowing down, breathing hard. Sam's eyelids opened halfway as she smiled at him and rotated her hips around and around.

Trace hardly dared make a sound for fear of being discovered. Because then they might stop. And he didn't want them to stop.

The air smelled of sex and lilacs mixed with Micah. Sweet and sultry. Heavenly.

Then it happened. Sam's gaze lifted and caught his. He froze, unable to turn away, unable to move, and unable to speak. He barely even breathed.

Almost immediately, Sam's body seized and shuddered as she fell into orgasm. Her eyes rolled back as her body collapsed forward against Micah, her breathing erratic and choked as she wrapped her arms around Micah's head and held his face against her chest before opening her eyes and staring right into Trace's once more. Then she came again, gasping, but not looking away from him.

Oh fuck! Fuck! He was dead. Micah was going to kill him.

HE'S WATCHING US. *Trace is standing in the hall watching us.*

Micah heard Sam's thoughts as clearly as if she'd spoken them, and he grinned against her breast before taking her nipple in his mouth and sucking.

Now he knew why she had come so hard. Twice no less. He thought he had sensed Trace's presence, and now Sam had confirmed it.

She continued rocking against him through her second orgasm and then finally pulled away and kissed him, her gaze still averted toward the hallway.

His little Sam wanted to put on a show, did she? Well, Micah was more than game for that.

Pushing her away, he stood up, jumped around behind her, and shoved her forward against the back of the couch. He pressed in behind her and pulled her hair, jerking back her head. She moaned loudly and gripped the top of the back cushions, her fingers curling over the fabric.

"Are you my little minx, Sam? Do you like to play?" He dove his hand between her legs and clamped down.

Sam cried out and shivered, her arousal spiking. "Yes. God, yes!"

Micah looked up and caught Trace's eye. Trace looked positively besmirched, but in the way a child plays in the mud and thinks it's the greatest thing since Lego blocks and bubble wrap. Sneering, Micah thrust into Sam, pulling her back to meet him with one arm while releasing her hair and pushing her upper body forward.

She splayed against the back of the couch, her knees split wide on the cushions as he climbed up behind her and fucked her hard.

With one hand pressed against her spine, holding her down, he spanked the side of her ass with the other.

"Mine, little one. You're mine." He glanced up at Trace again, leering for effect. It made his blood boil in such an incredibly erotic way to see Trace watching him fuck Sam, but pretending to play the possessive mate intensified their three-way fire into a pending volcanic eruption.

What a fucking turn-on! Nobody else but Trace could get away with watching him fuck Sam. Nobody! But with Trace, he liked it. Sam liked it. And clearly, Trace liked it, even though all he did was stand in the shadows and watch. Trace didn't even go for the obvious erection in his boxers, but Micah wouldn't have cared if he did. Hell, it might have upped the ante even more to watch him jack off.

"Micah! Oh God, Micah!" Sam's body tightened yet again, and he could tell she was looking at Trace, too.

"That's it, baby. Come for me. Come for both of us." He met Trace's gaze again, making it clear who *both of us* meant. "Come for Trace and me, baby."

Their plan had turned out better than they had expected. Neither of them had dreamed Trace would actually come out to watch them. They had just thought it would be sexy fun to flirt with the possibility. But the reality was turning out to be hot as hell.

And Micah was about to lose control and go over with his on-fire mate.

Locking his gaze with Trace's, Micah felt his orgasm tighten his balls and coil inside his body, and then he exploded just as Sam fell into spasms again. He came so hard he practically shoved Sam over the back of the couch as he collapsed against her and pushed her forward.

Then it was over, the two of them a heap of spent flesh draped over the back of the couch, his cock still twitching inside her quivering core.

"Oh baby. Fuck." He could hardly breathe, and his hair hung over his face.

"That was...." Sam's voice trailed off.

"Fucking hot." Micah finished for her.

Micah slowly lifted his head and looked at Trace, who was still rooted in place against the wall, his chest rising and falling deeply.

Trace was clearly lost for words, probably wondering why Micah hadn't ripped his head off for looking on his mate's naked body. Fact was, something was happening among the three of them. A bond was forming, connecting them to one another at a level deeper than mere friendship, and it was happening quickly.

Micah pulled out of Sam and helped her off the couch.

She joined him and wrapped her arms loosely around his waist as she nuzzled her face against his neck and shoulder. She was still turned on. He could feel it. Hell, he could smell it. What they had just done in front of Trace had startled her and set her aflame all at once, as if she couldn't believe how hot being watched made her.

They walked arm-in-arm toward Trace, who didn't turn or retreat back to his room. Hell, he didn't even look away. It was as if he didn't realize he wasn't actually a shadow and that they could see him.

As they got closer, Micah let go of Sam and held out his arm as she ducked shyly behind him. Trace took his arm, his expression calm but wary, joining their hands together as if they were about to arm wrestle. But Micah just leaned in slightly and clapped him on the back of the shoulder with his free hand.

"Night, bro."

Trace seemed to be in a state of dismay or confusion and nodded feebly. "Night."

Micah let him go and glanced over his shoulder at Sam, who smiled bashfully at Trace before her gaze flickered away. Micah could tell her face was flushed. Apparently, the reality of their actions was dawning on her as the passion of the moment ebbed.

"Night," she said softly.

Trace's gaze darted to Micah's, and he looked almost fearful.

If Micah could read Trace's thoughts, he would probably hear a lot of *Why hasn't Micah killed me, yet?* bouncing around.

"It's okay, Trace. Don't ask me why or how, but I don't mind if you look at her." He paused and shook his head in disbelief before huffing out a burst of laughter. "Fuck, but I don't even think I'd mind if you touched her." The notion was just as shocking to him as the look on Trace's face.

Sam's hand slid around his waist, but she remained silently hidden behind his body.

"I don't know what to say," Trace said, fidgeting.

"I know." Micah looked down, an odd sense of comfort and contentment coming over him. "If you were anyone else, Trace, you'd already be dead for laying eyes on her."

Trace fidgeted again and Sam's grip tightened.

"But..." Micah looked up. "I don't mind with you. I can't explain why, but I don't. All I know is that what just happened was very exciting. For both of us." He bobbed his head toward Sam.

Trace's eyes darted to his in surprise. They stared at each for a long moment. Then Trace said, "What are you saying?"

Micah looked back at Sam, who was still grinning, then turned back to Trace. "I think what I'm saying is that Sam and I wouldn't mind having you spend your days with us more often. Right, Sam?"

She nodded bashfully. "Yes. I'd like that." She squirmed and her slender fingers curled so that her nails scratched Micah's stomach.

Trace glanced back and forth between them, his expression making it clear he wasn't sure if he had heard them right.

"Would you like that, Trace?" Micah's eyes narrowed. Would Trace agree to do again what they'd all just done, or had this been a one-time act of spontaneity he didn't want to repeat?

After considering Micah's question, Trace finally lifted his chin and cleared his throat. "Okay, yeah. Sure."

Trace's tone indicated to Micah that he was more interested than his lackadaisical demeanor implied. Trace was just as hot for an encore as Micah and Sam were. Maybe even hotter.

"Well then. That's settled." Micah turned away and pulled Sam in front of him to protect her sudden modesty. "Good night, Trace."

Trace didn't immediately respond and Micah looked over his shoulder. His friend looked positively stymied, staring at the floor.

"Trace?"

Trace looked up. "What? Oh…yeah. Good night."

Despite Trace's befuddled expression, one thing was clear. Whatever had just happened among the three of them was a good thing. A very good thing. And Micah got the feeling it was another piece of the puzzle he was slowly putting together about mysterious Traceon.

CHAPTER 8

TRACE STOOD IN THE HALL for at least two minutes after Micah closed his bedroom door.

He was still alive. Micah hadn't killed him. In fact, it seemed as though Micah had actually approved. Had he somehow slipped into Micah's inner circle without knowing it? Did Micah even *have* an inner circle?

Seems he did now. And Trace had just been inducted.

In all the time Trace had known Micah, he had never seen that male be anything but a hard-ass to everybody. The Lone Ranger, some called him, because he was supremely independent and followed no one's rules but his own. The guy didn't *do* friends. Yet, suddenly, that's exactly how Trace felt: like Micah's friend.

Well, maybe more than friends. Because if Trace wasn't mistaken, Micah had just invited Trace to watch him and Sam have sex again. As in, he had kind of sounded like he wanted this scene they'd just played out to become a regular thing. And Sam seemed to want that, as well.

Trace swallowed hard and leaned his head back against the wall. Because, yeah, he wanted it, too. And so did his dick. And his inner beast, which was all kinds of mellow right now. Could this be part of the solution to controlling his inner beast without succumbing to total submission as frequently as he had been?

He looked down at his erection and breathed out a soft snort. He needed to take advantage of the moment before his power raised its hackles and got all bristly again.

No sense letting all this wood go to waste.

Turning on his heel, he went back into the spare room, closed the door, and got ready for a little personal time.

CHAPTER 9

SAM QUICKLY CLEANED UP IN THE BATHROOM then joined Micah. He was already in bed and held the covers open for her. She climbed in next to him, and his arm slid around her, pulling her close as he settled onto his back.

"What just happened out there?" She caressed his chest and stomach as she rested her chin on his shoulder.

The look in his eyes was absolutely stunning. Content, yet wanton. Sublime, yet humble. His lips twitched into a whimsical grin.

"What do you mean? We had fucking great sex."

He truly was incorrigible.

"Well, yes, but that's not what I'm talking about."

"Oh, you mean with Trace?" His eyes twinkled. Of course he knew that's what she meant.

"Well, yeah. I mean, hell, Micah. I've only known you a short time, but even I already know that if another guy even so much as looked at me, you'd kill him." She searched his face, but he gave nothing away in his expression. "Trace just saw me naked. He watched us having sex." She smiled sweetly. "And you didn't lay a hand on him."

Micah kept his gaze on hers for several seconds then shifted and stared up at the ceiling as he took a deep breath. Sam couldn't be positive, but it sure seemed as though Micah was as perplexed as she was over the events of the past half-hour.

"I don't know," he said, "but there's something different about Trace." Micah rolled his head back toward her on the pillow. "I don't feel threatened by him. I know that sounds odd, but I actually *liked* it."

The way Micah's brow furrowed as he said it emphasized just how strange all this was even for him.

"You liked it?" Sam lifted herself on her elbow, inspecting him more closely.

"Yes." He smirked. "Well, no. I didn't just like it. I fucking got off on it big time, if I'm being honest." He seemed to be on the tip of some revelation. "Didn't you?"

Sam bit her lip. "Well...yes. It was surprisingly exciting."

Micah turned onto his side and faced her. "Would you do it again?"

Hadn't they hinted as much to Trace in the hallway?

She nodded. "Absolutely."

This was so weird for her. She had spent a year dancing at the Black Garter, hating every minute of it. She'd had to wear those masks and fall into a role just to be able to get up on stage every night and take her clothes off for those perverted men. And yet the moment she had seen Trace standing in the hall watching her having sex with Micah, the most amazing decadent arousal flashed through her, making her come almost instantly.

She had enjoyed the exhibitionism of being seen in such an intimate, lascivious moment. And when she looked up and saw him enthralled with the orgasm she'd just had, she came undone a second time. In a blink, seeing him watching her had spiked lust deep at the heart of her. She had no interest in fucking Trace, but damn if she didn't want to put on a sex show for him, with Micah as her co-star. But she couldn't make any sense out of her feelings.

"I can hear what you're thinking," Micah said.

"I figured." She smiled, getting used to his mind-probe nature. "Do you have any answers?"

"You mean, why would you hate dancing for a room full of men and yet find having sex for Trace so exciting?"

She nodded.

Micah cleared his throat and sighed heavily. "I'm not sure. Maybe you're a closet exhibitionist."

"But then why would I hate dancing?"

"Was it the dancing you hated? Or the perverted men and the looks they gave you?"

Sam thought about that a moment. She did enjoy dancing. When she had first discovered exotic dancing when she was eighteen, she had really liked it. It excited her. But, little-by-little, it began to lose its charm because the men creeped her out. Some of them scared her. Those who did looked at her as if they wanted to do horrible, nasty things to her. She remembered leaving the club every night feeling as though one of those guys, or even a group of them, would attack and rape her. So, yeah, it wasn't the dancing she had hated.

"It was the men," she said.

She could see by the look on Micah's face that he had been following along in her head as she came to her conclusion.

He nodded. "So what makes Trace different, baby?" He caressed the backs of his fingers over her cheek.

She recalled the look on Trace's face. He had been aroused, yes, but he hadn't been lewd. In fact, Trace had looked more enthralled, maybe even a little scared, but certainly grateful, as if she and Micah had given him a gift. For Trace, what had happened hadn't been about lust. It had been about something else. Relief, gratitude, something Sam couldn't put her finger on. But a measure of surprise had shown in Trace's eyes as he'd watched them, as if he was learning something new about himself the same way she was learning something new about herself.

The way he had behaved afterward, so sweetly and platonically, also impressed Sam. She'd been naked, and yet Trace hadn't gawked at her nudity, despite his obvious erection. He behaved respectfully. Maybe even somewhat apologetic.

Sam's gaze met Micah's, and he grinned knowingly.

"That's why he's different, Micah. Because...well, because he *is* different."

"I know." He tenderly brushed her short, blond hair off her forehead. "I don't think Trace has had many lovers, if any at all. I'm beginning to think this power of his has robbed him of something he desperately wants."

"I wish you could see inside his head." Sam sighed sadly. She liked Trace. A lot. Between Micah and Trace, she felt like the safest person on the planet. These two seemed ready to live and die to save her life.

"Me, too," Micah said. "If I could see Trace's thoughts, I could know better how to help him." He hesitated. "And I get the feeling somehow that I'm supposed to. Help him, that is."

"What do you mean?"

He laid his hand over hers on the short span of mattress separating them, weaving their fingers together.

"I'm not sure," he said, frowning subtly. "But I feel like he found me for a reason. Like he needs me or something."

Sam didn't know what to say to that. What could Trace possibly need from Micah?

"I don't know," he said, reading her thoughts.

They lay staring at each other for a couple of minutes, and then the blinds and drapes kicked on and began to close over the windows.

"Here comes the daylight," he said, smiling.

"Yep." Her eyes adjusted to the darkness as the small night light plugged into the bathroom socket cast a faint glow into the bedroom.

Daylight. Something Micah had never known.

"Oh no. I knew it as a child," he said.

Sam's eyebrows popped with surprise. Micah had been a child?

He laughed. Just threw his head back and laughed. "Of course I was child. Where do you think vampires come from? Didn't I already tell you we have babies?" He placed his hand over Sam's stomach and gently pushed her to her back, rising up on his elbow, looking down at her.

He kept his hand on her belly, almost as if he were trying to feel a tiny life moving inside of her. As if he wanted more than anything to feel that.

"I just can't imagine you as a child, Micah." She smiled up at him and brushed his long hair out of his face before tucking it behind his ear.

He leaned his head into her hand and briefly closed his eyes.

"Well, I was. A long time ago."

"How long?" He still hadn't told her his age.

"I can't remember exactly, but over a thousand years."

She gasped.

"Don't look so surprised," he said.

Still holding his face in her palm, she made an appraising sound that embedded deep in her throat. "You look good for a thousand-year-old man."

"Male."

"Whatever."

He laughed. "And I'm older than that, I just can't remember exactly. You know, you kinda stop counting at a certain age."

Sam shook her head. "Well, can you take a guess?"

Micah blinked appeasingly. "It's just driving you crazy not knowing how old I am, isn't it?"

"I'm just curious is all." She patiently caressed his cheek with the pad of her thumb.

He took a deep breath and appeared to be thinking back over his life, adding up the years in his head. Finally, he said, "It was after the collapse of Rome in 410, I know that much. Drecks hid inside barbarian hordes and attacked vampire villages." Micah seemed lost in thought for a moment then smiled at her. "Let's call it fifteen hundred years."

Sam planted a sweet kiss on his lips. "Well, like I said, you look good for being an old fart."

"What can I say, I age well." He kissed her back.

"*Very* well. I daresay you're the best looking fifteen hundred-year-old man I've ever seen."

Micah rolled his eyes. "As if you've seen many."

"Hey, how do you know?"

He tapped her temple. "Because I can see all, remember?"

"Not if you're staying out of my memories, as you promised you would." She raised an eyebrow at him, challenging him.

"Difficult female." He bent down and kissed her neck.

"Incorrigible male."

"Touché." He left a trail of nectar bites down the side of her neck to her shoulder.

"What kind of child were you, anyway?" She wrapped one arm around him as he nibbled away and slid one of his long, powerful legs between hers.

"Rowdy."

She giggled. "Why do I sooo believe that?"

"Because it's true."

"Seriously, what else. If I'm going to have your children someday, I want to know what to expect."

The mention of children practically melted Micah against her as he snuggled even closer and rubbed her stomach. She had to admit, she loved this *calling* thing and how affectionate it made him. He was so attentive and reverent toward her body.

"I was an active child," he said. "Curious about everything."

"How did your parents raise you if they were vampires and you could go out in the sun?" She turned her face into his and kissed the side of his mouth.

"We had human caretakers. The humans raised us during the day. Our parents raised us at night."

"Us?"

"The children of the clan."

"Oh. Do you have brothers and sisters?"

He shook his head. "Only child."

"So humans cared for you?"

"Only during the day." He settled in closer against her, his hand skimming up the side of her body.

"Are your parents still alive?" She dreaded the answer to the question.

"No." He laid his cheek on her shoulder.

"What happened?"

"The war. Drecks killed them."

"I'm sorry." Sam kissed his forehead as he looked up at her.

"It's okay. I grieved for them a long time ago. I've accepted what happened."

"Still, it must be hard. Do you have any family left?"

"I'm not sure. My father had a brother, my Uncle Rory, but I haven't seen him in centuries. We lost touch after…well, after everything happened."

She could only assume he was referring to the death of his first mate, Katarina. From what little he had told her, Sam knew that Micah's life had fallen into despair after Katarina's death, and he hadn't fully recovered until she had come along.

What a life Micah had lived. She couldn't imagine what it must have been like for him growing up. Hell, what did kids do for fun in the Middle Ages? She didn't even know.

"What kind of games did you play as a child?"

Micah laughed, and she felt the low rumble through her rib cage, right into her heart.

"You'd be amazed at how active we were." He propped his chin on her chest and the whiskers from his new goatee tickled her skin. "We played all kinds of games and got into all kinds of trouble."

"Really now?"

He nodded, making her giggle as his soft whiskers teased her.

"I got very good at Chess, and while I prefer knives and guns today, my archery skills were the best of anyone in my clan. At the age of twelve, I was doing most of the hunting." He gave her a look that indicated she should be impressed.

She was.

With a quirky smile, he continued. "We played hide-and-seek, dice games, card games…we wrestled and had foot races. And we learned how to fight and protect ourselves."

"When did you get to the point where you couldn't go out into the sun, anymore?"

Micah settled in beside her again and pulled her back so he was spooning her, both of them on their sides facing the heavily draped windows.

"I started becoming sensitive to the sun in my early twenties. By the time I was in my late twenties, when I went through the change to an adult, I couldn't endure it, anymore."

"Do you miss it?"

"I did at first. But now…" he paused. "I'm used to it."

"I'm not sure I could ever get used to being without the

sun." She played her fingertips up and down Micah's forearm. "I enjoy it too much."

"I don't want you to ever be without something you enjoy." Micah's breath warmed the nape of her neck then he kissed it.

"You do take good care of me, don't you?"

"I plan on it, Mrs. Black."

She felt him smile against her skin as if he was waiting for her reaction.

"Um...we've discussed this," she said.

"Yes, we have, and you know you're mine, so why can't I call you Mrs. Black?"

"You know why." She shook her head, amused. Incorrigible should be his nickname.

He chuckled. "But you love me this way."

"You're pushing your luck." She playfully smacked his arm.

Micah's laughter made her smile. Damn, but she loved his laugh. So rich and deep. How sad that he hadn't laughed for so long before she came along. The world had been robbed of a sound more precious than birds singing.

"You flatter me, Miss Garrett."

"That's better," she said. "And it's not flattery. It's true. You really do have a wonderful laugh, but then I'm repeating myself, aren't I?"

His arms tightened around her. "Yes, but I love it. And I love laughing for you."

"Why, thank you, Mr. Black."

He squeezed her as he nuzzled closer, getting more comfortable as drowsiness began to settle over them both. She knew he would awake her in only a few hours, when the *calling* reared its head again and demanded he make another deposit in her infertile-for-now womb, but for the moment, she was still awake enough to broach one more topic.

"Are you going to talk to me about the room in your basement, Micah?"

He tensed only briefly then relaxed again. "What do you want to know?"

Loaded question. She wanted to know everything. How long had he been into BDSM? What did he do with all that equipment? Did he want to use it on her? Who else did he use it with? Was it purely about sex? Did he want to get back into BDSM with more people than just her? Would he teach her?

His arms tightened around her. "About sixty years, whatever I want, yes, nobody, no, maybe, yes."

"Huh?" Had he really just answered all her questions?

"Do I need to take it slower for you, love?"

With a nod, she rolled her eyes and smiled. "Yes, that would be good."

His lips pressed against the back of her shoulder. "Okay." He kissed her again. "Here's the deal. I got into the lifestyle about sixty years ago. Seems I had a knack for it, and I built up quite a reputation in the community, which was mostly underground then. You didn't really hear much about BDSM in open circles in the 1950s. Honestly, though, I had always gotten a bit of a sexual thrill by spanking and binding my partners. Diving into BDSM just took my interests to another level."

Sam wasn't sure she wanted to hear about his other partners.

"Hey," he said. "I'm not with them, anymore. I'm with you, Sam. Now and forever. You're it for me, okay?"

She knew it was stupid to be jealous of those Micah had been with before she had even been born, but she couldn't help herself. Micah belonged to her now, and damn anyone else.

"I feel the same way, Sam. Believe me. I hate thinking about Steve or any of the men you've been with before me. But that's the past." He snuggled against her and kissed her neck. "We're together now. I don't want anyone else but you."

In a way, it was nice being able to talk to Micah without having to speak. He saw inside her thoughts and immediately addressed her concerns. Talk about an open line of communication.

"I don't want anyone else but you, either," she said. "So, okay, go on. Give me all the gory details about your wicked past." She huffed and resigned herself to the reality that a fifteen-hundred-year-old-male would have been with a lot of partners. Fact. Of. Life. Not much she could do about it being that her parents' parents' parents hadn't even been born, yet, when Micah had become an adult.

Micah smoothed his hand over her hip and back up to her shoulder reassuringly before going on.

"Domination started out being more about sex for me, but then I realized it wasn't so much about sex as it was about trust. That's what really drew me in. Trusting someone and having them put their trust in me. It creating an intense high and made me feel alive and important again." He paused and drew in a tender inhale. "I really enjoyed providing the pain and, more often than not, the mental torture people needed. After a while, being a Dom became less about the sex and more about helping others achieve what they needed to feel free. For some of my subs, it was the only thing that gave them sexual fulfillment, but I didn't necessarily have sex with all of them. Some of them didn't need me for that part of it."

"What about with me?" Sam couldn't help wondering why he wanted to invite her into his dungeon of dastardly deeds.

"With you it's *very* sexual." He pressed up against her and briefly cupped her breast as he nibbled her ear.

She grinned. "Oh?"

"Mm-hm. With you, I'd like to exercise the kind of Domination that would give us both a *great* deal of pleasure."

"Really now." She didn't state it as a question.

"Oh yes. Really." He purred and the vibration rumbled gently through her back.

"What other kinds of domination are there?" This was all very fascinating.

"Like I said," he flicked the tip of his warm, soft tongue against her neck, "the kind where I provide a service."

"And that's not sexual?"

"Not for me." He crowded her, obviously becoming aroused. "At least not anymore."

"But for them…your subs?"

"Sometimes," he said, his voice soft and wispy. "Well, usually yes. For my subs, it usually was sexual. Submission is the only way a lot of subs get aroused."

"And you've been out of the, um, practice of Domination for how long?"

"A few years now."

"Why do you suddenly want back in?"

His hand skimmed lower, teasing her as he purred. "You woke me up."

"Do you want to Dom others?"

"Maybe, but not sexually." His lips were pure evil on her skin. "If I worked with a partner, he or she could provide the sexual component." He nipped her shoulder and brushed his lips up the side of her neck. "I could just...." He licked her nape. "Do what I do."

She was losing her willpower to resist. As if she ever could. "And what do you do?" she asked, turning into melted butter.

"Would you like to see?"

Did she? Did she really want to see him whipping or tying up, or whatever he did, another person? And if she did, how and where? At his house? She wasn't sure she'd like that.

"No, not at my house." He pulled away and rolled her toward him until she was on her back, and then he slid on top of her, pushing her legs apart.

"Where then?" She wrapped her arms and legs around him as he glided smoothly inside her.

"There are parties." He closed his eyes to savor the moment his pubic bone met hers then opened them again and looked at her. "Scene parties. I can take you to one and show you what I do."

She wasn't sure about this. Micah spanking her was one thing. Him spanking another was something totally altogether different.

"Oh, I wouldn't be spanking anyone but you, baby." He rocked gently against her. "But it's up to you. I don't have to do it. Playing with you would be enough, but I wouldn't play as hard with you as I would with someone else. Say, a true submissive who thrives on the pain."

"Do you need that?" She tilted her hips as he pushed forward.

"I don't *need* it." His body stilled and he looked down into her eyes. "Part of me does kind of want to show off for you, though."

Why the idea of Micah turning into a cocky rooster to strut his whip-lashing feathers excited her so much, she couldn't guess. But it did.

He grinned and ground deeply into her. "You like that."

There was no hiding the truth from him as the ache in the pit of her belly softened and made her feel loose and gushy at her core. "Yes."

"I'm glad." He lowered his mouth to hers and latched onto her top lip, sucking softly before breaking away. "I want everyone at that party to know I'm with you." His body surged forward again, claiming her. "I want them all to envy you when they see what I'm capable of."

She arched an eyebrow, feeling her insides clench at his words. Was it wrong to get so hot over such egotistical possessiveness? "So sure of yourself, Mr. Black?"

"I know my reputation." He pressed her hands into the mattress and out to the sides. "I know what I'm capable of. And so do they."

"And they'll want you for it." She was going to come. Micah was going to make her come with just his words and his voice.

"And all I'll want is you."

As he said the words, he rotated his hips just once while buried deep inside her, and her orgasm unfurled. She arched off the mattress, stretching against the restraint of his hands holding down her arms, and came undone in about ten different ways.

He pumped his hips three times in rapid succession then grunted as he joined her in climax as she crashed back down against the mattress.

Slowly, he released her hands and she wrapped her arms around his back, both of them breathing hard.

"Okay," she said, gasping for air.

"Okay, what?"

"I'll go with you. To a party. I want to see."

His body shivered in victory.

CHAPTER 10

A WEEK LATER, ON FRIDAY NIGHT, two weeks after Sam had moved in with him, Micah pulled onto the long, winding driveway of northside mansion. He was driving the new midnight blue Camaro he had bought Sam. She had chosen the color, saying it reminded her of his eyes, which of course gave his ego a hefty boost.

"Here?" Sam's astonished gaze swung to his. "The party is here?"

Micah nodded. "Many in the BDSM community are quite affluent." In fact, he couldn't recall a time he'd met anyone else in the lifestyle who didn't live comfortably.

She looked back out the window at the Colonial-style home as Micah pulled around the circular driveway and came to a stop. No doubt the valet who greeted him was one of the Domme's submissives, hired for the night with the promise of his reward later.

Micah had already prepped Sam on proper etiquette. If she recognized someone from the outside world, she wasn't allowed to acknowledge them. When observing a scene, there was no talking. No pictures. No touching the equipment unless given permission. Basic rules.

"Is this Domme a vampire?" Sam stepped to Micah's side and took his hand as the valet drove the Camaro around back.

He nodded. "The one hosting the party is, but not the one who invited me."

"And you know her? The hostess?"

"Yes."

"How?"

"I've attended her parties before." He led her up the steps to the entrance.

"You've never…?"

He paused with his hand on the door. "Sam, she and I both work on the same side of the switch."

"What's that mean, exactly?"

Micah squeezed her hand. "I've never Dom'd her and she's never Dom'd me."

Sam nodded awkwardly.

"Are you sure you're okay with this?" Micah said.

With a nod, Sam pursed her lips. "Yes. I'm just nervous."

He let go of the door and pushed her to the side, up against the smooth brick of the house, before pressing into her. He caressed her cheek. "Baby, I'll be by your side the whole time. And I don't want anyone in there besides you. You know that, right?"

"Yes," she said. "It's just that I'm still getting used to this."

"Are you jealous?" He may as well get to the meat of the issue right now. He'd already seen as much in her thoughts.

She didn't answer right away.

"Sam?" He swept his fingers around the side of her face and down to her chin before gently lifting so she was forced to look into his eyes. "Are you?"

With a sheepish roll of her eyes, she nodded. "Yes. A little."

He grinned. "I thought so."

Micah kissed her softly so as not to smudge her burnished red lipstick. "Baby, you so do not have anything to be jealous of. You're my mate. My biological other half."

Her eyes softened as her plump lips twisted into a shy smile.

He ran his palm lightly down her neck, over the side of her breast, and then around to the small of her back before tugging her toward him.

"And you're just about the sexiest thing I've ever laid eyes on," he said. "Inside," he nodded toward the entrance, "I'll only have eyes for you."

Her smile widened, and she skimmed her hands up his chest. "You do say the sweetest things."

"I only speak the truth."

"And the truth is very sweet."

Micah grinned wickedly. "You ready?"

She nodded. "Okay. Yes. I'm ready."

He lifted one of her hands to his lips and kissed the back of her knuckles. "Shall we go inside then, Mrs. Black?"

She rolled her eyes at him. "Is that how you're going to introduce me in there?"

"If you want me to." He arched one eyebrow.

Her green eyes sparkled with mischief. "Just introduce me as your girlfriend, Sam *Garrett*."

Oh, someday he would convince her she was indeed Mrs. Black, but until then, he would play along. With a chuckle of surrender, he gestured toward the door.

"After you then, Miss Garrett."

"That's better."

He followed her to the front door, reached around her, pushed on the handle, then ushered her in. He hoped she wouldn't find the goings-on here tonight disturbing. Micah really wanted her to embrace his lifestyle. But if she didn't, he would give it up for her. In a heartbeat, he would give up anything she asked him to. She was his world, after all, even if she did insist on being called Miss Garrett instead of taking his name.

WHAT GREETED SAM WAS...well, pretty normal. Except for the leather-clad servers wearing studded collars around their necks and carrying trays of Hors D'oeuvres and flutes of champagne, most everyone else she saw looked relatively normal.

Micah guided her to a parlor off to the right that served as a coat check, and he helped her out of her leather coat. As he took care of getting them tickets, she glanced back toward the main room.

Most everyone was wearing black, just like she and Micah. Still, she felt self-conscious, as if everyone would be able to tell with one look that she had never been to one of these parties.

She felt like she was wearing a blinking neon sign: *Scene Party Virgin.*

She ran her fingers through her boy-short hair, nervously re-teasing the soft peaks.

When Micah's hand landed on the small of her back, she jumped then laughed at herself for being so twitchy.

"Just relax," he said, leaning in and whispering into her ear.

"Okay." She felt like such a noob.

"You look lovely, by the way."

She turned and gazed into his slightly-hooded eyes. His mouth lifted seductively at the edges.

He had helped her pick out what to wear. *Black. You have to wear black,* he had said. So, she had selected a pair of black, flair-legged slacks and stylish, black patent leather, platform pumps. He had chosen a scoop-necked, black knit blouse for her to wear. One he'd bought her a few days before. The material was so thin and fine it felt like butter between her fingers and against her skin. It had long sleeves, but even though it was warm inside the house, it wasn't uncomfortable.

The final touch to her outfit had been given to her right before they left when Micah secured a platinum choker around her neck. It was designed to look like a dog's collar, but was much too exquisite, with three onyx stones set at the front.

"So that everyone knows you're mine," he had said with a sexy smile on his face.

She wasn't sure if that was true or if he just wanted to see her in a fancy dog collar, but it was a striking piece of jewelry either way.

"Very sexy," Micah said, staying close as he directed her toward the main room. "I might get jealous myself."

"Oh? Why's that?" She tried to act like she fit in, glancing around as nonchalantly as possible.

"Because every male here will have his eyes on you."

"Well, don't hurt anyone." She plucked a flute of

champagne from a passing silver tray as the waiter nodded
and smiled at her.

Micah glared at the waiter as he continued through the
room. "I'll try to keep that in mind."

She giggled up at him as his gaze followed the server
almost threateningly.

"Down boy."

He looked back at her. "Funny. I thought that was my line."

She shook her head. He really needed to get the word
incorrigible tattooed on his forehead.

"I'll think about it," he said, reading her mind.

"So, when does everything start?" She sipped her drink as
he navigated her through a throng of people.

He checked his watch. "In about ten minutes. That's
when the doors will be locked and everyone will retreat to
the basement. That's when the action really gets underway."

She took a deep breath. It was getting a little easier being
here. No one had jumped out and pointed a finger at her,
yet, announcing that she was a BDSM scene party virgin, so
maybe she would make it through the evening unscathed.

"No one is going to point you out, baby," Micah said.

She glanced at him. He really did look good tonight. He
had chosen an Under Armor, long-sleeved, skintight shirt
that hugged his body like a second skin. She could actually
count the muscular ridges in his abdomen. His tailored
black slacks hung low on his hips, and he wore a thick, black
leather belt with a brushed silver buckle. He looked good
enough to eat. It was easy to see why a sub would want
him as his or her Dom. He looked as good as his reputation
claimed he was.

When he glanced askance at her and licked his lips, she
knew he'd heard every word of her thoughts.

She blushed.

"You sure know how to boost a guy's ego." His arm
slipped more securely around her waist.

"Don't go getting a big head about it," she quipped,
smirking with amusement and taking a drink of her
champagne.

"Wouldn't dream of it, Miss Garrett." He steered her toward the back of the house. "We should head downstairs."

She linked hands with him and let him lead her. He had warned her about what she would see. There would be naked men and women here, tied and bound and on display as they were worked over for the others in attendance. Apparently, some submissives enjoyed the public humiliation.

They were exhibitionists like she was, only different.

Micah nodded to a male dressed in leather, who nodded back.

"Do you know him?" Sam said, turning and watching the man walk away.

"Yes."

She lowered her voice. "Is he another Dom?"

"Yes."

They reached an open staircase made of brown stone, which spiraled around a circular wall. Murmuring noise and soft music echoed up from the basement, and they began the descent into what Sam could only imagine calling the Temple of Doom.

"It's not the Temple of Doom," Micah said quietly.

"I know, but I don't know what else to call it."

"Just call it the dungeon."

"The dungeon." Sam let the two syllables fall off her tongue, contemplating all that the simple word implied.

She imagined medieval wickedness, maces, iron maidens, and odd contraptions where prisoners and criminals were tied down and punished.

"That's more like it," Micah said quietly as they reached the bottom of the stairs. "But not quite as primitive." He gave her a crooked grin.

"Micah." A blonde in black leather and very red lipstick smiled and broke from a group of other leather-clad individuals and walked over.

Sam bristled, and Micah secured her more firmly to his side, his strong hand nestled against her hip.

"Mistress Diamond." Micah bowed his head in greeting. "Meet my..." he glanced at Sam, "girlfriend. Sam, this is

Mistress Diamond. She's the one who invited us."

Mistress Diamond? How apropos. Her teeth were so white they sparkled like diamonds. *Bleach much?* At least Miss D was human, which meant that with her new immortal strength, Sam could take Miss Diamond if she made a move on her man — male, whatever.

Micah cleared his throat and tightened his grip. The message was clear. *Behave!*

Sam smiled sweetly, fighting her urge to stake her claim on Micah, and held out her hand. "Hi. Nice to meet you."

"My pleasure." Mistress Diamond flashed a genuine, congenial smile, non-threatened and non-threatening. But Sam still didn't like her.

Perhaps Micah had a point with that whole taking-his-last-name thing. If she started calling herself Mrs. Black, the message would be clear to potential usurpers that she and Micah were a unified pair. Of course, when Micah saw that thought roll through her mind, he looked at her with a self-satisfied grin plastered on his puss. *I told you so* was written all over his expression. Sam issued him a mock glower to let him know not to even think about rubbing her nose in this one later.

"Thank you for the last-minute invitation," Micah said, smugly turning his attention back toward Miss D.

"It was no problem." Mistress Queen of the Night looked between her and Micah. "Will you two be playing out a scene tonight?"

"No," Micah said. "Sam and I are only here to watch."

Mistress D nodded and looked at Sam. "Micah's introducing you to the lifestyle then?"

"Something like that, yes." Sam tried not to stare at those unbelievably white teeth.

"Well, you've got the best here," she said, glancing back at Micah. "He'll take excellent care of you." Mistress White Teeth turned toward Micah. "I was so pleased to hear you were coming out of retirement, by the way."

Micah patted Sam's hip gently. "Not exactly out of retirement, but close enough."

The mistress's bright eyes lit up and those perfectly reddened lips curved into a secretive smile. "Would you like to join me during a scene? I have the most incredible submissive here with me. The guy can take more than I can give him, to be honest. I think he'd like you a lot, Micah."

He looked over at Sam and shrugged. "I don't know, Diamond. He's your sub, and that's your equipment. I wouldn't want to impose."

Sam got the impression Micah was trying to ask for her permission.

"No imposition, Micah. It would be an honor to do a scene with you."

Micah kept his gaze on Sam's.

Well, she had come here in hopes of seeing Micah in action, hadn't she? This was her chance.

Finally, she nodded. "You should, Micah. I want to see. I want to watch."

Micah turned back to she-who-hath-the-white-teeth. "Okay. Sure."

Mistress D grinned victoriously. "Excellent. I was just about to get started." She motioned for them to follow her as she headed off into the depths of the dungeon. "I'm set up back here."

She walked toward an ornate, heavy, black curtain embellished with gold embroidery and tassels as if it had come out of some Elizabethan palace. Miss D held it aside.

Sam's eyes opened wide as she ducked around the curtain into a darkened walkway and passed a large room in which a topless woman danced to exotic music while a rather brusque male lounged on a mound of large pillows of various colors and watched.

Micah leaned down and whispered, "Gorean scene."

She frowned up at him, not knowing a Gorean scene from the Dance of the Sugar Plum fairies. He shook his head and rolled his eyes as if to say he'd explain later.

Mistress Diamond quietly directed them past the room and farther back into a more open area.

"There are four rooms set up down here," the mistress

said. "Two on the other side, and two this way."

Micah nodded as if this all made perfect sense to him, so Sam nodded, too. Sure, she could pretend to know what she was doing.

They stepped past another heavy curtain into a room where a small gathering had begun to form around an open area. Large, heavy hooks hung from the ceiling, similar to the ones she had seen in Micah's basement. A dark-skinned male knelt on his knees in the corner, with a black, fabric bag over his head. He was naked and his hands rested on his thighs.

Mistress D fell into character as she grabbed a whip off a nearby shelf and cracked it against the concrete floor. The man in the corner twitched at the sound of the whip and lifted his covered head, obviously aware that his Mistress had returned. She marched toward him in her knee-high, shiny black boots.

Micah leaned in and whispered, "That's her submissive."

She whispered back, "And she wants you to work him over or whatever?"

He nodded.

Micah's eyes narrowed on the submissive, and he tilted his head studiously. Then he looked up at the ceiling and over at the toys and other items Mistress D had laid out.

"Quit calling her Mistress D," he said softly.

"Get out of my head, and you won't have to hear me call her Mistress D."

Micah huffed with exasperation but turned admiring eyes on her. "You're sexy when you're feisty."

Sam grinned sweetly. "Why, thank you, honey."

He smirked at her obvious sarcasm.

Mistress *Diamond* knelt beside her submissive and whispered something in his ear. Then the sub nodded. Sam heard him say something, but couldn't hear what. The mistress looked up at Micah and nodded, motioning him to join her.

"Well, here goes." He gave her a quick kiss and smiled.

His smile was all for her. Micah's chest puffed up and

he held his head high and his back straight as if he wanted to honor her with his pending performance. He obviously wanted to impress her. And wasn't that the sweetest thing ever? Chivalry and all that.

As he sauntered away from her and inspected several coils of rope on the shelf, every female eye in the room focused on him like hawks to a field mouse. Oh yes, they wanted her man — male, whatever. He was pure hotness. Sensuality and sexuality personified. And he was all hers.

His eyes flicked sideways to her as one brow arched in reply to her thoughts.

I love you.

He smiled darkly and placed his palm surreptitiously over his heart in reply.

When he turned around, he came to an abrupt stop and his face blanked.

Sam frowned. What was wrong?

She turned in the direction he was looking and gasped before snapping her mouth shut.

The submissive. Mistress Diamond had removed the hood.

It was Trace.

CHAPTER 11

EVEN WITH MICAH'S BACK TO HIM, Trace could tell it was him by that luscious hair falling like black silk over his shoulders. Seeing Sam among the onlookers confirmed it.

Cat. Out of the bag. Oops.

Now they knew more about him than anyone else. They had just joined an elite group of people that included only the three of them. Trace, Micah, and Sam.

And it shamed him. Which was really quite perfect since that was why he was here. To be shamed and humiliated in front of a group of people. His cock instantly swelled as his immense power laughed at him and shrank into the shadows.

When Micah finally did turn around, he froze in place.

Surprise!

Wasn't this just perfect? Trace had sought Micah out for his reputation as a true master of the art, and now he was going to get a taste of Micah's abilities first-hand.

As long as Micah didn't back down.

His mistress whipped him with a horse hair flogger, the coarseness stinging his skin, making it feel as though a hundred tiny lacerations had ripped his flesh. He knew from experience that they hadn't, but the pain still smarted. Again, she struck him. Then once more for good measure.

"We have a guest today, slave," Mistress Diamond crooned, prowling around him, digging her long nails into his chest and torso as she scratched him and continued around behind him. When her nails reached the place on his back she had struck a moment earlier, Trace winced.

His skin was already raw.

"Yes, Mistress." Trace eyed Micah, who only glared back at him.

What was Micah thinking?

"What do you think of him, slave? Do you think he can hurt you more than I can?"

Trace knew Micah could and would, but he also knew he could never admit that to his Mistress.

"No one can hurt me more than you can, my Mistress."

"Good answer, slave." She whipped his bare ass as his reward for pleasing her.

Meanwhile, Micah scoffed. He knew the truth as well as Trace did. No one would bring the pain like Micah could, and even Mistress Diamond had to know that as the truth.

"Give me your arms, slave," she commanded.

Trace did as he was told, watching Micah retrieve the whip his mistress had used earlier. The nine-foot coil unfurled, the leather landing on the floor with a satisfying slap.

Mistress Diamond often used the whip for effect only. She never used it on Trace, because she didn't trust herself with such a precise accoutrement. Pull back too late, and the leather would rip open his skin. Pull back too soon, and the whip cracked too far away from the body to elicit fear. Why did he get the feeling that Micah knew exactly how to handle a whip—and that he would use it on Trace?

After binding his wrists, his mistress fastened him to a chain hanging from a hook in the ceiling.

Let the pain begin.

Trace's cock was already hard and standing straight out in front of him, tight and solid.

A look passed between Micah and his Mistress as she picked up a second horse hair flogger and stepped behind Trace.

"Do you think you can take me, slave?" Micah said, flicking the whip so that it cracked against the floor.

Trace licked his lips, eyeing the whip. It had been a long time since someone had used one on him, and he had missed its painful lick. Still, his heart was racing. This was Micah, for God's sake. Micah. The vampire with a reputation for bringing submissives to their knees.

"Answer him!" His Mistress struck his back in a criss-cross pattern with the floggers.

He shook violently, swinging forward and grunting. His back was already raw from earlier, and now it practically burned with pain.

Through gritted teeth, he said, "Yes. I can take whatever you give me, Sir."

Micah grinned, his eyes narrowing with satisfaction. "I'm not so sure, slave." He cracked the whip twice more, obviously getting a feel for it, studying its movement.

Trace licked his lips again, eager to feel what Micah could give him.

The horse hair floggers sliced the air and bit into his hips and ass, and he cried out. Micah seemed to delight in Trace's reaction as he stepped back and cracked the whip toward him. The tip snapped in the air only an inch in front of Trace's chest, causing his eyes to bulge as a collective gasp rose up from the crowd. Mostly likely, few of them had seen such expert whip action.

Mistress Diamond and Micah fell into a rhythmic pattern. First she flogged him, having traded in the horse hair floggers for a bamboo rod, which she struck him with against the ass and the back of his legs. Before Trace could recover from her lashing, Micah reared back and unleashed a wicked flick of the whip. Back and forth they traded punishment, and with each crack of the whip, the tip grew closer to striking his skin until finally...

Trace threw his head back and cried out as the tip licked his left pec. A welt rose up almost immediately, and Trace thought he had died and gone to Heaven.

If he hadn't been strung up by his wrists, he would have fallen at Micah's feet and sworn submissive fealty for the rest of his life. The urge to bow before him and beg him to be his Master nearly overpowered his thoughts, and tears of gratitude welled in his eyes.

All from a single lashing of the whip.

But Trace didn't have much time to think about pledging eternal service to Micah before the next round began with a strike of the bamboo rod to his hamstrings, followed by another subtle, yet painful, kiss of the whip across his right pec.

After another minute of blessed pain, his mistress finally halted the action and lowered him to the floor.

"Don't think we're finished with you, slave," she said, scratching his scalp with her nails as he fell to his knees in a breathless, bruised heap, covered in sweat and eager to come.

As if reading his thoughts, Mistress Diamond knelt and wrapped her hand around his cock. He groaned and issued her a pleading glance as she squeezed hard then raked her nails up his shaft as he winced and growled with frustration. He knew she wouldn't let him come, yet.

"Now, do as Master Micah tells you, slave, or I will be very displeased." His mistress stood and sank into the shadows to the side. She obviously didn't know that Trace already knew Micah.

Clearing his throat and gasping through another heavy panting session, Trace swung his eager, drunken gaze toward Micah, ready for more. Needing more.

Micah re-coiled the whip and set it back on the shelf, grabbed a bundle of rope, then stepped forward, his eyes narrowing hard on Trace's. Trace dutifully looked down, instinctively knowing not to look Micah in the eye.

"That's right, slave. You haven't earned the right to look at me." Micah drew near and leaned toward him until his mouth was right beside Trace's ear. "Do not look at me unless I give you permission. Do you understand?" He sounded like a drill sergeant.

Trace nodded. "Yes."

"Yes, what?" Micah's voice commanded respect.

"Yes, Sir."

Micah drew back. "Yes, *Master*. Now stand, slave."

Trace bowed his head and corrected himself as he stood. "Yes, Master."

Micah paced around him, and Trace could feel his eyes slicing through his soul. What did Micah think of him? Was he disgusted? Angry? Did he feel betrayed that Trace had kept his submissive status a secret? Would he refuse to speak to Trace after this?

"Come here." Micah snapped his fingers and pointed to the floor beside him a few feet away.

Trace complied and stepped toward him.

"Put your hands behind your back."

Again, he did as he was told.

Micah stepped around him and began binding his wrists, wrapping and knotting the rope around his body, hips, arms, legs, and finally his ankles until Trace was bound so securely he couldn't move.

Fuck, Micah was good. He'd been bound before, but not so expertly and so swiftly.

Suddenly, Micah gripped the rope around his wrists and yanked him back. Unable to move his feet to catch himself, Trace freefell backward. *Shit!* He cried out, just knowing he was going to crack his skull on the concrete.

At the last second, Micah caught him and placed him gently on the floor.

Mindfuck much!

"Silence, slave." Micah leaned over him and the barest hint of a smile quirked his lips as if he were enjoying himself a bit too much.

"Did I give you permission to look at me, slave?"

Trace quickly averted his gaze. "No, sir — *Master!*"

Mistress Diamond stood at the side, smiling proudly. Of him or Micah? That was the question.

Meanwhile, Trace's dick was having all kinds of fun, sticking out like a third leg, only shorter. But the damn thing sure was trying like hell to make him a tripod.

Fuck, this concrete floor was cold.

Micah walked back to the Mistress's toys and poked around for a second then turned back, holding a violet wand.

Fuck. Me.

Trace wasn't a fan of the violet wand, even though it got

the job done well enough.

Micah tsked. "Since you refuse to obey me, slave, I'll have to force you not to look at me."

A few seconds later, Micah was covering his eyes with a soft, black blindfold.

"Try looking at me now, slave."

The violet wand struck his chest, and Trace jerked. And again. Pause. And again. Another pause, then ZAP! as the wand tapped lower on his torso, then his hip. Trace grunted louder with each touch of the wand, his teeth clenched, his arms and legs straining against the rope as he squirmed and slithered on the floor, trying to get away from the electrical current. But Micah was relentless, taking him to the brink. When Trace cried out, Micah finally stopped.

Trace heard him walk away, then he heard him whisper something to Mistress Diamond.

"His safe word?" she said. "Red."

"Red." Micah's voice sounded contemplative. "Okay."

Footsteps came back toward him and he felt Micah's warmth as if he'd knelt beside him.

"Do you know your safe word, slave?"

"Yes." Trace panted heavily, the pain of the wand an echo for the moment, but his muscles hadn't yet released from the most recent onslaught.

"Yes, what?"

"Yes, Master."

"What is it?"

"Red, Master."

"Good." Micah paused. "Are you afraid to use it?"

Trace hesitated. He had rarely used his safe word. What the hell was Micah getting at? "No, Master."

"Good."

And then Micah was gone again. But only for a moment. Then he was back.

"I've got a knife in my hand, slave." Micah's voice dropped to a low hiss, a malicious timbre. "Feel it?"

Trace felt cold, flat metal against his chest. Holy fuck! What was Micah doing? Trace had never engaged in knife play. Hard to believe that in all his years as a sub, no Master or Mistress had used a knife on him.

"Do you feel it, slave?" Micah's voice sounded irritated.

"Yes, Master."

"It's a very sharp blade, slave. From my personal collection. And I can assure you, I keep my knives razor sharp. Do you understand?"

Trace swallowed as the cold metal caressed his chest in his world of darkness. He wished he could see, but he knew Micah wasn't lying. Trace had seen his knives. He knew how lethal they were.

"Yes, Master."

Abruptly, the knife was gone, and a second later the edge pressed into his throat.

Jesus!

"Now, if you move, you will be cut," Micah said, holding the knife steadily against his Adam's apple. "Do you understand?"

"Y-yes, Master."

Fuck, fuck, fuck! What was Micah doing? What was about to happen? Panic crept into his muscles, but he was helpless. Utterly helpless, bound as he was.

The violet wand crackled once more, zapping his thigh. Trace clenched, but didn't move, feeling the pressure of the knife.

Relax, Trace. Relax.

The violent wand hit him again, higher. Then again on his hip after a short pause. And again an inch higher up.

The pain was near excruciating, but he couldn't move. If he moved, the knife would slice into his throat.

Zap! Zap!

Micah was relentless, pushing him closer and closer to the edge of sanity. The knife, the wand, the pain, the fear, the panic!

Zap!

Holy Mother of God! He couldn't take much more. Micah needed to stop. He needed to give Trace a break, for God's sake!

The wand crackled his skin again, near his cock.

And still Trace remained still. Every muscle in his body was clenched and quivering, ready to snap. But Trace denied his natural impulse to cry out and escape the pain.

Zap!

The wand struck his cock, and that was it. Trace was about to lose consciousness.

"Red!" He hated using his safe word. This hadn't been the first time he had, but he had never used it so soon in a scene. Never. And within minutes, Micah had taken him to the edge.

Immediately, the knife was withdrawn from his neck and the violet wand stopped zapping him. The blindfold was removed and Trace blinked up in horror at Micah, who smiled down at him.

Then he held up a credit card. "Not a knife." He said. "American Express."

He looked down and saw the knife on the floor. "You mean...?"

"Mindfuck. I never had the knife at your neck. It was my credit card."

Trace glanced at the onlookers. Many looked as flabbergasted as he felt. When he hazarded a look toward his Mistress, she seemed awestruck. Probably because she was shocked he had used his safe word.

Granted, part of the reason he felt he needed to stop the scene was because he wasn't sure what Micah was capable of. Knowing his reputation and experiencing his abilities first-hand were two very separate things, and there had been too many unknowns at work here tonight for him to continue on. But Damn! Micah was good.

Fuck me! That was hot.

As Micah quickly untied him, Trace looked down. His cock was positively straining for release. But this scene was over. He'd used his safe word. He wasn't coming tonight. Well, at least not out here in front of the crowd.

The audience that had gathered began murmuring, and several leaned in to compliment Micah before wandering off. Sam stood in the back hugging herself, concern etching her face.

"Diamond, can I have a moment with him? Alone somewhere?" Micah said to Mistress Diamond. "I want to make sure he's okay."

"Of course."

A good Dom always tended to his or her submissive after a scene. But Trace had a feeling Micah also wanted to talk to him on a more personal level about what had just gone down.

Micah helped him up and turned toward Sam. "Sam, join us?"

Sam pressed the fingers of her right hand to her throat as her left arm hugged her waist, but she immediately nodded.

With his Mistress in front of him and Micah and Sam behind, they slipped into the back room where he had stashed his clothes along with his Mistress's things.

"Here you go," Diamond said. "I'll be back in the playroom cleaning up." She left and closed the door, leaving the three of them in silence.

For a couple of minutes, no one said a word, and then Micah shut off the light and nodded toward his boner.

"You need to take care of that?"

Trace immediately glanced toward Sam, who modestly looked away, trying to give him the impression she hadn't been staring. Nothing like pointing out the pink, polka-dotted elephant in the room to draw everyone's attention to it. He looked down at his hard-as-a-rock cock and nodded, feeling his face heat as he glanced once more toward Sam before looking back at Micah.

"In front of Sam?" he said.

Micah turned and looked at his mate. "Do you mind, baby? He needs this or he's gonna be keeled over when he leaves."

Only another male could truly understand a bad case of blue balls.

She fluttered her hand toward them and shrugged, tightening her hold around her waist with her other arm as her gaze met his. "I'm fine. Go ahead."

Micah turned back toward Trace, his dark eyes soft with patience and understanding. "Anything I can do to help?"

"You did enough back there, don't you think?" Trace didn't mean it maliciously. If anything, he was grateful for what Micah had done. That had been the absolute best scene he'd had in years. Fucking hell, he was on the verge of coming just thinking about it.

Trace gave Sam one last glance before turning his back to her and wrapping his hand around his shaft. He needed to come. His balls were hard as stones and aching.

Out of the corner of his eye, he saw Micah lean back against the wall as he combed his fingers through his hair. "Yeah, well…."

Trace glanced down and saw a cat o' nines sticking out of his Mistress's bag.

"Grab that, would you?" He nodded his head toward the bag. "Use it on me."

With his back turned, he heard Micah push away from the wall. Then he heard the leather flogger rustle out of the bag.

"You sure?"

"Yes." Trace began stroking feverishly. It should only take a couple of strikes and he would come. He reached for a hand towel on the shelf next to him.

He heard another rustle of the cat o' nines a second before it struck his raw back.

"Again." He clenched his teeth as his orgasm coiled tightly in his scrotum.

The flash of pain blistered him in such a pleasant way.

"Again!" His voice cracked.

The leather tails whipped down over his back at a diagonal a third time, and then a fourth, but his orgasm stalled. Nestled into his balls, his release kicked its feet up and smiled, making itself right at home.

Fuck!

Micah continued whipping him, but it was no use. No matter how hard he stroked or how fast, his orgasm wouldn't budge.

He growled violently in frustration.

Everyone in the room knew he was stuck as he reached for the wall and leaned on his outstretched arm, out of breath, in pain, gripped by the overwhelming need to release but unable to do so.

"Can I help?"

He and Micah whipped around to see Sam standing only a few feet away, her face painted with compassion.

"Do you want to?" Micah frowned curiously. He looked almost awed that Sam had offered.

And wasn't that about as expected as a flood in the desert? Micah allowing his mate to assist in making him come? Holy fucking ball busters, but Trace thought he could hear Hell freezing over this very instant.

Sam nodded, her eyes meeting Trace's.

"What can I do?" She tentatively touched his bare back.

Just her touch eased him. Trace craved the feminine. He longed for a female's touch to be enough to bring him to completion, but he feared it never would be. He would always need the pain, harsh brutality, and humiliation to give him sexual pleasure.

Micah seemed to sense the change in him as Sam brushed her fingers down his back, because he took a step back.

"Sam, I want you to hold him," Micah said. "Trace, back up. Come here."

Trace pushed away from the wall and did as Micah told him, making enough room so Sam could slip between him and the wall in front of him. Her eyes met his with a beautiful innocence that shamed him. Sam didn't deserve to be exposed to his depravity like this.

"I'm sorry," he said softly to her.

She smiled and cradled his cheek in her palm. "It's okay, Trace. I'm a big girl. I can handle it."

"You shouldn't have to."

"Never you mind that. I want to help or I wouldn't have offered. Especially after…"

Trace was sure she was referring to when he had watched her and Micah on the couch. They had been undeniably thankful for what he'd given them that night. Maybe this was Sam's way of showing it.

Trace would never understand the relationship between Micah and Sam, or the one he was forming with them both. But he was grateful for it. It had been a long time since he'd had friends who were there for him when he needed them.

Micah's hand pressed against Trace's back. "Let her hold you, Trace."

Sam opened her arms until he relinquished and stepped into her embrace. She wrapped her arms around him and held him close as he bowed his head against her shoulder. He didn't deserve them. He wasn't good enough to have earned such unconditional acceptance.

"Continue, Trace." Micah's hand smoothed down his spine and then was gone.

Trace felt tears sting his eyes. "I can't."

"Yes, you can." Sam's arms tightened around him, feeling like a safety net as her small breasts pressed against his chest.

He shook his head, struggling with his desire to feel the warmth of her feminine energy by pulling her even closer. He couldn't insult Micah like that. This was already too much. Trace was already taking advantage beyond propriety.

The cat o' nines struck his bare back and he flinched. Sam smoothed one of her palms over his shoulder and up his neck before cradling the back of his shaved head.

"Use her!" Micah struck him again. "Do what you need to do, Trace."

Trace was about to break. The pain of the flogger combined with Sam's pure, feminine touch was more than he could stand, but still he refused to touch himself.

"Trace," Sam's gentle voice pried him like a crowbar against a locked door. "Touch yourself."

Her fingers brushed along the length of his shaft, and he nearly fell over as he gasped gruffly. Sam's strong arms swiftly pushed back around him, supporting him. The wick had been lit. Trace's hand slammed down on his cock and he began pumping furiously, crowding her, pushing against her, growling, his head still bent and resting against her shoulder as his free arm wound around her waist.

Micah struck him again, and again, almost as punishment for touching his mate so inappropriately. But Trace knew that wasn't it. Micah only wanted him to think he was upset when he wasn't, but it added to the mini-scene they had working here, where no audience watched. The mix of sensations was what he needed. The pain of the cat o' nines pushed him while Sam's soft femininity eased him. Between the two, he knew he wouldn't last long.

With a surge of unbidden strength, he shoved Sam backward against the wall, drawing deathly close to coming. Her grasp on him never wavered, despite a sudden growl from Micah that he quickly silenced.

The flogger lashed him again, and just like that, the first wave of release unfurled.

His cock let loose, spurting semen against Sam's black blouse. Trace's whole body jerked as he came harder than he'd come in years. So hard, in fact, that his legs gave out. Micah caught him under the arms and kept him from falling. Then he dragged him backward onto his lap as he sat down on the small couch against the wall.

Sam came with them, easing herself up onto Trace's lap and laying down on him like a blanket, holding him as his orgasm continued quaking his body. He laid his head back on Micah's shoulder, unable to do much else than lie there and simply *feel*...and twitch.

"It's okay. I've got you, buddy." Micah ran his hand over Trace's shaved head as he wrapped his other arm around both him and Sam.

I've got you buddy. Usually it was Trace saying that or something similar to Micah. Or at least thinking it. He had pulled Micah's ass out of the fire several times in the past few weeks, and every time he said or thought, *I've got you buddy.*

Now it was Micah's turn to return the favor. Well, Micah's and Sam's. He couldn't forget Sam's role in all this. Without her, he'd still be suffering a case of the blue balls.

They rested like that for a while, all three of them nestled together, until Trace's orgasm finally diminished and left his body spent and completely undone.

Trace took a deep breath and blew it out. "I'm a fucked up mess."

"We all are, Trace." Micah affectionately dipped his forehead against Trace's temple.

"I wasn't ready for you guys to see me like this."

"Well, we did." Micah gently rocked him as Sam slowly peeled herself away, stood, and reached for a towel to wipe off her blouse. She smiled endearingly at him.

"You okay?" she said.

Trace bowed his head sadly. He was ashamed. This wasn't how he had wanted them to find out his secret. "Yeah. I'm okay."

"You sure?" Micah asked. "I worked you pretty hard back there."

Trace disengaged from Micah's hold and sat down on the floor in front of him, facing him. "I needed to be worked hard."

"Why?" Micah leaned forward, his elbows on his knees.

Sam sat down next to Micah and wrapped one arm around his back. Micah reached over and tucked his hand between her knees. They were completely devoted to each other, even after what had just happened.

"I shouldn't have used you like that," Trace said to Sam, looking down shamefully.

Micah tsked and growled. "She's okay, Trace. And you're avoiding the question."

"What about you?" Trace looked up at him, knowing what Micah wanted to hear but not ready to say it. "She's your mate. I took advantage of our friendship. I never should have allowed —"

Micah held up his hand, cutting him off. "Trace. I'm fine with it. You didn't do anything wrong. Sam and I are both okay. Now, tell me. Why do you need to be worked so hard like that?"

Trace took a deep breath and looked down. "It's how I keep my power from consuming me. If I don't, I'll go rogue."

Micah slowly sat back. "Fuuuuuck me."

It was clear Micah understood what he was saying.

"Yeah, brother. If I don't do this, I'll turn into a fucking mutant."

Micah bent over again and rubbed his hands over his face before combing them back through his hair and looking at Sam as if pulling from her strength. "Fuck, Trace. I didn't know. I thought...shit, I don't know what I thought. I guess I didn't realize your powers were so strong. I mean, I knew, but...I didn't know."

"Nobody knows. Just me. And, well, now you. Don't tell Tristan or anyone else."

"Fuck them. They don't have to know. Your secret's safe with me, buddy."

Trace looked at Sam, who seemed to be following along as best as she could. "Are you sure you're okay with this?"

What she had just witnessed had been pretty intense.

She nodded. "Actually, yes. More than okay. I feel...." she hesitated and looked at Micah, searching for the right word.

"She feels...wow, really?" Micah's eyebrows popped at Sam as if he were surprised. He had to be in her head again, seeing her thoughts.

"What?" Trace was suddenly curious. How did Sam feel about what she'd witnessed?

Micah turned toward him. "She liked it."

Sam blushed and looked away.

"Like the other night at the apartment, when you caught us in the living room," Micah said. "She's surprised by how much she enjoyed it."

Sam leaned in and hid her face against Micah's shoulder.

Micah grinned and glanced down at her. "It's okay, Sam." He caressed the side of her face and her hair.

Trace bit his lip and looked down. What did all this mean? What was happening among the three of them? He clearly wasn't forming a mating connection to either of them, but a powerful bond was obviously joining them on a higher level.

"She'll be okay." Micah turned back toward Trace, still

holding Sam's face in his palm. "I want you to come back to the apartment tonight, Trace. I want you with us after what I just did to you, okay?"

Trace reached out his right hand and clasped it with Micah's as he briefly let go of Sam. "If you're sure it won't make Sam uncomfortable and it won't be an imposition, sure. I'll hang with you guys tonight."

Sam finally pulled away from Micah's shoulder, still flushed. "It won't make me uncomfortable, and it's no imposition. I'm with Micah on this one. Come home with us, okay?" She blew out puff of air. "I think I need it as much as you do."

Micah leaned forward and man-hugged him. "I agree. I think we'll all feel better if you stay with us tonight. You're as important to Sam as you are to me." He exchanged glances with Sam, and she nodded. "She needs to see you're okay and that I didn't hurt you, and I think she wants to know you're okay with her, too. She needs to know this is normal for you—for us." He let go of Trace's hand.

Sam's expression made it clear Micah had hit the nail on the head. But then, if Micah was in her thoughts as much as he suspected, he knew everything about Sam.

"Thanks," Trace said.

"We'll be out front waiting for you." Micah stood and helped Sam up.

Trace frowned. "I can drive myself over."

"No. You'll come with us." Micah's tone was final. Clearly, he was a Dom worth his weight in salt. The guy intended on taking care of him on every level after what he'd just done to him. "I'll handle Diamond."

In other words, Micah would compel his Mistress's mind so she didn't expect Trace to return home with her.

Like a lost soul who had just been found, Trace suddenly felt like he fit in somewhere. After what had happened the other night at Micah's apartment, he had felt a deepening bond with both Micah and Sam, and now, after this, despite the shame rolling through him, he had a feeling the three of them would become even closer.

He hoped so.

Micah and Sam were the most important people in his life, being that he no longer had any family left.

CHAPTER 12

SAM STOOD TO THE SIDE while Mistress She of the White Teeth got her mind jimmied to alter her memory of who should be going home with whom. Queen Dominatrix might have come to the party with Trace, but she wasn't leaving with him. Trace was going home with her and Micah. They could take better care of him than this woman, who would likely send him on his way.

The last person Sam had expected to see here tonight had been Trace. Sam glanced toward the hall that led back to the storage room. She couldn't deny that events back there had excited her, which was surprising. She didn't want to have sex with Trace or anything like that, but she felt protective of him. Protective in a way that felt sort of like a lover and sort of like family. Based on Micah's behavior, so did he

Was this normal? Was she feeling this way because Micah's blood coursed through her veins and she would automatically be tied to his feelings?

There was so much about this mystical world she didn't understand, and maybe she never would, but she did know that she wanted to help Trace. She also wouldn't mind being involved if Micah ever had to work him over again, which she hoped he did.

Seeing Micah put Trace through the paces had been both stimulating and unnerving, but not unnerving enough to make her want to stop. And Micah had been damn sexy to watch. She totally understood why subs wanted him. The guy controlled the room from his presence alone. Her chest lifted proudly as she glanced around the room and realized that of all the guests who would probably kill to be in her shoes, she was the one with the honor of leaving on Micah's arm.

Eat your heart out, ladies and gentlemen. That male is mine.

Micah smiled and hugged Mistress D, and she hugged him back. Clearly, the mind job was complete.

"It was nice to meet you, Sam." Mistress Diamond turned toward her pleasantly.

"Uh, nice to meet you, too." Sam gave those pearly whites one last, fixated stare.

Micah joined her, took her hand, and began to lead her out of the room.

"Are we set?" she said.

"She now thinks Trace arrived at the party with us." Micah ushered her back through the basement.

"So she won't think it's odd Trace is leaving with us."

"Exactly."

Sam stopped and pulled him back. "Should we talk about this first?" She needed to know what Micah expected of her once they left here.

"Upstairs." Micah motioned for her to come with him.

Once upstairs, Micah pulled her into a quiet corner. Most of the party attendees were still downstairs watching the other scenes being played out.

"Is Trace okay?" She kept her voice quiet despite the lack of an audience.

"Yes. He's better than okay, actually." Micah looked a bit unnerved. Obviously, he hadn't expected to see Trace here either, and hadn't counted on having to help his friend get off.

"No, I didn't," he said, answering her unasked question.

Micah wasn't acting like himself. He seemed upset, which wasn't how he'd acted downstairs.

Sam touched his arm. "Are you okay that I was involved?"

Micah nodded. "Yes, oddly enough, I enjoyed that you helped. It was...sexy." His navy eyes darkened and flitted away from hers almost as if he felt guilty.

"Then why are you so agitated?"

Micah's gaze found hers again. "Because I didn't know

how fucked up he is."

"Fucked up how?"

"His mixed-blood powers are stronger than I realized."

So, Micah wasn't upset about that mindfuck thing he'd pulled on Trace or about what had gone on in the storage room. He was upset because Trace was more powerful than he thought.

"That's right," Micah said, keeping his voice hushed.

"Why is that a problem?" And then Sam remembered what Micah had told her about mixed-bloods and mutants. "Oh, God!" She covered her mouth and gazed up at him, suddenly scared for Trace. "You don't think…?"

"No, Trace isn't going mutant." Micah smoothed his hands over her arms to reassure her, but he was obviously worried. "Being a submissive is how he keeps his power under control so he doesn't tip the scale."

"Is he going to be okay?"

Micah shrugged. "I don't know. I hope so."

She had only known Trace for a few weeks, but the thought of losing him was intolerable. "So, now what? After what just happened down there, what am I supposed to do?"

Micah glanced over her shoulder as if looking for him then he turned back to her. "Actually, I think it would make Trace feel better for you to talk to him. I think he's relieved that you and I know his secret, now."

"Okay. Do I pull him aside? Do I ask him questions?"

Micah shook his head. "No, nothing like that. Just be conversational. Can you do that?"

She nodded.

"Oh, and one more thing." Micah glanced over her shoulder again. "He's going to be tired. After he comes down off his high, he's going to be exhausted. And he needs caring for. I've never Dom'd him, and I take care of those I Dom. If he had been anyone else, though, I would have turned him back over to Diamond to tend to. I would have sat with him for a while and made sure he was okay, but I would have let Diamond care for him. But since it's Trace, I'm going to do that. I want you to help. Do you mind? He seems to be as attached to you as he is to me."

"No, I don't mind." No question about it. Sam would do whatever Micah needed her to do. "How can I help?"

"Just reassure him. Make him comfortable. He needs to know he's okay with us and that we're okay with him...that his secret doesn't change how we feel about him."

No problem. She could do that. This was Trace, after all. And Trace was already closer than a brother to her. Almost as close as a lover, really.

Micah waved and Sam turned around. Trace had just walked into the room and was glancing around as if looking for them. He bobbed his head in their direction when he saw them.

She and Micah walked toward him.

"You ready, buddy?" Micah took his duffel bag.

"Yeah." Trace looked at her and nodded in gratitude but said nothing further, his expression conveying his appreciation.

"Hi, Trace." She smiled up at him and took his hand. Doing so just felt natural.

"Come on, let's go home." Micah led them out.

She kept her hand linked with Trace's as they followed Micah outside. The valet took their ticket and hurried off for their car.

"How you feeling?" Sam looked up at Trace's dark face, his pale eyes unreadable but heavy.

"Tired, actually."

"Yes, Micah mentioned you might be tired."

Trace stretched. "Yes, but I feel good. You?"

Sam squeezed his hand and smiled at him as he glanced down at her. "I'm good."

Trace nodded and grinned sheepishly before turning away.

The Camaro pulled up and Micah headed around to the driver's side.

"Um, when did you buy this fine piece of automobile?" Trace let Sam lead him down the steps.

She let go of his hand and opened the passenger door.

"Couple days ago," Micah said. "It's Sam's."

Sam rolled her eyes. "Yeah, but he wouldn't let me drive it tonight." She waved her hand at Micah as if he were a big kid with a shiny new toy then gestured toward the inside of the car. "You want the front or back?"

"Back's fine." Trace ducked down and climbed in after Sam pushed the front seat up for him.

"It's a tight fit for a giant like you," she said as he got situated.

"Yeah, but I can sprawl out a bit. Relax."

Sam blinked and smiled at him then stood and looked over the car at Micah, who gave her a look as if to say *I told you so.* Then they both climbed in, Micah put the car in gear, and they pulled away from the mansion.

No one spoke the entire trip back to the apartment, but Sam peered in the back seat a couple of times to see that Trace had closed his eyes and was rocking gently with the motion of the car.

He looks exhausted.

Micah's gaze flicked to her briefly, and he reached for her hand.

Here they were, the Three Musketeers of S&M. Well, Sam felt more like part of the Three Stooges for all her knowledge, or lack thereof, in what Micah and Trace seemed to be experts.

An amused expression swept over Micah's face, and he laughed quietly but didn't say a word. Obviously, he found her comparison to Curly, Larry, and Moe funny.

With narrowed eyes, she huffed at him.

Well, it's true. I can't hold a candle to you two.

His expression softened and he lifted her hand to his mouth and kissed it before turning toward her at a stoplight and mouthing, *I love you.*

Okay, so Micah knew how to allay her trepidation and her fears, and he knew just what to say to make her all better.

I love you, too.

TRACE WAS EXHAUSTED. The combination of Micah's mindfuck and the powerful orgasm afterward pushed him to the brink of sleep. The hum of the Camaro's engine, as well as the soft rocking as Micah navigated them through the streets of Chicago, lulled him even further.

He knew Micah and Sam were having some kind of silent communication, but he didn't have the energy to question them. Were they concerned about him? Worried? Was Sam upset? She hadn't acted upset.

That female never ceased to amaze him. She was a stalwart rock, unmoving and resistant to the hardest pounding anyone could give her. She'd been through a shit storm in the past month, finding out vampires exist, almost dying from a dreck bite, saved from death by Micah's venom, and coming face-to-face with her abusive ex-husband who had wanted to drag her back to her former life.

Maybe that was why she was taking this latest development so well. After surviving what she'd been through, seeing a guy get mindfucked and then holding him through a monumental orgasm was child's play.

The car slowed and turned, and when Trace blinked his eyes open, he saw they were in the parking garage at the Sentinel. Within moments, Micah parked, shut off the engine, got out, and pushed up his seat.

"Come on, buddy. Time to get you to bed."

Trace swatted away Micah's outstretched hand. "I'm fine."

Fuck, he hated moving. He just wanted to stay in the car and sleep.

"Yeah, uh-huh." Micah chuckled. "I can see that."

Trace flipped him the bird then slowly peeled himself out of near-slumber to climb out of the car.

Micah shut the driver's side door, and Sam joined them as they headed toward the elevators.

"I'll make you some tea and fill a bath for you." Micah rubbed his hand affectionately over Trace's bald head.

"No. I just want to sit and rest a bit."

"I can do that, too."

They rode up the elevator in silence, got out on the

eighteenth floor, and Sam linked her hand with his as they headed down the hall to Micah's apartment.

"I love you guys." Trace looked down as they reached Micah's door.

"We love you, too, buddy." Micah unlocked the door and let it swing open before wrapping his arm around Trace's shoulders. "Now, come on. Inside with your ugly ass."

He grinned and flipped Micah off again as he trudged drowsily inside, feeling like he finally had a family again.

CHAPTER 13

"Go have a seat on the couch, Trace." Micah released him and extended his arm toward the living room. "I'll make you a sandwich."

Trace didn't protest and walked into the living room and grabbed the TV remote and clicked it on to ESPN.

Sam rubbed Micah's arm to catch his attention. "I'm going to change. I'll be right back."

As Sam slipped down the hall to the bedroom, Micah went to the kitchen and prepared a pot of chamomile tea and started making sandwiches. Turkey with lettuce, tomato, mayo, and mustard.

His gaze lifted toward Trace, who sat with his back to him. For all Trace's toughness, the guy really was troubled. Micah would never have guessed it was so bad for Trace, but then he couldn't get inside that cranium to see whatever pain Trace was dealing with. Was it really so bad?

Micah felt as if he was only just touching the surface of Trace's secrets. How many more were there waiting to be discovered?

How surreal. Only a few weeks ago, Micah had been the one who was monumentally fucked up. But Trace and Sam had pulled him out of that fire, and the scars he had carried for centuries were finally healing. Micah was becoming the male he had been before Katarina's death.

Unfortunately, one of his two saviors now seemed to be revealing that *he* needed saving, too. But Micah didn't know how to save him. How did you remove a threat that couldn't be removed? If what Trace said was true, his power could destroy him at any moment. If he didn't subject himself to submission and receive his fix of pain and degradation, his power could eat him alive like cancer.

Was this why Trace needed him? Was this what Trace wanted from him?

Micah wouldn't assume anything, but if Trace ever came to him and asked him to be his Dom, Micah would do it in a heartbeat. In no way would he let Trace fall prey to his powers. Micah wouldn't lose his new and best friend—his brother—to such despair. No way. Trace had taken care of Micah, now he would take care of Trace. If that's what it came to, Trace would become his charge, just as Micah had become Trace's.

They would find a way to overcome this together.

SAM CHANGED INTO SWEATS AND A T-SHIRT then returned to the living room, offering a smile to Micah as she passed the kitchen before joining Trace on the couch.

"You look like you're about to fall asleep," she said.

He nodded.

"Does doing a scene always do that to you?" She might as well speak candidly. Micah had told her it might help him if she showed him what she had seen didn't bother her.

Micah quietly entered and set a tray of sandwiches and tea on the large ottoman in front of them then sat down beside her.

Trace chanced a cautious glance at her as he picked up one of the sandwiches.

"Yes. Scenes are pretty exhausting."

"How come?" She grabbed a sandwich and sank her teeth into a mile-high stack of turkey and lettuce.

Micah's arm wrapped around her shoulders, but he kept quiet, almost as if he purposely wanted to stay out of the conversation.

Trace shrugged and kept his gaze averted. "The pain is a lot to deal with." He took a bite of his sandwich, chewed, and swallowed. "And when I'm in a scene is the only time I can truly relax, so I guess that naturally makes me tired."

"Go on." The more he talked, the more she wanted to know.

He turned and searched her face, his brow furrowing curiously. "Are you sure?"

She nodded. She knew from what Micah had said that this wasn't the normal and usual way to react after a scene, but more seemed to be brewing inside Trace and she got a sense he wanted to talk about it.

Trace glanced between her and Micah. "Well, it's my powers," he said slowly. "Being a submissive and putting myself through that is the only way I can..." He hesitated. "It's the only way I can actually feel free."

"Free?" she said.

He nodded. "Most of the time, my powers keep me locked in a state of tension. But when I'm in a scene, the pain and humiliation push my powers back. For just a little while, I feel normal."

Sam nodded. "And you can relax."

"Yes."

No wonder he was tired. It sounded like he spent most of his time tied in stressful knots until he endured a scene such as the one Micah had just put him through. With all the tension dissolved, he would probably sleep like a baby tonight.

They finished their midnight snack, watching SportsCenter, and Trace seemed to grow sleepier by the second.

"Come on, Trace, lie down." Sam tugged him toward her as Micah pulled a throw pillow from the side and set it on her lap.

Trace didn't even try to fight his weariness and lay down, his head settling on her lap. Micah's hand joined hers as she stroked his face with her fingers. "Just sleep, Trace."

"We've got you," Micah added quietly, scooting closer and caressing Trace's scalp.

Sam laid her head on Micah's shoulder, and turned her face toward his. He kissed her then snuggled her against him as they lulled Trace to sleep with their caresses.

An hour later, with Trace sound asleep, Micah shut off the TV, quietly got up, lifted Trace in his arms, and cradled him. Trace didn't even stir. The guy was out cold.

Sam stood up and followed him to the spare room and pulled the covers back on the bed so Micah could set him down. She pulled off his shoes and set them on the floor at the foot of the bed, and then Micah tucked him in.

"He looks so innocent," she said, watching Trace sleep.

"Yeah, he does." Micah ushered her to the door and out into the hall before silently closing Trace in for the day.

After going to their own bedroom, Micah went to the restroom and started getting ready for bed as she put on her pajamas.

"So, is that what you would do to me in your dungeon?" she said as she joined him in the bathroom and grabbed her toothbrush.

He rinsed toothpaste out of his mouth and looked at her in the mirror. His *calling* was all but finished, with only a lingering touch of arousal that flared up about once a day.

"No. I wouldn't be that hardcore with you," he said.

"Why not?" She started brushing her teeth.

Micah slipped behind her and wrapped his arms around her waist. "It would just be different with you, that's all."

She recalled their earlier conversation about this topic. He had told her scenes with her would be more sexual than with others. With others, it would be about providing a service. With her, it would be more intimate. Just for them.

She spit and rinsed as he loosened his grip so she could bend over the sink.

After she wiped her mouth, he shut off the light and followed her to bed.

"Why do you ask?" he said. "Are you having second thoughts?"

She nestled beside him. "No."

"So, you still want to—"

"Yes." She propped herself on her elbow and gazed down at him. "Yes, more than ever I want to play with you in your dungeon of depravity." She grinned.

"Are you sure?"

"Absolutely." She trailed the tip of her fingertip around his nipple, biting her bottom lip.

"Come here. I'll show you depravity." He pulled her on top of him and shut off the light on the nightstand.

Oh, Micah, Micah, Micah. What a bad boy he was.

CHAPTER 14

Trace awoke feeling refreshed late in the afternoon. He could already feel his powers flowing back to life after the raw working over Micah had given him, but the restful sleep had done him wonders.

With a stretch, he sat up and realized he was still wearing the same clothes he had worn last night.

He spent the night here often enough now that he had a few changes of clothes tucked into the top drawer of the bureau. Standing, he stretched again then pattered barefoot across the carpet, pulled open the drawer, grabbed out a pair of jeans, and hit the bathroom for a shower.

Last night's events still rattled through his thoughts, and it would probably be a while before he fully grasped what had happened, but after a good, long sleep he felt better about how things had gone down.

After shutting off the water, he did a half-assed job drying off then yanked on his jeans commando-style and headed to the kitchen for some coffee and grub.

The apartment was silent, which meant Sam and Micah were still sleeping, so he tried to keep quiet as he pulled out the coffee and started brewing a pot. He knew the apartment well enough by now that he knew where everything was and easily made his way around the kitchen.

Trace was whipping up a batch of homemade pancakes when Sam appeared, wearing a pair of grey yoga pants and a long-sleeved, raspberry-colored knit top. Her hair was wet.

"Morning," she said, despite the time on the clock showing it was nearly three in the afternoon.

"Morning. Hungry?" Trace stirred the pancake batter then spooned four equal portions onto the hot griddle he'd plugged in on the counter.

"Mmm, yes. I love pancakes." Sam shuffled to the cabinet, grabbed a mug, and poured a cup of coffee before turning around and topping off his own mug.

"Thanks." Trace smiled as he looked down at his cup, spinning a spatula around in his hand.

"How you feelin' this morning?" Sam opened the fridge, pulled out her French vanilla creamer, and poured a dose into her coffee.

"Good." Trace grinned. "Rested."

Sam parked against the counter next to him and lifted her mug to her lips and blew over the hot liquid. "Is that unusual?" Her green eyes turned up to his.

He nodded, checking the pancakes. "Sort of. I usually get a decent sleep after getting worked, but I haven't slept as well as I did today in ages."

Sam's pink lips curved into a proud smile. "That's my Micah, always taking good care of the people he cares about."

Trace flipped the pancakes then glanced sideways at Sam. She was tall but still stood a good four inches shorter than he did.

"Micah's a good friend. I bet he's an even better mate," he said.

Sam's smile broadened. "He's damn near perfect."

The two stared at each other for a moment.

"Yeah, he is, isn't he?" Trace held Sam's gaze. "And you're damn near perfect for him, too." Would he ever have what Micah had with Sam? "Maybe...someday...if I'm lucky...I'll meet someone like you, and she'll be *my* mate." He lowered his gaze and softly cleared his throat as he fidgeted with the spatula.

Sam gently touched his arm. "Trace, there's someone out there for you, and she'll be perfect. She'll be exactly what you need and then some."

"I don't know, Sam. What I need is a lot, as you saw last night."

"What are you saying?" Sam slid closer, sipping her coffee. "You don't think God created someone just for you?"

"Maybe." He flipped the pancakes. "But honestly, Sam, there aren't many females who can dish out the kind of pain I need. If any at all."

Sam gazed into her coffee, appearing uncomfortable. "So, what? Do you think you need a...man?" She glanced back up at him.

He shook his head. "No, I already know that if I ever take a mate, it will be a female. But I need her to be willing to hurt me. Physically, you know? And even mentally."

Sam set her coffee down and turned toward him, rubbing his arm. "Yeah, I know, sweetie."

Trace sighed and took up the pancakes, stacking them on a plate. Then turned toward her. "I'm pretty fucked up, huh?"

Sam frowned and shook her head. "Not any more than the rest of us." She smiled compassionately. "You're actually pretty normal, Trace. Except for that whole I'm-a-vampire thing." She bit her lip as if she was trying not to giggle. "And, of course, then there's that whole mind control stuff you've got going on. Other than that, you're pretty much a regular guy."

With a chuckle, Trace took her hand and squeezed it. "Regular guy. Yep, that's me."

Micah entered the kitchen, scratching his bare chest and yawning. "You making a move on my girl, Trace?"

Trace did the unthinkable under any other circumstance and pulled Sam into his arms, hugging her tightly. "Absolutely. I might not give her back."

Micah froze and shot Trace a lethal glare. Both Trace and Sam went starkly still, then Sam scrambled out of his arms.

"He was only kidding, Micah," she said, trying to placate him.

Micah busted out laughing. "Oh God, Trace! If you could have seen your face." He reached over and clocked Trace with a playful smack on the cheek. "Seriously, do you think after what we've been through I'd give a shit if you gave my babe a hug?"

"Hell, I don't know!" Trace exhaled heavily in relief, throwing one hand against his chest as he steadied himself with the other by placing it on the counter. "Fucker. You scared the shit out of me."

Micah waved a hand at him. "Ah, whatever man." He turned toward Sam and pulled her in for a kiss. "Morning, sexy."

"Morning." Sam swatted Micah on the arm. "And be nice."

"I'm always nice."

Trace snorted. "What-the-fuck-ever." He poured more batter onto the griddle.

Sam smacked Micah again. "Yeah. What Trace said."

"Hey!" Micah laughed and pulled back as Sam went for him again. "Watch it, Iron Mike."

"I'll Iron Mike you," Sam chased Micah out of the kitchen, both of them laughing.

Trace smiled to himself, listening to them and thinking back to what Sam had said earlier. One day he would have what they had. Surely, someone who had been made just for him was out in the world. He only had to find her.

Easier said than done, but Trace had been through worse.

CHAPTER 15

WITH THE SCENE PARTY TWO DAYS BEHIND HIM, and things settling down where Trace was concerned, Micah wanted his last night off from work to be special. The honeymoon was over now that his *calling* had officially ended, but that didn't mean he couldn't give Sam one last night to remember before he got back to the task of enforcing and policing the drecks or any other criminal element that needed a firm hand.

He flipped on the light switches in the foyer of his suburban home and shut the door then stepped behind Sam.

"Are you nervous?" He brushed his fingertips over her neck as he helped her out of her coat.

"Not really." She turned and gazed up at him. "I trust you."

She looked beautiful, her face only showing the barest hint of makeup, her short hair standing out in soft, piecy tufts. She wore a simple blouse with comfortable yoga pants and tennis shoes. Not your average S&M attire, but whips and bondage wasn't what tonight was about. Tonight was merely an introduction.

He hung their coats in the hall closet then took her hand and led her through the kitchen to the door that led to the basement.

"Do I have to call you Sir or Master?" Sam stood back as he unlocked the door and opened it.

With a smile, he pulled her roughly against him, making her gasp and suck in her breath.

"That's not what tonight is about, Sam. That's not what this about between us." His gaze swept over every inch of her face. Sam was exquisite. So perfect. Too perfect for him.

How had he been so lucky that Fate had matched *her* to someone like *him?*

He bent and kissed her softly, sweetly. "You're not my slave, and you're not my servant. You're not even my submissive."

She stared up at him through her lashes, and Micah couldn't resist. He lifted his mouth, and she closed her eyes just as he planted a tender kiss on one eyelid then the other. "You're my mate, Sam. You never have to call me Sir." *Kiss.* "Or Master." *Kiss.* "You call me Micah. Always call me Micah, because I love how my name sounds falling from your lips. Especially when you're about to come."

Lifting up on her tiptoes, Sam found his mouth with hers, and her kiss was as feverish as a fire on an autumn night, stirring Micah's arousal to a higher altitude, driving his yearning for her right up to the limits of his tolerance. Micah was so unbelievably, madly, deeply in love with this woman. Fuck the mating and the *calling.* He simply wanted to be with her forever, to share his entire life and heart with her. Yes, he longed for her to bear him a child, but if she never did, his feelings for her would still remain as powerful as they were right now.

They broke apart, and shadows of desire passed through her eyes before she rested her forehead against his chest, her body rising and falling heavily in want for him.

Mmm, the way she held him, and the way she made him feel. Micah was a stronger man with her love. The idea of marring her flesh even in play was abhorrent, which was one reason why he refused to call her a submissive. Sam was most definitely not a submissive. Micah considered the thought for a moment and grinned to himself. Perhaps she was the very epitome of a submissive, because didn't a true submissive have all the control? And didn't Sam have complete and total control over him?

In the most bizarre way, Sam was his master and he was her servant, because he would do anything for her if she only asked. Which she rarely did, and that made him want to please her even more.

He took a deep breath and turned his gaze down the stairs

before looking back at Sam as she pulled away.

"What we do down there is for your pleasure, and for mine. It's not about who is in charge." He lifted her hand to his heart and pressed it against him. "Because, Sam, you are in absolute control in every way."

He didn't need to explain his meaning any further than that. She nodded with understanding then followed him as he wrapped his hand around hers and descended the stairs.

In his dungeon, he turned off the overhead lights and lit three candles set in front of mirrors. Light flickered and reflected around the room with a magical, almost otherworldly effect, casting alluring shadows.

With deliberate, reverent steps, Micah approached Sam as if she were a goddess he had to approach with care, who could strike him down with one look if he displeased her. But she didn't strike him down. As he reached her, she lifted her hands and combed her fingers through his hair while he slowly knelt down in front of her, pushing her pants down until she stepped out of them and toed off her shoes.

The light shone off her naked legs, long and lean. He loved her legs. He loved running his hands over them, loved feeling them wrapped around his body as he took her with his.

As he slowly stood back up, he dragged his hands up the outside of her thighs, over the gentle curves of her hips, and under her blouse. Dutifully, she lifted her arms over her head and let him easily remove it.

Sam wore no undergarments, just as he had requested, and her pale pink nipples—almost invisible against her porcelain skin—puckered instantly, the candlelight flickering over her breasts and casting captivating shadows on her body.

Micah clutched the back of his shirt and pulled it forward over his head before tossing it on the nearby couch. In one sure, solid movement, he had her in one arm while the other grabbed one of her legs and lifted. She hopped up and locked her legs around his waist, her breasts pressed firmly against his chest, her lips open against his in a breathless caress.

"I'm giving you a safe word," he said.

"I didn't think you were going to hurt me." Her eyes sizzled with a mix of arousal and fear.

"I don't plan to." He carried her to the large bed with the wrought iron frame. "But I don't want to take any chances. I want to make sure I don't hurt you or push you too far, because I want this to be about pleasure, not pain."

He climbed onto the bed with her still wrapped around him and set her on top of the satin comforter before sitting back on his heels between her legs to feast his gaze on her glorious flesh.

"Mmm, you're beautiful." He pushed his palms up her torso and over her breasts before dragging them back down her body.

To her credit, she reached up and took hold of one of the iron rails of the headboard.

"Jesus." Shit, she was sexy splayed out for him, falling into the character of being bound and helpless.

She undulated over the comforter, shifting her body and tightening her grip on the headboard. "Do you like, Mr. Black?"

"Very much, Mrs. Black."

She tilted her head and arched one eyebrow.

"Very well, Miss *Garrett*. Yes, I like."

He got up off the bed, still wearing his black, nylon sweats. "Turn over for me, Miss Garrett."

"What?"

"You heard me. Turn over like a good girl." He smiled over his shoulder at her, grabbing a pair of leather cuffs connected by a short chain from a shelf. He unhooked them from one another.

By the time he returned to the bed, she was on her stomach, her perfect ass beckoning him to smack it.

"Get up on you knees for me. And grab the headboard again."

He eased up behind her, pressing his chest into the back of her shoulders while his erection pushed against his sweats and bumped against the soft curves of her ass.

"What are you going to do to me, Mr. Black?" She looked over her shoulder, her green eyes sparkling with innocence.

"I'm going to tie you to this headboard, Miss Garret, that's what I'm going to do."

"Why would you do something like that?" She arched her back and swayed her hips side-to-side against his groin.

Little minx. Damn, she knew how to rile him up. Oh, but he would get her back. She didn't know who she was messing with. He was Micah, master of the mindfuck. He would have to play with her a little. Just to enhance her reaction, of course. Nothing harmful or too traumatic.

He secured the leather cuffs around her wrists, slid the hook and chain through a loop in the headboard, then attached the hook to the other cuff. She pulled and the metal clanked and rattled, but she couldn't pull free.

The grin on his face had to be pure satisfaction as she glanced back at him again.

"Is this all?" she said, challenging him. "You're just going to tie me to the bed?"

His grin widened. "Oh no, that's not all." He reached down and picked up a pair of clothespins. "Remember that safe word I mentioned?"

She frowned at the clothespins. "Yes?"

"It's *stop*. Your safe word is *stop*. Repeat it."

"Stop." Her gaze turned wary.

It wasn't very inventive as far as safe words go, but for tonight, it was satisfactory. He didn't really think she would need to use it, though. He had every intention of going easy on her being it was their first play session, but he had a feeling a little bit of pain would excite her.

"Trust me?"

She paused and looked back the clothespins. "What are you going to do with those?"

"Nothing you don't want me to do. Now, do you trust me?"

She took a deep breath. "Yes."

"Will you use the safe word if you have to?"

She paused then nodded. "Yes."

"Okay. If you use your safe word, I will stop immediately and the scene will end."

She bit her lip. "Completely end?"

"Yes."

"What if I don't want it to completely end and simply just want you stop what you're doing?"

"Then say 'too much.' If you say that, I'll know that what I'm doing is uncomfortable, but won't stop the whole scene, just what I'm doing at that moment. Deal?"

She nodded. "Okay."

He kissed the back of her shoulder. "Okay."

Crowding her, he reached around and tweaked her left nipple between his thumb and fingers until it formed a tight peak. She breathed heavily, getting an idea of what he was about to do with the clothespin.

"Ssshhh. Just relax," he said, swirling his palm over her raised nipple.

"This is going to hurt, isn't it?"

"It'll pinch, yes. But it'll be okay. Just breathe." He pressed the clothespin open and poised it over her nipple while she held her breath and tensed.

Slowly, he closed the clamp over her nipple.

"Ouch! Oh my God!" She flinched and strained against the headboard. "That hurts!"

"Do you want me to stop?"

She hissed and rocked back against him as if she could get away from the stinging pain.

After a moment, she shook her head. "No. Don't stop."

He repeated the process on her right nipple with the same results as she cried out from the pinch of the clamp.

The way she cavorted and yanked against her bindings excited him. He loved watching her lithe, limber body twist and squirm. She was exceptionally flexible, anyway, and to see all that flexibility bend her was like watching moving art. Sam was built for fluidity and motion, to be watched, which was one reason why she had been the star performer at the Black Garter in her dancing days.

But now she only danced for him. His own private, exotic dancer.

His hands shot around her and down her stomach to her inner thighs and she stilled. For all their discomfort, the bite of pain created by the clothespins turned her on. He could see it in her mind. And with his hands massaging up and down so near the juncture of her legs as he ground against her backside, she was soon moaning and rotating her hips involuntarily.

"Micah…" She laid her head back on his shoulder, exposing the graceful arch of her neck to his eager fangs.

Yes, he wanted to taste her tonight. He hadn't taken her blood since last week. But first…he let go of her and quickly backed away so that she nearly fell backward from his abrupt departure.

"Where are you going?"

"Quiet." Micah wouldn't Dom her, but he could play act a little. And right now, he wanted to show her how good it could be.

With a blindfold in his hand, he returned to the bed and gently placed it over her eyes and secured it in place.

"Is that comfortable, baby?"

She leaned into his hand. "Yes."

"Good."

Time to play. He returned to his bureau of toys and pulled out a violet wand and one of his Hitachi Magic Wands. Oh, she would love this. The idea of what he was about to do made him smile.

"You like pain, love?"

"I didn't say that." She sounded nervous with her sense of sight effectively shut off.

"But I can see it in your mind." With the violet wand, he zapped a piece of leather wrapped around a block of wood.

The electric crackle of sound made Sam jump.

"No, wait. You're not really going to…?"

"Just try it." He lowered his voice seductively. "For me." He circled her on the bed, watching her strain and turn her head in the direction of his voice. "You know what this is, don't you?" He licked the tip of the violet wand on the leather again.

"Yes."

He had used one of these on Trace the other night, and

she had seen what it had done to him.

"What if I don't want you to use that on me?"

"Use your safe word." Micah spoke matter-of-factly.

"I don't want to use my safe word."

He zapped the leather one last time before setting the violet wand aside and picking up the Hitachi Magic Wand. She was too scared to realize he would never use the violet wand on her while he was on the bed with her or touching her. If he did, he could be shocked, too.

She tensed and panted as he drew up behind her.

"It's okay. It will only sting a moment," he said. "Are you ready?" He wrapped his left arm around her waist and held the vibrator in front of her but several inches from her body.

Her breath came in sharp bursts through her nose and every muscle in her body tightened before she nodded stiffly. Damn, she was ready to let him go forward with pain. Was she in for a surprise!

SAM WAS HELPLESS. Her hands were cuffed and tied to the bed frame, and she had the most incredible sensations shooting through her nipples. A cross between pain and pleasure. And now Micah was going to zap her with one of the electrical wand things he had used on Trace.

She remembered how tortured Trace had been from the pain the other night. So much so, in fact, that he had used his own safe word, something Sam found out later Trace had rarely done before.

God, was she crazy? Was she really going to let Micah do this to her?

She had to try. She didn't want to deny him this. And she trusted him, right? If she didn't like it, she would tell him she didn't want to do it again, but she could endure it just this once.

Suddenly, Micah's entire body grasped her hard and the tip of the wand came down on her, right between the legs.

She screamed, just like in the movies, terror gripping her.

"It hurts! Micah!"

But it didn't hurt. Not really. Sam quieted and frowned behind the soft blindfold. Pulsing vibrations stimulated her core, deep and all the way through her vagina, not just her clit.

Realization dawned on her as fiery heat swarmed within her core. He had mindfucked her. He had only wanted her to *think* he was using the electric thingy on her, when in fact he had replaced it with a vibrator.

"Yes." He confirmed what she had just deduced, following the syllable with a deep purr as he licked the back of her neck. "But you're a wonderful screamer. So sexy."

"Asshole." But no malice backed up her insult as her insides throbbed in time to the deep vibrations. She moaned, laying her head back against his shoulder as her hips involuntarily rocked forward. "You tricked me."

"Mm-hm." He massaged the vibrator head up down her clit and then down deep between her legs. "But trickery leads to fear, and fear heightens the pleasure."

She nodded eagerly, completely understanding this heightened pleasure he spoke of as her core tingled and clenched hungrily. She readily gave in to his persuasions with the vibrator, pressing her hips forward and moaning again as she felt him shift behind her. She heard rustling fabric, and then the head of his cock nudged between her legs as he forced them open with his knees. With his free hand, he slicked the velvety head up and down her opening, coating himself with her juices, then abruptly drove inside her.

They both gasped harshly.

Between his cock inside her and the vibrator pressed against her clit, and with the added pain licking through her nipples, Sam was already near orgasm.

And from the sound of it, so was Micah.

"Come for me, baby. Don't make me wait." His hips thrust forward in deep, hastened strokes.

The building orgasm quickening within her would unravel her. It was going to blow her mind and her body to pieces. She'd never felt anything like this.

"Neither have I." Micah practically groaned the words out as he stepped up his pace. "I'm already so close, baby."

The sparks of pain in her nipples. The vibrator. Micah's guttural moans and arousing purrs. His strong body behind her. His thick cock working with the vibrator to stimulate her vagina.

"Oh fuck!" The build was unreal. The rising crescendo of pleasure almost supernatural. "Micah! Oh God! Micah!"

She pulled against her restraints, wanting to touch him, desperate for him. One breath short of terrified at how powerfully she was about to come.

"I've got you, baby."

And just as she was on the verge of coming, he pulled away the vibrator, reached up with both hands, removed the clothespins from her nipples, and clamped his hands over both breasts, pulling and kneading.

"Aaaaauuuuhhhh!" Fire shot through her nipples and mainlined to her core as the most unbelievable orgasm she'd ever had shattered her soul.

Micah came the moment she did, slamming into her and crying out, filling her with liquid heat that made her insides feel even more like molten lava.

Releasing one of her breasts, he reached up and removed the blindfold then unhooked the cuffs. They collapsed face-first onto the bed, his hips still surging against her backside, his stomach tightening with each contraction of his cock.

"Jesus!" Sam breathed out the exclamation, in awe that she could come that hard. Her body still shivered spasmodically, and the pain in her nipples still radiated throughout her breasts.

And then Micah bit into her shoulder. Euphoria from his venom loosened her body and the room swam wondrously until she came again with him still inside her.

MICAH HUGGED HIMSELF to Sam's body as he fed. He didn't take all that he wanted, because he knew after what they had just done, she would already be exhausted. She would need her blood to recover. All-too-soon, he released her shoulder and watched the bite mark heal from the tiny dose of venom he had injected.

She had come again during his feeding, which wasn't uncommon. The euphoric high of vampire venom often had that effect, even on other vampires.

"Are you okay?" he said, his nose pressed into her hair.

"Mmm." She maneuvered, tightened, and unwound beneath him as if she were settling into a warm bed or snuggling into a blanket.

He smiled. "I take that as a yes?"

She was still feeling the effects of the euphoria, but they were beginning to fade. "Uh-huh."

"No safe word."

She grinned contentedly, her cheek pressed against the pillow. "No. No safe word. That was," she sighed, "incredible."

They lay like that for several minutes, Micah on top of her, still inside her, snuggled together as he peppered kisses over the back of her neck, her shoulders, in her hair, and finally down her back as he pulled out of her and sat up.

"Come on, beautiful. Let me get you cleaned up and tucked in."

He took her hand and helped her off the bed, then lifted her in his arms and carried her to the bathroom. After setting her on the counter, he started filling a lilac-scented bubble bath and joined her by the counter, slipping into place between her knees.

"Lilacs?" She smiled up at him as she draped her arms over his shoulders.

"Yes. I swung by here the other night when I was out so I could supply the house with a few things for you."

His lips brushed over hers and she deepened the kiss before pulling away once more.

"Why, thank you, Mr. Black. You do take good care of me."

"You're most welcome, Miss Garrett." He gently caressed his palm over her nipple then bent down and kissed one breast then the other. "Are they sore?"

Her fingers combed through his hair, and she moaned as his tongue found her right nipple and swirled softly around it.

"A little, but in a good way."

He switched sides and caressed her left nipple before tenderly brushing his lips over it, as well.

"This is part of the scene, by the way." He grinned up at her.

"Oh? What's that? Getting me turned on again?"

He chuckled and stood, taking her face in his hands. "No. Tending to you afterward. Caring for you." *Kiss.* "Cleaning you." *Kiss.* "Making sure you're okay."

She arched on eyebrow and nodded dramatically. "Oh, I can assure you. I'm very okay."

"I'm sure you are." With a final, sweet kiss on her lips, he went to the bathtub and checked the water then returned to her, lifted her in his arms, and settled her into the sudsy, hot bath.

"How's that? Too hot?"

She shook her head. "It's perfect. Join me?"

He climbed into the tub with her, cleaned her, smoothed his palms over every inch of her perfect, exquisite body, then pulled her back into the frame of his torso and held her as they both laid back and closed their eyes, content to enjoy the feel of the other in the soothing water.

CHAPTER 16

LATE THE FOLLOWING MORNING, with the house shuttered in darkness, Micah navigated around his kitchen, preparing breakfast for Sam while she slept. He wore only a pair of sweats and a smile.

In fact, he couldn't stop smiling. Not even the knowledge that he had to return to work tonight could ruin his good mood.

After loading a tray with homemade pancakes, syrup, eggs, bacon, sausage, fresh-squeezed orange juice, coffee and tea, he carried it downstairs and set it on the massive bed where they had spent the day.

"Good morning, love." He leaned over and kissed Sam's forehead.

She had slept like the dead after their stint in the dungeon last night. So had he, but today was special, and when he had awakened, he couldn't contain himself before hurrying upstairs to get everything ready.

Sam stretched and opened her clover-green eyes then grinned sleepily. "Good morning."

"Are you hungry?"

She rolled her eyes. "I just woke up. I'm never hungry right when I wake up."

"Well, I'm hungry." He climbed into bed beside her and took a drink of orange juice.

Sam smiled at him. "What's up with you?"

"Oh nothing, Mrs. Black."

She sat up and huffed. "How many times do I have—?"

"Ah!" Micah held up his hand to stop her. "You're Mrs.

Black. End of discussion."

She held up her left hand and flashed her empty ring finger. "Not until I see a ring on this finger, Mr. Black."

Micah pulled his other hand out of his pocket and held up a platinum band with nine diamonds around the top.

"You mean like this one?"

Sam gasped, her eyes opening so wide they looked like saucers. She stared at the ring for several seconds before tearing her gaze away to meet his.

"Give me your hand, Sam." He reached for her left hand.

She slowly lifted it to him. Her fingers were shaking.

"I may have flaws, and I may not be human, but I want you to share my name for the rest of our days in the human traditions to which you were born." He held the ring poised in front of her finger. "Will you be mine forever, Sam? Through sickness and health and all the rest?"

Tears threatened to fall, but she held them back. "Yes."

He slid the ring in place, lifted her hand to his mouth, and kissed the row of diamonds, his lips pressing against the soft skin of her finger as he did. "Can I finally call you Mrs. Black now?"

"You play dirty."

"I like to win."

"Do you now?"

"Uh-huh." Micah kept hold of her hand. "So? Can I? Call you Mrs. Black?"

Sam didn't answer right away then said. "You really are incorrigible, you know that?"

"Just answer my question." He grinned, feeling victory within his reach.

"Okay. Fine. You can call me Mrs. Black. Happy now?"

She looked adorable in mock-pissed-off mode.

"Yes. Very." He squeezed her hand.

She shook her head and tried to hide her smile by turning away from him. A moment later, she brought her gaze back to his. "I love you. I *really* love you."

"I love you, too. *Mrs. Black.*"

She rolled her eyes and laughed. "What have I gotten

myself into with you?"

"A lifetime of love, happiness, and devotion...with the occasional possibility of danger, death, and mayhem."

"Oh, of course." She rolled her eyes as if to say *how silly of me.* "What relationship wouldn't be complete without a little threat to life and limb?"

Micah tugged her hand. "Come here, you."

She was in his arms in an instant, holding him so tightly he could feel her heartbeat against his chest.

"I'll take good care of you, baby."

She exhaled as if she'd been holding her breath. "I know. And I'll take good care of you."

Micah held onto her and breathed her in. If anyone was up to the task of taking care of him, it was Sam. His Sam. Fearless and strong. The mother of his future children.

Micah couldn't wait until his next *calling.*

DID YOU ENJOY READING THIS BOOK?

If you did, please help others enjoy it, too:

Recommend it.

Review it at Amazon, iBooks, or Goodreads

If you leave a review, please send me an email at donya@donyalynne.com or message me on Facebook so that I can thank you with a personal e-mail.

ABOUT THE AUTHOR

DONYA LYNNE is the bestselling author of the award winning All the King's Men Series and a member of Romance Writers of America. Making her home in a wooded suburb north of Indianapolis with her husband, Donya has lived in Indiana most of her life and knew at a young age that she was destined to be a writer. She started writing poetry in grade school and won her first short story contest in fourth grade. In junior high, she began writing romantic stories for her friends, and by her sophomore year, she'd been dubbed *Most Likely to Become a Romance Novelist*. In 2012, she made that dream come true by publishing her first two novels and a novella. Her work has earned her two IPPYs (one gold, one silver) and two eLit Awards (one gold, one silver) as well as numerous accolades. When she's not writing, she can be found cheering on the Indianapolis Colts or doing her cats' bidding.

For more information on Donya's books or just to say hello, visit her on Facebook or swing by her website.

www.facebook.com/DonyaLynne

www.donyalynne.com